CHRISTMAS
KISSES

Happy Reading!

Tracy Summers

<u>BOOK YOUR PLACE ON OUR WEBSITE</u> <u>AND MAKE THE</u> <u>READING CONNECTION!</u>

We've created a customized website just for our very special readers, where you can get the inside scoop on everything that's going on with Zebra, Pinnacle and Kensington books.

When you come online, you'll have the exciting opportunity to:

- View covers of upcoming books

- Read sample chapters

- Learn about our future publishing schedule (listed by publication month *and author*)

- Find out when your favorite authors will be visiting a city near you

- Search for and order backlist books from our online catalog

- Check out author bios and background information

- Send e-mail to your favorite authors

- Meet the Kensington staff online

- Join us in weekly chats with authors, readers and other guests

- Get writing guidelines

- AND MUCH MORE!

CHRISTMAS KISSES

Christine Cameron
Jill Henry
Tracy Sumner

Zebra Books
Kensington Publishing Corp.
http://www.zebrabooks.com

ZEBRA BOOKS are published by

Kensington Publishing Corp.
850 Third Avenue
New York, NY 10022

First Printing: November, 1999
10 9 8 7 6 5 4 3 2 1

Printed in the United States of America

CONTENTS

A HIGHLAND CHRISTMAS

by

Christine Cameron

Chapter One

Her heart in her throat, Cassandra gripped the tartan around her shoulders, ran up the tower steps, and stopped beside a window to listen. Horses' hooves sounded on the drawbridge. Turning to the window, she leaned out. Snowflakes landed softly on her face. She strained to hear the words a masculine voice shouted.

"What godforsaken place is this that King George has tossed to me like a scrap to a dog after all my loyalty to him? I know Cedric is behind this. I'll kill him—brother or not."

It could only be the voice of her intended, Baron Drake Bancroft. Heat swept through her at the words he'd spoken. Cassandra tried to see the shouting man's face but his fur hood blocked her view. *Churlish man. Ach, I'll not be in the hall to greet him.* Gathering her skirts, she descended the stairs and ran through her beloved castle's corridors. How could he liken her home to scraps thrown to dogs?

She thought of his brother and Drake's seneschal who'd arrived a few weeks ago; she'd have to warn Cedric.

Pascal approached her from behind, clearly panicked. "Quickly, milady. What kind of man must you wed?"

"An ogre from the sound of him." Cassandra pursed her lips tightly and matched her steward's pace as they continued to the Great Hall.

"You've heard him then?"

"From the tower window." Her cheeks heated.

"Cassandra, get that temper of yours in check at once." Pascal gripped her arm, stopping her before she entered the hall.

She forced herself to smile sweetly. And in truth, her face seemed to cool with the effort. Pascal released her and they entered the hall just as her intended bore down on his brother. Her eyes focused on the baron's broad back as she moved around the army of men who attended this ill-tempered man. She could see Cedric's frown.

She moved closer, whispering to Pascal, "He's intent on harming his own brother." She remembered how Cedric kept to himself most of the time, but at meals his quick wit had helped her feel better about the arrangement.

The baron towered over his brother's much smaller build. "You petitioned King George, didn't you?"

"I don't know what you mean, brother. Just look at the wealth of this castle. You'll soon see the lands. And the lady is very fair." Cedric's expression lightened and his eyes seemed to plead with the baron.

"The lady who doesn't even see fit to greet her future husband?" The larger man's hands reached for his brother's throat as his seneschal tried to come between them.

Cassandra stepped forward. "Pardon, my lord, I arrived as quickly as I could." She waited for him to turn to her, but he was too intent on strangling Cedric. All she could see of Drake Bancroft was a mass of black hair, which glistened with moisture from the snow and cascaded over his fur cloak. She could feel her color rising again at his inattention.

Pascal put a hand on her arm but she slipped by him and raged over to Drake. Gripping his arm with both her hands she swung him around to face her. She nearly recoiled from the powerful response his touch sent her. She quickly released her hold.

"I said—" She glanced up at his face.

He was the most strikingly handsome man she'd ever seen.

"Pardon me. I arrived as quickly as I could." Cassandra suddenly found it hard to stand. Her legs wobbled as his green eyes seemed to bore into her. Her fear foolishly spurred on more accusations. "Although I can see you're not so worried about manners at this moment. So far I've heard you insult my home and I've seen you leave your men standing in puddles waiting for your bad temper to be spent."

Drake advanced on her, looking at her as if he'd never seen anything quite so distasteful. Cassandra's valor failed as she backed away from his advances.

Drake's seneschal cleared his throat. "Baron, let me introduce Lady Cassandra MacIntyre of Sedgewick Castle. Milady, Baron Drake Bancroft of our fair England."

Cassandra curtsied, her cheeks flaming hot now, but not from anger. He stood tall and broad with damp tendrils of hair over his forehead. His anger made him look roguishly alluring. But would she have to face his boorish temper for the rest of her days? She would have to make the best of it, but she wouldn't bow down to the man. She smiled up at him.

"Please let me take your cloak. We've a feast prepared. Let us settle your men." Cassandra drew his cloak from his shoulders and tried not to stare at his fine stature.

He shrugged out of it and continued to glare. "I can see I've some hard work ahead of me."

"Only as hard as you make it." Cassandra tossed his coat to Pascal and led the procession to the tables of the Great Hall. She looked at her handiwork as from a stranger's eye, admiring the festive trestles draped with holly and evergreen boughs decked with ribbons and sugarplums.

Glancing at Drake, she noticed his gaze still rested on her. She quickly looked away. He didn't appear impressed—just angry. They sat at the high table as her staff seated his men. Then her clan members, having heard the signal horn, filled the rest of the tables. As was their custom, her clan looked to her and quieted before beginning the meal.

Cassandra stood. She looked at Drake as she spoke. "Welcome to Sedgewick Castle. We offer you all the comforts we enjoy. If you don't mind, my chaplain will pray over the meal."

His crystal glare continued in her direction but he nodded his consent. After the prayer, Cassandra and Drake ate without comment as the hall came alive with conversation.

She breathed in the pine aroma from the garlands and found it difficult to swallow the spiced beef she chewed. Drawing in a deep breath, she tried to relax and turned her attention to her surroundings. The Yule log crackled in the enormous fireplace, offering its heat to the open hall. Looking subdued, Cedric sat quietly opposite them.

At least now Drake's glaring eyes no longer fell on her. But she could still see his dark brooding expression.

Finally he spoke. "Tell me true, Cedric. I know you had an audience with the king. What transpired?" His tone sounded calm.

Cassandra decided the food must have soothed the beast.

But poor Cedric looked as if he'd rather not say. "Drake, the king merely stated that a man of your strength would fare much better protecting the Crown's interests here in the Highlands. And that my slight build suited English society. From what I've seen of this place and what I know of you, it's clear that Sedgewick Castle does suit you. And it's much grander than Wellington."

Drake didn't look convinced.

His seneschal, Thurston, lent a hand. "They learned to rotate crops from Pascal here." He pointed to Cassandra's steward, sitting on the other side of her. "I've not seen a Scottish keep with such a bounty of food."

Drake looked at Pascal. "Who is Pascal?"

"Pascal is my steward. He's from France and came to my family when I was a child." Her hand shook as she reached for her chalice of wine.

He stared menacingly into her eyes. "I have no need of his services. He's dismissed." Drake turned back to his meal.

Everyone began protesting at once.

"You can't dismiss my steward."

"We couldn't do without him—"

"What? When a chief speaks in this castle his word is not law? I'm your equivalent of a chief and what I say is law." Drake finished his meal in the ensuing silence and stood to leave.

Cassandra sent a pleading expression to Thurston.

Thurston valiantly stood up beside him and spoke quietly. "Baron, I've never seen you behave so. Pascal is a valuable servant."

"You haven't seen the start of it either." He glared at his brother and then at Cassandra, and left the hall with Thurston jabbering beside him.

Cassandra frowned at Cedric and reached again for the comfort of her wine. "You could've at least warned me. Did you cuckold him out of his inheritance?"

She thought that, if anyone deserved it, Drake did. A

sudden notion struck her—if she'd had a choice of a husband she wouldn't have picked spindly Cedric.

Pascal stood slowly. "I'll take my leave then." He nodded to Cassandra. "Milady." He looked grim.

"Pascal, have a little faith in my feminine wiles, would you? I won't be without you and neither will our lands. Even Thurston stood up for you—now that's progress. Cedric, did you know that I found Thurston and Pascal throwing punches one day in the library? I've had my hands full solving their disagreements."

"That doesn't surprise me." Cedric nodded. "But be careful using those wiles on my brother. I've never seen him in such a rage. I certainly wouldn't have done what I did if I didn't truly believe my actions were for the best."

Pascal spoke up. "I wouldn't be breathing those words aloud again. Stick with your original story."

Cassandra agreed, thinking of the firm muscles of the baron's arms and his broad chest. The king was right. Drake was built more like a Scotsman. Audacious excitement filled her regardless of her predicament and caused her to smile. But when she caught Cedric and Pascal shaking their heads sadly for her, she sobered.

She wouldn't be in this position if not for her love of clan and home. She would marry this Englishman to see that her family remained in their rightful home. The wedding would take place on the morrow and the beast would be her husband. Tomorrow night she would face him in their marriage bed. Her stomach fluttered. Although inexperienced, she knew the ways of a man and a woman.

"Don't worry about me." She raised her chalice, toasting herself. "To my wedding night—I'm a brave Highland lass." But now her stomach churned and the feast turned sour within her. She strode over to the fire and sat on the hearth.

Pascal brought her another chalice of wine, leaving her

with her thoughts. The drink warmed her and settled her churning stomach. Although the hall was full of people she felt alone. She'd been alone for a long time. A cry caught in her throat. She needed some fresh air.

Cassandra walked from the hall, wrapping her woolen plaid over her head and shoulders. She moved through the corridor and out to the courtyard. The chapel, her source of comfort, beckoned her. Her footsteps crunched in the freshly fallen snow. Snowflakes caught on her eyelashes. Her breath appeared in white clouds before her.

It seemed she was cursed and blessed in the same breath. Blessed with her home, cursed with marriage to a man from the people who had killed her family. Cassandra's devastated clan numbered many woman and few men. Drake's men far outnumbered her own. As she entered the church the scent of the freshly waxed pews calmed her turbulent thoughts. Stepping past them she walked to the wall of candles.

Saying a prayer for her mother's soul, she ended with a plea for the comfort that only her mother could give. Tears filled her eyes as she lit the next candle for her father, praying for the courage that only her father could give. The last she lit for her brother, praying for the hope that only her brother could give. She ended with a Hail Mary and asked a blessing on the Christmas feast.

Drake walked the rampart and looked down at the snowy-white grounds. Then he recognized Cassandra walking across the courtyard to a small building. *Probably trysting with a lover.* The chill in his body diminished as he remembered her raven hair, its glistening blue highlights, and her sparkling blue eyes as she boldly faced him.

He had behaved poorly but with good reason. Somehow he'd get back to England and his beloved estate. He would send Cedric packing on that errand shortly. He descended the narrow stairs to the ground and walked to the building Cassandra had entered.

Opening the door without a sound, he realized that he entered a chapel. Cassandra's voice quaked as she spoke prayers for the dead and herself. She prayed in Latin to St. Mary. *Imagine a Highland woman knowing Latin.* He listened to her words, understanding the loss she'd suffered. He'd also lost his parents—to bloodthirsty Highlanders bent on revenge.

Disquiet settled in his conscience. His people had wronged her. But her people had wronged him as well. And they would marry? He didn't have a choice. King George's verdict had been clear. But Wellington was meant to be his. The estate was the only thing on this earth he cared for. The only thing he had left. There must be something he could do to return there.

The whisper of her skirts brought his thoughts back to Cassandra. He watched her from the shadows. Guilt washed over him and he resolved to make the experience as painless as he could for her. Somehow they would both have what they wanted.

Cassandra hurried back to the hall. She approached Pascal, who still spoke with Cedric.

"Milady, I'll stay with some acquaintances in the village. Send young Gavin with a message, should you need me." Pascal bowed to her and turned to leave.

Panic gripped her. "Pascal—what will I do without you? Do you really need to leave the castle?" Cassandra had never cried before her clan, but found herself dangerously close now as a sob escaped her throat.

Clan members nearby looked up in surprise.

Cassandra steeled herself, drawing on her father's spirit

of courage and reversed her words. "Aye, you must go. I'll be fine." She glared around her, daring anyone to say any differently.

A man cleared his throat. Looking to the sound, she noticed the baron stood at the door a short distance away. "Pardon, milady, perhaps I spoke too hastily. It seems Pascal has earned Thurston's respect. He may stay."

Cassandra looked to the baron and nodded her thanks. For the first time a soft kindness showed in his expression. He turned from her and to Pascal, who expressed his deep gratitude. She couldn't bring her gaze from his face and feared at that moment she'd lost her heart to this man.

As he turned to her again she noticed how he backed away form her warmth and became cold and distant. She in turn backed from him as if he'd struck her. Excusing herself, she left their company.

When he followed, calling her name, it sounded like music. She turned and waited for him. No one had ever spoken her name so beautifully.

"Let me walk you to your chamber. We've gotten off on a bad note. Again, please excuse my behavior." Drake took her hand and looked into her eyes.

His touch seemed to melt her soul. She struggled to control the need to feel more of him. His lips lightly kissed her palm. Then he tucked her hand in the crook of his arm as they walked to the archway in the far corner of the hall, leading to their tower. Traveling down the dark hall, the torchlight winked at her. They stepped up the spiral stairs, in the center of the tower, which brought them to the corridor outside her chamber.

Cassandra glanced up and nearly gasped when she saw the warmth in his eyes. His smile sent her emotions dancing around her heart. They stopped before her door.

Taking her hand in his, he leaned down and touched a light kiss to her lips. Cassandra closed her eyes against the enchanting onslaught his touch caused. When she opened her eyes the warmth was gone from his eyes, replaced again by that detached coolness. Her heart constricted in her chest when he spoke.

"Cassandra. I must be perfectly honest with you. I have no intention of taking this marriage any farther than the vows forced upon us by King George. Don't expect me in your chamber tomorrow night. I don't belong here and I will do my utmost to see myself back at Wellington. Good night." Drake raised her hand, bowed over it, then dropped it. Turning on his heel he strode around the corridor toward his assigned chamber.

Cassandra stared after his departing figure. Nothing could have prepared her for the crushing blow his words had dealt her. Opening her door she managed to close it and sink to the ground, her back against its solid comfort.

Slowly all the emotions she'd held in all day fell from her, leaving only rage toward this man who'd come so forcefully into her life. Who'd made her respond to him, and then—all in one evening—left her with bitter loneliness as her only companion.

Chapter Two

"I don't care how you do it—just get it done." Cassandra stormed from her chamber and collided very neatly with the baron. Still in a rage, she yelled, "Watch where you're going." Pushing away from him, she continued through the hallway and down the stairs.

Whatever he thought of her actions, she wouldn't wait to find out. Today was her wedding day and she had too much to do. Imagine demanding she stay in her chamber with the Christmas feast to oversee and . . . an insensitive beast to marry. Her pulse raced.

Pascal came up quickly from behind. "Ah, Cassandra, *Joyeux Noël*. Calm yourself. Your intended is ready to have you put in stocks. Get back to your chamber." He turned her around and tried to lead her back up the stairs.

"Who'll see to—"

"It's being taken care of." He managed to march her up the stairs and to her door.

"But you don't understand." Cassandra pulled from his grasp.

"I understand perfectly. Go and get ready ... sssh." Pascal shooed her away waving his hand. "Go." He opened the door.

She knew he waited patiently for her to enter on her own accord. "This is too much," she whispered as she followed his order.

"*Oui*, it is, *ma petite.*" He bowed his head and quietly closed the door.

Still facing the door she fisted her hands and screamed an oath. A chorus of gasps resounded from behind. She froze in place, not wanting to turn.

A feminine voice spoke. "Milady, is that any way to speak on your wedding day? And Christmas too?"

Whirling around, Cassandra realized that during her absence her chamber had filled up with English ladies. They stood with their mouths agape. At that moment she would have gladly jumped from her chamber window and been done with it. A young woman about her own age glided over and took her hand.

"I am Leigh, your lady's maid. We are your first Christmas present from Lord Bancroft. Ladies in waiting." Her free hand swept in the ladies' direction. Then tightening her grip on Cassandra's hand, she addressed the other women in the room. "Leave us alone for a while."

They all filed out of the room, looking at Cassandra much as Drake had the day before. She watched as the last one left and snatched her hand from the woman's grasp.

"What is the meaning of this?" Cassandra narrowed her eyes at the woman.

"Exactly as I've said."

"I don't need a lady's maid. I've never needed a lady's maid. Please leave." Cassandra turned her back to Leigh.

"Whether you need one or not, you've got me. The *lord* of Sedgewick Castle insists."

Cassandra shivered at her words. "He is not the lord of my castle yet." She glared at Leigh, daring her to disobey her order. "I asked you to leave."

"I will not leave—to do so would be disobeying Lord Bancroft's direct order." Leigh stood as if planted to the floor. "Please, Lady Cassandra. Disrobe and I'll prepare your bath."

Cassandra sighed, brushed past her, and began to undress. "I can bathe myself and wash my hair. You might as well have a seat."

"You misunderstand, my lady. I've been assigned a duty and I will do it." Leigh tipped the caldron of steaming water that hung in the fireplace into the tub that stood next to it, following that with large buckets of cold water.

Cassandra timidly wrapped herself in a blanket and walked to the tub. She tried to quell Leigh with another glare. "I need some food and a drink."

"You don't need food right now. We'll have a feast in a short while." Leigh took her arm and helped her into the tub.

Cassandra's covering dropped to the floor as she stepped into the water.

Leigh handed her soap and set to preparing her clothes. "Let me know when you need me to wash your hair."

Cassandra didn't answer and began washing her own hair.

"My lady?" Leigh hurried over and grabbed at Cassandra's hair, pulling it so hard that Cassandra screamed.

Livid with rage, she splashed at Leigh. "I told you I'd do it myself! Leave me be!" She splashed her again and noticed Leigh's face had turned a dark, angry shade.

"Stop it! You're such a child!" Leigh pulled at her hair again.

"And *you* are an insolent sop of a girl!" Cassandra stood in the tub ready to do battle if she grabbed her again.

"I was told to help you with—"

"I don't care what you were told—" Cassandra watched her chamber door open and there stood Drake, looking annoyed. She immediately sat, plunging herself into the depths of the tub.

"What is all this caterwauling? Leigh, what's the problem?" He strode toward the women.

Cassandra and Leigh both yelled at once, making it impossible for Drake to understand either one of them. The louder Cassandra complained, the louder Leigh matched her volume. Drake's eyes opened wide, and he grabbed Leigh's arm as they both continued to protest, even after he pushed Leigh into the corridor and closed the chamber door in her face.

Cassandra's mouth snapped shut and she sank farther into the water, closing her eyes. Trapped, she was trapped. She couldn't flee. She squeezed her eyes shut tighter. Maybe he would go away.

Suddenly she felt his hands on her hair and the sweet smell of perfumed soap drifted to her nose. He was washing her hair. Her eyes flew open.

"Shut your eyes or you'll have soap in them." Drake stared down at her.

Enraged, she could hardly speak her words. "Get out!"

"Oh? You're ready for your lady's maid?" His voice sounded smooth and controlled.

Cassandra clamped her mouth and eyes shut. His laughter filled the room as he continued to wash her hair.

"Aye!" She thought the water would boil with her ire.

"Aye?"

"Aye, I'm ready for Leigh."

"The proper answer is, 'Yes, would you please send in

my lady's maid? And what a thoughtful gift, thank you.' "
Drake continued to lather her hair.

"Just send in the damn maid." Cassandra knew she'd made a mistake as soon as she'd spoken the words.

Drake's hand stilled in her hair and he gripped it tightly, lifting her toward him. Her hands flew to cover her now exposed breasts.

"What did you say?" Drake hissed the words into her ear.

Cassandra squeaked, "Yes, would you please send in my lady's maid?"

"And you'll not upset her again?" Drake didn't release her.

"Nay . . . no, I won't."

"That's better." Releasing her suddenly, he strode from the room.

Water sloshed around Cassandra and her body shook as she rubbed her smarting head and tried to rinse the soap from her hair.

A short time later Leigh entered the chamber. "What kind of day shall we have, milady?"

"Oh, be quiet, Leigh. I've already had enough of this day and it has only begun. I thought I could accept this." For the first time, Cassandra looked into Leigh's brown eyes.

Leigh smiled. "Why not accept it? Do you find Lord Bancroft hard to look at? It would be the happiest day of my life if I were in your place." Gently she finished rinsing the soap from Cassandra's hair.

Cassandra studied Leigh's face as the Englishwoman concentrated on her mass of hair. Could she trust her? She'd never had a woman to talk to. "That's the problem. He's very desirable but he doesn't desire me. He doesn't even want to be here." She took a deep breath in, fearful that she'd trusted too soon.

Leigh sighed as she draped Cassandra's hair over the rim of the tub, drying it with a cloth. "It may appear that way. But appearances are not always the real truth. For one thing, I can't imagine Lord Bancroft not desiring you."

"He's said as much. He just wants away from here. I think he loves his home in England and maybe has a lady there."

Leigh laughed as she brushed her hair dry. "Not one lady . . . many. But none that could ever find his heart."

"Have you known him long?" Cassandra looked at Leigh again and realized how bonnie she was. *And how well have you known him?* She was probably his mistress. Her eyes narrowed.

"Now don't be thinking that. We're too closely related and he wants me to make a good marriage." Leigh seemed to be disappointed.

"And how did you know I was thinking that?" Standing, she wrapped herself in the blanket Leigh offered.

"You have a very expressive face and it was expressing that perhaps you'd like to scratch my eyes out."

"Nay . . . "

"Very clearly, milady." Leigh left her side and bustled around fetching layer after layer of clothing.

Cassandra liked her frank way of speaking. A sudden pounding on the door startled her. Unceremoniously the other ladies filed in and swarmed around her. She was pushed, prodded, and fit into the various pieces of clothing. Finally, when the swarm parted, she stood facing her looking glass. She hardly recognized the woman she'd become. Voices in the room expressed awe.

"Oh, my." Leigh leaned close to her ear and whispered, "And see if the man doesn't desire you now."

The sleeves puffed at the shoulders and tightened just below the elbow with silky ribbon to lace them closed down to her wrist. The body of the dress also laced down her back to an expansive skirt that flowed to her feet. Her low-cut bodice made her chest far too bare.

The corset pushed her breasts up, revealing an expanse of bosom she never knew she possessed. The round fullness showed above a strip of beautiful French lace that exposed more flesh, but in a much more chaste way. Satin covered the essential areas.

"Shall I wear a scarf?" Cassandra's hand brushed nervously over her bared skin.

Murmurs of disagreement fell on her ears.

"Pearls—I'll wear my mother's pearls."

Everyone seemed to agree. She took them from her wooden jewelry box and let Leigh fasten them on. Although they didn't cover up much, they added a delicate beauty to her ensemble. She tried to breathe as she walked away from the mirror, but the corset made that nearly impossible. Exactly why she never wanted a lady's maid— she'd never had to wear a corset before.

"Watch out. She's swooning!" Leigh and another lady grabbed for her. "Haven't you ever worn a corset?"

Cassandra shook her head. "Loosen it please . . . ."

They fussed some more, untying this, loosening that, and finally she could breathe again. A quick glance at the mirror on her way out of the room told her that the effect hadn't been diminished with the loosening.

She traveled through the halls of her beloved castle in the middle of a throng of women. They seemed to be moving in the direction of the chapel. Panic gripped her and she nearly pushed away from them all to flee for her life. But her clan must stay in their home.

She must marry the beast.

Panic threatened to drown his senses as he stood facing the long aisle of the chapel. Visions of his home swam before his eyes. What did he have back in England? Not a lady or even a close friend. He'd been so involved with Wellington he'd never had time for friends. All that ever gave him reason to live was his grand home . . . his spreading lands that made for the best hunt in England . . . pride of his name and ancestry.

He glared at Cedric, who'd spent a good part of the day pointing out the riches of Sedgewick Castle to him. Cedric smiled reassuringly. Drake would love to just—Wiping the thought from his mind, he wondered what he had in the cold Highlands.

As if in answer to his question, the pipe organ announced the arrival of Cassandra. Remembering the hurtful expression she'd worn when he told her his wish, he looked away. Anywhere, but at the innocent face of his Scottish bride.

Cedric's warning glare made him glance once again toward Cassandra. A short veil hid her face from him. He sighed his relief. At least he'd have a reprieve from looking at those eyes . . . so blue you could drown in their beauty. He closed his eyes only to open them and gaze lower at her rounded breasts, covered only partly with lace.

He trained his face into nothingness although what he could feel was far more. The emotion, so foreign, made his frown deepen. Roiling around within him, something he couldn't understand tried to surface.

His chest tightened as the priest told him to join his bride and lift her veil. Pascal led her to him, releasing her; he gave Drake a clear message with his expressive eyes. *The man must not trust me with his ward's happiness.*

Slowly he lifted the veil to see her bewitching eyes, one moment pleading with him, the next icy with contempt. He wasn't the only confused person this day. But when he witnessed their bitter sadness he nearly wept, having to gird his raging emotions even more.

* * *

Cassandra walked slowly down the aisle toward Drake. He wouldn't even look at her. She gripped tightly to Pascal's arm and vowed to be brave. No one would see the tears she longed to shed. Each minute of Drake's refusal to look at her fired the steel of her will.

Finally, he glanced her way, his face a guarded mask of nothingness. Why did she desire this man of ice?

Pascal met her gaze and whispered to her. "You've always wanted what you couldn't have. Use that—draw on it. And if I remember . . . you always get what you want."

His warm smile melted some of the ice that had begun to freeze her heart. She clung desperately to Pascal as he guided her hand into Drake's. But no one else witnessed her desperation, just she and her mentor. Contrary to the coldness in his glazed expression the touch of Drake's hand nearly burned her alive.

It seemed that his touch tried to tell her something important, giving her the impression of great need. She'd often been able to tell what people could feel by touching them. Was that what it was now? Or did she just wish it?

Then the feeling seemed to disappear and its loss left her aching more painfully than she had from the loss of her family. Her already battered heart seemed to break even more.

The priest talked overlong as she knelt beside her future husband. They spoke their vows with cold rhythm. The kiss that sealed their joining, however, burned through Cassandra with a searing sureness. Her eyes opened just in time to see the same desire gleaming in his eyes. But as quick as a glance, it too vanished.

She walked from the chapel, her arm linked with his, followed by their throng. Two different breeds of people joined together by their union. Thoughts circled in her mind as she nodded to all the well wishers. Did he desire her? Why would he hide it? Even as she perceived his emotions thrumming for her, he denied it.

The wondrous aroma of roasted meats, bread pudding, and cinnamon-baked apples met her as she entered the Great Hall. Her trained eye told her that her orders had been carried out to the letter, and without her constant vigilance. Relief flooded her and she decided to enjoy the day of feasts. Pascal was right. She would get what she wanted.

Cassandra watched Drake talk to her people and knew it would take some doing, but in the end he would be worth it. Touching his arm she could again feel a very timid happiness and as his gaze met hers a very real passion surged from him.

She'd never told anyone of her talent to *know* feelings, but the people of Sedgewick knew never to say a false word to her because somehow she always knew the truth. She treasured that knowledge and it gave her the power that she needed to control and lead her people. Some even figured out that as long as she didn't touch them, they could play her false. But those people never stayed in the castle walls for very long.

Cassandra smiled at Drake as they took their seats at the table to begin the feast. Thurston and Pascal sat beside each other, looking for all the world like best of friends.

Across the table, Pascal seemed to suspect her thoughts and shook his finger at her. "Get that mischief out of your mind, milady."

"Mischief? I merely wondered at the amiable behavior of you and Thurston after weeks of, shall we say, less than friendly behavior." She had to laugh at the expressions on the men's faces as they glanced nervously at Drake and back to her. "Why, Pascal's black eye faded just a day ago."

Pascal, usually full of lectures and wise words for her, sputtered and Drake's smile rewarded her frankness.

Thurston cleared his throat, looking uncomfortable. "Just getting to know each other's ways, milord."

Pascal's expression promised retribution. Much like when she was a child. Where her parents coddled he would admonish. Cassandra smiled charmingly at him. "Pascal, I'm no longer your charge. Relax." Her words, innocently spoken, betrayed her.

Drake immediately made use of the opportunity. "Yes, Pascal. Consider yourself freed of Lady Cassandra's mischievous ways. I'll take it from here." Drake's and Pascal's chalices clanked together sending a bell of doom to her ears. She met Pascal's broad smile with a wide frown.

Pascal winked at her. "Never fear, Cassandra. He seems like a reasonable man." The men laughed together.

She tried to control the heat rising in her cheeks. Being ill-tempered would not win Drake's approval. But by the way her cheeks burned, her emotions once again must be evident. Approval or not, she would not be ordered about.

Drake perused her and took hold of her hand. "Is the feast as you planned?"

Cassandra looked at him, wondering, and then she knew by his touch that he had made sure her orders were carried out. "Aye, Lord Bancroft. To the very letter."

"Good." He released her hand, suddenly looking uncomfortable.

The rest of the feast went along happily. She found herself laughing along with Drake. His laughter added a special music that had been missing all her life. The wine flowed and her musicians played well. Pascal had schooled her well. He'd passed his love for music on to her. She became adept at all the instruments he'd brought from France.

Her favorite was the violin. She drew comfort from that

simple instrument in her hands. She'd often venture into the mountains, bringing the violin with her, and she would play for hours. It was a musician's worry over the castle violin that led him to follow her and discover her talent.

From that day forward she was asked to play when the musicians performed. Her talent had been her mother's pride. Cassandra's eyes pricked with the threat of tears as she thought of her mother. Memories swarmed back to her as she listened to the sweet sounds of a Corelli composition. The blending of the violin, harp, bagpipe, flute, and timbrel wove its magic through the Great Hall.

Sipping her wine, she studied Drake's reaction to the music. He seemed pleased. He turned to her and gifted her with another smile. The music ended, breaking the spell. They looked away from each other. Cassandra did not miss the sly exchange between Cedric and Pascal.

The violin player walked over, holding the instrument out to her. She stood, accepted the offer and joined the other musicians. Savoring the cheering from her clan, she quickly chose a song she'd written and had taught to the other musicians. A song inspired from the mountains themselves in the springtime, a melody of warmth to quell the wintry stillness.

She was an angel or a witch—Drake couldn't decide which. Her hair swayed as she held the violin to her chin and played. The lively tune seemed to lift the already light spirits even higher. He'd never heard such a tune, not even in England's finest courts. It was magic and though it lasted for a long while it ended far too soon.

As Cassandra started to go back to her seat the people begged for more. She smiled and glanced at him. For approval? He nodded his agreement and she spoke to the musicians. They played an Old English Christmas tune that wrenched his heart, bringing back far too many painful memories. Memories he'd buried deeply within and had no wish to uncover. He rose quietly and left the hall. When he walked out to the courtyard, Cedric followed.

Drake turned to Cedric. "Give a man some peace," he muttered. He breathed in the cold air and then let out a misty breath.

"You can't run away from those emotions forever. Mother would have wanted you to live—really live—and enjoy the heart of life she taught so gently."

"That heart died with her."

Cedric placed his hand on his brother's sleeve. "And it does her no honor."

"And you've done *me* no honor. We both know that Wellington is mine by birthright." Drake's throat tightened as he forced out his next words. "You will leave in the morning and relinquish your hold on Wellington and offer to take Sedgewick."

Cedric huffed in exasperation, sending his breath before him in a white mist. "You're married to Sedgewick's lady already. Try to look past your pride and anger. You need this wild place. You need the love Cassandra can give you. I'll not relinquish Wellington."

"The marriage will be annulled and Wellington will be mine or I will no longer call you brother."

"I beg your pardon?" Cedric paled.

"You heard me." Feeling wretched for even speaking those words, Drake turned swiftly from his brother only to discover Cassandra standing there.

Her trembling hand covered her mouth, and unshed tears glistened in her eyes. As she dropped her hand to her side, Cassandra's face reddened. "If marriage to me is so distasteful and you can not appreciate this beautiful land, you don't deserve either one. You don't even deserve

the dedication your brother shows you." Her breasts
heaved as she fought for air after her speech.

Cedric looked at Drake. "Hah! She sounds like mother!"

Anguish pulsed through Drake. He aimed his fist at
Cedric, punching him squarely in the jaw. Swiftly turning
to Cassandra, he watched her expression turn from anger
to fear. He stopped himself from raising a hand to her
and stormed away from them both. His words fell in his
wake. "Tomorrow, Cedric."

He couldn't believe Cassandra's gall as she shouted after
him. "Look what you've done—Cedric will not be going
anywhere on the morrow. At least until the holiday's are
over, perhaps even until winter is past, you unfeeling
beast!"

He turned back to see her kneeling next to Cedric's
prone body. *Good Lord, the man couldn't even take a punch.*
He strode back to them.

"Beast? You think I'm a beast?" Drake bent down. Grabbing Cedric's shirt, he heaved him to his feet.

Cedric's eyes flew open and for the first time in a good
long while Drake could detect rage in their depths. He let
Cedric go and turned to hear Cassandra's answer.

"Aye, an English beast, and none worse." Her hands
fisted at her sides.

Drake stood stunned to silence, his body responding to
her wild beauty as the peaceful snow fell around them. A
movement at his side made him turn, only to meet Cedric's
fist as it contacted with the side of his jaw. His head snapped
back with the blow. Pain shot through his jaw.

When his vision cleared he observed Cedric ready for a
fight, his fists in the air. Rubbing his jaw, Drake said,
"Cedric, you know I always win these skirmishes. Put away
your fists. The lady has a point. You can stay until Twelfth
Day. But then the deed will be done." Drake couldn't
resist another glance at Cassandra. Confusion shot through

him like a thunderbolt. "We best return to our feast."
Taking her by the hand he continued as if nothing were
amiss. "You play violin divinely." Tucking her hand in the
crook of his arm, he escorted her to the Great Hall with
Cedric following behind.

"You spend your anger and now lapse into pleasantries?" Her color was still up.

"Yes, and be glad of it." His smile faded as they entered
the hall.

Thurston accosted them. "They've been waiting for the
last dance."

The musicians struck up a lively song as Drake pulled
Cassandra onto the dance area. He took her hand in his
own and placed his other hand on her waist, leading her.
Her touch heated his arm, as her palm rested there. Looking in the depths of her eyes he imagined that he could
feel her thoughts.

It had happened when he'd touched her before. The
beauty of the pure love he sensed enthralled him. How
had she kept so pure with so much grief? She made it
seem so simple, but try as he might, when he reached into
the depths of his own heart he found only pain—guilty
pain at the sight of his mother's lifeless body. If only he
hadn't dallied. He shook his head to clear away the tor-
menting memory. Becoming aware of Cassandra, he
couldn't help but smile.

Although Drake tried, he couldn't conjure up his usual
grim expression. Being in this woman's arms was far too
pleasant. Drake was used to getting what he wanted. But
he couldn't have Cassandra. There was too much to lose.
He must not consummate this marriage or his home in
England would be forever lost to him.

The music ended and he parted from her, noticing the
blush on her face. Unable to control his actions, he gently

brushed his thumb over her cheek. The people in the hall quieted.

Then loud calls and drumming on the tables startled Drake. But it sent his blood singing toward his lower regions. He'd heard of how the Highland people sent their lord and lady to the marriage bed. Cassandra blushed even more and took his hand, leading him hastily to the entrance of their tower. Her action raised peals of laughter throughout the hall.

As soon as they passed under the arch and into the corridor the noise died down to the normal festive sounds. She released his hand and continued toward the stairs.

Once he was in the corridor, Drake's thoughts warred. Wasn't she rightly his? After all, they were married. But he couldn't risk the annulment. She looked so full of sorrow. Her eyes sparkled with tears. Why? Afraid to touch her he bowed his good night and fled down the hall to his chamber, pausing at his door until he heard hers close.

Chapter Three

After leaving Drake in the corridor, Cassandra closed her door. She could not stand the desolate feeling of rejection. He acted as though he didn't love her, but his touch told her differently. Her emotions alternated between rage and sorrow. She removed her gown.

Suddenly the rounded walls of her chamber and the gay spread of holly and ribbons above the fireplace closed in on her. Her chest constricted, threatening to halt her breath. She donned a shirt and a pair of boy's trews that she kept for dueling. Finding some woolen socks for her feet, she pulled on her boots. Lastly, she found her fur cape and walked to the fireplace.

Lighting a lantern that hung there, she stealthily climbed beside the fire in her fireplace and pressed the wall. It swiveled inward, allowing her into the walls of the castle.

The musty smell in the narrow passageway immediately brought back memories of her childhood. How she'd played within the walls and learned the path to every part of the castle. Her brother had been surprised when she showed him her discovery. Their parents had been proud and encouraged the exploration.

She wound her way down the stairs within the walls of the tower and followed the path to the stables. Finding her way to the wooden panel that led to the barn, she shifted it aside and entered the barn. Nighthawk whinnied as she neared his stall. Hefting the saddle onto him, she tightened the cinch and adjusted the stirrup. "Happy Christmas, Nighthawk." Cassandra always put away a carrot and an apple during meals for her horse. Pulling a carrot from her satchel, she fed it to him. "Let's go for a good run."

She led her mount through the deserted courtyard. Her cape's hood covered her face. Nighthawk's hooves clip-clopped over the stone walkway, echoing in the still night. Making her way to the guardhouses, she was at once happy but concerned to find the gate unguarded and wide open. The Yule always made her clan lax. It would make her escape easier.

Escape? Nay, she'd never abandon her family and home. Tying a sword that hung from the wall of the guardhouse onto the saddle, she mounted and rode across the bridge. The bitter wind gave her blessed relief. Just let a chill try to enter her heated body—it wouldn't happen this night.

She watched the raging torrent below the bridge and looked up to the full moon that shone on the waters surrounding her castle's island. The beauty of it eased her pain. The mountainous country that rose beyond always inspired her.

Cassandra took her favorite path to the frozen meadows and let Nighthawk have his freedom. Her horse, aptly named, loved a run in the dead of night. He reveled in his independence and his joy eased her plight a little more. Horse and rider shot across the land to the rocky shore of Loch Earn. The stillness of the loch contrasted sharply to the firth it emptied into and raged past her castle, protecting it.

Nighthawk stopped to eat some dried wild oats that still stood near the edge of the water. Cassandra dismounted and walked along the shoreline. The night air stilled around her and as she stood quietly her thoughts transcended time and place. An almost sultry wind blew into her face. Pushing the cape's hood from her head, she gazed into the depths of the water and imagined her mother, father, and brother smiling up at her.

Their smiles seemed to encourage her, renew her belief in herself, and they seemed to say, "Find his heart, Cassandra. You can do it." A tear drifted down her mother's cheek. As the image faded she blew a kiss at them. Tears streamed down her cheeks but a peace settled in her soul.

The clip-clop of Nighthawk's hooves on the rocky shore jarred her back to reality. His warm breath fell on her cheek, as he nudged against her.

"What makes you think I brought you another treat?" she teased as her horse nudged her cape pocket.

Sticking his nose into the folds he was rewarded with an apple. Cassandra's laughter sent a healing to her heart. She and her horse had performed this ritual for years, even back when he stood shorter than she did. The familiar act comforted her.

Her gift couldn't be wrong. Although the baron's love was buried deep within him, she sensed a passion there that needed release. Her own passion flared. A new determination entered her. They would love well and prosper together, she and this man from the other side—this Drake Bancroft. "Drake." His name sounded well aloud.

Mounting Nighthawk, she spoke into the night. "I'll find his heart. I'll find his love." She ended with a whispered, "I will." She had until Epiphany.

* * *

Safely ensconced in his chamber Drake realized his raging thirst. He knocked on his chamberlain's door. The elderly man immediately answered by opening the door between their chambers.

"Milord?"

"Have some mead sent up to my chamber and plenty of it." The man's eyes opened wide, but he nodded.

Drake had already come to like the taste of the rough way the Highlanders brewed their mead. It would dull his senses and the ache within him. Sitting before the fire on a large chair he thought of Cassandra's sweetness. With an oath he strode to the heavy curtain that concealed his chamber window. Pushing it aside he let the air cool his ardor.

Finally the mead arrived and he drank his fill of it. But it didn't help his restless yearning. Cassandra must be a witch of sorts. She had bewitched his body and only she could put out the fire within him.

He walked unsteadily to the chamber door, trying not to think of reason. He went directly to her chamber, opened the door, and searched the room for the object of his need. She wasn't within. His fury, dulled only by the mead, led him to her bed, where he lay down. He would wait for her and demand to know where she'd been. The fireplace spewed forth heat. Drake removed his clothing and settled himself under her blankets.

Cassandra crept up the spiral stairs to her chamber, glad that she wouldn't have to pass his room. Or maybe she should go to him. Nay, she'd too much pride for that.

She'd never go begging. But she paused at the entrance to the corridor, his image invading her senses. She'd been acquainted with many bonny men, but none had set such a fire within her. None had made her happy and sad at once. She continued on to her chamber.

Why did this English man intrigue her so? Had he fought against her people? Had he killed them? Oddly enough, her intuitions seemed to assure her that he hadn't. But this she would also find out.

Quietly swinging her chamber door open, she stepped inside and shut it again. In the shadowy darkness she laid her cape on a chair by the fire and played through her nightly routine. After disrobing, she splashed her face with water from a wooden bowl on her dresser. Wrapping her soft robe around herself, she climbed the steps to her bed.

Movement startled her as she parted the curtain. Being very still, she listened for the sound again. *It must have been nothing.* Lifting the blankets she slid into their warmth. Had Leigh warmed her bed with a stone? Cassandra's hand brushed across the bed, suddenly feeling warm flesh that sparked her thoughts. She nearly screamed out. *Drake.*

He'd come to her bed? Oh, Lord, and she'd not been here. What could he think? Her racing heart threatened to burst. Sliding carefully from the bed, she found a candle. Lighting it, she climbed back up and placed the candle on the wooden frame above their heads. She just had to see him.

The soft light fell on Drake's sleeping form. His chest rose and fell slowly. The blanket covered him from his waist down. *Pity.* Cassandra blushed at her own thoughts. She remembered the curiosity of her youth that caused her to slip into her parents' chamber one night to learn about the ways of a man and woman.

They never discovered her and had taught her well.

Although she had been glad to finally know, her guilt sent her scurrying to confession the next morning, landing her with serious penance that lasted a month. Regardless of how she'd pleaded with the father that she needed to know what she'd learned for her own future, he would not let her off lightly.

Now she gazed at Drake as if hypnotized. Wanting to touch him, but afraid to wake him. She caught the scent of Highland brew on his breath and leaned closer, careful not to make the bed move too much. Watching his eyes, she let her lips touch his lightly. He stirred, causing her to move away.

It was Christmas and her wedding night and this wonderful gift had appeared in her bed. Did she dare wake him? Sighing deeply, she gathered together all her grit. As her hands smoothed over his chest hair, an explosion of emotions flowed from Drake's heart to Cassandra's mind. Emotions so full of sorrow, she had to draw away.

He'd suffered great loss. Tears stung her eyes. Slowly she caressed his firm arms. Sitting beside him, she leaned closer. She continued to stroke him lightly with both hands up the sides of his neck, lacing her fingers through his hair. He still didn't awaken.

"And just how much o' our fine Highland ale did ye drink?" But she didn't mind. It gave her time to gather her courage and *feel* his inner thoughts.

A vision of his mother ravaged his soul with guilt, dark and cruel. His guilt seemed to ease as she smoothed his brow. Stretching out beside him, she moved her knee to rest on his lower body.

Gradually, his body and thoughts started to change with her administrations, revealing his desire. A boldness she'd never known invaded her. Her hand reached under the blanket to hold his arousal as it throbbed—she sensed he'd had many women along with a shallow lust.

She rested her head on his chest and his lust turned to a burning desire to be loved. Letting him go she lifted her head only to gaze into the green depths of his eyes.

Cassandra continued to rest against Drake, gazing into his eyes. She hoped that neither would speak and listened to what his touch told her. His thoughts flitted nervously about, full of fear one moment and hope the next. She closed her eyes and laid her head on his chest. His fearful thoughts lessened and the hope blossomed. He didn't want to leave her bed. His new emotions seemed to be like a savory wine that he dared to sip just slightly.

Drake's voice sent wisps of breath that fell on her hair. "I beg your pardon. I should leave."

"You don't have to." Cassandra knew not to move or he would likely dart away like a startled buck in the snow.

Drake sighed. "No—I should."

"I don't want you to." She closed her eyes tightly, hoping.

"Why don't you want me to?" Drake's hands cradled her as he moved her so that she would have to look at him.

"Because you don't want to." She knew she must always speak the truth to him.

"How would you know that?" Although he let her go, his eyes still held hers with a longing she could easily read.

"I just know." Cassandra smoothed his brow and tried to send comfort to all his dark memories. "Sleep."

He relaxed in her arms, his eyes closed, and a peaceful expression stole over his face. Even as she snuffed the candle and drifted off to sleep herself, Cassandra became aware of Drake's thoughts and sensed that he might even know hers. He tried to push her away and when that didn't work he led her into the darkest recesses of his mind.

Drake was ten years old. He playfully explored the crystal-white mountainside on lanky legs. Christmas night was one of his favorite nights of the year and the feast lay heavy in his stomach, keeping him warm.

A nagging reminder not to stray far and to come right home when the last ewe was gathered came to his mind often. But he didn't heed it. Instead, he shrugged it off and climbed higher. His energy was boundless and he just had to spend it before he'd be cooped up in the family rooms.

He picked holly to appease his mother when he returned later than he should have. By the time he left the shelter of the trees and could see the estate, he knew something was wrong.

Running in through the open front door he realized that in his absence his home had been raided. People ran here and there trying to help the wounded. *Mother? Father? Cedric?* A younger Thurston stood before him blocking his view of a body at the foot of the stairs. Drake pushed past Thurston. His heart, beating loudly in his ears, drowned out the noise around him.

"Father." Drake clutched the branches of holly to his chest. His father's lifeless eyes stared up at him, accusing him. Unable to stand the reality, Drake ran for the only comfort he'd ever known. But when he reached his mother's room, he had to force himself through a crowd of people. Once at her side he found her bloody body also beyond life.

A sob from beneath the bed made him realize that at least Cedric lived. Cedric, a year and a day younger than himself, and beyond comforting . . .

Tears streamed down Cassandra's cheeks and even in her sleep she could feel the tears that fell from Drake's eyes. Sorrow, deep and deadly, engulfed her. She fought to bring some light to Drake. But each time he turned his back, in their dreamlike state, and drifted from her, leaving her agitated and sad.

* * *

"Cussed Highland ale," Drake muttered through a painful fog in his head. Groaning, he rolled over onto something soft. "What the—" His eyes popped open and beheld the beautiful creature who lay beneath him as she responded to his words.

"Is there anything you do like about our beautiful Highlands, Baron Bancroft?" Cassandra's eyes twinkled with a playful light.

"Only one thing. And that I'll not tell." Groaning, he rolled away from her.

"You'd better tell or I'll have to guess. Let's see . . . could it be the breathtaking way the snow brightens the mountainside? Or the fresh air as it breezes over the loch? Or maybe—"

Drake put his finger to her lips. "Between you and Cedric you'd think this place was heaven. No, I think it's the ladies. I rather like the ladies." Drake's finger left her lips and he leaned back, closing his eyes.

Cassandra sat up and pushed at his shoulder. "*All* the ladies?"

"No—just one." He grabbed her hand.

"Who?"

"The fairest—that's all I'll say. Have you tea?" Letting go of her hand, he rubbed his forehead.

Satisfied, Cassandra gently left the bed and went to her kettle. Searching the herbs, never far from her, she found the willow bark and hung a kettle of water over the fire.

Yet another groan ensued from the bed. "Oh, Cassandra. We didn't—"

Looking up from her chore, she smiled slyly. "Didn't what?"

"I'm not for jesting. Tell me what happened last night."

He gripped the bed linen, hopped off the bed, and wrapped it around his waist, advancing on her.

"You don't remember?" As he got closer she hurried to say, "Oh, you mean—" Cassandra wished she could tell him just a little white lie, but they always managed to turn black. "Nothing like that happened." She turned again to the herbs.

Drake towered over her. "No? That is—are you quite sure?"

"Quite sure." Her tone mocked his proper English speech. "Don't worry. I won't spoil your plans," she replied waspishly, nearly biting her tongue for letting her words and tone betray her sentiments. Instead, she lowered her head over the herbs.

"See that you don't. Forgive my intrusion." He turned to leave.

Cassandra grabbed to control her temper but it slipped from her grasp. She followed him to the door. "If I were you, I'd take a good look around Sedgewick and pay closer attention to the wishes of King George and Cedric. I hear that this place is far grander than Wellington, and I have more to offer than your mistresses in *bonnie* England do." At the sight of his dark expression she took a sharp breath.

"More to offer, have you? Only as much as any *witch* has."

She pushed past him and opened the door. Unable to speak, she stood at the door waiting for him to leave. Drake glared at her, and then took his time pouring heated water over the herbs she'd prepared in a cup. Finally, he strode to the door.

"I do suggest you keep that temper of yours in check. I am your husband and you will treat me as such."

"My husband—how so?" She laughed bitterly.

"As much as I have to be—for now." He shook his finger at her. "Don't test me." He slammed the door behind him.

Cassandra's teeth gripped so tightly together she feared they wouldn't separate. And they didn't for a long time after he'd left. She donned her black trews with a linen shirt.

Poor Pascal happened to be the first person to enter her chamber afterward. Her colorful language in earlier days would have landed her a cuff in the ear. Instead Pascal stood patiently by until her ire was spent.

"Cassandra, was it so bad?" He walked over to her, an expression of pity on his face.

She gave him an incredulous look and stalked past him. "I've a need for vigorous exercise." Gathering all her strength, she put on her proud posture even as her wounded pride ached within her.

Pascal followed her, as she knew he would, to the library, where he'd taught her to duel. She immediately took her rapier from the wall and swept the thin blade through the air in arcs. She stood ready.

Donning his dueling gear he said, "Get your gear."

Petulantly, Cassandra found her mask and glove and tugged them on impatiently.

"Do you want to talk about it?" Pascal took up his rapier and faced her.

"There's nothing to talk about." She started her attack determined once and for all to best her mentor. Using her unspent ire she sent him fast attacks, never giving him the chance to riposte. But at his warning glare, she politely allowed his counterattack.

A sound at the entranceway nearly distracted her, but she refused to look away from her duel. Pascal laughed as she faltered slightly and rallied even harder. Cassandra marveled as she scored the winning hit.

Her mentor bowed nobly. "And I always thought you'd best me if only you put more passion into your fight. So there you go."

She laughed and let out a Highland whoop. Lunging for Pascal, she hugged him gleefully and he spun her around as he had when she was a child.

A booming voice stopped their revelry. "What is the meaning of this?" Drake stood across the room glowering at Pascal.

Cassandra smiled proudly as she bowed. "A friendly duel with my mentor, whom I've finally bested."

Drake strode toward them. "What's that you're wearing? You're not properly covered."

Her sudden burst of nervous laughter didn't seem to amuse him. She handed Pascal her gear and rapier "These, sir, are trews. Suitable attire for dueling."

"Not suitable for a lady."

"Oh, ho. This is where I leave." Pascal bowed politely and attempted to leave, but Drake stopped him with a gesture.

Cassandra's heart raced. She stepped up to face Drake. "It's certainly none of your concern. And as for what is or is not suitable for a lady—"

"*You* will not trounce about this castle dressed like that." Drake gripped her arms.

"*You* canna tell *me* what to do." Cassandra glared into his eyes just daring him to do something about it.

"I am your husband and you will obey me." He released her.

She drew in a quick breath and noticed how Pascal paled. "Until you act as a husband, I will not obey you."

Drake's grasp just grazed her arm as Cassandra took that

moment to dash for the door. She never looked back as emotions tumbled within her.

Pascal's voice cut through Drake's urge to pursue her. "Sir, if I may offer you some advice, with all respect."

He turned his anger on the elderly Frenchman. "And what's between you and Cassandra?"

Although older, the man looked to be in exquisite health.

"We are only mentor and student. I've known Cassandra since she was a wee one. She's always been spirited and free willed. At first I tried to curb her ways until I realized how to reason with her and show her the way of things."

"And you taught her to duel?" Drake's hands fisted at his sides.

"Women duel. And I've been able to bring the world to her. She's intelligent and wise and has been leading this clan successfully for five years now. It's a hard change for her to answer to a jealous husband."

"I am not a jealous husband." Drake glared at Pascal, wishing he could just punch the man and be done with him. But deep within himself, he sensed the truth of Pascal's words and he respected him.

Drake watched as Pascal prepared a chalice of wassail for him on a side table. Walking over to his side, he excepted the glass. The smell of the mixture brought memories of Christmases past. Sipping the drink, he was delighted at its taste.

"Your cook makes a good wassail." Drake sipped again and it warmed him, making life seem a lot grander. He cast a suspicious glare at Pascal.

"The best I've tasted and I've tasted quite a few." Pascal grinned at Drake's glare, cleared his throat, and simply said, "Reason with her."

A commotion from the courtyard caught their attention

and they went out to investigate. Drake scrutinized the
mass of masked people and noise that jumbled onto the
castle grounds. He caught sight of Cassandra atop a huge
horse waving gayly at the throng. *Mummers.*

Chapter Four

Drake stopped to watch her as she rode through the brightly clothed visitors in the courtyard. She seemed to be searching for someone. Then, with a mighty shove, she nearly unseated a large man from his horse. She whipped off his mask and hugged the man, who promptly drew her onto his own horse.

Beside Drake, Pascal laughed and waved. "She's done it again."

However, his smile froze when his gaze met Drake's glare. Turning from Pascal, he walked swiftly to the stable. He got as far as saddling his horse to ride into the throng and see to his wife when Pascal caught up with him.

"Lord Bancroft, it's a game she plays with the head mummer. They're childhood pals. Artair's but a brother to her. My word. And if you don't think you're a jealous husband you'd better step aside and take a look at yourself now." Pascal bowed slightly to show his respect even as his words stung.

"A game." Drake stopped tightening the cinch.

"He tries to trick her each year with a different costume and mask." Pascal motioned for a stable boy to unsaddle the horse and led Drake to the courtyard.

By that time Cassandra and Artair were on the rampart over the castle gate, waving at the last of the assembly as they entered. His wife and the mummer descended the stairs laughing together. Pascal's knowing expression became an annoyance.

Drake walked toward them just as they said farewell. Cassandra nearly walked right past him. The most beautiful smile lit her face.

She stopped short as soon as she saw him and her smile turned sour. "Drake, the mummers are here. I've a feast to see to and—Oh, my, so much to do. They'll be setting up tents and fires in the courtyard. Maybe you could help oversee that?" With a quick touch to his arm she darted away from him as quickly as she'd spoken.

Now she's telling me what to do?

As he watched her leave, she turned back to him and yelled, "I'll send for you when it's time for us to greet them in the hall." She smiled again and this time it was for him.

She'd been running the castle for five years. Why hadn't a man taken over? Then he remembered Cedric telling him that the king wouldn't let their chief appoint a chieftain.

Still, the display she'd made with that man set his temper a notch higher. Walking back inside, Drake noticed Thurston smiling ear to ear. It irritated him that his seneschal seemed happy here.

"Ah, there you are. I've been looking for you all morning. I couldn't wait to tell you that the rents are flowing in and the people seem healthy and prosperous. We'll have a full castle tonight with the mummers and the extra watchmen. But I tell you, this castle can handle it." Thurston's smile seemed to fade and turned uncertain.

Drake glared at him. "Good. Then you can stay behind when I leave."

"What's got you in such a temper?" Thurston spoke without malice.

"I'm not in a temper!" Drake stalked away, making for his chamber and away from all the madness. He rounded the stairs that led to his chamber and paused to listen at Cassandra's door. Hearing feminine laughter, he listened a moment longer and imagined that she and Leigh were getting on better. If that was Leigh she laughed with. Then he pictured the great redheaded brute of a man called Artair with her. Shaking his head free of the torturous thoughts, he stopped himself from barging into her chamber. Jealous husband indeed. He'd never been jealous in his life.

After glowering in his room for a while, he changed into his holiday finery. Hearing a light knock on the door, he opened it. His eyes savored the beautiful sight before him. Her eyes twinkled at him and her mouth fell open, just a bit.

"Milord, I thought we'd walk down together. What an extraordinary outfit." Cassandra actually curtsied.

So the lady does have manners. He smoothed the green velvet of his waistcoat. "Thank you. And yours is quite nice." He glanced nervously at her rounded breasts above the silky fabric the same deep shade of green as his own.

Drake offered her his arm. When her hand slipped under his arm, he prepared himself for the effect she always caused. Right away a connection. What was that? Could he read her mind? An emotion he'd suppressed for a long time came to him. The smell, the sights, and the spirit of Christmas flowed through him.

When he looked down at her face, she smiled up at him.

"I do so love the Christmas season. The mummers always bring the true spirit back to me. I love their plays and music. Do you enjoy them?"

"Yes." He helped her step down the stairs before him and released her.

Her full dress billowed out with a lace overskirt cascading on its satin. Cautiously, she descended the stairs.

They walked to the hall. It was set up with trestle tables from wall to wall. A large area in the center of the room was left empty except for a few props for the performers. Standing at the door, they greeted the mummers and castle occupants until everyone was seated.

Various mummers brought dice to the people who played against the traveling minstrels and always won. Cassandra watched how Artair spoke to Drake and tried to sense his opinion. Artair's guarded expression didn't help. Then she touched his arm and was rewarded with the perception of respect and envy.

After that the groups of mummers took turns feasting and performing plays about the Christ child. Their exotic music filled the hall. Some of the plays were old legends. Artair sat on the other side of Cassandra. They talked and chatted happily. Drake's mood got bleaker as the night wore on. But at least the wassail still tasted good.

Cassandra excused herself and he thought he saw mischief in her eyes. When he would follow her, Artair's hand fell on his arm, like a great claw, clamping him back down on his seat. The man was round and bearish.

Artair's face came much too close to Drake's. "Stay in your seat, Lord Bancroft. You'll not want to miss this." He released Drake's arm and left.

Pascal leaned across the table. "The last play is always the most elaborate."

Cassandra entered, playing a sweet tune on the violin. She sat beside the manger. The long lace that covered her

skirt folded up over her head, making her Mary. The play-
ers entered dressed as the beasts of the forest: birds, deer,
bear, pheasant, hare, fox, and a cat. They paid homage to
Mary and the babe.

Drake was very amused when Artair showed up as the
bear with the great head atop his own and brown fur
around his ample build. His appearance brought a smile
to Drake's face. Then all the animals left except the cat.
Cassandra started to sing. *She is an angel.* Her voice, clear
and true, sang to the cat, blessing it for all time.

At the end of the play her clan, his people, and all the
mummers cheered. She bowed and let the lace fall back
to her skirt. Artair emerged with a little white kitten, a red
bow tied around its neck. He handed it to Cassandra. Her
eyes lit up as she held the fluffy bundle to her heart.

The expression in her eyes touched Drake's heart so
much it hurt. His heart actually ached for the nurturing
and love he saw there. But when she stood on tiptoe and
kissed Artair full on the mouth, his heart froze. He stood
as his face heated.

Thurston left his seat and came to Drake's side. "Milord,
whatever argument you may have with the lady, please
keep it in your chambers."

Thurston's logic knotted Drake's stomach. And then
he remembered his gift for the second day of Christmas.
Quickly summoning his men he ordered them to bring it
in. They left as Cassandra sat down beside him.

The warmth in her eyes melted his heart, but he still
couldn't smile. He nodded and sipped his drink. His men
summoned her to the clearing and brought in a large
crate. Drake pried it open with his knife and presented
her with the newest musical instrument in the kingdom.
A *piano e forte.*

She marveled at the instrument. "A harpsichord!" Her

fingers wiggled in the air as if in anticipation and she swept open the lid, revealing the ivory-and-onyx keys.

"No, actually it's a *piano e forte*, by the inventor Cristofori. Try it." Drake stood close behind her and brought her hand to the keys. The crowd was silent.

Her hand touched a tentative chord. And suddenly the hall filled with a musical sound that most of them had never heard before. His body still touched hers as he witnessed the music that came from within her soul. The pure love that flowed from her as she turned to thank him warmed him. And the evidence of his warming rose beneath his breeches.

Never in his life had he been so overcome. She put her hands on his shoulder and pulled herself up as she hugged him. Her lips met his and all his self-control left him as he took her in his arms, for all to see, and kissed her. His tongue parted her lips as he sipped at the ambrosial taste of her mouth.

The hall and its occupants seemed to swim around Cassandra as her senses reeled with the sensations his kiss caused. The people erupted with cheers that fell silent as the passionate kiss continued. She could hear the astonished whispers. Drake's lips hardly parted from hers as he picked her up and carried her up to her chamber.

Ladies scurried from her chamber as they entered. In the distance she thought she might have heard Leigh sputtering, "Lord Bancroft!" as if he were doing something he shouldn't. At that thought Drake's lips left hers and he nudged the door closed in Leigh's face.

The intense look he gave Cassandra made everything else leave her mind. She sensed his desperate need. Not just to be with her, but to be loved. She dared not think as he carried her toward the bed. Gazing intently into her eyes, he placed her on her feet.

His hand swept over the swell of her breasts, leaving a hot trail. Gently he turned her around and unbuttoned her gown. Each feathery touch of his fingers heightened her awareness. Cassandra could feel an almost painful melting of his heart as it shed its fear and shame.

She wanted to cradle him in her arms and comfort him. But it wasn't comfort his body screamed for. He wanted her with a passion that scared her. Yet he moved slowly with a calm sureness that she wished she shared.

With her last thought his hands smoothed her gown from her and he turned her again to face him. His hands caressed her face and comfort flowed from his mind to hers. As soon as she calmed he reached around and unlaced her corset.

Cassandra wondered at his knowledge of her need to be calmed and his control of the urgency she could feel building within him. Could he read her feelings as well? As soon as he had all of her clothing removed, he placed her on the bed and moved on top of her, worshiping her body with his hands.

Just before she thought her body would burst from how he touched her, he stopped. His eyes opened wide as if he were waking. The vision of a beautiful manor house flowed from his mind to hers an emotion that seemed to have been born long ago about his home being all that should matter to him. It was all he had left. He yanked himself from her and paced the room. Then he turned, glaring at her.

Cassandra drew a blanket around herself. Her pleasure turned to a dull ache.

He pointed his finger at her. "You almost had me, witch."

Her face flushed, and she gathered the blanket taking

it with her as she left the bed. "I didn't do anything. You were but acting from your heart." She advanced on him, not caring that a storm brewed in his expression.

He looked like he wanted to bolt from the room, so Cassandra moved to block his escape.

"When you touch me," he began.

She clutched the blanket to her heart and tried to change the subject. "You set a fire within me and run like a coward?"

"I told you before, I can't stay in this godforsaken place. I've had too many wassails. I'll bid you good night." He tried to walk past her.

She stood in front of him and pushed his chest. "If you call my home 'godforsaken' again, I'll—" Cassandra's hand fisted at her sides.

He looked down at her hand and laughed. "You'll what?"

His scornful face and laughter rankled. She drew her hand back and sent a stinging slap to his cheek. "Don't laugh at me." Not wanting to receive a reciprocal slap, she quickly moved away from him. She strode to her wardrobe. The ensuing silence made her nervous. Turning, she saw that he had left the room without closing the door.

Leigh walked in, looking concerned.

Cassandra lashed out at her. "It's not your affair. And why were you so shocked when my husband brought me to my chamber as he should?"

Leigh's face reddened and she stammered, "I—I wasn't shocked."

Cassandra pretended to be sorry. "I must be mistaken." She put her hand on Leigh's shoulder but when the woman backed away from her touch she said, "I'm sorry. What's wrong?" Laying her hand on Leigh's arm, Cassandra took in a deep breath. Her touch told her that Leigh had been

Drake's lover and was slighted by him. "Jesus, Mary, and Joseph." Cassandra's oath filled the chamber.

"They say you have a knowing." Leigh cowered from her.

"Oh? Is that what they say?" Cassandra carefully put her anger in check. She rummaged through her wardrobe. Finding the first gown that would cover her, she tossed it over her head.

Leigh moved to help her. "Well, do you?"

"Get away from me." Cassandra tied the simple gown. Grabbing her tartan shawl, she walked to the door.

Leigh followed and stepped in front of her. "You can't leave your chamber. Lord Bancroft has forbidden it. And you never answered my question."

"I simply know what is before my eyes. And I don't give a fig what Lord Bancroft forbids." She marched past her, storming down the stairs. *Serves me right for missing Mass.* Maybe it was still on. All at once her throat got tight and tears threatened. Her clan spoke of her gift?

Entering the hall on her way to the church she noticed the group of mummers dicing and enjoying the wassail. Artair sat on a bench, bellowing with laughter. It brought a smile to her face. Too late, she thought of the ribald comments he would have for her.

"Have ye had your fill already, lass? Easily satisfied, are ye?" Artair bellowed some more.

Cassandra slapped the back of his large head. "Hold your tongue, Artair, or I'll feed your drunken body to the wolves." She slumped onto the bench beside him.

"Ho, ho. I'd best bide by her words, don't ye think?" He nodded to his companions. "We were just thinking about visiting yer orchard with some wassail for another plentiful year."

Cassandra's spirits perked up with the thought. She'd always slunk from her bed without her parents' knowledge to join them in blessing the apple trees. Thinking she'd join them, she looked for a cup. As she reached for it, one of Artair's men grabbed the chalice before she could and took it to the bowl for her.

"I'm ready if you are." She put her hand on Artair's sleeve.

"Drink a warm cup first." His blue eyes twinkled at her.

"I think we should leave before my husband finds me gone." Cassandra stood and took her cup from the man who filled it.

They all took her words as a cue and moved quickly from the hall. Stopping at the mesnie, they equipped themselves with belts and swords, a habit that was born from years of clan wars and many unfriendly neighbors.

As Cassandra buckled her belt, Artair watched the courtyard for signs of Drake. Artair had always loved a challenge. She finished and moved stealthily behind him and then spoke loudly, "Should we saddle the horses?"

The huge man jumped, drew his sword, and turned on her, but she was ready. Pascal might have taught her to duel, but Artair taught her real sword fighting.

"Little girls with puny swords could get hurt playing tricks like that."

"My sword is not so puny."

"Aye, it is." They laughed together and Artair said, "Let's not bother with the horses. I could use a brisk walk."

Cassandra nodded her agreement and led the men out of the castle and across the bridge. She turned to see her guards following. "What? And you'll leave the castle unattended? Just like last night when I came and went as I pleased. And so could've any MacCrory or McDermott!"

They nodded and turned back to watch the gate. The apple orchards stood on both sides of the road that led to Sedgewick. Tonight they reflected the full moon with a ghostly quality that didn't sit right with her. She sipped her cup and listened to the mummers' stories of the nether-worlds as they walked.

Suddenly the apple trees seemed to come alive. Men jumped at them from the cover of the trees. Artair's arm immediately blocked Cassandra. All of Cassandra's party drew their swords.

She called out, "It is I, Cassandra of Sedgewick. Who goes there?"

"There she is—the whore who married the English bas-tard." The voice sounded familiar.

"Nay, I am still a virgin. And he had a father and mother married to each other." She glanced at Artair, trying not to laugh.

Artair raised his brows at her. "The lady asked, 'Who goes there?'"

"You sound Scottish to me. Where is the English baron?"

Cassandra finally placed the voice and spoke loudly. "It's the MacCrory clan."

Pleasantries done, the MacCrory clan sprang into action. Cassandra and her company quickly matched swords. Artair never left her side.

In the fray she shouted directly to their chieftain's son, "I'll not shed Scottish blood on my land. Stop this fight. We're allied with the English now. Accept it or be damned."

"We'd rather take Sedgewick than see it in the Crown's hands." The MacCrory's son matched her sword.

They fought on. Just as Cassandra tired she heard the thunder of horses' hooves and gunfire rang into the night air.

She shouted over the din to the man she fought. "My guess is the English are approaching."

He nearly cut her arm, but she blocked it just in time. Blow after blow left her no choice other than to lunge when she had the chance. Her sword entered the man's leg with a sickening sound. The other MacCrorys fled into the trees.

Cassandra withdrew her sword and quickly tore her dress. Taking the cloth, she knelt down next to the man and stopped the flow of his blood.

Artair loomed over them. "Let me finish him."

"Leave him be." She continued to try to help the man.

Drake rode up to her pointing his sword. "Move away, Cassandra."

"Nay, I'll not have Scottish blood shed on my land. This is the MacCrory chieftain's first son. You kill him and we'll have a war on our hands. Now help me get him to the castle."

While Drake stared, the other men immediately followed her order and carried the wounded man up the path to the castle. Cassandra followed behind, out of breath and aching in every part of her body. Suddenly, the sound of hooves pounded toward her. Drake scooped her up into his lap. His stern look stilled her protest.

She rested her head on his chest and listened to his heart, sensing his emotions as they tumbled within him. Anger, jealousy, and fear. But the one she heard the most, always finding its way to the top, was shear ecstatic relief that she'd not been hurt.

Then a question surfaced. What could he do to make sure she never disobeyed his orders again? Cassandra answered it, hoping he'd hear her heart. *Just love me, Drake.* She looked up at his face.

His frown deepened. "Did you say something?"

"No. Drake, I—"

"What were you doing out there?"

Cassandra turned her face from his and concentrated on the clip-clop of the horses' hooves on the drawbridge. "We were going to bless the apple trees with the wassail. I did it as a child. It's a tradition."

"Didn't Leigh tell you I said to stay in your chamber?"

She swung around to look at him as the horse entered the courtyard. "I'll not have your mistress as a lady's maid. I told you once and I'll tell you again: I do not need a lady's maid."

"No, you wouldn't need one because in truth you're not a lady." Drake swung down off the horse and lifted her after him. He scrutinized her tattered attire.

Annoyed that he hadn't let her dismount on her own, she glanced down to see if she was covered properly and stomped away.

"Wife!" Drake's voice stopped her.

A hot flush shot through her. Turning, she stalked back to him. "I have a name. And you haven't yet made me your wife."

He gripped her arm and started to march her through the hall. "We weren't done with our conversation. Did Leigh tell you she'd been with me?"

Sheer green rage threatened to overcome her. She tried to free herself from his grasp. "I must take care of the MacCrory."

"Answer my question. What did Leigh tell you?" Drake's grip on her arm tightened.

Cassandra yelled in his face. "She didn't have to tell me anything."

They walked into the hall and toward their tower. Some of her clan ladies looked their way as they passed. They looked ready to defend her. She smiled at the thought.

Drake yelled to them. "Get your lady a bath immediately. Tell Leigh to keep the MacCrory alive."

The fight in their eyes vanished as they scattered to do his will. *Cowards.*

He let go of her arm. Cassandra rubbed it and opened her mouth to disagree with his order.

Drake held up his hand. "Don't even speak. Leigh is

skilled in the healing arts. Get up to your chamber." His glare promised retribution should she not listen.

With control she didn't think she possessed, she turned from him and walked up to her chamber, shouting oaths to the rafters all the way up. Until she heard his shouted warning from behind.

"Cassandra!"

He made her feel like a child. Regardless of his station as her husband, she was still the lady of this castle.

"She is the most audacious woman I have ever met. She could have been killed." Drake paced in front of Thurston. "I don't know whether to put her in stocks, beat her or—"

"Love her?" Thurston laughed.

"That's not what I was going to say." Drake glared at the older man. Sometimes he suspected that Thurston knew him better than he knew himself. Was the pain in his chest love? And that desperate feeling when he saw Cassandra fighting for her life? Was that love too? Yes, it seemed that throughout his life, loving had always brought him pain and desperation.

But did he love Cassandra or just feel lustful toward her? He certainly wanted to have her beneath him. When he lost control and carried her to her chamber it was like nothing he'd ever felt before. The only love he'd known before was his mother's gentle caring and the love of Wellington his father had instilled in him.

Chapter Five

When Cassandra entered the Great Hall early the next morning, the light just barely filtered in through the upper windows. As she walked over to the wounded man she noticed his color seemed good. Leigh slept on a pallet beside him. Cassandra was surprised that she knew the healing arts, and by the look of it she knew them well.

Cassandra's stomach growled, so she strode into the crowded kitchen, which was full of early morning activities and the fresh smell of baked breads. Holding her morning tea out to her, a kitchen boy scampered to do her bidding.

"Thank you. Run and fetch a messenger." She watched the boy run off, looking proud of his important mission. Taking some bread and cheese, Cassandra headed back to the hall. The ever full wassail bowl mocked her. She reached for her herbal bag, looking for something to stop the pounding in her head. Sitting at her table, she sprinkled some powdered white willow bark into her tea.

Cassandra laughed at the memory of Artair finding his

way into her chamber through the secret passage after she'd been banished there. His simple, "We havena' blessed the trees yet—ye don't want to cause an apple blight, do ye?" had her laughing all the way to the orchards, where the rest of the mummers waited. They drank more wassails and happily poured the rest at the base of the trees.

On her way back through the hall, she'd cautiously checked on Leigh and the MacCrory. He would live. Thank God. Thurston had caught her gaze from the balcony under the windows and his eyebrows raised. She mouthed, "Don't tell," putting her finger to her lips, and went up to her chamber.

Now she glanced up to see Drake saunter into the hall. He looked like the cat that had finally caught the bird. The bird, most likely, was she. "Good morning, Cassandra."

She slanted a glance at him. "Good morning."

Drake sat beside her and motioned for a serving girl. After telling her what he wanted, he turned back to Cassandra. "So you didn't run into any more MacCrorys? When you went out again?"

His calm words shook her to attention. "Nay, only the owls and the night moon."

He confidently stated, "I'll be leaving today for an audience with King George to straighten this situation out. No sense setting down my laws if I'll not be staying."

Just as his words sank into her startled mind, the messenger she'd sent for walked up. Wrenching her attention from Drake, she turned to the other man. "Bring some men with you to notify the MacCrory that his son is well and is being cared for. We'll take him home when he's able to travel. Tell him he's welcome to come see him."

The messenger nodded and left the hall.

Drake's smile was cool. "There, you see. You don't need

me." He began to eat the stew the serving girl had just brought him.

Cassandra tried desperately to conceal her response to his declaration as her heart began to sob. With a calm she didn't feel, she ate quietly beside him. She couldn't think of any words to say, aside from pleading. Far too proud for that, at least in public, she sat searching for the right words. After all, she couldn't *make* him love her and her home. But he already did. Her touch had never told her falsely.

Thurston sat down opposite them and Cassandra sent him a glare. His questioning expression made her mouth the word, "Traitor." She frowned.

Thurston shrugged and said, "What?"

Drake laughed at the man's confusion and turned to Cassandra. "It wasn't Thurston who told me. Actually, I came to your chamber—only to find it empty. Again."

Cassandra nearly choked on the bread she chewed and refused to look at him. Instead she glanced up at Thurston. "Did you know Lord Bancroft is leaving today? Will you be going with him?"

She had to smile at the disconcerted look on Thurston's face. Daring a sidelong glance at Drake, she was happy to see his gloating smile turn into an annoyed line.

"Drake, there's no use doing that," Thurston said. "I told you before to just accept this as your fate. I know you well enough—I feel strongly about this. It's for the best."

Thurston's understanding of Drake's loss reflected in his eyes. Cassandra longed to touch Thurston to see how deeply he felt. But she would appear odd and most likely raise some unwelcome questions.

"We'll leave today. I'll not discuss it further."

Thurston rummaged through his pockets and produced a rumpled piece of parchment. He tossed it in front of

Drake. "I don't believe you finished reading the king's order before you threw it to the wind. Luckily, I found it."

Drake pushed it away as if it were poison. "I read enough of it."

"I've never known you to be a foolish man." Thurston nodded to Cassandra as she reached for the parchment.

She opened the order and the familiar seal and script reminded her of the day she had received hers. Quietly, Cassandra read it and smiled. Her cause was not yet lost. "It says here that after the initial order you should not seek an audience with King George about this matter.

"He realizes what you're forfeiting and will greatly reward your loyal service to the Crown. But he feels you would be more comfortable in the Highlands since your family, after all, is Catholic. The king also adds that he hopes he'll not have to take Wellington from Cedric—should you decide to disagree with his order."

Fury stained Drake's face. He stood, pounding his hand on the table. "And you can smile at this?" Without another look at her, he strode from the hall.

Cassandra's heart could feel his disappointment even though she wasn't touching him. Tears welled in her eyes.

"He does you a great injustice. No one could hope for a better wife." Thurston seemed to be having a time with his own emotions.

"Oh, Thurston, he's lost the only thing he's allowed himself to love since his mother and father died." Cassandra left the hall and headed for the stables. She arrived in the courtyard just in time to see Drake ride out through the castle's open gates.

Hastily she saddled Nighthawk, grabbing an extra tartan for warmth, a weapon, and a belt. As she left the castle on her mount, she could see Drake heading for the moor. His horse didn't know the moor the way hers did. Spurring Nighthawk into a gallop, she quickly caught up.

He tried to urge his horse on faster.

Cassandra shouted to him, "Give a care—for your mount at least. Follow me." She passed him and led them for a brisk run.

They continued to thunder down the frozen moor for miles. The air chilled her lungs. Cassandra and her mount skillfully led them through the rough land. The majestic mountains surrounding them silently watched their flight. Just before the moor ended at the base of a mountainside, she reined in.

The horses' sides heaved from the run. Silently she led Drake up the path to her favorite waterfall. It stood frozen in glistening white cascades. Although it wasn't a very large fall she loved how it froze in the winter. The faint sound of water flowing within the ice fell on her ears. Proof that the fall still lived. She likened it to Drake's heart.

His eyes widened at the sight. They dismounted, leaving the horses to nibble at the barks of the trees. She led Drake to a cave beneath the falls' frozen cascades.

"Amazing. I've never seen anything quite like it." Drake's gaze settled on her with a warmth that threatened to melt the mighty fall. "Or quite like you, for that matter." His arms surrounded her as he pulled her to him.

Cassandra buried her face into the fur of his cape. His surrender seemed to make his heart shudder within him. Although she doubted actual tears would fall from his eyes, she knew his heart wept. In her mind she could discern his lament: *Wellington is no longer mine.* Her own tears wet her face.

Drake suddenly stood back from her and asked, "How do I know what you're feeling?" His hands gently dried her tears. "You're crying for me." His eyes glistened brightly.

"I know how much you love Wellington. I know how I would feel if someone took Sedgewick from me."

He pulled her close again. She knew his tears finally fell

and she could feel his heart beginning to thaw. Cassandra put her extra tartan down on a stony ledge and they sat together.

"Cedric will have it. It's not like I'll never see the estate again. But I was the firstborn. My father instilled his passion for the place in me—he raised me to run Wellington. Not Cedric." He turned his sad eyes to her.

Cassandra nodded her understanding and traced the path of his recent tears with her finger. "I can't blame Leigh for wanting you. You're a bonny man, Drake Bancroft." She rested her hand on his.

"I never loved her."

"You've never loved anyone, have you?" She tilted her head to him and grinned.

"I don't know." He lifted her onto his lap so she straddled him with her wide skirt billowing around his legs. His gaze memorized her as he kissed a path across her cheeks.

"I know that you do." Placing her hands on his shoulders, she moved from his kiss to gauge his reaction to her words.

"And whom do I love?" His mouth quirked into a smile.

"I'll nay tell." Cassandra shook her head. Then she took that opportunity to kiss him full on the lips.

She drew in a quick breath as he answered her kiss with his tongue playfully entering her mouth. She drew in another breath that kindled the fire building within her. For the first time Cassandra didn't try to stop the feelings that flowed to Drake.

The center of her being awoke to an aching need. She moved closer to him, creating wonderful sensations. His body reacted to hers. His kiss deepened. Immediately she could feel him hardening beneath his clothing.

Setting her abruptly onto her feet, he spoke a little breathlessly and adjusted his trousers. "Let's get back to the castle." The warmth in his eyes didn't dim, but deepened as he gazed into hers.

"Aye, and make haste." Cassandra ran down the path to the horses, laughing.

Drake followed, his laughter echoing hers. "It's lucky we didn't melt this fall and send it pounding on our heads."

Mounting the horses, they rode briskly down the trail and across the moor.

By the time they reached the castle, a light snow had begun to fall and the inhabitants were in a state of alarm. A watchman had spotted an army of MacCrorys headed their way.

"They could be coming to collect the chieftain's son. And to make sure he's really alive. I did invite them." Cassandra looked up at Drake, who was all too ready for battle.

But then he seemed to compose himself. "We'll greet them as guests. Cautiously."

"Maybe you should stay out of sight." Cassandra shrugged, trying to seem nonchalant.

"I'll *not* stay out of sight." The expression on his face made her unwilling to disagree with him.

"Just remember, the MacCrory clan still has a strong dislike for anyone of English blood. Let me speak to the MacCrory."

Soon the courtyard filled with her men-at-arms, all the able mummers, and the English soldiers Drake brought. Cassandra and Drake stood on the rampart above the guardhouse, with shields and crossbows hidden beside them.

When she caught sight of the leader she leaned closer to Drake and pointed out the chieftain of the MacCrory clan. He nodded as they waited for the army to arrive at the castle gate. Cassandra was amazed at the inner strength Drake possessed. She could sense no fear.

But she did notice a certain pride. Reaching to touch his arm, she tried to sense what made him proud. Her heart leapt at the answer. He'd finally taken a good look around and realized what a magnificent castle Sedgewick is. She hooked her arm around his and smiled up at his questioning expression.

That is good, because I'd like to keep you.

Drake laughed, but looked down at her a little startled. "How do you do that?"

At that moment the MacCrory chieftain stopped in front of them. "Lady Cassandra MacIntyre"—he gestured a bow from atop his horse—"how do I know this isn't a trap?"

"You know because, if I'd wanted to trap you, I'd have done so a long time ago."

The chieftain laughed. "You haven't changed, lass. But now you've stabbed my son?"

"Regretfully, and entirely in self-defense. I did ask him to stop the fight before I gave him the unfortunate wound."

"As it happens, the raid was not ordered by me and would not have been. My apologies, Lady Cassandra, and to you also, Lord Bancroft. How is my son?"

Cassandra nodded to acknowledge his apology. "He is mending."

"Can he travel in a wagon?"

"Aye, if you take care and travel slow. I'll have the mummer Artair bring him to you."

"So be it." The chieftain motioned his men to move back across the drawbridge. "My thanks." He waved a farewell.

Drake had stiffened next to her.

"Don't pout. It's a lot more difficult to deal with the MacCrory if you don't know him. He bounced me on his lap when I was a babe. If you'd spoken, it could have turned out differently. It's good he purposely let us know he's not going to forcefully disagree with the marriage as his son did.

"But know this: It doesn't sit well with him. He was behaving well today. I've seen his manners much worse. And against the English, he is brutal."

Drake's brow creased as Cassandra and he turned to leave the rampart. "It could be a trick to get his son out before they try another attack."

"That would be a possibility except that isn't how the MacCrory operates, although he probably did order the attack." Cassandra walked down the narrow stairs that hugged the castle wall.

Artair appeared with another man, carrying the man on a plank. Cassandra laughed as she heard Artair muttering, "Ye best breathe heavy or they'll think you're dead."

She and Drake walked to the Great Hall in silence. Placing her hand in the crook of his arm, she looked up at him. "Scotland is a different land. You'll learn her ways and I'll wager she'll learn some of yours."

"Will she?" His mien darkened with a frown. "You never did answer my question. How do you know what I'm feeling and I you?"

"You can sense what I'm feeling?" Cassandra's suspicion was correct. But how could she explain her gift to him? She'd never explained it to anyone. She walked faster, concentrating on her feet so as not to trip on her skirt.

Drake turned to her and caught her arm, stopping her before they entered the hall. "I distinctly heard you say, 'I'd like to keep you.' "

"I don't know how I do it. I just always have. For a great part of my life I thought everyone could sense each other by touch. Then I realized it was a trait only I possessed." She shrugged. "When you touch others, can you hear them?"

"No. You sense what everyone feels? You know my every thought?" Drake took a step back and away from her touch.

"If I touch you." Dread filled Cassandra, but she couldn't touch him to see what he felt about all this. However, before he released her, her last perception of him was reluctance.

"Why didn't you tell me this before?" Drake's color deepened.

"I've never told anyone. Do you think I wish to be burned as a witch? And would you have understood?" She tried to touch him and he lurched away.

"You deceived me." He turned to briskly walk into the Great Hall.

Cassandra's heart could not take much more of this. She walked directly to the kitchen and asked a boy to bring food up to her room. No sooner had she given the order than Drake, who stood behind her, canceled it. Deciding she wasn't hungry anyway, she calmly left the gaping kitchen boy and ignored Drake. As she strode across the hall, she noticed that people who would normally stop her to talk avoided her.

Good. The heat in her cheeks cooled only under the onslaught of tears. At least she'd made it to the tower before the torrent started.

After running up the stairs to her chamber, she slammed the door and fell on her bed. There she was again. He'd reduced her to a tearful child—but her anger would not surface. Instead, she mourned the love she was sure she'd lost, and all because of her peculiarity. She'd never lied to him, yet he called her deceitful.

Cassandra always prided herself on being sure of a good outcome, even in the darkest of times. Moping around didn't appeal to her. Drying her tears, she climbed off her bed and walked to her water bowl. She splashed the chilly water on her face and decided to calm herself and have a tea.

With a powerful whoosh her chamber door opened. She spun to see Drake striding toward her. He purposefully flung her over his shoulder and strode from the chamber.

"Put me down!" She kicked against his hands, which gripped her thighs. "Right now!"

"Let your clan see who is the weaker of us two and who they should heed." Drake descended the stairs.

Cassandra fought to push through his pulsing fury. What motivated such behavior? Finally, she determined the problem through his touch. The kitchen boy—he'd been bringing her food, regardless of Drake's order. The fool. But she would expect no less from her clan. "Humiliating me in front of my clan is not the way to handle this. What did you do with the kitchen boy?"

At the last step Drake froze and dumped her onto her feet. The fury in his glare heated her own.

"Answer my question." Her words held as much menace as his glower.

"I sent him back to the kitchen." He grabbed her shoulders and quickly let go, apparently remembering her gift. As he crossed his arms in front of his chest, confusion seemed to play over his stern expression.

Cassandra also crossed her arms. "You've won. My clan will acknowledge that, if I simply enter the hall with you. By now the tale has made it to the mice themselves. The people of Sedgewick watch out for me. They know and trust me." She started to lay her hand on his arm and quickly withdrew it before she touched him.

He nodded and offered his arm to her. His thoughts as she touched him remained guarded.

Cassandra cursed his insensitive arse and watched his eyebrows rise. "You see? I have just as much at stake at our perceptiveness as you do. You can sense my thoughts. Don't be so quick to disregard your heart."

"My heart causes me naught but pain. I choose to disregard it."

They reached the arched doorway to the hall and stepped through it. Although the people continued to talk, she could tell they noticed their entrance. Drake seated her and she smiled sweetly at Pascal.

"Pascal, where have you been keeping yourself? We nearly had a siege and you were not to be found." Cassandra took a sip from the cup of wassail Artair so dutifully brought her.

Pascal blanched. "I rode out to help Leigh deliver a baby."

Cassandra's glare snapped up to impale Pascal. "Why wasn't I called?"

"You were out on the moor when we received the message and Leigh insisted on leaving immediately." He reached a hand across the table and patted her arm.

"Don't patronize me. In truth, I've had about as much as I can stand." She wondered if Pascal could hear her words as she spoke through gritted teeth.

His hand squeezed her arm.

"So no one in this castle is to listen to my words? Leigh leaves the MacCrory to tend to a baby that I was supposed to deliver?" Her body shook.

"Your people have a lord now. They honor you by following your husband's orders. And Leigh is a worthy midwife. The baby was delivered without incident." Pascal always knew how to tell her the way of things.

"They do me no honor and I have no husband." She put her hands on the table, ready to stand. Suddenly Drake's arm was around her shoulder in an affectionate fashion, ceasing her effort to rise.

He whispered in her ear, "You complain overlong about

my ineptitude at being a husband to you. Perhaps it's time
to remedy that?''

Drake's whisper sent a bolt of awareness through her,
striking a flame of desire within her. Artair offered her a
violin at that moment. *God bless, Artair.*

She stopped the bitter words forming in her mouth and
simply asked, ''May I?''

Drake murmured, ''Please.''

The mood that she discerned from his touch made her
ire melt, sending liquid fire to her feminine regions. She
took one last sip of her drink and waited for Drake to
remove his arm.

Before he did, a vivid picture of what he would do to
her flicked through her awareness. She took a startled
breath and glared at him, shocked.

He chortled. ''Maybe it is a gift to consider more seriously.''

''And secretly,'' she whispered in his ear.

Chapter Six

As the sweet lilt of the violin went on and on, Drake wondered if his breeches would be able to stand the volume of his arousal much longer. Did she play overlong, or was it his imagination? He watched how she made the bow stroke the strings. They sounded slow and seductive. *The temptress.* She was doing that on purpose.

When she finished, he would assure the inhabitants of the castle and the guests that their marriage was true. He called one of his guards to bring his third gift for her into the courtyard. He sent Leah for Cassandra's fur cape and his own. Finally, the music stopped. Amid the cheers, he rose to escort her back to her seat.

Her knowing smile raised his ardor even more. He knelt on one knee before her and took her hands. Kissing her palms, he worshiped her fingers for the music they'd made. The people quieted and a collective sigh could be heard. Cassandra's blush heightened her beauty.

Standing, Drake announced that the assemblage should

come to see Cassandra's third-day-of-Christmas gift out in the courtyard. He wrapped her cape around her shoulders and fastened the front. Then he donned his own. They led the merrymakers out to the courtyard.

Before them stood the sleigh that Drake had taken pains to bring through the wild Highlands. It was ornately carved and painted white with a golden trim. Four horses were harnessed in front. Drake watched Cassandra's expression. Her eyes opened wide.

"How beautiful!" Cassandra ran her hand over the smooth grooves in the large spiral that led to the sleigh's polished blade. Drake helped her onto the wooden seat and sat beside her. He lifted a large tartan plaid and covered their legs.

She raised a questioning brow at the unfamiliar plaid.

"Distant Scottish relatives. You see, some Highland blood flows in my veins." His grin went straight to her heart.

"I knew there was something I liked about you." Her laugh was cut short by his lips covering her own. She was unprepared for his kiss, and the desire that had been building since their romp on the moor burst within her. When he stopped the kiss to look at her, the alluring expression on his face reminded her that he could sense her desire.

The promise in his eyes as he took up the reins made her happiness soar. The crowd cheered them on as he shook the bells that adorned the reins, sending the horses into action. They leapt forward and out of the castle gate with a steady jingle. The drawbridge covered with freshly fallen snow led them into the pure white world beyond.

Cassandra huddled close to her husband and wondered how he would feel when they finished the day. Would he come to her bed? Drake nodded, but didn't look at her. It was still difficult for him. She sensed his pain returning.

Sending soothing thoughts to him, she realized that this time he didn't close himself to the healing.

The frosty air nibbled at her cheeks and the light ping of snowflakes fell and stuck on her lashes. When the apple trees ended, a meadow surrounded them. He steered the horses into a wide arc and headed back to the castle. Halfway there he urged the horses to a halt, making the bells sing loudly. He took her into his arms.

Instead of kissing her, he motioned toward the castle with another nod of his head and whispered, "Look at her." A sigh escaped him, sending a frosty mist before them. "She's a grand lady you would share with me."

"Aye, grand and in need of some loving care."

Lights glittered from its windows, as snow fell lightly about the looming walls of the castle. Guards walked the rampart like great stuffed bears. She could almost see their breath.

In silence, Cassandra savored the camaraderie of their shared thoughts. Almost subconsciously they communicated and bonded. At that moment she knew that loving this man would fill all her emptiness and her soul wouldn't have room for sorrow. And neither would his. But was he ready for it?

Drake broke their thoughts as he moved from her and jingled the reins. The horses pranced back to the castle. A blanket of darkness gently enveloped Sedgewick as they rode through the gates. But the steadily falling snow lightened the night.

Thurston met them in the courtyard looking concerned. "A word, Lord Bancroft."

Drake huffed in annoyance. "Not now, Thurston."

"It *is* important, milord."

"Nothing you couldn't handle, I'm sure." He smiled down at Cassandra.

She frowned, trying to ignore the worry that threatened to ruin her mood.

"Very good. I'll see you at your convenience." Thurston's guarded expression further worried her.

Drake swept her into a waltz to the door of the hall, lightening her mood. Thurston opened the door and Drake strolled her passed him and up to the wassail bowl. Cassandra's eyes widened, but then she decided she was ready again for the potent spiced drink.

He ladled some of the spiced brew into a chalice and held it up to her lips. His eyes glowed with a happy light and the intensity of their green sent anticipation coursing through her. She pushed away a wave of disharmony that she sensed in the air as she sipped the drink. Now she would think only of Drake. Her due, she decided after years of lonely leadership.

The mummers announced their last performance. They would leave in the morning. Cassandra reached up to kiss Artair farewell. By his touch she sensed that he knew he wouldn't be seeing her until next Christmas.

"Go with God, Artair."

"And you." Artair shook Drake's hand and joined his group.

"Why must you do that?" The annoyance in Drake's voice assaulted her ears.

"Artair is a dear old friend and I will always do that. But never this." Cassandra put her hands behind Drake's head and tilted it so their lips met, using her tongue to make her point.

Drake's deep laugh vibrated against her lips. He drew back from her. "I concede." With that he swept her into his arms and made his way across the crowded hall, winking at the women he passed. "I'll not wait through another performance."

The thrill of his words made her squirm. A sudden fear of something relatively unknown invaded her senses.

Drake kissed her ear and whispered, "Relax. I won't bite." Teasing, he nibbled her ear. "Too much."

Cassandra moaned. As he mounted the stairs, she leaned her head back dramatically, exposing her neck to his kisses. His hand worked away the bindings in her hair, leaving it to flow freely.

He spoke between kisses. "You shouldn't bind your hair."

Cassandra found herself unable to speak. Her desire threatened to drown her. He kicked her chamber door open and shut again, placing her on her feet before the fireplace. She could barely stop her wobbly legs from buckling. He let her go and their gazes locked. Facing him as he circled her, she moved so they wouldn't lose eye contact. His seductive scrutiny never wavered, sending a shiver down her spine.

The intensity of his eyes softened. He stopped and slowly plucked open the hooks on her bodice. The thick cloth fell away to reveal her shoulders and breasts. She heard him take a deep breath as he lowered his mouth to rain light kisses on her bared skin.

Cassandra's desperate need made her grasp Drake's shoulders. He responded by lowering her gown to her waist and caressing her back as he continued to taste her. She needed more.

Pushing him away, she grinned at his foreboding glare. "I want some too." She moved her hand to unbutton his shirt. His quick breath fell on the top of her head as she steadily worked her way to his breeches. Her hands stilled at the sight of his arousal.

Sensing his need she knelt and kissed him, slowly lowering his trousers. Abruptly, he brought her to her feet as he kicked free of his clothing.

He clucked his pleasure. "I've a bold lass."

She reached for him and he playfully caught her hands and placed them on his chest. As she smoothed her fingers up the line of dark hair that branched at his collarbone, he freed her from the rest of her clothing. With a tug on her skirt her petticoats ruffled to the floor.

Moving from her touch, he knelt and smoothed her hose down to her leather shoes. Cassandra lifted a foot at a time, allowing him to remove them. Slowly caressing his way up her leg, his hand found the root of her desire. Her breath caught in her throat and she didn't dare breathe again and end the torturous pleasure.

As he stood, his hand continued its exploration. His finger encountered moisture there and then her tender bud. As he kissed her, his finger moved slowly into her. Cassandra's legs swayed with the intense sensations building within her. Her stomach tightened pleasantly.

Drake's low moan as he pressed himself against her nearly sent her over the precipice on which she balanced so precariously. With one graceful movement, he lifted her so her belly met his lips. Carrying her to the bed, he placed her there and climbed up.

Fear slipped into her mind and threatened to engulf her enjoyment until he smoothed his hand over her forehead and kissed her eyes. His manhood probed gently against her moist center. Drake's desire-filled eyes met hers as he thrust quickly and precisely.

With a stab of pain her maidenhead gave quickly to their ardor. As he moved slowly within her, she watched his eyes close with intense pleasure. And she experienced his passion, as well as her own, until they were completely absorbed in one another.

Everything else ceased to exist but the two of them in utter and complete surrender. She could feel the beauty of his discovery. There was no pain in loving her.

A sudden tightening and intensity of their passion exploded into a pulsing silken heat, filling her and emptying him. They lay still and she sensed his pleasure dissipating. The pain that ripped from his soul at his loss returned. She pulled from him. Was she not enough to quell his pain?

"There are times when a woman shouldn't know the thoughts of a man. If you didn't have your gift you would never have known."

"Never have known what? That you don't love me?" Cassandra's heart plummeted down that precipice that earlier had caused her such joy.

"We never spoke of love." Drake left the bed, gathered his clothes, and walked from the chamber without dressing.

She followed, her ire just beginning to erupt. "It's there you fool—I know it is. It is—" A sob ended her words.

He stood before her again, closing the door. "Cassandra." Carrying her to the bed, he placed her under the covers. "I'm sorry. I've given you what I can."

Cassandra closed her eyes to the searing anger that threatened to devour her. *Just leave before you see my true colors.*

In response, Drake turned and strode from the room.

For a long time she clamped her eyes shut in an attempt to still her rage. Finally she rose, dressed in a heavy woolen gown with a hood, and made her way to the chapel.

The darkness of the night welcomed her. The chill air did nothing to quell her heated body. Stars twinkled down at her from a clear sky. Walking into the chapel, she decided not to miss Mass another day. The door echoed shut behind her and the sound of her steps resounded through the empty church.

The perfume of incense hung lightly in the air. Lighting her family candles, she murmured her prayers in Latin. The rich sound of the words gave her courage. She rose and walked to the pipe organ. Sitting down, her feet began to pump the billow pedals. She played the steady melody of a Bach two-part invention. The music centered her thoughts.

She would no longer mourn Drake's inability to admit his love. Weariness struck her with such force she wished she could sleep here in the peaceful sanctuary. Instead, she walked steadily to the passage, not wanting anyone to see her.

As she stepped through her secret door within the fireplace and into the chamber, a shadow startled her. Suddenly Drake's viselike grip took her shoulders and pulled her out of the fireplace. She struggled, all her peace evaporating. Drake pushed her from him.

"Had I not just taken your maidenhead, I would be anxious to know where you slink off to each night."

"I've been to chapel to try to gain some peace of mind." Cassandra nearly spat the words. "And now I'm tired." She'd meant to ask him to leave, but she couldn't form the words. Turning, she strode to her bed and settled herself under the covers. Then she removed her gown.

Drake turned from her to gaze into the fire's embers. Slowly, he walked back to the door.

"Drake?" She didn't want to be alone.

He stopped walking and looked at her.

"Don't leave."

Surprisingly, he strode to her, removed his nightshirt, and joined her in the bed.

Drake awoke to a sweet freshness. Cassandra's sweetness. His arousal reminded him of what they shared the night before. And then his mind reminded him of his pain afterward. *Damn.* But somehow the pain had lessened considerably.

He began to remember dreams of seedtime. His home and Sedgewick in the springtime. He'd never been at the castle in the spring, but the images were real. He breathed in her freshness and caressed her arm with his fingertips, watching her eyelids flutter open.

Cassandra's sleepy smile plucked at his heart painfully. He didn't want to hurt her again. She moved so her body was up against his and her hand found his swollen member. Stroking it, she gazed into his eyes. Her blue depths . . . so knowing. His hand caressed her breast. He took her into his arms, not willing to wait.

The pressure of her lips on his further inflamed him. He lifted her above him as they continued to kiss. She didn't move, although he sensed that she knew he wanted her to. He cupped her behind, pulling her closer and burying himself deeply within her.

Their kiss ended as she arched her back and moved on top of him. Her eyes widened in amazement as she brought them both to the pinnacle of pleasure. Right before he would release his seed within her, she stilled. Drake's eyes snapped open.

"Say you love me." Cassandra smiled wickedly.

He teetered on the edge—at once enraged and amused. His manhood pulsed within her, aching for release. He grinned back. "Why?" Even to his own ears his voice sounded tight.

"Because you do."

"I love you."

His admission sent them both over the brink as she moved on top of him. Drake rolled her over, pinning her beneath him. "That was a dirty trick."

"You didn't enjoy our lovemaking?" Cassandra smiled teasingly at him.

Even in her precarious position she would tease him? His anger melted with her smile. "You'll pay for that."

"I hope so." Her head tilted. "Did you hear something?"

Drake listened and heard loud banging and crashing sounds coming from the hall. They both vaulted from the bed and dressed hastily. Running out of the chamber and down the stairs with Cassandra at his heels, he was shocked at the sight that met his eyes.

Thurston and Pascal stood yelling and waving their arms in the midst of brawling men and women.

Cassandra met his glare. "Oh, my God." And she flew into action, pulling one of her own women from the back of an Englishman. She ordered her from the hall. When the lady nearly refused, Cassandra moved toward her menacingly. The woman scurried away.

Drake set on his men, each of them ordered to stop their fight. Thurston and Pascal followed Drake's lead and soon the hall was cleared of people.

Drake looked around at the broken benches and tables and confronted Thurston. "What is the meaning of this?"

"I tried to tell you last night." Thurston stood his ground, glowering back at him.

Glancing over at Cassandra, he saw her railing at Pascal as he tried to calm her. Finally she yelled in his face. "Call a meeting in the library." When he hesitated, looking to Drake, she demanded his attention. "Now, Pascal!"

Turning on his heel, Pascal stormed over to Drake.

One look at his wife's glaring countenance heading his way inspired Drake's words. "Do as the lady asks. But just call the people of Sedgewick. I'll deal with my own."

"I think we should deal with them together." Cassandra snapped at him.

Drake forced himself to be calm as he answered. "I said we'll deal with them separately."

"And I said we deal with them together."

Drake nearly laughed at the picture they made. With

Pascal behind her ready to defend her. And Thurston? Turning, he noticed Thurston backing him in the same fashion. "Why? So our people can watch *us* battle and destroy the library as well?" He rested his hands on his hips and ducked his head to her smaller stature, face-to-face.

Cassandra didn't flinch. "All right. I'll see what my people are fighting about, and you see to yours. And then we'll battle it out in private." Her finger stabbed at his chest.

Drake smiled. His body reacted to her, as he remembered their lovemaking. "My men will meet in here. Why would they be brawling so early in the morning anyway?" Scratching his head, he glanced at Thurston.

Thurston looked at him as if he were demented. "It's well past the midday meal."

"Is it?" Drake answered sheepishly as the men departed to call the meetings.

Cassandra strode toward the hall's entrance, her laughter dancing behind her as she walked out. He had to smile at her mirth. Then he turned to see the shambles. Striding to the kitchen, he ordered a boy to bring him as many tools as he could find.

Chapter Seven

Cassandra pulled her blankets up over her head to quell the chill in her chamber. The fire burned low. The chapel bell rang for early morning Mass. Hastily she left her bed and donned her woolen gown over her light chemise. After pulling on her boots, she hurried out of her chamber and down the stairs.

The sounds of hammers and saws fell on her ears. Rich smells of wood and stain met her nose. Drake had ordered his men to work all night, without rest, to restore the hall. After discussing improvements with her, he gave his men instructions. The wassail bowl was put away for the day. Spirits would be low on this, the fifth day of Christmas.

It seemed the people didn't feel properly housed with a tower for Bancroft, one for MacIntyre, and splitting the third between the two. The people claimed that the accommodations didn't match their individual stations.

During her discussion with Drake the night before, she had suggested mixing the two groups so the chambers would be appropriately assigned. Cassandra was surprised when Drake took her suggestion as law and proceeded to set restrictions and penalties on the men who brawled.

Now she rushed past the weary men. Recognizing some of her own, she nodded her approval. She entered the corridor and hastened out the wooden doors, across the courtyard, and into the chapel. The small building was full of sullen women folk, looking ashamed. Walking up the aisle, she curtsied before her front pew, crossed herself, and knelt.

Her traitorous mind couldn't focus on the Latin words being spoken in reverence. Instead, she pictured Drake's glowering countenance as he had told the people his orders. Pascal and Thurston must have been up all night figuring out the housing.

She had ordered her women to attend Mass and recommence duties normally put aside during the holidays. Glancing around the church, she assured herself that they'd all followed her orders. Unexpectedly, her gaze fell on the large sad eyes of a child.

Cassandra realized her decree would affect the innocents as well as the adults. She smiled at the lad and made a mental note to take it upon herself to give the children a kind of celebration. He looked confused at first, but when she winked, he brightened. She was no stranger to the young members of her clan.

Unwittingly, Drake came back into her mind. He hadn't come to her last night, but he had sent her a fourth day Christmas gift: a large trunk full of fashions from Paris.

She'd stayed up a large part of the night looking at them all. A red-and-gold riding jacket and skirt, Steinkirk neckwear, silk chemises, petticoats, morning gowns of Oriental design, and fancy gowns that gripped the body instead of flaring away from it.

The sound of a bell and incense passing by her nose

brought her out of her revery. She noticed that everyone waited for her to begin the communion procession. Rising, she led them to the altar.

Finally, Mass came to an end. Cassandra stood at the door with the father, greeting her people. She whispered to the children as she hugged them. When the church cleared she hurried to the courtyard, where excited young voices met her. Young lads and lassies clambered for her attention.

"Hush now. Let's see who can build the bonniest warrior from the snow."

They all set to work. The skies seemed to support their efforts as the courtyard filled with large flurries and excited laughter.

She started to work on her own warrior, wrapping her hands in her scarves as the children had. Laughing at her own hastily built snow warrior, she helped the younger children erect theirs. Soon the great mounds of snow served as shields as they all threw snowballs at each other. Cassandra seemed to be the favorite target.

A musical sound found its way to Drake's ears. It was her laughter. *The vixen.* Even when he kept away from her, she affected him. As he stopped at a window that looked out over the courtyard, the sight below mesmerized him.

Cassandra and the children. As he watched, a smile grew on his face and suddenly he laughed. Her abounding energy and loving nature targeted his heart with a bitter-sweet arrow. He could see her rosy cheeks and hear her laughter as it drifted above the other sounds. He imagined her special perfume mingling with the fresh scent of the snow.

"I do believe you're smitten." Cedric's voice broke the

spell. Drake's fist swished through the air and Cedric ducked just in time.

"Now, brother. . ."

"Shut up, Cedric. You're the cause of all my problems. Where have you been keeping yourself?" Drake continued to walk along the corridor.

Cedric followed beside him. "Far away from you."

Absently, Drake nodded. "The snow is coming down so steadily, I think we're in for quite a bit more. Cedric, there are things in which I must instruct you. Wellington is a fine estate—in order to keep it that way you'll have to—"

"I know how to run Wellington."

"No, you don't."

"I most certainly do."

"No, you don't. Don't argue with me."

As the snow began to fall thickly, blinding them, Cassandra called a halt to the play and instructed the children to get dry clothing and meet her in the library for hot mulled cider and stories.

Soaking wet and freezing, she stopped in the kitchen to order a pot of cider and went to her chamber to change. As she left the stairs and lifted the bolt on her chamber door, masculine voices caught her attention.

Drake argued with Cedric about Wellington—what else? Her spirits plummeted. Drake still couldn't let go. However long it took him, she would wait.

Shedding her wet clothing before the fire, she breathed deeply to smell the pine garland displayed on her mantel. She smiled as she remembered the children's laughter. Cassandra remembered how her mother had played with them as children in much the same way.

Gazing down at her nude body, she thought about the way Drake had touched her and wondered when motherhood would come to her. She took the few steps to her wardrobe, picked out a long sleeved linen chemise, and pulled it over her head. It hadn't been that long since she'd been a child herself. She still loved to take out the doll her father had made her.

Choosing a blue flannel tunic, she put it on and reached over her shoulders to the buttons behind her back. Tentative knocks sounded at her door. Still struggling with the buttons, she strode to the door.

"Who is it?" She buttoned a few more straining and then reached under to finish the lower buttons.

The door opened at the same time he announced, "Drake." Closing the door behind him, he looked at her strangely. "What are you doing?"

"Buttoning my dress, and I didn't give you permission to come in." She continued her struggle.

"And you don't think you need a lady's maid?" He turned her around to help.

"No. I don't need a lady's maid. There're just a few more . . . " She moved away from him. "There. See?"

"Uh, you missed one." He put his hands on her waist and pulled her toward him.

"I didn't." She tried to look behind.

"Aye, you did." His large fingers fumbled with the small button. "There." He swirled her around to face him.

Their brief contact gave her the reassurance she needed. Drake's need for her was just as great as her need for him. His hand smoothed her tussled hair and caressed her cheek. Cassandra savored the warmth and comfort that flowed between them.

"I've been ordered to tell Lady Cassandra that the children are awaiting her in the library." Drake's smile reflected the feelings she sensed.

"Then we must be to the library." Regretting her promise, she wished they could stay in her chamber.

Drake laughed at her thoughts. "Ah, but duty calls."

They walked arm in arm to the library. The children quickly hushed when they saw Drake with Cassandra. He stood back as she served them hot cider and they gathered in front of the fire, sitting on the rug. She sat on the hearth and began to weave the most extraordinary tale of elves and Father Christmas.

Drake leaned on the mantel, sipping his cider and watching her animated face. He studied each line, the way she spoke, the way the firelight played on her face. But the discovery of her perfection sent an ache to his heart. As he thought of his brother and Wellington he realized he would have to leave. He owed it to his parents to set everything right. And then his happiness could come—but not until then.

When she finished her story, he presented her with her fifth-day gift: a small book bound with a leather cover. The children cheered and Cassandra kissed his cheeks. Her eyes glittered in the firelight. Her face flushed from the fires heat and something more.

Drake peered from the window of his chamber into the early morning. The world outside was covered with a thick blanket of white. Apparently, the snow had not lessened during the night. Letting the heavy drapery cover the window again, he walked to the fireside.

His body ached for Cassandra, but his confusion rankled even more. Blaming the empty pit in his stomach on lack of food, he made his way to the Great Hall.

He met Thurston on the way and they talked amiably as they rambled down the circular stairway. The corridor looked dark as if it were still night. Lanterns lit their way. The hall also had a strange glow.

Glancing at the Great Hall's upper windows, Drake saw

that they were almost entirely covered with snow. The fireplaces roared with welcoming warmth. Cassandra strode toward them, carrying a tray brimming with sweet rolls and hot oats.

"Good morning, Lord Bancroft, Thurston." She nodded at them and set the tray down. "A large breakfast is good on a cold morning like this one. I've assigned men to shovel the roofs."

Drake frowned. He had just as much to learn about Sedgewick Castle as his brother had about running Wellington. He searched the room and got a glimpse of Cedric, asleep on a pallet, wrapped around a serving wench. "Did anyone think to awaken my brother before the hall filled?" Heat suffused his face as he raged over to him.

He stood over his brother, contemplating the best action. Seeing an urn of icy water, he poured it in his face.

Cedric screamed, sputtered, and glared up to see who had assaulted him. "Bloody hell! What's your problem, Drake?"

"My problem, again, is you. Since when do we dally with serving wenches for all to see?" Waving the flustered girl to her work, he continued. "Today you'll attend me in the library and I will attempt to instill some of the learning that Father gave me before he died."

"I already know what he taught you, dear brother. I have better things to do." Cedric headed to the table, sitting opposite Cassandra.

Drake followed, taking his seat beside her. "Go right ahead, and I'll be heading back with you to Wellington after New Year's. I refuse to leave the estate in your hands until I'm sure of your capability."

Cassandra's head, previously bowed over her food, snapped up and she faced him with alarm. Her reaction to his proclamation gave him a startling satisfaction.

"I'm sure Cedric is capable. We'll be needing you here."

She patted his hand, resting hers on top of his, and giving him an all too clear perception of just how she needed him.

Ignoring her intrusive thoughts, he said, "You don't need me, Lady Cassandra. I know nothing of the workings of your castle. The roofs would have collapsed on us all if I'd been in charge."

Her frown set his heart on edge. The blue depths of her eyes darkened, reflecting her distress. "Then let me show you how the castle runs. My ladies are still at their normal tasks awaiting permission to celebrate the holidays once again. Come. We'll free them of their duties as we go." Cassandra stood, waiting for him to follow.

Drake shrugged and stood. They walked to the corridor, where small doorways led to rooms he'd never seen. The first was the candlemaker. The fetid smell of tallow met his nose. A woman stirring a large vat smiled up at them. As he watched she poured a bucketful of herbs into the tallow mixture, and the odor lessened, even turning pleasant.

Drake wondered why their candles held a fragrance, but he wouldn't concede his wonder to Cassandra. "Lead on."

"Our soaps are also made here. In the next room fabrics are woven together and the clan tartan is created." She told the woman to finish her batch of candles and resume her holiday. Stepping aside, Cassandra followed Drake to the weaving room.

He couldn't hide his interest when he watched the spinning wheel form the thread, which was then dipped in the dye. Various colors hung drying. A frowning child worked a wooden mechanism that wound the thread on a spindle. His heart went out to the lass who'd had her holiday cut short.

He knelt on one knee to see her progress. "May I try?"

Looking first for her mother's approval, the child nodded. She showed him how it was done and laughed when he made a tangle. Unraveling the thread, she watched him and smiled as he mastered the skill. He could hear Cassandra telling the lady to lay off for the day. The timbre of her voice set his blood thrumming. He quickly focused his attention back to the child so it wouldn't thrum to the wrong place.

"Go and play now. Your work is done." Drake smiled as the child curtsied and scurried to her mother's side.

Her mother shooed her out the door and finished placing her last thread in the loom. Drake watched in amazement as the plaid took shape.

"How do you get it the same every time?" He leaned over to watch closer. The thick green stripes appeared with thin blue and white stripes crossing it.

"Got a marked stick—see here?" She smiled up at him revealing her gap-toothed mouth.

Cassandra interrupted to lead him into the potter's room, where an old man turned a wheel and shaped clay into an urn within seconds. They announced the commencement of the holiday and went into the seamstress's room.

Heaps of cloth lay on tables and women chatted, quieting when they beheld their guests. Giving them the announcement, Cassandra took him to the smithy. Weapons lined the walls as a large man heated and pounded a sword into shape on his anvil.

Like a small boy who'd just discovered a most interesting bug, he moved into the room. "Incredible."

Cassandra's hand stopped him. "I'll leave you here to ogle the weapons." A fresh scent met his nose as she breezed by him.

Drake watched her leave. He was very impressed with the organization of her castle.

* * *

Cassandra tried to shrug away the ire that continuously built within her. He'd do anything to leave here, to run away from his heart.

Frustrations threatened to ruin her day as she sat at the table watching the English mingle with her clan. At least they looked happier with one another. Her men had helped Drake's men work all night and the next day, even though they hadn't been ordered. Today the refurbished hall filled with merrymakers and once again the wassail flowed.

She'd just have to take the initiative. If he didn't come to her tonight, she would go to him in the morning.

Drake came into the hall leading a procession of men who carried a large rolled tapestry. He strode to her side, tilted her chin up, and leaned down to kiss her. The spark of desire added to her frustration, but she smiled pleasantly.

For a moment he looked concerned but he seemed to shrug it off and presented her with her sixth-day gift. The men unrolled the tapestry and stood on chairs so she could see its splendor. She gazed at a magnificent English manor surrounded by trees and gardens fit for a king. The artwork on the tapestry made it look so real. *Wellington.*

Cassandra's throat dried. She took in a breath trying to quell her jealousy. It was as if she looked at a grand portrait of her husband's mistress. When she dared a glance at Drake, the love in his eyes infuriated her. Then, taking firm control of her emotions, she murmured, "She's a grand lady."

Drake seemed to puff his chest up with pride. "Oh, yes. That's Wellington." He motioned for the men to hang it across the hall on a wall.

Pascal sat beside Cassandra. "Is that Cedric's manor?"

The corners of her mouth quirked up. "Yes, that is *Cedric's* manor."

Drake glowered at them both, his proud smile a thing of the past.

Pascal stood and scrutinized the tapestry from their table. Tilting his head this way and that, looking confused. "It seems to be missing something." His expression was full of mischief. "Ah, yes. It's missing the magnificent mountains. Look how flat and without character the land is."

Cassandra sat biting her lip, trying to contain her laughter, but the cast of Drake's face undid her. Her laughter floated into the air and her spirit soared with the wonderful feel of it.

Chapter Eight

The morning of the seventh day of Christmas just barely dawned with the winter sun diminished further by steadily falling snow. Teams of Bancrofts and MacIntyres wrestled around the clock to shovel snow from roofs and window ledges.

Cassandra took a wistful breath and stepped from her vantage point at the window. The heavy curtain swished back into place. As she splashed her face with frigid water, her mind awoke to the promise she'd made herself the night before.

Drake hadn't come to her chamber. She would go to him this morning. As she considered the wisdom of her decision, her body blazed with the memory of their love-making, sealing her resolution—wise or not. With an annoyed frown she realized that her chamberlain hadn't brought water for a bath up for the last two days.

Tired of bathing herself with a cloth, she rang her chamberlain. It took a while before the woman entered her room with sleep evident in her eyes. Maybe it was earlier than Cassandra thought.

"Please fetch a bath for me."

A voice from behind the woman quipped, "I'll fetch the water."

In annoyance Cassandra realized it was Leigh. Biting back a retort, she nodded grimly. Leigh worked fast and soon a steaming tub of water awaited Cassandra. Thanking Leigh, she dismissed her, pleased that she didn't insist on helping. The warm water soothed her, but she didn't tarry.

With her bath finished, she sat nervously brushing her hair dry by the fireside. Impatient to get to Drake's bed before he rose, she rang the bell again. This time Leigh answered.

Cassandra tried not to show her annoyance. "Is the hall awake yet?"

"No, milady. It's still quite early."

"Thank you. That will be all." She watched Leigh leave.

Her hair was still a bit damp. She clothed herself in a flannel robe. Her body trembled as she went to the door. *This is preposterous. Why should I be afraid to enter my husband's chamber . . . unannounced . . . to seduce him?* The corners of her mouth raised. Foolish as she seemed, the seduction would be worth it.

Her feet brought her to his door, quicker than she would have liked. Smoothing the back of her hand over her lips uneasily, she opened the chamber door. The breeze that met her held a pine aroma she remembered from when she'd nuzzled against Drake's neck.

Tiptoeing to his bed, she pulled the curtain aside and peered in. He slept peacefully, his chest steadily rising and falling. Breathing in deeply, for courage, his essence filled her with sweet yearning. Her stomach tensed. If he rejected her advances he would experience her wrath. She resolved not to leave without a fight.

Discarding her robe, she slid beneath the covers. Her body touched his and he stirred, but his eyes remained closed. Gently, she pressed her leg against his male member and slid her hands over his chest. She kissed his neck. As her lips touched him a low moan vibrated in his throat.

She didn't know if he opened his eyes as his body awoke, stiffening slightly, but she began to perceive a sweet and almost sorrowful need within him. Finally, she gathered enough courage to look up into his eyes.

His green gaze bore into her, as he grabbed her closer and started to graze her neck with his lips. Sensing his need to be even greater than hers, she wrapped her legs around his hips.

Drake lifted his head to look into her eyes. "You thought I wouldn't want you?"

The bittersweet sound of his words brought tears to her eyes. He kissed them away and entered her slowly. Rolling her beneath him, he set a steady rhythm above her. Cassandra matched his movement, savoring the exquisite pleasure within her. Then abandoning the rhythmic pulse, his thrusts quickened and his release pulsed within her.

Losing control of her emotions, she cried out, "I love you, Drake."

He tensed and moved away from her. "Don't. I can't give you what you need." Drake quickly left the bed and pulled on his breeches.

Cassandra's throat tightened, nearly stopping her breath. Pulling on her robe, she trailed him as he walked to his washing bowl and splashed his face. Her sorrow turned to anger. "You just gave me what I need. Why can't you admit it? You feel the same about me. I know you do."

Swiveling to face her, he gripped her arms and backed her up against the wall. "Maybe you just feel what you want to feel."

"Drake, I know about your mother's death. I know you

blame yourself. But you were just a boy—it wasn't your fault. You deserve to love and be loved." Cassandra nearly cowered at the rage she saw building in his eyes.

Taking her roughly away from the wall, he nearly flung her to the door. She stumbled away from him, but swung back to face him, her fists clenched.

Drake advanced, meeting her with the same passion. "You had better leave before I do something else I'll regret for the rest of my life."

"You go right ahead." She taunted him even as his composure faded. "Maybe it'll make you feel again. Maybe it'll melt that icy heart of yours." She punched his shoulder.

Shock registered on his face. "You don't want to do this, Cassandra."

"Why not? What have I got to lose? Not you." She punched his other shoulder. "Did you feel that, Drake? Or are you still so frozen you can't feel a thing?"

"Just barely, and if you think your puny little punches will knock some sense into me, you're greatly mistaken. They may land you over my knee, but that is all. Now leave, with whatever dignity you have left." He turned from her.

Cassandra raged at his back with her fists. Dignity or not, it did her heart good to take her ire out on him. Her fists stilled in midair when he turned to glare at her. Common sense told her to flee, but she refused to back down.

Grabbing her wrists, he propelled her to the door. He released one hand to open the door and she took that opportunity to strike his face with her open palm.

Cassandra watched as he froze and his face paled. He marched her to a chair and pushed her into it with a thump. At least now he wasn't throwing her out of his chamber. Drake paced in front of her raking his fingers through his hair.

Stopping in front of her he railed, "That's enough!" He glared at her and placed both his hands on the arms of the chair. His face met hers, nearly nose to nose. "You will not strike me again. Because if you do I will go against my own beliefs and you"—he gripped her chin—"will be sorry."

His touch told her what he would not reveal with words. Cassandra began to have more respect for him, realizing she didn't know the man before her as much as she thought. She'd grown up in the rough Highlands, where a man backhanding a wife was not rare. She'd expected it, wanted some kind of reaction from him.

But the gentleness in his stare as he understood her thoughts was more than she'd hoped for. His hand caressed her cheek.

She swallowed a lump of pride and murmured. "I'm sorry."

Drake regarded Cassandra's blue eyes as they pooled with moisture. Her generous lips pouted. That extraordinary pain returned, holding his heart in a viselike grip. The same pain he'd felt at his parents' graveside, when he'd finally realized he loved them. Too late.

His fierce independence had put him at odds with his parents more often than not. He'd never been able to show them his love. He didn't know he'd never have the chance.

Tears spilled from her eyes and onto his hand. He knew she understood. His lips met hers, gently caressing, surface to surface. The sensual feel of their lips touching soothed away his torment.

Cassandra clutched his arms and tried to pull herself closer to deepen the kiss.

Drake pulled away from her. "Aye, my Scottish lass. Ye are a vixen, witch, and angel—all rolled into one."

"Oh? And are ye wishin' ye were a Scot?" She shrieked

playfully as he put on a fierce expression and pulled her to her feet.

"I'm an Englishman, and lucky for you I am." Taking her hand he led her to his door again. "Go and dress." Their lips met again briefly and she did as he asked.

Drake finished dressing and planned his day. After walking down to the Great Hall, he ate a few bites of bread, then set to work.

He picked a group of men who would travel out with Cedric and himself after the storm cleared. In the stables he examined the horses and notified the grooms about their travel. He'd not have to worry about his brother's safety if he went with him. Of course Cassandra could handle Sedgewick. Maybe he'd sort out his thoughts by the time he returned. God, he needed to get away and straighten out his thoughts.

Cassandra checked on her residents, those who had been sick and the very old. They all told her how wonderful Leigh treated them and they seemed very happy. Fighting a twinge of jealousy, she had to admit that another healer in the castle certainly helped. She made sure all of her families were getting enough to eat.

The day passed quickly. She'd seen Drake a few times instructing his men. She nearly laughed when she realized he was still preparing them for travel, even in the midst of the storm. She kept well out of his sight.

Sighing, she realized that at least for now God was seeing that no one left Sedgewick. The storm raged outside the castle's sturdy walls. Pascal had checked on the wood and peat stores and they were plentiful. She always made everyone set aside enough to burn for two winters and then they never ran out.

As she wound her way up to her chamber, the hall

echoed behind her with lighthearted merriment. She shared the wonderful French wine that Drake gave her for the seventh day of Christmas. Pascal had never smiled so wide as he did when she allotted an entire bottle to him.

Tired, but still restless, she made herself a sleeping draft and settled into her bed. Her heart knew Drake wouldn't come to her and she wouldn't go to him again. She'd shown him how strongly she felt. What more could she do?

Regardless of the sleeping draft, she tossed and turned through the night. Finally giving up, Cassandra rose to face the early morning. As she left her room, the chill air of the corridor made her shiver. Then she heard a woman's voice come from the direction of Drake's chamber. Staying in her doorway, she waited to see who would pass.

Leigh nearly skipped past her, feigning satisfaction with a flippant attitude Cassandra read as "I bested you."

Clenching her teeth tightly, she tried to subdue her raging emotions. The corridor no longer chilled her. She wanted to go after Leigh and ask her what exactly had transpired. But she just couldn't conjure up the courage to hear the truth.

When Drake's pine scent drifted to her nose in Leigh's wake, rage pounded in her ears. She would not be so humiliated. She strode toward Drake's chamber, but her courage faltered again.

Returning to her room, she took the passageway to the stables. Nighthawk whinnied as she entered. Men looked up in surprise. She smiled, wrested a carrot from her pocket, and fed it to her horse.

Cedric approached her from the far side of the barn, a frown staining his visage. "He means to drive us through the snow to Wellington."

"Surely not until the storm subsides?" Cassandra began to worry. But after her discovery this morning she almost wished he would go.

Almost.

Chapter Nine

Chapter Nine

Drake paced the library. His brother stubbornly refused to listen to his advice. "Is it not enough that you've stolen Wellington from me?"

"I never stole Wellington from you. You're too stubborn to see what's right in front of you. If you insist on leaving here, I'll know you for a fool. And then we'll agree that our brotherhood is ended."

Cedric wouldn't look him in the eye and quickly stormed from the room. Knowing his brother as well as he did made Drake realize that Cedric was hiding something. Drake had spent the entire morning trying to explain what made Wellington prosper. But Cedric had different opinions and would bring it to ruin with his ignorant arrogance.

The library door opened and Leigh walked toward him. "Milord, I've left the herbal wash in your chamber." Leigh's smile seemed a bit sly. She left, humming happily.

He'd have to tell Thurston to keep an eye on her. He rued the day he'd ever let her into his chamber, but had vowed to see that she married well or held a high position in his household. He never forgave himself for taking her innocence.

And now he'd taken Cassandra's. How could he make it up to her? Leaving would probably be the best way. She could still run her castle the way she wanted. If he stayed she'd be unhappy with the changes he'd make. Unease crept into his rationalizing. She'd gotten under his skin. The thought of not seeing her daily did not appeal to him.

The library door opened yet again, sending a chill to his back. When it slammed, he turned around to see a red-faced Cassandra, her hair hanging free and full over her shoulders. He smiled.

"When are you planning on leaving, Lord Bancroft?" She walked to him, clearly in a rage.

"When the celebrations end." Drake moved toward her. She moved away. "On Epiphany?"

"Yes. What's the matter?" Lifting his hand to touch her, he hoped the contact would give him the insight he needed.

"Nothing. Just be sure you take Leigh." Cassandra turned abruptly, her hair swirling behind her.

"Leigh? No, actually, I hadn't planned on taking her. Your castle needs more than one healer. It would give you more time to attend to other matters." Following her, Drake tried to touch her and failed again when she spun to face him.

"How noble of you. Are you sure your carnal appetite could stand it?"

Grabbing for her again his hand finally made contact with her arm, as he stopped her from leaving. "What are you in such a rage about?"

"I'm sure you know. Don't insult me more by feigning innocence." Cassandra tried to pull free. "Let go of me."

A vision of Leigh leaving his chamber assaulted Drake's

consciousness. So vivid was the picture that he could nearly detect a pine scent. Leigh's misleading mien surprised him into letting go of Cassandra. She thought . . . "Cassandra, come back here." Her jealousy sent a thrill of excitement through him.

Leaving the library, he searched up and down the corridor, but couldn't find her anywhere. She would just have to stew for a while longer then. Maybe next time she wouldn't be so quick to abandon an argument. Did she really care? Or was it just her pride? He pushed away the disconcerting notion that she really did love him.

Entering the Great Hall, he perused the people, who nodded politely as he passed. Cassandra was not in evidence. Leigh helped an elderly woman sip her tea. Sedgewick would be a good place for her. But he would have to deal with her deceptive behavior toward Cassandra.

Drake watched Leigh look up as he approached. Her whole body seemed to stiffen and her movements became stilted. He stood beside her in silence until the other woman left.

"Perhaps you could tell me why my wife is in such a rage this morning." He glared down at her.

"Isn't she always in a rage?" Leigh seemed bitter.

"You may not speak of Cassandra in that way. Now tell me what you've done."

"I simply put your herbal wash in your chamber. Can I help it if she saw me leave?" Leigh gazed into the fire.

"And you didn't explain that to her, did you?" Drake gripped her arm. "You will tell her why you came from my chamber this morning and that I was not within. Is that clear?" He released her.

"Yes." Leigh's face reddened as she strode to the tower's corridor.

* * *

Cassandra's face perspired under her fencing mask. Frustration engulfed her as she tried to gain the winning hit. Pascal eluded her again and finished the duel by scoring the hit himself.

"Damn!" She threw off her mask and watched it skip across the library floor.

Pascal's eyebrows raised. "Perhaps going to Mass would help."

She bit her tongue to keep from uttering the impudent words that entered her mind. "Perhaps." Retrieving her mask, she plopped down in a chair by the fire. "Pascal?"

"Oui?" He walked to her and took her gear, putting it away.

Finally, some courage for the truth came to her. "Have you questioned Thurston about Drake's part in fighting the Scots?"

"Aye, he served mostly in the border towns and never came to the Highlands until now." Pascal sat beside her.

Relief flooded through her. "And Cedric?"

"The same. But Cedric did visit here. He realized that you and your castle would be better suited to his brother. And then he had an audience with King George to give him his opinion."

Cassandra laughed. "I wonder how he drew that conclusion?"

"He was right. Whether Drake realizes it or not, his brother acted out of love." Pascal rose. "I've duties to attend to." He strode from the room.

Cassandra stood and stretched before the fire. She drew her cape around her, remembering Drake's warning about trouncing about the castle in her fencing attire. Why should she appease Drake by doing so? She must be getting soft. Remembering Leigh, she whipped off the cape and marched boldly from the library.

Leigh met her in the corridor. "I've been looking for you. I've been told to make amends for this morning. My behavior purposefully misled you. You see, Drake was not even in his chamber. I just left his herbal wash."

When Cassandra touched Leigh's arm she knew her adversary spoke the truth. "Why did you mislead me?"

"I told you what I've been asked to." Leigh walked briskly away.

Cassandra imagined Leigh's next move would probably be to poison her—or Drake. She'd assign someone to watch her and check her herbal supply. She disliked mistrusting anyone in her castle. Changing direction in the corridor, she walked to the guardrooms.

There sat one of her most loyal, albeit most unruly men-at-arms. Although ruggedly handsome, he lacked any amount of gentleness and always glowered. Perfect. She'd put him on a constant vigil of Leigh.

"Can you find someone to fill your duties? I've an important task for you."

"Aye, milady."

Cassandra explained his duty and left the guardroom. She met Drake walking from the library. He scrutinized her appearance and sauntered up to her.

"Did Leigh speak with you?" Gently he took her cape from her hands and draped it over her shoulders.

His closeness aroused her and his feather light touch enchanted her. "Aye."

"Good." He tied her cape and grinned.

The spell broken, Cassandra swept away, ripping the cape off. Drake's laughter sang out in the corridor.

*   *   *

Sounds of celebration and happy dancing echoed through the hall. With the trestle tables cleared two lines of dancers formed. The men faced the women. Cassandra and Drake moved to the music, changing partners, and twirling one another around.

Even Drake smiled. After the dance he led Cassandra to the wassail bowl for refreshment. "Who's the henchman you've assigned to Leigh?"

Cassandra's gaze met his. "His name is Beathen. Why? Are you jealous?"

"Never. They make a good couple. You're a wise lass." Drake grinned wryly.

"She doesn't seem very pleased with him." Cassandra's smiling lips were met with Drake's quick kiss.

He shrugged, seeming uninterested. "Is this your favorite of the Paris gowns?"

"Aye, it is." Cassandra loved the startling blue of the gown and the myriad silk-covered buttons in the front going all the way to the triangle of white silk over her stomach. It was as if a wide belt were sewn into the dress.

The blue velvet skirt swelled from the waist with a white silk petticoat beneath that peeked out at the hem. The velvet at her shoulders puffed and gathered closer to her arms at the elbow, ending at the wrist with a point of fabric covering the top of her hands.

Some of her drink splashed onto the floor as he took the cup from her hand, placed it down, and led her back into the dance. Holding her close, a slow and sad melody sang from the violin and harp.

Cassandra leaned against his chest, her ear and mind to his heart. He wondered if the snow had stopped. Pushing away from him, she pouted. "Why don't you go and check the weather? Then you can leave tonight on your all-important jaunt."

Drake's hold on her tightened and he drew her up

against himself once more. His fingertips caressed her neck, beneath her coiled hair bun, to sooth her. Releasing the hair comb, he let her tresses cascade down her back. "I thought I told you not to bind your hair."

Cassandra forced away the pleasant sensations, replacing them with bitterness and fear. "Shall we check the snow?"

"Yes, let's."

She realized her mistake too late. At least in the hall he couldn't make her weaken. Why should she satisfy his yearnings if he would abandon her in a few days? Her heart lurched.

Leading her by the hand, quicker than she could walk in her cumbersome skirts, they clambered up the stairs on the sidewall of the hall and to the balcony that skirted the upper windows of the castle. The columns gave them privacy.

Cassandra yanked her hands from his grasp. "What're ye tryin' to do, kill me?"

"Do you have any idea how charming you are when your ire is up? Your brogue is more pronounced. Positively charming." Drake caught her up in his arms and pulled her close.

His kiss softened the grim lines of her lips. His hands roamed her body. She savored the feel of him and marveled at the warmth radiating from his heart to her senses. Gripping him tightly, she searched his heart and could detect no ice there. When had it all melted?

His low laugh set her body ablaze. "Cassandra, I love you."

His mouth claimed hers and her tongue played with his. She sent her message of love to him, pressing closer.

He murmured, "I know," against her mouth and deepened their kiss.

Stopping the kiss, he urged her toward the door to their tower. He draped his arm around her, and tilted his head to rest against hers. They made their way through the narrow upper corridors that led to their tower.

"Then why? Why do you want to leave?"

"Sssh. I don't want to leave. It's my duty. I owe it to my father. I have to see Wellington safe."

"No." Cassandra tried to pull from him.

"Please don't argue about this now." Drake propelled her into his chamber. "Not another word. We'll discuss it later. Trust me?" He stopped in front of the fireplace.

"Aye." The timbre of his voice soothed her worries as she placed her trust in him.

Reaching into a vest pocket he pulled out a golden ring. Her heart raced as he took her hand and put it on her finger.

"Beautiful." The Celtic knotted ring glittered and her heart soared. But a ring would be a shallow talisman if her husband didn't return from Wellington.

"Close your eyes." Drake's hand brushed over her eyes, as if to shut them himself. He plucked at the buttons of her gown. "Eh, eh, keep 'em closed."

She kept her eyes closed, and the cool air hit her skin as he pushed the bodice over her shoulders. Something soft stroked her breasts, making her nipples tighten. Cassandra opened her eyes and caught sight of a feather in Drake's mouth. His hands worked to untie her petticoat.

She laughed at how his eyes widened as he tried to tell her to close her eyes again, with the feather gripped between his teeth. Taking the feather from him, she opened his jacket and shirt and smoothed them from his body. Then she took the feather in her own teeth and stroked his chest as he had hers. Her hands worked to free him from his trousers. Green sparks of desire danced in his eyes.

Cassandra wiggled out of her dress as Drake finished removing his clothing. She laid the gown over the end of his bed. The shifting shadows from the fire moved hauntingly about the room as they climbed into bed.

The fresh pine essence of him floated to her nose as she nuzzled and kissed his neck. He slowly entered her. They rocked together, building the tempestuous flames within. Cassandra struggled to get ever closer to him, as their beings melded together—body and soul.

Closing her eyes, she could almost see the colors their passion created within them, and with one great burst, they both lost themselves in the wonder of their love.

Chapter Ten

Cassandra snuggled closer to Drake. Warmth and love surrounded her, but she still couldn't sleep. She wouldn't rest until she and Drake discussed his leaving Sedgewick. Even though he planned to return, she held a great apprehension that he never would. And she couldn't get rid of the feeling.

Listening to Drake's steady and slow breathing, she couldn't bear to think of being without him. Not even for a time. Restless and growing more anxious with each breath, she decided to go for a brisk run on Nighthawk.

As she eased herself from Drake's side, loneliness seeped into her being. She almost crawled back into bed, but her restless nature demanded release. Donning his robe, she quietly left his chamber and went to her own.

Before taking the robe off, she brought its lapel to her nose and breathed in his musky scent. She'd return before he awoke and her mind would be clear and ready for their discussion. Somehow she had to convince him to trust

Cedric and stay with her. She pulled on some breeches and socks and tugged on a lamb's wool sweater. After slipping her feet into her warmest boots and gathering her fur cape, she made her way to the stables.

Cassandra didn't bother to use the passageway. Instead, she descended the tower steps and walked through the silent hall. Out in the courtyard the clear night sky twinkled down at her. The wind swept the snow into drifts, clearing some areas for passage and creating giant walls in others.

As she opened the barn door, the familiar smell of the stabled animals met her nose. No grooms seemed to be about, which was just as well. They'd probably try to stop her. Nothing else but a ride in the silent snow would soothe her. The familiar whinny of Nighthawk made her smile.

"Aye, lad. I've always a carrot for you." Pulling out a carrot, she fed him and patted his nose. She turned to get the saddle that Drake had given her for the eighth day of Christmas. When she hefted the saddle onto her horse, her heart soared in anticipation of a good run as she secured the cinch.

Pulling on her cape, she walked her horse out to the crystal night. The guards, remiss again, didn't see her leave. She hopped onto her mount and they clopped across the drawbridge. The moon reflected on the snow, lighting her way.

Nighthawk hedged restlessly until she gave him his lead. He took off into the night toward their favorite shore. Suddenly, a shout startled Cassandra. Men on horseback charged her, blocking her return to the castle. She'd forgotten her sword—the realization nearly strangled her.

She fled toward the water, because the frigid depths of the river seemed more appealing than facing the strangers without a weapon. But before she could reach the shore, a man snatched her off her mount. As she fought, she gasped to see another man catch Nighthawk and fasten a parchment on his saddle with a dagger. Then the man cracked a whip beside her horse to send it back to the castle.

Nighthawk stood wild-eyed for a moment, then turned to gallop back.

Drake started awake. The same apprehension that had filled him when he returned to his home as a child—to find his parents dead—struck him with a sickening blow. Reaching for Cassandra in the dark, he found her gone.

"Cassandra?" He quickly left his bed and lit a lantern. Pulling on some breeches, he walked down the corridor to her chamber and pounded on the door. "Cassandra!" His dread deepened.

Growing frustrated with his old fears, he pushed his uneasiness away. She was probably in the hall eating or at Mass. He opened her chamber door, and a cool breeze met him. His robe lay on a chair by the fire, which was almost out. A chill crawled up his spine. Absentmindedly, he threw another log on the fire.

Tracing his steps back to his chamber, he quickly clothed himself, pulled on his boots, and belted on his sword. Loping down the tower stairs and into the hall, he inquired after Cassandra. He was met with, "Nay, milord," and several wide-eyed stares. Growing impatient, Drake walked out into the courtyard. The snow had stopped and the morning dawned with a gray light.

Suddenly, a guard bustled into the yard. He led Cassandra's mount. *Oh, dear God.* Drake stormed up to the man, causing Nighthawk to rear. By the time they got the horse under control Drake was ready to burst.

"There's a note, Lord Bancroft." After handing Drake the missive, the guard drew back from him. He seemed to want to flee.

And rightly so. Drake slapped the parchment on his leg as he spoke. "When did Lady Cassandra leave the castle?" He clenched his teeth and moved toward the man, making Nighthawk shy again. "Bring the horse to the grooms and meet me in the guardroom." Flashes of warmth flooded through his body, moisture beaded on his face.

Pascal walked up to Drake. "Is something amiss?"

"Amiss? I would say so." He threw the parchment at Pascal and strode to the guardroom.

The sight before him sent him reeling and grabbing objects to throw at the slumbering guards. "Can anyone here tell me when the Lady Cassandra left the castle?" Drake's rage thundered through the chamber.

The guards—most of them hired, housed, and fed for the holidays—sprung to their feet, fleeing from the chairs, bowls, and even weapons that Drake threw at them. Throwing things around didn't altered the cluttered room's appearance.

After his tirade, Drake stopped to glare at the silent men. "Alert every man to meet in the Great Hall. Immediately. Lady Cassandra has been taken. Kidnapped." He didn't dare reveal the ransom demanded: his own head.

But it wasn't Drake's head that would roll. It was the MacCrorys', as many as possible, until they returned Cassandra untouched. Thurston and Pascal accosted him as he entered the hall.

Pascal's face looked pale. "It is not hopeless, Lord Bancroft. We've rescued men from their castle before. Look here. I've drawn a layout of the castle. Cassandra also knows it well. I wouldn't put it past her to escape even before we ride out."

Drake gazed down at Pascal's sketch. The Frenchman still held the blackened stick he'd drawn with between his fingers as he pointed out the castle's weaknesses. They studied the map together, devising a plan as the hall filled with men.

Thurston had served as a tactical soldier for some years before he'd left the field and settled down with the Bancrofts. He suggested a plan. Pascal used his knowledge of the MacCrory clan. Together they worked quickly to plot each step of Cassandra's rescue.

Drake assigned men to seal up Sedgewick. No one would enter or leave until the army left to complete their mission. No spies would have a chance to relay the plan. The three men then explained the scheme to the other men. The day was spent learning the strategy and the castle layout.

As night descended, the army left the castle on horseback in a dark line that tracked across the white snow to the MacCrory stronghold. Drake sent a scouting party, not privy to their scheme, to assure the demise of the Mac-Crorys at the outposts. If they were caught they wouldn't be able to reveal their tactics.

As the army threaded its way to the neighboring castle, Drake fought his own battle within. At one moment, he was enraged with Cassandra for being so careless, and the next devastated by the thought of her being harmed.

And he would leave her at Sedgewick while he saw to Wellington? Suddenly, Drake lost his taste for *that* idea. King George was right. They needed him at Sedgewick. Cassandra needed him. The thought warmed his heart, but the warmth quickly soured.

If anything happened to her, his life may as well end. If the plan went awry they could have his head for her life. He wouldn't live with the blood of another women he loved on his hands.

The pounding in her head was so great that Cassandra couldn't open her eyes. She groaned, rolling on the cold stone floor. Memory tumbled back to her. How could she have been so foolish? And now Drake's life could be in danger. He'd never get back to his beloved Wellington.

Slowly she forced her eyes open. The dim light from a torch outside her cell allowed her to see. She lay in a small narrow room with a barred door at one end. As she sat up, her body screamed in pain, reminding her of the fight she'd given the MacCrory men. As she pulled her fur cape around her, her lips quivered. It would be a relief to cry, but instead she pressed her lips together. Tears would have to wait.

Standing, she peered out of her cell. The circular chamber, surrounded by similar rooms, sported a gory wood block with a wicked-looking ax next to it. Dizziness threatened to steal her awareness. But her mind snapped into action. She knew the layout of this castle and even the passageways.

Just last summer she'd seen an army of MacCrorys heading north. She'd petitioned three Sedgewick men to join her in a recognizance mission. They had discovered passages and explored the entire MacCrory castle and had never been apprehended.

She'd found passages to different cells. She prayed they were all the same. At the far end of the small room, she used her sturdy belt buckle to pry a slab of stone away from a wooden trap door in the floor. Suddenly, a sound came from the outer chamber. Cassandra rushed to cover the door with straw that lay in the corner.

"There's no need to hold me. I come willingly." The sound of Drake's voice sent her pulse racing.

"Drake?"

Cassandra clutched the bars of her prison. They walked him into the center chamber with his hands tied behind his back. Pushing him onto his knees, they forced his head down onto the block.

"Release her to my men first." The green of Drake's eyes darted toward her.

"No! Drake!" Cassandra gripped the metal bars and threw all her weight against them. The sound of their rattle against the stone echoed in the center chamber.

"Proceed." It was the MacCrory chieftain ordering Drake's death.

"Are you mad?" Cassandra screamed. "Don't!" She covered her eyes as the executioner raised the ax.

"Hold. Take the lady out of her cell. Make her watch."

Cassandra struggled with the men who held her arms. "No, take my life. I'll give you Sedgewick—take my life instead." She glanced at Drake, who shook his head.

The chieftain's laughter echoed in the stale air. A torch on the wall flickered. "How noble. Has little Cassandra found true love? Then let us take her love from her as her father took mine. Did you not know? My true love was your own ma. Aye, and your da took her from me." He pointed his finger at her as if he blamed Cassandra for the deed.

"Nay, he didn't. She went on her own, and now I see why." Cassandra gathered her strength and broke free of the guards, throwing herself over Drake's kneeling form.

"Get away, Cassandra." Drake's cold voice ground into her as he shoved her away with his shoulder.

Cassandra fell to her knees, begging. "I'll marry your son. You'll have Sedgewick. Lord Bancroft wants to go back to England. Don't do this—"

The MacCrory chieftain's hand ended her tirade, landing her on the ground. Cassandra leapt to her feet to attack him as the guards grabbed her again. Drake straightened up, his eyes sparking with rage, his mouth a thin line of anguish.

All at once the chamber filled with Drake's and Cassandra's men wielding swords. The executioner was the first to fall. She watched in amazement as Drake jumped to his feet, kicking and shoving to defend himself. Her clan protected him, fiercely battling the MacCrory clan.

The guards holding her released her arms to assist their chieftain. Cassandra grabbed Drake's arm and pulled him to the passage. Her men would know to follow, and they'd best hurry. She could hear the footfalls of MacCrory reinforcements coming to outflank them.

A sword slid across the stone floor to her feet as a MacCrory came at her. She grabbed it just in time to parry his blow. One of her men distracted her attacker. She quickly cut Drake's bonds.

He grabbed the sword from her hands. "You've done enough this day."

Ignoring his heated glare, she turned to the trap door and heaved it open. She descended the ladder. Drake called a retreat and followed her. They ran through the passage, trailed by their men.

The dark tunnel loomed ahead of her as she tried to remember each turn. Turning to the left, she became unsure of her direction. Drake's arm reached out for her in the dark, grabbing her tightly.

"This way." Now Drake led. "Be ready. They might have a force of men meeting us at the other end."

"We should be able to get there first. They have a longer way to go." Cassandra struggled for breath as Drake pulled her on. Reading his thoughts as he remembered the path helped her follow him more swiftly.

Finally, they reached the end of the passage. Drake let her hand go and hefted up a wooden hatch. Dirt and snow fell onto them. He climbed out slowly and reached for her.

"It's clear. Hurry."

MacIntyres and Bancrofts scrambled out of the passage

and headed for a stand of trees in the distance. Shouts from the castle behind them urged them onward.

Cassandra's lungs nearly burst with the effort. Men and horses greeted them as they entered the woods, and in seconds, they rode free to Sedgewick. She tried to regain her breath as her mount galloped beneath her. Her horse stayed in the lead. She couldn't see Drake and prayed that he followed behind her.

With her castle in view, she turned to see Drake close at her heels. A glower stained his countenance.

Chapter Eleven

Drake dashed across the moor, and his heart raced when Sedgewick came into view. The morning mist cleared slowly, drifting across River Earn. Then the wind blew, revealing an ominous sign. Now it seemed his possession of this castle would be challenged.

Cassandra gasped. "God in heaven, Sedgewick is flying the MacKay colors!" She turned, glaring at him as if it were his fault.

The MacKay plaid flapped in the wind in place of the MacIntyre crested flag. Cassandra called a halt and the army stopped. Drake protested as she ordered the men to retreat.

Her nostrils flared as she accused him. "What did you do? Leave the castle defenseless to rescue me?" Her mount circled around his, seeming as agitated as Cassandra herself.

His face heated. "Not entirely. Aren't you allied with the MacKay clan?"

Cassandra steadied her horse and glanced from the castle to the river. "Aye. Those whoresons planned this with the MacCrorys. We'll have to retreat. I'm sure they've seen us—the drawbridge is up—we must enter the castle from the river passage." She glared back at the plaid that flew over her castle.

Drake signaled the retreat, not missing Cassandra's sardonic expression. He rode beside her and yelled through the wind. "The Earn is running high and swift. How can we travel it?"

"Our horses are trained to withstand the waters. We'll have to move quickly." She spurred her horse to lead the men to the tree-lined cove on the north side facing the castle's island.

Drake looked to the river and thanked God for the mist that still floated over the water. As she urged her horse into the River Earn, she seemed fearless. He followed her, glad that he'd chosen a MacIntyre warhorse. The current tore at his boots and his mount stumbled along with the force. Cassandra kept a tight rein. He emulated her movements.

Their army struggled behind them. Cassandra's horse faltered. For a heart-stopping moment the raging water washed over her mount. But she stayed upright while the palfrey regained its footing.

The frigid waters numbed his legs as the animal beneath him forged on. Just a short distance from the island's bank the horses were forced to swim. He concentrated on moving with his mount to assist its efforts.

Finally, Cassandra's horse climbed the riverbank to a narrow strip of land in the shadow of the castle wall. His steed's swift movement out of the water nearly unseated him. Drake's legs gripped the saddle tightly. Moving along the bank, they waited for each horse to ascend from the treacherous waters.

When the army lined the shore, she led the men around the castle. The strip of land ended up ahead, where a tower jutted out on sheer rocks that vanished in the river's depths. Cassandra dismounted and began to dig with her sword in the sandy earth within the stones. Drake jumped down to assist her. She unearthed a lever. They both pulled it, but only after two other men helped by pushing the wall did the passage door yield.

A large portion of the wall swung inward to allow entrance. They rode into a cavernous cellar with archways that led to a broad stairway. Large vats lined the walls, their content scenting the air with hops and brewing ale. Dismounting, they drew their swords and prepared to battle.

The stairs led to the winecellar. The army crept past the resting bottles and up the stairway to the kitchens. An unusual quiet from the normally bustling kitchens met Drake as he peered from the doorway. Two MacKay guards stood with their backs to them, sampling the wassail. Drake turned to Cassandra, putting his finger to his lips. She gave his arm an impatient shove.

Creeping up behind the guards, they knocked them in the back of their heads—Drake with his fist and Cassandra with the handle of her sword. The men slumped to the floor without even a mutter.

Cassandra and Drake's army filled the kitchen. She peeked out a viewing loophole that allowed her to see the Great Hall without being seen herself. "They're holding our people in the hall." She gazed through the hole from different angles. "All the entrances are guarded."

Within the hall a baby cried. Drake noticed how Cassandra's face turned rigid with concern.

"We'll take the passage to the mesnie and better equip our men." Drake turned to Cassandra. "You travel to our tower and stay there."

She nodded her understanding, but had no intention of following his order. The men entered the passage within the inner walls of the castle. She trailed behind, keeping out of Drake's sight. The passage took them to the weapons room.

Drake and his men swept up shields and weapons and swiftly descended on the guards at the chamber's entrance. The clank of swords sounded as they fought their way through the MacKay men. Each man, and Cassandra, confronted the enemy, forcing them into the courtyard.

Suddenly, a familiar voice exclaimed, "Cassandra?" She stood face-to-face with the chieftain of the MacKay clan. He shouted to his men to stop the fight. Cassandra called to hers and the fighting stopped.

The MacKay chieftain looked startled. "They said that Lord Bancroft had killed you."

Drake appeared at her side with anger snapping in the depths of his eyes. He grabbed her arm. "I thought I told you to get to the tower."

The MacKay glared at Drake. "It's a good thing she didn't or it would have meant your demise."

Drake moved Cassandra away from the man and faced him. "I doubt it."

She immediately thrust her way between them again and demanded, "Why are you flying the MacKay colors over my castle?"

Without answering, he turned to his men and ordered their colors down and the MacIntyre flag returned to its rightful position. "Those MacCrory swine lied to me. I was only attempting to avenge your death."

Cassandra curtsied slightly. "My thanks to you then." A smile lit her face.

Drake cleared his throat. "Will you join us in the Great Hall?"

"With pleasure, Lord Bancroft."

Excusing herself, Cassandra went to her chamber to remove her torn clothing and clean herself. She made sure to take a chalice of wassail with her, sipping it along the way.

Leigh met her on the stairway. "Lady Cassandra! My God, what happened to you?" Clucking like a mother hen, she changed direction and escorted her to her chamber.

Cassandra accepted her help and marveled at the thoughts she sensed from Leigh. Apparently the guard she'd been assigned brought her happiness. Cassandra perceived grateful emotions flowing from her one-time rival. They entered her rooms.

Leigh set to work heating water. "Milady?"

Cassandra turned to her as she removed her soiled clothing. "Aye?"

Leigh blushed. "Would it be remiss if I married a guard?"

"Beathen?" Cassandra grinned.

"It is remiss, isn't it?" Leigh frowned and her body sagged.

Cassandra moved toward her. "Nay. Not if the feelings are there."

"We both feel the same about each other. But Drake would never allow it."

"What has Drake to say about it? This is your life. You should do what makes you happy. I'll speak with Drake."

Leigh looked ashamed. "You would do that for me?"

"Aye." Cassandra patted her shoulder and helped set the bath.

After the tub was full of steaming water, Leigh gave Cassandra a quick hug and hurried off to tell Beathen the good news. Soaking in the warm water soothed her aches, and her heart filled with yearning. She would have to convince Drake to stay at Sedgewick. Stepping from the water, she donned a new gown and she went to the hall to enjoy the time she had left of the season.

Cassandra walked into the Great Hall. Everyone grew quiet.

Drake stood raising his glass. "Long live Lady Cassandra."

The hall erupted with agreement. "Long live Lady Cassandra." They cheered.

Cassandra swept her skirt into a curtsy. She smiled until her bruised jaw pained her, stealing her smile. Drake came to her side and escorted her to their table.

He leaned down to speak in her ear. "I didn't think you would come down again tonight. Are you all right? Did Leigh see to you?"

"Aye, I'm just a little sore. I've got some herbs to mix with my wassail that will help."

Drake nodded and pulled out her chair. His touch told her that his ire was still a bit up. She touched him purposefully, admitting her foolishness. Her face heated as she sat down. They no longer touched but Cassandra detected a satisfied smile just beneath his stoic expression.

She tipped the herbs into her drink and laid her hand along Drake's strong forearm. Letting her fingertips convey, in their private way, that she may need some help getting up the stairs after drinking the pain-relieving herbs. But her thoughts caught him in the middle of a sip and he choked on his drink. When the others looked at him, he patted his mouth dry with the table's cloth and pardoned himself.

Drake gave Cassandra a murderous, but playful glare. She tried desperately not to laugh as she sipped her golden chalice. His eyes suddenly turned merry and he put his arm around her shoulders and pulled her close. *Don't worry, love. I'll take care of you.*

Before long Cassandra sagged against him. He picked her up and brought her to his chamber. Taking her clothes off, he wrapped her gently in his robe and tucked her into the blankets.

The recent threat to Cassandra's life and his own still set his pulse racing. Walking quietly from his room, he returned to the Great Hall. Even after many wassails he couldn't seem to relax. He approached his brother, who sat beside his favorite serving wench.

Cedric stood abruptly and went to Drake motioning for him to sit. "All right, brother. I'll listen to your advice. In exchange for a favor."

"You want the wench." Drake knew his brother well and always suspected that he drowned his sorrow by bedding women.

"Aye."

"As long as it's all right with Cassandra, she's yours. Will you marry her?"

"Aye. No one in England need know her station here. I'll make a lady of her." Cedric smiled.

Drake looked seriously at his brother and detected a sincerity he'd never seen before in his countenance. He nodded and proceeded to impart his knowledge of Wellington on Cedric. His brother listened carefully and seemed to agree.

Appeased and finally ready to sleep, Drake glanced up at the early morning light that shone through the upper windows. He strode to his chamber.

When he entered, the fire in the grate gave off the only light. Disrobing, he slid under the covers. He watched each breath Cassandra took and finally succumbed to his exhaustion.

Chapter Twelve

Cassandra awoke. As she stretched, her body rebelled with pain. Groaning, she rolled over and vowed not to leave her bed for the day. Holidays be damned. Drake be damned. He could just leave then, and he probably would not even say good-bye. Her ire sent her sitting up. Glaring at Drake, she shook his sleeping form.

Drake's eyelids flew open and he sat up. "What's wrong?" His head glanced frantically from side to side, stopping to stare wildly at Cassandra.

"I'm not leaving the bed this tenth day of Christmas." She rolled over and shut her eyes.

"You woke me to tell me *that?*" Drake leaned over her, jarring her sore body.

Cassandra pushed him away angrily.

"Oh, pardon. I just wanted to inform you that I'll not leave the bed this tenth day of Christmas either. Maybe you should reside in your own bed."

"This is my bed." She rolled over dismissing him. "Now close your mouth so I can sleep."

Drake, now fully awake, rang loudly for his chamberlain. Cassandra let out an exasperated yell and covered her head with the pillow. A satisfied smile tugged at his lips.

When his man entered Drake ordered him to send Leigh in with a draft for Lady Cassandra's pain and some hot pottage for them both.

"You'd best sit up and ready yourself for a draft and food." Drake pulled her limp body to a sitting position. "Then maybe the next time you wake you'll be a little more pleasant." He laughed at her irritable bearing. When she opened her mouth to speak he placed his finger to her lips and warned, "Don't let those mutinous words leave your lips, milady."

Her mouth snapped shut. Drake strode to the door, desperate for Leigh to bring the tea and rid his wife of her sour disposition. Glancing down the hall, he saw her coming and turned back to Cassandra.

"Leigh is here, Cassandra. Behave yourself."

"Don't tell me to behave myself."

Drake shook his finger at her. "And don't make me shame you in front of Leigh."

Leigh breezed past him without a word and proceeded to pamper Cassandra pitifully. "Milady, you poor thing. Let Leigh make it better."

Drake couldn't believe his ears.

She pointed a shaky finger at Drake. "Oh, aye, and make that beast leave." Cassandra burst into laughter.

Smoothing his fingers through his hair, he strode toward them. "That's enough, you two. I'm the one she shook awake as if the castle were afire."

Cassandra ignored him and continued her complaints. "He's such a brutal man. Look at these bruises."

Drake suddenly joined their laughter. "Aye, and there'll be more if you don't stop this caterwauling."

A kitchen boy arrived with the stew and Leigh went to see to her other patients. Cassandra and Drake ate the thick vegetable and beef mixture and then curled up together.

"I feel much better. Thank you for insisting."

"Thank goodness. Before you sleep, here's your tenth-day gift." Drake reached beside the bed and handed her a leather pouch.

"What a charming bag. Thank you." She planted a kiss on his cheek.

Drake beamed. "Open it."

Cassandra gasped as she pulled out a beautiful golden brush. Taking it from her hand, Drake brushed her hair.

Cassandra awoke and drank the draft that Leigh had left for her. Moving the window curtain aside, she gazed into the dark night. She left the bedchamber for a quick jaunt to the Great Hall, and she saw that all was well. Cassandra climbed back into bed and was met with his green-eyed gaze.

"All is well?"

"Aye."

"I'm hungry. I'm to the kitchen." Drake hopped from bed.

Cassandra snuggled deeper into the cover, already missing his warmth.

"Lady Cassandra, Lord Bancroft, how are you feeling?" Pascal stood as Drake and Cassandra strode to the table.

"Much better, Pascal." She looked up at the windows to gauge the weather.

Drake nodded as they sat. A serving woman brought cheese and bread, and they ate. The hall seemed quiet. Today was the eleventh day of Christmas. Dread filled Cassandra and sudden panic gripped her.

"Drake, would you ride with me this morning? My muscles need to stretch and the fresh air would be most welcome."

"Splendid idea. And bring your sword."

Cassandra glared at Drake, wondering if he knew she'd forgotten it before. After ducking her head so their eyes wouldn't meet, she glanced with chagrin at Pascal. The fury in her mentor's eyes shamed her. She quickly left the table to return to her chamber. Changing into her new riding outfit, she picked up her sword. She would rather die than forget her weapon a second time.

Drake waited for her at the stable with their horses saddled. Mounting, they rode through the open castle gate. Cassandra led him to her favorite shore. The day was clear and brisk. She marveled at her homeland.

Drake broke the silence. "Pascal is right. These mountains are awe inspiring, far more picturesque than the plains."

"I never tire of them." Halting at the shoreline, Cassandra dismounted and fed Nighthawk his carrot. And this time the apple went to Drake's horse.

He dismounted and walked beside her to stand on a large rock next to the river's current. "Cedric wants to take that wench he's so smitten with. He says he'll marry her. Would that be all right with you?"

"Yes, if you also agree to allowing Leigh's marriage to Beathen." Cassandra grinned at her cunning.

"I thought they'd warmed up to each other. That would be fine." Drake kissed her lips lightly, sealing their agreement.

* * *

The night passed swiftly with the bond between the Scottish and the English solidified.

In the early morning, Drake walked silently beside Cassandra into her chamber. Pretending to ignore his presence, she observed him from the corner of her eye. He removed his belts and seemed to be examining her hairbrush, which lay on the dressing table. She found her herb salve and rubbed the ointment into her bumps and bruises. Her pulse quickened at his approach.

He rested his hands on her shoulders and kissed her hair. Reaching for the salve he asked, "May I?"

Cassandra's heart ached more than her wounds. She wanted to pull away, shout hurtful accusations . . . beg him not to leave. But instead, she turned and relinquished the salve to him. His fingers smoothed away her pain, replacing it with a hunger for him to fill her. A throaty moan escaped her.

Drake smiled and continued to smooth her clothes from her body as he soothed her wounds. His hand stilled suddenly. Following the path of his vision, she realized he noticed her sword hanging on the wall.

"You did forgot your sword that night, didn't you?" After her nod he continued. "Ah, I wondered how they took you. If you'd remembered your sword, they never would have taken you. Who taught you to fight like a man?" Drake's eyes held a great respect for her.

"Artair." Cassandra fingered the buttons on Drake's shirt, opening them slowly. She smoothed her hands through his chest hair. She wanted him so fiercely. But in another day he would be gone.

Drake sensed Cassandra's mood. Keeping his thoughts closed to her, he sighed. "Our last night together. Will you miss me?"

The pleasant expression on her face turned ominously dark.

Without demanding a reply, he continued. "It will be a rough journey, but worth it." His smile taunted her as he held on to his secret. Without warning, his joy slipped a little, breaking down his guarded thoughts.

Her hands gripped his chest hairs painfully. "You're playing with me." She gripped tighter.

"Aye, ow, Cassandra!" He laughed. "I'm staying—let go."

She waited a moment longer and then released him. Her face reddened. "Had you gone, you wouldn't have returned."

"I would have." Drake smoothed the worried lines from her brow and kissed every part of her face. "The very hounds of Hades couldn't keep me away from you."

Slowly, he led her to the bed and they lay down together. He traced a path with his finger from her lips, down her neck, between her breasts, over her belly, and into her womanhood. She was ready for him.

Rising above her, he entered her silky folds. She gripped and surrounded him with her womanly heat. Moving within her, he watched as her expression dissolved into pleasure. His member became even tauter as they moved rhythmically together and apart. He slid out of her to his tip and plunged back in over and over until she tightened in spasms around him, making his pleasure complete.

Maintaining his movement within her as her muscles continued to contract around him, his own release came. His seed spilled into her and he drove even deeper. Her rhythm renewed its pulsing. Sobbing, Cassandra clung to him in her pleasure.

Holding her in his arms, he realized his love for Wellington was shallow compared to how deeply he loved this exquisite woman.

Her voice interrupted his newfound wonderment. "And will you think thus when you are not in the aftermath of our lovemaking?" Her solemn blue eyes accused him.

"I will. Over and over again." Drake nudged her neck, wetting it with kisses. "I am a tyrant, you know."

Cassandra laughed. "As am I. We'll have full days dealing with each other."

"And nights full of another kind of dealing." He chuckled deeply.

"Only if the daytime is dealt with in fairness." Cassandra grinned her meaning and touched his nose with her finger.

"Blackmail? You would resort to such soul-wrenching blackmail?" Drake gazed into her eyes.

"If need be." Cassandra ended her sentence with a scream as Drake's fingers found her most ticklish spots. "Stop!"

Drake continued to tickle her. "Yield?"

"Never." Her fingers fought to find his ticklish areas as she fought back with the same tactics.

They rolled in a heap to the floor and continued wrestling. Then Cassandra's hands found Drake's most sensitive area and started to squeeze.

He squeaked, "I yield."

She released him.

"That was *not* nice." His brows set in firm lines over his admonishing glare.

"I was just evening the score. You're bigger than I." Cassandra tried to untangle herself from Drake's family quilt, her eleventh-day gift from him.

"Aye, and don't forget it." He playfully slapped her backside as she freed herself.

She grimaced at him. "Get ye gone to Wellington," she teased.

"Too late now, lass. You've changed my mind."

"Ach, no." She fell back onto Drake pretending exasperation.

They rolled together laughing.

And now the twelfth day of Christmas dawned with the most beautiful light. Wrapped in her Oriental morning gown, Cassandra leaned out of her tower window. "Saints be praised," she breathed. She remembered the night she'd first heard Drake's unyielding voice from another tower window. Sitting on the window seat, she brought her knees to her chest and rested her chin on her folded arms above them. She gazed at the River Earn, amazed at what the sprites of Christmas had brought her. But something else felt different.

Drake came to sit behind her, his legs on either side of her. She leaned back against his chest. They communicated without words. Suddenly Cassandra knew what it was: another presence, one growing within her. Her heart soared with the knowledge.

She turned her head to see Drake's eyes glistening with the shared awareness. Beneath the folds of his robe he produced a small porcelain doll. Her twelfth-day gift. Joyful tears tracked down her cheeks. Drake pulled her closer, and in their silent way, he promised to love her always.

SARA'S GIFT

by

Jill Henry

Chapter One

Disappointment wrapped around Sara's heart. Hours had passed while the train stood motionless on the tracks as the howling blizzard battered it, and there was no sign of help. The conductor assured them the crew was attempting to dig through the snowdrift, solid as ice and six feet high, that blocked the tracks, but she could see how fast the snow fell on the other side of the frosty window. It looked like an impossible task.

I should never have taken this train. Sara snapped open the silver locket at her neck and ran a careful fingertip over the single black curl tucked inside. The tiny lock of hair still felt fine and silky after four long years. The baby she'd given birth to would be a child now, talking and laughing, running and playing. *Maybe I have no right to see her.*

But how could she go on if she didn't? A new life awaited her ahead in Missoula, and it was time to let go of the past, of what could never be. She had dreamed of this chance, and now, she was not ten miles away from seeing the little girl her baby had become.

How many times had Sara imagined what she might look like? Probably thousands. Those fine black curls would be thick and lustrous now, maybe hanging halfway down her back, curling in tangles like her own. But would she have Andrew's eyes? Or chin? Or the way he cocked his head when he smiled?

Her heart cracked with too many memories. Nothing hurt like lost dreams, like love buried and gone forever.

"Someone's coming!" a man, who had been nervously watching for the rescue party, announced from the front of the car. "I see lanterns. I bet it's help."

"Finally," another answered. "It's freezing in here. I'm writing a formal complaint to the railroad company."

The drum of angry voices faded to a faint blur in Sara's mind. The rescue party had come. That meant she was on her way to Moose Creek, where her daughter lived. Men's voices rumbled outside the car, and Sara gathered her satchels. The thought of a long trek to the next town was sobering, and with the way the wind howled, she wondered about the dangerous storm.

"You'll be fine, missy," the conductor assured her as he handed down her largest satchel, heavy with her sewing box inside. "The sheriff and his men will take good care of you. Sheriff, we got a lady here. She's a might delicate. Keep a good eye on her. Make sure she doesn't get too cold."

"Right you are," a low, rumbling voice answered. A flicker of lantern light splashed across his face, and Sara saw dark eyes, a strong slash of a mouth, and shoulders wide and capable. A man's hand reached out, well shaped and strong; then the lash of light retreated to cast her rescuer in darkness again. "Come on down. I've got you."

She'd seen his face before. Sara stepped out of the car,

and the howling wind struck her hard. Ice pellets scoured her face and drove straight through her wool cloak. Her foot hit ice on the steps and she slid, but the strong man's grip held her up until she caught the next step and landed solidly on the drifted bank of snow.

"Here, climb up with me." He took her arm and led the way through the confusion of swirling wind and blackness.

A gust of wind hit her full force, and she fought to keep from buckling backward. His hands gripped her arms, holding her up, keeping her from falling. How strong he was. She noticed that right away.

The storm kept her off balance. The cold tore the heat from her body, and teeth rattling, she clawed her way up to the top of the embankment. Mittened hands reached out and grabbed her, and she felt frozen through already, not having taken more than ten steps in this weather.

"Do you have her?" The sheriff towered over her, sheltering her from the battering wind with his big steely body. Lantern light flickered close, cutting a thin slash of gold through the dark, illuminating the whole of his face. Of his familiar, handsome face.

Gabe Chapman. Sara's heart shuddered to a stop. It was this man and his wife who had adopted her baby. She dipped her chin. What if he recognized her? The taint of shame at having to give up her baby still hung heavy on her shoulders.

"This way." A man tugged her to a sleigh, the storm engulfing both the light and the sight of the strong sheriff.

Gabe watched the woman go, his chest tight. He'd caught the look of sadness in eyes a bleak color of blue, like a stormy twilight sky. He caught hold of Clancy. "Put her in my sleigh. She's delicate. She won't last long in this storm. And give her an extra blanket."

"You got it, boss."

Gabe rushed to help the last passenger from the cars, a

thirteen-year-old boy. He helped the lad locate his family, all tucked in a sled together, and Clancy took the reins. It wouldn't take much for all of them to become lost in this storm, confused by the wind, frozen by the subzero temperatures. He had to get these people to shelter as fast as he could.

Through the swirl of black ice he saw the shape of the woman in his sleigh, huddled beneath buffalo robes. "This trip is going to get awful rough," he leaned close to tell her. "If you get too cold, you tell me. I don't want you freezing."

"Okay."

Her teeth chattered; he could hear the clacking when she spoke. How small she was. His chest tightened with worry. There were no more blankets. He could do nothing but grab his team by the bit.

"Let's move out!"

His shout was snatched by the wind, but the sleds and sleighs behind him followed in single file, keeping to the tracks he made. Responsibility settled heavily on his shoulders. Where he led, everyone followed. Already the powerful wind was knocking him off course, and he found the slope of the railroad grade by luck.

He headed into the wind, nearly blinded by the storm. Once the lantern swinging from his sleigh cast a faint glow, and for a brief instant, between the curtain of snow and darkness, he could see the woman's face. Fragile and striking, with eyes dark and clear.

Yes, she was depending on him too. Braced against the biting cold, he faced the wind and turned the horses with him, heading, he hoped, down the middle of the grade. The howling winds were worse here at the peak of the mountain, as was the snow. It seemed as if they walked through clouds, for the world around had faded until there was only the numbing crystals of driven ice and the packed snow at his feet.

When he was certain they had crested the mountain and were still on the railroad grade, he took hold of the reins and fell back to check on the woman in his sleigh. The lantern cast her in brief silhouette. She was huddled tight beneath the bundle of wool and skins, her face wrapped with a muffler so only her dark eyes showed, eyes full of questions.

"It's a long way yet to go." He bent close to her, fighting the ache in his joints put there by the brutal wind. "Can you wiggle your toes?"

Her eyes squinted with an unmistakable smile. He couldn't see it, but he remembered the sight of her face as she'd descended from the railroad car, oval and soft, cheekbones high but not too prominent, the soft lush cut of her mouth. He would lay down good wagering money that she had a beautiful smile.

Her nod confirmed she was holding her own, at least so far. He looked back to see the outline of horses nosing the back of his sleigh, for ropes tied the sleighs from stern to trace.

"The wind's pickin' up." Clancy covered his mouth, shouting to be heard over the howling storm.

"Check on our passengers, will you? Don't want anyone freezing on the way home."

"Least of all you. Get in that sleigh and beneath those blankets before you're an icicle."

"Same goes for you." Gabe had to make certain their course was true, and when he did, he would be more than happy to share the sleigh with the pretty young woman. Since Ann's death, he'd been mighty lonely—the kind of loneliness that hit at night when sleep would not come and the empty place at his side was harder to ignore.

The wind gusted, knocking him to his knees. He struggled back to his feet, determined to keep his course. Overhead he could hear the creak of battered trees and knew the only danger wasn't from the cold or losing direction. The steep fall of the mountainside sent the team in a panic and he caught the bit, speaking low and steady to Rebel. The black quieted, his hooves sliding, struggling to breathe as the ice crusted his velvet muzzle.

Gabe rubbed the ice from both horses' noses and led them, kept them calm. Already he was so cold inside he ached and his stomach muscles coiled tight. Ice struck him and clung to his eyes, his face, his chest. The ten-mile trek stretched ahead as if it were a hundred.

"We don't have much farther to go now." The sheriff's voice broke through the wave of sleepiness washing over her, threatening to pull her under. "Are you awake?"

"I'm awake." Sara made herself speak. A cold knot clamped in the middle of her stomach, and she knew, if she fell asleep, she could freeze to death in these temperatures, even buried in the layers of robes and wool. Her jaw ached from clenching her teeth to keep them from chattering.

Think of your daughter, she told herself, again cradling the much remembered images of the baby in her arms, moments after she'd been born, face red and wrinkled, fingers so tiny it was hard to believe they were real. Sara's heart squeezed with a fondness grown greater over time. How sorry she was Andrew had not lived to see his daughter born. How proud he would have been, how much in love with her.

When she looked up, she saw the blur of a street, the faint impression of dark windows and roof lines through the blinding storm. The sleigh skidded to a halt in the shelter of a tall building. Lights burned in the windows, warm and cozy within. Sara, numb from the cold, began pushing off the robes.

A gloved hand caught hers. The sheriff, Gabe Chapman, shook his head. A muffler covered his face, frozen white and caked with ice. "Let me make sure there is room at the hotel before you climb out. It's damn cold out here."

Sara nodded, careful to keep her chin down, afraid. But he could not see her through the layers of the wool scarf wrapped around her face and know the secrets she hid. Still, the shame and uncertainty clung to her, as cold and desolate as the storm.

Finally, Sheriff Gabe Chapman strode back into sight, broad shouldered and powerfully agile. Just watching him hop down the steps and extend a hand to the family in the sled behind her made her heart skip a little. He was her daughter's adopted father.

There was a strong sense of caring about him, masculine but tender as he helped the middle-aged woman from the sled, catching her elbow when she stumbled, keeping her safe. He escorted her up the steps while the family followed, the father seeing after their son, all looking as frozen as she felt.

Now that they had stopped, her nerves crackled. She didn't feel right about what she was doing—not right at all. When she'd handed her baby to her father that last time and watched him ride away from the shanty, it had felt as if he'd taken her entire soul with him. Now all she wanted was one look, even if she had agreed never to contact the little girl or her family.

"The hotel's full." His voice startled her. He stood by the side of the sleigh, broad shoulders and the cut of his profile limned by the gleam of lighted windows. "My deputy and I will see you to the boardinghouse. They could have room."

"And if they don't?"

"Don't worry. We'll find you a warm place for the night. Here in Moose Creek, we don't let pretty ladies stranded by a blizzard sleep out in the street." Even though it was dark and stormy, she could see the flicker in his eyes, a bright snap of humor and charm that set her heart racing.

Why, he was flirting with her! What kind of man was he? He was a husband and a father. Sara bowed her chin and clenched her frozen hands.

The sleigh bumped to a start as Gabe Chapman led the team out of the shelter between the hotel and stables and into the unprotected street. Ice drove at her, cutting and scouring the exposed part of her face. The sleigh stopped again, but this time there was no shelter from the bitter misery of the storm. She could not even see the light in the windows, only the smallest glow as the front door opened. She waited for minutes but it seemed like hours before the sheriff reappeared at her side.

"The boardinghouse has a vacant bed, but it's sharing a room with our local teamster." It was too dark to see his face, but his voice sounded serious. "You might be more comfortable at my sister's house. She has a warm, cozy place and a spare guest room. Will that do?"

Sara remembered Connie from her childhood, although she hadn't seen her in many years. She recalled a friendly girl with red hair and freckles. But Connie was Gabe's sister and her daughter's aunt. "Is there anyplace else?"

"Not that I can find this time of night. It's two in the morning. Unless you want to stay with me."

"No." Goodness, she hadn't come to town to install herself in the Chapman household. She was a woman of her word. She had agreed never to interfere in her baby's life, and she would keep that promise. But looking wasn't interfering. And where else was she to stay?

"Then I'll take you on to my sister's house?"

There were no more sleds trailing them. The rest of the

passengers from the train—all men—had found shelter at the boardinghouse. Without another solution, Sara nodded.

That was all the answer the sheriff seemed to need. He trudged away from her side to lead the horses home.

Chapter Two

"I brought you a visitor." Gabe took one look at his sister in her flowered wrapper, her hair sleep rumpled and exhaustion ringing her eyes. "The hotel was full up. If there was another solution, I would have found it."

"I'll get the bed ready. Goodness, I'm a sight. I could scare off mice at twenty paces."

"Only at four," he teased, shouldering through the door to set the three satchels on the floor. "Did Mary have a hard night?"

Connie shrugged, a simple casual movement. "She was just missing her pa."

"I missed her too." Gabe's chest tightened. "I appreciate you looking after her."

"It's the least I can do for my precious niece." Connie's smile lit her face, and it was all the assurance Gabe needed. His sister was generous, but she was newly married and he hated imposing. "Who did you bring me?"

"A lady heading to Missoula—that's all I know about

her." Gabe glanced outside to see the woman, who'd only accepted his help in carrying her bags, quietly step up onto the porch behind him. "That, and she's shy."

"Why, she looks frozen, the poor dear." Connie rushed on past him, clucking her tongue, her hands outstretched to help the frozen woman into the house.

He had tried twice to assist her, but she only shook her head, stubbornly insisting that she could manage on her own. He held the door for her as she hobbled into the swath of lamplight in Connie's parlor. Her dark skirts were frosted with a layer of ice and frozen stiff. Stooped, she looked as if each step caused her pain. But she didn't complain.

"I'll build up the fire," he said as he closed the door, then crossed the room despite his aching joints and numb hands.

"I kept the fire going in the kitchen," Connie said, holding the woman's arm as they made slow progress across the room. "I thought you might need some hot tea."

"You're a lifesaver, sis." Gabe found the range lit, but the fire dying. He grabbed a few sticks of wood with his clumsy fingers and added them to the flames. How good the heat felt.

"Sit right down here." He dragged a chair from the table and set it before the stove. He caught the woman's arm, so fragile beneath the layers of wool she wore. Here, in the light, he could see that, while her cloak was not worn thin, it was not new either, but patched neatly at the right elbow.

"Thank you." Her words were soft beneath the muffler that still covered her face, caked with ice. "I can manage from here."

"Oh, no, you can't." Connie caught hold of one snowy hand.

The mittens came off easily, bits of snow crackling to

the polished floor. But the muffler stuck, layers frozen together. They unwound with a bit of work, revealing more of those dark stormy eyes and a face as soft as he'd remembered.

The gentle light brushed her alabaster skin with golden caresses. She wore no ring on her left hand, he noticed in a glance. Why was a woman so young and pretty traveling unescorted, especially this time of year? Gabe knelt before her.

"I can see to my own shoes. Thank you." Her voice sounded prim, but the way her mouth shaped the words did not. His gaze snagged hers, and he could swear he caught the look of panic before she bowed her chin, working intently at her cloak's wooden buttons.

"You're scaring the poor girl," Connie whispered in his ear. "She's been through an ordeal and doesn't need an overeager bachelor trying to play with her feet."

He only meant to be polite, and rolled his eyes at his sister. "Go ahead and joke. If I'm not wanted, I'll head on upstairs and see my daughter."

The woman's head snapped up, one delicate brow crooked with interest. He wondered at that. Well, maybe he didn't look like the father type.

"It's pretty cold out to take her home this time of night," Connie commented.

"I know. That's why I'm going to leave her here." Gabe grabbed a biscuit from the covered basket on the counter and headed through the house. He heard Connie's voice, low and merry, probably making some comment about him, thinking she was funny. Sibling teasing never died— it just took on a different form.

The upstairs hall was unlit, but Gabe knew the way by memory. This wasn't the first time his job had forced him from his home late at night. Good thing Connie lived so close and didn't mind watching after his girl. He curled his hand around the knob and turned it slowly.

The door creaked open just enough for him to see his daughter, asleep in the bed, a shadowed form in the dark room. His eyes adjusted as he stood there, listening to the reassuring rhythm of her relaxed breathing, glad that, as she slept undisturbed, her dreams were apparently good ones.

It was far too cold to take her home. He only lived across the street. But it was hard closing the door and walking away, even though he knew she was better off sleeping here in the warm house.

"Sara's cold straight through, poor thing." Connie stopped him at the base of the stairs. "I have her in a lukewarm bath in the kitchen to help her thaw a bit, so you'll have to use the front door."

"The train might not be running tomorrow. I can find another place for her then. I know this is an imposition."

"Nonsense. Why don't you stay the night here? Mary does better with her papa close, and the storm is worse. Look, you might not even make it across the street."

"With your houseguest, I don't think I should be sleeping on your sofa, or next thing we know the whole town will be talking." He winked.

She grabbed a warm muffler. "Wrap up good then. I don't want to lose my only brother."

"You can't get rid of me that easily." He wound the scarf around his throat and headed outside into the darkness.

He saw the glow of the kitchen window, where the woman with the sad eyes bathed. He would wager she was a sight, all alabaster skin and delicate curves.

Hell, he'd been too long without a woman, for the thought made his blood heat, made the bitter arctic air less cold. A few more steps and the lighted window faded, swallowed by the night and the storm, until there was nothing but darkness.

I'll head on upstairs and see my daughter. Gabe Chapman's words haunted Sara. Was her little girl upstairs? In this very house? It had to be, unless the Chapmans had adopted a second child.

Sara settled into the tub, the lukewarm water like fire against her skin, and tried to quiet her racing thoughts. She could still hear Connie's voice, mumbling through the kitchen walls, even though she spoke low to her brother. *Mary does better with her papa close.*

Sara's heart twisted. They had named her baby Mary. Elation and longing spun through her. Ever since she'd had to let her daughter go, she had held close the impossible dream of seeing her again.

And now, it could truly happen. She would get to see her little girl. From the instant she'd traded in Aunt Ester's train ticket for a stop in Moose Creek, she'd harbored so many fears. That what she was doing wasn't right. That someone would recognize her. Then the blizzard hit, stopping the train.

But now she could see how events had brought her here, to this shining hope. Tomorrow, she could leave, and maybe the sleepless nights would end now that the emptiness in her heart had filled.

A new life awaited her in Missoula. Maybe, with the knowledge her child was loved and well, with a strong kind man like Gabe Chapman as her father, Sara could move on, maybe try to find love and marriage, have another baby.

"Goodness, but it's cold out there. I hope my brother doesn't freeze solid on his way across the street." With a glitter of humor, Connie breezed through the door and into the room, all bustling energy even in her nightgown and wrapper. "How are your feet feeling?"

"Like they're on fire." Sara wiggled her toes. "I'm lucky I'm not frostbitten."

"I can heat the water up for you. The teakettle is full and steaming."

"No, I'm ready to get out." Sara reached for the length of linen, soft and neatly folded. "I'm sorry to impose on you like this. You must have a family to look after—"

"No, we have no children yet, and my husband is upstairs snoring up a storm. I brought you some things of mine, since your satchels look frozen solid."

"That is mighty generous of you." Sara could not remember the last time someone had shown her kindness, true kindness. Not since Andrew died. Her legs were stiff and clumsy as she climbed out of the tub, but she didn't trip.

"Now tell me why you look so familiar," Connie started as she lifted the steaming teakettle from the stove. "I know, you're Sara Reece from over in Oak's Grove."

Sara grew cold at the woman's words, and her hopes faded one by one. She did not look up as she fumbled with the buttons on her borrowed nightgown, the flannel soft against her skin.

"Am I right?"

"Yes, but it's Sara Mercer now."

How could she admit why she'd come? They wouldn't understand. How could they? She had given up her child, made from love, to perfect strangers to raise. But the ties of the heart remained, so strong and solid she could not sleep a night through or survive a day without regrets.

"We were in the same class in school, those few years before your mother died." Connie plinked a pot on the cloth-covered table and set the tea to steeping. "Whatever are you doing traveling out this way?"

Sara's knees wobbled, and she dropped into a nearby chair. "I'm on my way to Missoula."

"And you got stuck on the pass in this nasty blizzard," Connie finished, checking the teapot. "That looks ready enough. Here, this will help you sleep. Where's your husband?"

Sara watched the woman pour, the scents of peppermint and chamomile steaming in the air between them, and she did not know what to say about her past, about the truth she did not wish to tell. "Andrew died five years ago."

"I'm sorry, Sara." The brightness in Connie's dark eyes faded to sympathy and understanding.

Later, after she'd taken the tea upstairs and sipped it until she was warm from the inside out, sleep eluded her as it often did. The winds had quieted and she took refuge at the window seat, staring out at the sheen of falling snow. The world seemed dark and mysterious, strangely beautiful.

And at odds with the fears balled high in her chest. What mess had she gotten herself into? Connie had recognized her. What if Gabe had too?

Ashamed at the weakness in her own heart, of a mother's need she had no right to, she watched the snow fall, a continuous cascade of wind-battered specks against the endless night.

"Gabe, you don't have to haul in wood for us," Connie scolded as she swung open the back door. "But I won't argue since Jim had to leave early. You know he had to get the path shoveled and the schoolhouse toasty before the students arrive. I'm afraid I'm running low on what he left me—it's such a cold morning."

"And still storming." The bite of the wind had curled

itself around his bones in just the short walk across the road. He shouldered through the threshold and dumped the cedar in the wood box near the range. The door slapped closed behind him and he savored the warmth of the room. "Is that coffee I smell?"

"Strong, just the way you like it." Connie grabbed her broom. "Come over here and take off your boots. You're dripping on my clean floor."

"Pa!" Dark twin braids and blue skirts flying, Mary sprinted through the kitchen, all merriment and enthusiasm. "Pa, you *finally* came! I've been waitin' and waitin'."

He knelt to accept those small arms around his neck. He felt the need in them—how she'd missed him. And how he had missed her. "Look at you, all dressed and your hair braided. You never get up this early at home."

"Oh, Pa, I wasn't sleepy this morning." She hopped back, all little-girl energy. "Aunt Connie made me hot chocolate after you left last night."

"She did?" Gabe stood, shrugging off his bulky coat.

"Yep. And we worried and worried 'cause you were out in that blizzard."

"You worried about me, huh?"

Mary nodded, her dark eyes serious, twin braids bobbing up and down. " 'Cause I didn't want you to freeze up like an icicle, Pa."

"I'm too tough for that." Gabe winked as he hauled off one boot, then the other.

"Yeah, some tough guy." Connie's eyes twinkled as she set a cup on the table closest to the stove. "I heard the emotion in your voice last night when you asked me to look after Mary."

"I had a moment of weakness." Grinning, Gabe grabbed the sugar bowl, tipping it sideways to sweeten his coffee.

"Here's a spoon, barbarian," Connie dropped the utensil on the table in front of him. "A moment of weakness? You nearly teared up at having to leave your little girl."

"I did not. I caught a snowflake in my eye." Gabe took a sip. "This is damn good coffee."

"I cried when you left too, Pa." Mary leaned her head against his shoulder. " 'Cause people sometimes don't come back when they leave you."

Dealing with loss wasn't easy, especially for a small child. Gabe's chest tightened and the old grief—these days just a hard sadness—returned. This would be their second Christmas without Ann. "Well, I came back. And I always will."

"That's good, 'cause we gotta go shoppin' today." Mary dropped into the chair next to him. "Is it snowin' too hard to go?"

"Why don't you go check for us?" Gabe asked, and like lightning, she bolted up from the chair and dashed through the room to the parlor, where the big front windows offered the best view. "Connie, how's the woman from the train doing? She was pretty cold last night."

"Sara is just fine. I heard footsteps a few minutes ago. I should start breakfast." Connie set out a cup of tea.

"Sara, huh?" He took another gulp of steaming coffee, finally feeling warm.

"Didn't you recognize her? She's Sara Reece, from back home. Actually, she's Sara Mercer now. Widowed, poor thing, and traveling all alone."

Gabe recalled the sadness, so shadowed in those storm blue eyes. And he remembered a lot of things about the town they grew up in, where he married, and where he became a father. "She's Grant Reece's daughter. He was a tough son of a bitch."

Connie cracked an egg against the lip of a bowl. "He pulled her out of school when she was nine years old to do her mother's work after the poor woman died."

"I remember he was a harsh man. He was good friends with Ann's father. I saw him a couple of times at the yearly Christmas party Ann's family hosted. I don't remember Sara ever being there."

"She wasn't. She was probably home doing the work." Connie's voice rang low with contempt for a man who would treat his own child so harshly. "It still makes me furious that cruel people can have children they don't value, but that you and Ann went so long without a baby to call your own."

"We got Mary, and she made up for all that waiting and heartbreak." Gabe thanked his sister for the bowl of oatmeal she set before him.

"It's snowin' buckets and buckets." Mary dashed into the kitchen, her eyes shining. "When can we build snowmen, Pa, like we did yesterday? I wanna go now."

"Not until that wind dies down." Gabe patted the chair next to him. "Now sit on down and have some oatmeal. We have a lot of planning and shopping left to do before Christmas."

"We have to hurry. I wanna pick out my new dress first thing."

Gabe grabbed a jar of huckleberry preserves from the shelf behind him and broke the seal. "I don't remember saying you could have a new dress."

"Oh, Pa, you're not one bit funny."

While Mary shook her head, he plopped the jar on the table beside her. The scent of the sweet wild berries enticed her to pick up her spoon.

Gabe caught Connie's laughing gaze over the platter of bacon and eggs. The table had been set for five, the empty chair and plate reminding him of the woman upstairs—Sara Reece Mercer—and her sad eyes and quiet manner.

Looking after her welfare last night had left a warm spot in his chest, just a small one, but it was enough to force him to remember what it was like to hold a door for a lady or help her from a sleigh. He had been a widower a long time, and he had grieved Ann truly and well, but Mary needed a mother and he was a lonely man.

He cast his gaze to the generous window above the kitchen pump. He watched the snow fall steadily at a mean angle from the driving wind. Had to be over a new foot since last night. The train wasn't going to arrive today or anytime soon if this storm didn't end.

His gaze flicked to the stairs, the banister just visible from where he sat, and his heart picked up a quicker pace remembering Sara Mercer's gentle beauty.

Sara hesitated on the top step, startled by the rumble of voices coming from the kitchen below.

"Shopping?" a man's low voice rang with humor. "Are you going to make me suffer through another round of shopping? I think I have to work."

"You can't squirm out of this one, brother," Connie's merry voice answered.

How happy they sounded. If Gabe was here, then maybe his wife was too. This was a family, laughing over breakfast, for Sara could smell the aroma of fresh fried eggs and bacon, the sweet scent of tea and the deeper harshness of boiled coffee.

She had no right to intrude. She had never meant to wedge her way into the middle of the Chapman family.

"But, Pa, you gotta see my new dress," a child's bright voice pleaded, sweet like melody, merry as song.

Gabe Chapman's answer faded against the buzzing in her ears. Sara grabbed the rail, already stepping forward, hungry to hear more of the happy child's voice.

"Oh, Pa, I still gotta pick out a new ribbon."

"What? Don't you have enough ribbons? I suppose you want another hair clip too."

"And maybe new shoes."

"Shoes?" Gabe's protest sounded like nothing she'd ever heard before, not from a grown man and father. Warm as cocoa, rich as cream, brimming with love.

During all the long nights of worrying and wondering, she had never imagined something so wonderful for her helpless baby. A terrible ache tore through Sara's heart, so big and grateful it hurt. All the days of living without Mary in her arms was worth it to know she was so well treated.

"I think I hear a footstep on the stairs." Gabe's words broke through her thoughts.

Sara blinked. She was halfway down the staircase. Heavens, what did she do now? She had imagined being alone and unnoticed when she took the first look at her daughter, maybe from the street watching the child at play or shopping with her mother. But not like this. Not in front of Mary's family, who had brought Sara in out of the cold and given her a bed for the night. What if the years of longing showed in her eyes? How could she disguise the affection for a child she loved but could not have?

"Sara, is that you?" Connie called, friendly and expectant. "Breakfast is still hot. And I steeped some tea."

"Who's Sara, Pa?"

"A pretty lady who was stuck on the train last night."

"You mean, you rescued a pretty lady? Like in my fairy tale book?"

"Well, I'm no shining knight." Humor and humility tolled in Gabe's words.

He was a hero to her, a man who had provided for a baby not of his blood and raised her so that she could joke at the table, so that confidence twinkled in her voice as bright as sunlight.

Footsteps clattered on the wood floor, the gait of a running child. Sara didn't have time to retreat or to think or even to blink back the tears pooling in her eyes. There was Mary, with twin black braids hanging over her shoulders, with eyes as blue gray as a stormy sky and Andrew's chiseled chin.

"Are you the lady my pa rescued?" Mary tilted her head to one side when she smiled, curiosity bright and unmistakable.

"Yes, I was stuck on the train last night." How she found her voice, Sara didn't know, but words tumbled off her tongue in such a rush. "Your pa helped me from the train and tucked me into his sleigh and made sure everyone was safe."

"That's my pa." Pride swelled her shoulders, and Sara could see the love there, pure and true.

Mary was delicate and lean, and the blue flannel dress she wore with a red rosebud print had to be store bought. In all Sara's life, she had never owned a dress half so fine or made of such beautiful fabric, but for her daughter, why, this was a *play* dress.

More gratefulness wedged in her throat. Years of worry fled, like nighttime shadows at the first touch of dawn, because now Sara knew for certain. Giving up her baby had been the right thing to do.

"Aunt Connie made up some eggs and stuff, but I don't like eggs." Mary reached out and grabbed Sara's hand.

At the first touch of those slender little fingers, Sara's heart melted, just puddled in her chest. "I don't like eggs either."

"Mrs. Mercer." Gabe stood, his chair grating on the wood floor. He hadn't asked for her name last night, so Connie must have told him this morning.

Their gazes locked, and she tried to tuck away the emotion she knew showed. "Sheriff. I didn't expect to see you again."

"He's always showing up, begging for a hot meal." Connie rose, fetching the teapot from the counter.

"No, don't fuss over me," she said, lowering her eyes, seeing no other woman in the room.

"Don't let her give you the wrong impression about me." Gabe circled around to draw the empty chair away from the table, holding it out for her. "I may come and eat her out of house and home now and then, but I do it for Mary's sake."

"Yeah, Pa's cookin' is sorta bad sometimes." Mary traipsed over to her chair and dropped into it, braids swinging. "Unless he's makin' stew."

Connie set down a steaming cup and a bowl. "There now, don't be afraid to ask if you want anything more. I'm not the best of cooks, but I'm a far sight better than Gabe."

"It's the only reason Mary and I visit." He grinned, and she was close enough to see the smooth line of his freshly shaven jaw, the hint of dimples along his mouth, the flecks of indigo in eyes as dark as midnight.

There was no mention of a wife to cook supper, a mother to look after Mary. Sara settled down into the chair he held, his solid strength towering over her, sure and honorable.

"I asked Santa Claus for a new mother this year," Mary piped up as she dumped another spoonful of jam on her oatmeal. " 'Cause my real mother died. Sara, can you cook?"

"Excuse me?"

Then Gabe broke out in laughter so easy and hearty she felt mesmerized. He looked at ease as he circled around to his chair, moving with the powerful agility of a man comfortable with his body, aware of his strength. "Nice try, Mary, but that's not going to work. Mrs. Mercer is planning to leave as soon as the train comes."

Mrs. Mercer. It was friendly enough, but formal too, letting her know that Gabe had not guessed from her eyes why she was here, had not noticed the emotion strung so tight in her body she felt ready to snap.

Across the table, Mary granted her a smile and the jar of huckleberry preserves. "Oatmeal tastes yummy with jam on it."

Sara's favorite breakfast food was oatmeal with jam.

She tamped down every last bit of emotion and thanked Mary, no longer the baby she ached for, and knew she could leave. She could go on, holding this sweet moment in her heart, knowing the little girl with Andrew's chin and her eyes was happy and loved.

Chapter Three

There was a lonely look to her, Gabe decided as he pushed his empty plate away and reached for his second cup of coffee. Sara Mercer from Oak's Grove, a little farming town near the North Dakota border. He didn't remember her, nothing but a vague impression of a solemn little girl from his school days, but then he was older and had been several grades ahead.

He knew Grant Reece had a daughter, but had never noticed. He'd been married by the time Sara would have been in her teens, moved from Oak Grove to take a deputy job by the time she'd probably married. He felt sorry for her. Since she was Reece's daughter, her life would have been hard, and since she was a widow, he knew the pain of that breaking loss.

"What's in Missoula?" he asked, because he was curious and because he wanted to see her look up at him again.

She set her teacup down with a clatter. "A job. My

father's sister opened a dress shop and is in need of a seamstress. She offered me the job first."

True pride shone in her eyes, as gentle as twilight. How it drew him. "Sounds like a good opportunity."

"It is." She ran her forefinger, slim and beautifully shaped, around the rim of the china cup, her face bowed. Dark curls framed her delicate face. "I've been working in a laundry for the last few years."

"Did you still live with your father?" She looked up startled, and he regretted asking. "I just remember him, is all."

"You do?" Her eyes widened with what looked like fear.

Gabe remembered how cruel her father was. "I didn't know him well, just met him a few times. You spent your growing up years out on the farm. I just wondered."

"I came to live with him right after"—her voice dropped—"after my husband died. But eventually I found a job and could afford to rent a place in town. It wasn't much, but it was a home of my own."

"That's important," Connie spoke up.

"It is." So intelligent she was, and with the way she dipped her chin and smiled just a little, she made his heart thrum. "When Aunt Ester offered this job, it was like a dream come true. I think I can make a good living, and for the first time in as long as I can remember, I'll be working at something I enjoy."

What she didn't say struck him more. Gabe's throat tightened and he heard the dreams, unspoken but bright and shining—dreams for a happier future.

"Do you have to go to Missoula?" Mary asked, licking huckleberry jam from the back of her spoon.

Sara's smile gleamed, changing the solemn set of her face, chasing the sadness from her eyes. "I wish I didn't, but I do. I gave my word that I would be there."

"But the train ain't comin' today, is it, Pa?"

"Not if this snow keeps up. The crew won't be able to clear the tracks." Gabe drained his cup. "Your aunt will hold your job, won't she?"

"Not if I'm late." Sara's gaze strayed to the window, where snow fell with a dizzying speed. Worry lines crept across her forehead and his thumb ached to soothe them away. "I had no idea the trains couldn't run in this kind of weather."

"Not when we get blizzards the way we did yesterday. The wind drives the snow into drifts, and it's especially bad when the tracks have been cut through the mountainside and the snow just blows right in and fills the gully."

"When do you think the train will be running?"

"I don't know. Maybe late today, if the snow tapers off. Maybe tomorrow."

"I don't want to impose." Sara turned her gaze to Connie. "Let me help with the dishes. It's the least I can do. I guess I should try the hotel again. Maybe there'll be room today."

"Not as long as the train is stuck up on the pass." Gabe scooted out of his chair and stood.

"Well, I'm going to hope they do." She lifted her face and wisps of ebony curls, gossamer fine, brushed her brow and the curve of her cheek. "A person just never knows."

"I'll check for you." Her optimism touched him. "I'll need to stop by the hotel anyway and pay a visit to the train passengers."

"Thank you." She rose from the table and began gathering the plates.

It was time for him to leave. The parlor clock bonged. He had work to do, yet he wanted to linger here in the warmth, watching Sara clear the table, her movements graceful and lithe.

A widow with no children, making her way in the world alone. He fetched his boots, now dry, and carried them back to his chair. Sara brushed past him for the final time, the table picked clean, to join Connie at the counter, where they discussed who would wash and who would dry.

"Pa, do you gotta go?" Mary leaned against his shoulder, a frown tugging down her angel's face. "It's Saturday."

"I know Clancy normally takes care of things today, but with these extra people in town, they'll be unhappy. We can't have any of them heading off on their own."

"But what about my dress?" Mary whispered in his ear. "Aunt Connie ain't good at pickin' out dresses."

"True," Gabe admitted. His sister's fashion sense left a lot to be desired. Even now, her tan-and-brown-plaid skirt did not exactly match her calico shirtwaist. Connie just had never put much stock in appearances.

"I know." Mary's dark blue eyes sparkled with merriment, the little spite, as she skipped up to the work counter. She tilted her head back to gaze up at the woman holding a dishtowel, diligently wiping the spots from the china cup she held.

"Sara?"

"Why, Mary." Sara's face softened like the sky at sunrise when she looked at his girl. She clearly adored children. "Did you need a clean cup?"

Mary shook her head, slow and solemn. "You got an awfully pretty dress."

Sara flushed with pleasure, a soft pink caress of color across her delicate nose and cheekbones. "It's not nearly as pretty as yours."

"Uh-oh," Connie commented above the splash of soapy water. "I know what's coming next."

"So do I." Gabe, feet snug in his boots, stood to lift his coat from the peg. He was proud of his girl, pleased she had thought enough to include Sara in their midst, the woman with the lonely eyes and the quiet smile.

"Could you come help me pick out my Christmas dress?"

Mary swiped dark curls from her eyes, her unruly hair already escaping those tight braids. "Please, Sara?"

"Well, I—" The blush across her cheeks turned pinker. "No, I don't see how I can, Mary. I'm sorry. I don't want to disappoint you."

"Pretty, pretty please?"

"The train won't be coming this morning, Sara. You might as well give in." Gabe plopped his hat on his head and knuckled it back, so he could see the way her eyes widened, the worry dark and unveiled. "Go on. Save Connie from the torture of shopping alone with Mary."

A softness touched her mouth, a ghost of a grin. "I don't see how shopping with such a wonderful little girl could be difficult."

"Trust me, it's brutal." Connie feigned bleakness as she rinsed her fry pan.

Sara shook her head, determined to keep herself apart from them, but he could see in her eyes the argument was already won. She had a fondness for children and a big heart. So he stepped out into the frigid morning, feeling warmer for the smile she'd given him.

She should have said no in a way that meant it, Sara decided, but how on earth could she ever say no to Mary? The child was like a fairy, all wispy dark curls and energy, dashing around the kitchen.

"I hope Pa doesn't have to work too long." Mary ran with the small stack of saucers to the sideboard, the enamel rattling. "We gotta go get our tree."

"A Christmas tree?" Sara took the heavy stack of plates herself, afraid they would be too much for Mary.

"Yep. Pa and me are gonna string up popcorn and put candles on it." Mary skipped along beside her, blue skirts swishing, shoes drumming against the polished floor. "The best part is when Santa comes and leaves lots of presents."

"As long as you've been a good girl this year." Sara couldn't help teasing, couldn't help the thud of her heart at the sight of the joy and excitement sparkling in Mary's blue gray eyes.

"I've been a very good girl, right, Aunt Connie?"

"No way." Connie heaved up the washbasin and headed to the door. "A more terribly behaved girl doesn't exist."

"I'm awful," Mary giggled. "I don't eat my vegetables."

"A horrible crime. Santa never leaves gifts for little children who waste good vegetables." Connie went outside to dispose of the dishwater, then hopped back in, her cheeks red from the cold. "I guess that means you'd better try to reform yourself quick."

"And eat vegetables at dinner?"

"If you don't, Santa will be leaving coal for you, young lady." Connie's teasing made the kitchen warmer.

So this is what a happy family feels like, Sara realized, watching Mary, who was still debating the merits of green beans, then tromped across the kitchen to gather up the wet dishcloths and towels for Connie.

A cozy home, easy laughter, gentle banter. It was so different from the childhood she'd had, solemn and strict, where there had been no running in the house or leaving vegetables uneaten. The more she saw, the more grateful she was to Gabe. She had no more regrets. Not one.

"Sara, look out the window." Connie knelt to bank the fire in the cookstove. "The snow is stopping. This means you could be in Missoula before Christmas."

"Just as I'd hoped." Sara closed the etched glass doors of the beautiful sideboard. "Can I help?"

"Too late." Connie stood with a grin. "The embers are banked. Let's grab our coats and get on our way. I hope you don't mind walking? It's too cold to bring out the horses."

"I'm used to walking." Sara thought of her savings, hard earned and carefully tucked in her reticule upstairs. She had some money to spare, not much, but maybe she could find gifts for these wonderful people, for their hospitality, for the care they'd given Mary all her life. "I'll be right back."

Upstairs, in the room papered with tiny rosebuds, she stood before the bureau's beveled mirror and brushed the curls at her forehead and tried to stuff the escaped tendrils back into her braid with some success. She saw the window reflected in the mirror. The snowfall had tapered to just a few airy flakes. She felt cold inside at the thought of leaving, for this morning had been so wonderful.

But what was right for Mary and the promise she'd made long ago—never to interfere—made her course clear. She had to go. Before someone noticed they shared the same eye color, before she fell more in love with Mary.

"Sara?" Mary's face peeked around the doorframe. "Hurry up, okay? I got a lot of stuff to make Pa buy me."

At least she was honest. Sara laughed, treasuring the sight of the girl's smile, a ghost of Andrew's, gentle and sweet. "I've got my reticule and my gloves. I'm ready."

Mary grabbed her hand and Sara's chest squeezed with happiness as she raced down the stairs, making a horrible clatter as their feet drummed on the wood steps, echoing in the parlor's high ceilings.

"Goodness, you two sound like a wild stampede," Connie laughed as she shrugged into her wraps. "Mary, you bundle up now. If you don't, you'll only get more coal under that Christmas tree."

Mary grabbed her little cloak, beautifully cut and made of bright red wool. "I don't think Santa's sleigh can carry too much coal."

"I don't know. I've heard it's a pretty big sleigh." Connie knelt with little red mittens for those little girl hands and a matching scarf and hat.

Sara, unable to take her gaze from Mary, fetched her coat from the pegs. The child, cloak half buttoned and the scarf loose around her neck, pulled open the door. Cold air blew in, and outside sunshine glittered off drifts of sugar-white snow.

"That's more coal, young lady," Connie admonished with a grin as she rushed after Mary to fasten more of those buttons.

"But look! We got enough snow to make a whole family of snowmen." Mary spread her arms wide, sparkling like a ruby among diamonds.

Sara, squinting against the bright gleam of sun on snow, closed the door behind her. A sleigh sped by on the street ahead of them, its runners squeaking on the hard packed snow. A mild wind blew cold and crisp, and the scent of winter and pine teased her nose.

Moose Creek was a small town, pleasant with neatly painted storefronts and long awnings that covered freshly shoveled boardwalks. Shoppers were already crowding the streets, their bustling and excitement adding to the festive feeling.

Mary ran ahead, jumping and sliding and hopping about in the snow. Her delighted squeals tolled like birdsong. Lacking the same energy, she and Connie trudged through the deep snow behind her, then, when they reached the boardwalks, stomped the caked ice off their boots.

"Sara, where do you need to go?" Connie asked, catching Mary by the cap as she raced on by. "We need to drop by the mercantile for this wild one's new dress."

"That's fine with me."

Mary led the way inside. The brass bell above the door tinkled as they entered. The scent of coffee and pickles and leather clashed, and the warm stove in the center of the main aisle emitted the soothing scent of wood smoke.

There were so many things to choose from. Sara blinked, overwhelmed. The small dry goods store in Oak's Grove was a closet compared to this, and the variety—why, it was fun just to look at so many different kinds of ribbons and dishes and lamps.

"Over here, Sara!" Mary charged down the aisle. "Look at the candy."

Rows of glass canisters lined one whole section of the counter. As many different kinds of candy as Sara could imagine.

"I got a penny." Dark curls tumbled over Mary's brow as she dug through her pockets.

"So do I." Sara set a dime on the counter. The clerk counted out a dozen peppermint sticks and wrapped them in a striped paper sack. Pleasure pooled warm and cozy in her chest as she held the sack out to Mary.

"Sara, she's spoiled enough all ready," Connie scolded gently.

"She's got a little ways to go before she's good and truly spoiled." She heard the fondness shimmering in her own voice, but she could not be ashamed. She didn't belong here. She had never meant to so much as say a single word to Mary, but this sweetness was like nothing she had ever known.

"Thank you, Sara." Mary gazed up at her, tilting her head slightly to one side. "I'm glad you got stuck on that train."

"Me too." Her throat ached.

"Aunt Connie, can we go look for my dress now?"

"Here's where the agony begins." Connie winked at Sara as she chose a piece of candy. "Prepare yourself."

Mary led the way to the clothes racks, which sported an

array of colorful dresses. Beautiful calicos and ginghams, velvets and satin.

"Hello, Connie," a portly woman, an apron tied around her waist, said as she approached with a pleasant smile. "In to take a look at the new dresses, I see."

"I like the red one," Mary spoke up. "Can I try it on please?"

"Why of course you can." The sales clerk reached down the red velvet dress from the rack. "Is this the one you like?"

Mary's nod was serious, her eyes wide. "I'm gonna need new shoes."

Connie laughed. "See? She's torture."

Sara's chest felt so tight. "Yes, I can see the misery."

Clapping with excitement, Mary followed the clerk to the curtained partitions in the back wall. "I don't need any help," the girl announced.

"She's an independent one." Connie turned to study the selection of spooled ribbons.

"Like her father, I bet." Sara caught sight of the lace goods, laid out by the yard, and the stitched collars and cuffs. A bow caught her eye and she wondered how much it cost.

"I guess she does get that from Gabe. It's funny, the impact a parent can have on a child." Connie, perhaps in anticipation, picked up a roll of velvet red ribbon. "She's adopted."

Sara dropped the length of lace. "Adopted?"

"Yes. Not many people know that." Connie sighed, her gaze settling on Sara's face, on her eyes.

On eyes the same color as Mary's. Sara flicked her attention back to the lace goods, biting her lip. How foolish she'd been. She should have insisted on leaving after breakfast. Hadn't it been enough for her that no one had noticed the resemblance then?

"Ann died of cancer, and that was probably the reason she could never conceive, or so the doctor thought. It was hard on both Gabe and Mary. She withdrew and didn't flash that button smile of hers for an entire year. Gabe—well, he just looked half dead inside, but he tried hard to get past his grief, because of the love he has for their daughter."

Sara glanced up and saw Connie watching her. She felt terribly sad for their loss. "Ann must have been a kind person, to have loved an adopted child so much."

"She was. Kind and gentle, frail, actually. Like she never quite belonged on this earth." Connie looked away, sorting through the selection of stockings. "How she loved that child."

I owe Ann my thanks too. Sara looked up at the sound of Mary's shoes clattering on the polished floor. The girl skipped into sight, all rich crimson velvet and full swishing skirts.

"I love it." Sara couldn't stop the words; they just rolled right out of her heart. Maybe it was the little girl she thought so special, with her face pink with pleasure, her eyes shining, and her bow-shaped mouth flashing a beaming grin.

The dress—a princess-style cut with a round neckline and narrow waist—was adorable. The full skirt was trimmed with fine white lace and red ribbon, and when Mary swirled around, a big, fat bow hung at an odd angle in back, from her attempt to tie it herself.

"You look adorable." Connie dropped to her knees to retie the bow Sara ached to reach for.

Sara took a step back, remembering who she was. She was not Mary's mother, not the woman who cooked for her and watched over her by day, not the one who comforted her when nightmares interrupted her sleep.

"But this dress needs something. It's a little plain." Connie sounded puzzled. "What do you think, Sara?"

"It could maybe use more lace to offset the lace on the hem." Sara knelt beside Connie for a better view of the dress.

"I want a lace collar, like the one on that dress." Mary skipped to the rack and studied a deep blue sateen with cuffs and collar of cream lace.

"You know I can't sew a stitch." Connie inspected the delicate lace on the blue dress.

"I can." Sara's hand flew to her mouth. She had no right sewing for a child no longer hers, no right to steal such a pleasure.

"Oh, thank you!" Mary's arms wrapped around Sara's waist, all enthusiasm and joy.

"Sara, that's so nice of you. And you're a seamstress to boot!" Connie's smile told her gratefulness.

"I see you three are still standing." Gabe strolled down the aisle, his lanky gait unhurried. "Mary, you haven't given Connie an apoplexy yet, have you?"

"We haven't been shoppin' that long, Pa." She dashed into her father's strong arms. "I like this dress best."

"It sure looks pretty on you." Gabe brushed back tangled curls from his daughter's brow, a gentle gesture from so powerful a man. A father's love shone in his eyes, and Sara adored him all the more for it. Every time she saw the love he had for Mary, he became a bigger, better man in her eyes.

"And guess what? Sara's gonna put on a lace collar."

"She is?" Gabe's dark blue eyes flashed up to meet Sara's, full of humor too, and the joy of being with his daughter. "I hope Mary didn't railroad you into this?"

"I offered."

"So, she charmed you, did she?" A grin tugged at one side of his cheek, lopsided and charming.

"Just a little bit." My, but he was a handsome man, all dressed in black, from his hat to his wool jacket to his polished boots. "Any news on the train?"

"Still snowed in." Gabe swept off his hat. "The hotel's still full up. I wish I could offer better news."

Her heart hammered. How could she spend another night in Connie's home? "Maybe the boardinghouse . . . ?"

"What? You don't like staying with me?" Connie crunched on the last of her peppermint stick. "Or was my cooking that bad?"

"No, it's just that I"—her gaze fell to Mary—"can't impose. Christmas is almost here, and your family—"

"Would be honored to have such a lovely guest." Gabe stepped into the light, and there was no mistaking his honesty.

"That's right," Connie agreed. "You could just pretend we're family for as long as it takes for that train to get here. We have yet to decorate the Christmas tree and finish our shopping and, oh, help with the Christmas boxes for the needy—"

"And don't forget the Christmas pageant," Mary spoke up as she twirled round and round, her full red skirt flaring. "I want Sara to see me sing."

"There's a thrill she won't want to miss." Gabe winked, and Sara felt the impact of his lopsided grin across the narrow aisle. "I'm going to leave you ladies to shop and check back with you later."

"He's good for hauling our packages home," Connie confided. "And for buying three lovely ladies dinner."

"I heard the hint." Good humored, Gabe offered Sara his hand, palm up.

She laid her smaller hand on his, felt the male-hot texture of his skin, rough and calloused, but pleasant, saw deep in his eyes a longing she understood too well.

"If you truly want me to find other accommodations, I

can." He said the words low so that Mary and Connie, their heads bent over the lace goods, couldn't hear. "We want you to stay right where you are. With our family."

Her heart turned over and plummeted all the way down to her toes. No man had ever looked at her this way; no man had ever made her ache quite the way Gabe did.

"I'll stay where I am." Emotion ached in her throat.

"If the weather holds, we'll see the train in the morning."

In the morning. Sara had never dreamed for so much, this time spent with her daughter. "That will give me plenty of time to sew on that collar."

"Just the collar, huh?" Gabe's eyes laughed, such a dazzling shade of blue. "You don't know Mary. There's a word you need to learn if you spend any time around her at all. And it's the word *no.*"

"I bet it's a word she doesn't hear often." Sara watched as Mary held a delicate collar up to the dress's neckline.

"Thank you, Sara." Gabe released her hand, stepping back, and the air suddenly felt colder.

"It's my pleasure."

He strode away, and she could not tear her gaze from the line of his rock-hewn shoulders, not until he disappeared from her sight. But the way he made her feel, warm and treasured, remained.

Chapter Four

It was the light in Sara's eyes that drew his gaze back every time he looked down at his plate to cut his steak or over at Mary while she spoke of their adventures in shopping. Back to the shimmer of Sara's blue eyes, like sunlight on water, and the way happiness seemed to fill her, changing her face from pretty to beautiful.

The tinkling din of happy voices in the diner, the beaming joy on his daughter's face, the street beyond the sparkling window with its white streets and colorful shops faded to silent gray when Sara leaned forward to answer Connie's question.

"No, my father thought wrapped gifts and decorated trees frivolous." She toyed with her fork, bowing her chin, and dark curls fell around her face. "When she was alive, my mother would hang stockings for us above the hearth for Santa to fill with candy and pennies."

"I don't remember my mother much." Mary rubbed dark curls out of her eyes. "Did Ma put up stockings, Pa?"

"She did." It hurt to remember, but in a good way. Those were happy times too, but so far away, impossible to touch. "And she decorated the tree every year and played the piano. She loved Christmas carols. There was always music and presents piled beneath the tree."

Mary lifted her gaze, resonant with longing. "That's why I asked Santa to bring me a mother. I don't need no presents."

"Not even a doll?" Connie asked.

When Sara's eyes brimmed, his chest tightened, kicking up a new sense of longing with every beat of his heart. Not for times past, but for those yet to come.

"Not even a doll." Mary's solemn tone seemed at odds with the merry laughter somewhere else in the diner, with the exciting anticipation lingering in the air like the scent of cookies and pine, for the holiday was only days away. "Pa and me are real lonely. Other girls have got mothers to sew their dresses and tuck them in at night."

"I tuck you in at night," Gabe protested, reaching for his glass of cider before the emotion tight in his chest sounded raw in his voice. "I'm a pretty darn good tucker-inner."

"Yeah, but, Pa, a ma would be good too." Mary's gaze flicked to Sara, stormy eyes luminous. "Did you ever get a new mother, Sara?"

"Never. I would have liked one." How wistful her voice.

Gabe considered the little girl she must have been, kept home from school to take over the bulk of her mother's work. Her father, a stern, unbending man who took no pleasure in life. "Surely you celebrated Christmas when you were married."

"No. We were wed in February and he fell off the barn roof late that summer. He died soon after." The grief had passed, but its shadow remained, keen and spellbinding.

"We would have had a wonderful holiday if Andrew had lived. But some things are not to be, I guess."

"Is that when you moved back home to your father?" Connie asked.

Sara nodded. "And later, when I was on my own, I would decorate a small tree, but that was all."

"Then I'm glad you'll be with us, at least to share some of our fun." Connie's gaze warmed out of sympathy for the woman and her past.

"So am I." Sara kept her head bowed, maybe shy, maybe just uncomfortable that her feelings showed. "I will remember this time spent with you always."

Gabe could not stop looking at her, drawn by a beauty that grew with every moment. A gentle, radiant beauty, the kind that only came from within.

"It's starting to snow again." Mary spread her arms wide and spun in circles, the ends of her scarf and the hem of her blue dress twirling right along with her.

Entranced, Sara missed a step and nearly slid off the boardwalk.

"Careful." Gabe stepped down after her, his words rumbling with care.

She blushed, feeling foolish. Ice crackled beneath her shoes, where the day's brief sun had melted the snow, which had frozen again.

"Hey, Pa!" Mary skidded, almost falling the same way Sara had. "Oops."

"Yeah, oops. It's slick, angel." Gabe's gentle teasing could not hide his protective nature. He watched the traffic on the busy road, where horses and sleighs rushed by.

Sara blinked against the thick flakes batting her face as she turned at the intersection. Packages rattled as Gabe strode beside her, wide shoulders braced against the north wind.

"Mary, stop goofing around. You're going to end up on your fanny," Connie tsked. "Goodness, look at that sheen of ice. It's going to be a cold one tonight."

"Mary." Gabe's warning sent Sara turning.

"Oh, Pa. I don't fall. Much." Mary skipped up to take her hand. "Sara, do you like snowmen?"

"I haven't met one I haven't liked." How that button smile warmed the darkest places inside. Sara took a careful step, even as Mary, in her exuberance, pulled her along.

"Mary, you're going to wind up on the ground and take Sara with you." Gabe sounded breathless as he gazed over the top of the packages he carried.

His dark blue gaze sparkled, rare and easily, and she caught herself smiling back. "I'm likely to be the one falling and knocking Mary over."

The girl giggled, her face pink with delight.

"Goodness. Would you look at that?" Connie's airy wonder snared Sara's attention and she swung around.

She heard Gabe's "Whoa," the rustling of paper and packages, and the thud of something hitting the ground hard enough to rattle teeth. Then she saw the packages tumble into the snow.

"Gabe!" She rushed to his side, dropping to her knees. The ice was so hard, it would be no trick at all to break a bone. "Are you all right? Can you move your legs?"

"I'm fine, Sara. Just a little humiliated—that's all." He was a big man standing up, but spread out on the ground, his size and strength seemed more noticeable. Maybe it was because he was dressed in black, a stark contrast to the sugary-white snow. Or maybe it was because she saw the man he was, powerful and substantial, not just the father of her daughter.

"My pride's a bit bruised." He rubbed his elbow as he sat up.

"Here's your hat, Pa." Mary skipped close, offering the now battered Stetson. "It flew off your head when you hit."

"Thanks, smarty-pants." Shaking his head, scattering thick tantalizing dark locks over his brow, he tried to bend the hat's brim back into shape.

"You should have been watching where you were going, Pa," Mary reminded him with a giggle.

"Watch out, or I'm going to have a talk with Santa." With a rueful wink, he set the hat back on his head. Ice clung to him, along every inch that had contacted the ground.

"Pa, you look like a snowman from behind." Mary's helpful comments just didn't stop.

"That's it. You're getting only coal for Christmas." Tossing a sheepish grin Sara's way, he tried to brush off some of the more embarrassing snow chunks.

Sara felt the tickle deep in her chest and tried to stop it, but up it bubbled, growing stronger as it went. She erupted into giggles.

"A proper lady wouldn't find humor in a man's misfortune," Gabe reminded her, though he didn't scold, didn't find fault. No, his words came like a touch, tender and binding.

"You weren't misfortunate, Pa." Mary joined in retrieving the fallen packages. "You were walkin' too fast, and you didn't look where you were goin'. That's what you always tell me."

"Guilty as charged." Gabe did not see the need to mention he'd been watching Sara, noticing the swish of her dark skirts against her slim ankles, the fine set of her slender shoulders, the easy grace of her smile when she looked down at his daughter. Fine way to act now that he was in a pretty lady's company. "I'm gonna have to tell Santa all about this little incident here."

"More coal." Connie reached, but Sara grabbed the last package, straightening up carefully as her feet began to slip. "Gabe, would you mind telling me what in blazes all those men are doing standing around on my porch?"

"What men?" Over the stack of the packages, Sara stepped away from him, taking with her the scent of sweet apples and even sweeter woman.

"I should have guessed it." He took a step, readjusting his gun belt, which had twisted during the fall. "Looks like word has gotten out about Sara."

"What about me?" The rose-soft color pinkening her cheeks drained away.

"That you're stranded here." Gabe didn't mind stepping close to her to take the packages she carried. Her scent, innocent and enticing, tickled his nose, made his heart skip a beat. "Those vultures think one of them just might be lucky enough to take you out to supper."

"What?" She froze, stiff as an icicle. "Gabe, I don't think I could—" She paused, her gloved hand covering her mouth.

He could see the prospect of facing so many eager gentlemen, all sporting their Sunday best even in this frigid weather, daunted her. He liked that Sara Mercer was shy and unpretentious. "I'll handle it."

"Thank you." Her gratitude shone like sunlight through clouds, unveiled and genuine.

He tipped his hat to her, his chest tight, his blood thrumming through his veins.

"I should have suspected something like this could happen." Connie snuggled her hat over her ears and took a step, following her brother. "When I came to town to help out, when Ann was failing, I had six men bring me flowers before I'd walked from the train station to the house."

"Six men?" Sara lifted her skirts to step off the icy road and into the softer snow of Connie's yard. "I guess I should have figured on it too. In Oak's Grove there's a shortage of marriageable women."

"And yet look at you, still unmarried."

"For a long time after Andrew's death I wasn't ready." Sara thought of the gentle man, his loss made all the more difficult for the love he'd given her. Somehow, seeing a hint of Andrew every time Mary smiled made it easier now. "And then, when I was, my father felt he had the right to interfere."

"I'm glad you're free of him." Connie's touch was pure comfort, the kind that warmed from the inside out.

Sara was glad too. Returning home to her father, after she'd been widowed, had been difficult. Had she had one other choice, she would have taken it. And she'd worked hard to make her own life, a tough thing in a world where a woman couldn't vote, couldn't make a man's wages to support herself. "That's why this job offer from my aunt is so important to me."

"Don't you worry. The men will get the train running and you'll be on your way to a happier future. Although we're going to hate to see you go."

"Sara, you're gonna stay and watch me sing, right?" Mary spun around, a bright red angel against shimmering snow. The girl might have had Andrew's smile and Sara's eyes, but there was no mistaking that Mary's face was her own, soft and not quite oval, and so very dear.

"I would love to stay, but I can't risk being late. I never meant to stay so long in Moose Creek—" Her mouth clamped shut when she realized what she'd said. *I never meant to stay so long.*

"Who knew a blizzard was going to hit the mountains?" Connie reached out. "Come, Mary. Take my hand. Let the men pass."

Sara bit her lip, grateful. Connie hadn't noticed her slip. Her chest squeezed so that the cold air burning in her lungs could not escape. In today's happiness, in the excitement of shopping for gifts and keeping them secret, she had forgotten who she was. She didn't belong here. And if Connie and Gabe knew the truth, they couldn't help but hate her for every minute of her deception.

Ashamed, she bowed her face, unable to meet the men's gazes as they filed by, tipping their hats to her, murmuring hellos. Maybe in Missoula she could hope to find a man with broad shoulders and a kind smile, someone who could love her. Someone she could love in return.

"They were disappointed, but I chased them off, like the tough sheriff I am." Gabe held open the front door, his confidence as brazen as his smile. "I tell you, it was dangerous there for a few moments."

"Then they realized you weren't any competition." Connie tossed her brother a saucy grin. "They saw you land on your behind on the ice and thought, 'Hey, that clumsy sheriff isn't good enough for the lovely Sara.' "

Sara's face flamed as he winked at her.

Mary giggled. "Pa's not clumsy. Not all the time."

"That's a comfort to know." Sara stepped into the warm home, cozy with its papered walls and braided rugs. Connie already knelt before the potbellied stove in the parlor, stirring the embers to life.

"Pa, where'd you put my dress?"

"I hid the packages in the kitchen, because I knew someone would want to rifle through them." Gabe stepped close.

Sara's skin tingled at his nearness, at the way he towered over her, iron strong and dependable. Mary's shoes pounded against the wood floor as she raced to the kitchen, and Connie sprung up to catch her, reminding the girl there were surprises hidden in those packages and she would search for Mary's dress herself.

"Let me help you with your coat." How warm his voice was, deep but not dark, rich as hot chocolate after a long winter's day.

His hand settled at her shoulder, holding the heavy wool garment so she could slip out of it. Even though they did not touch, she could feel his body's heat, radiant and substantial like the man. He smelled of fresh snow and sharp cedar and faintly of soap. She could see the dark indigo flecks in his eyes, true blue and focused on her face. A small smile tugged dimples into his cheeks.

She stepped away, breathless, as if she'd run three miles. Still, his gaze did not leave hers and she turned away, tugging at her muffler to keep her hands busy. "I appreciate how you had those men leave. I'm not staying, and I'm just not . . . not looking for a reason to stay in Moose Creek."

"That's too bad." He took the ragged scarf from her fingers, slim and so beautiful. He hung the length of wool on a peg near her cloak. "Moose Creek is not a bad place to live. Friendly. Safe. Besides, we're here—Mary and me."

"Yes." How breathless she sounded, how magical. He hadn't realized quite how much he missed a woman in his life, not until he'd seen her walking home, snow clinging to her scarf and those wispy curls over her brow. Her laughter, low and pleasant, still rumbled through his memory and her sheer concern that he'd hurt himself on the ice.

His heart clenched. How long it had been since a woman, so beautiful and fine, had shown concern for him.

"Here's my dress, Sara." Mary bounded into the room, her velvet red dress scrunched in her arms. "Can you do the cuffs too?"

"Sure I can. It will take no time at all." Sara settled

down on the sofa, her soft skirts shivering around her. "I bet I could have this done today."

"Truly?" Mary's adoration shone. "You must be a really good sewer."

"I'm not bad." Pleasure pinkened Sara's face, and he could read her affection for this child as surely as if she'd said the words. She had a kind heart and was fond of children.

Gabe shrugged off his coat. Mary had been a great comfort after Ann's passing. How much harder had it been for Sara, who had no daughter of her own?

"Come over and have supper with us." The words tumbled out before he could call them back, before he lost his nerve.

"Yeah, Sara. Come have supper!" Mary hopped up and down.

Sara's dark-as-a-storm gaze flicked from the girl up to him. "I thought you said you couldn't cook."

"No, but I can make a tolerable stew. If you'd care to risk it." Gabe strode forward, encouraged at not hearing an instant no. After all, she hadn't screamed and bolted from the room at his invitation. That had to be a good sign. "We'd like to have you, Sara. In appreciation for sewing on Mary's dress. You're my sister's guest. You didn't have to agree to do this."

"It's no trouble at all. But a pleasure."

"I don't see how." He sat on the chair near her, unable to stop noticing she was a woman, all curves, slim but firm. "When Connie has to mend something, she curses and swears she's never done such tedious work in all her life."

"I don't find it tedious." Sara placed the lace collar at the dress's neckline. "I enjoy sewing. It beats scrubbing clothes in a laundry for a living."

"Ooh, it's so pretty!" Mary bent over Sara's knees. "Can you make it look that good?"

"Better. You just wait until I have the cuffs on it. You know, we have a bit extra of that matching ribbon you picked out. I could lay it here, over the cuffs, so that the trim at the sleeve matches the trim on the hem."

"Could you, Sara?"

"You bet I can."

"Thank you, thank you, thank you!" Mary hopped to her feet and charged back into the kitchen. "Aunt Connie, Aunt Connie, guess what Sara's gonna do?" The door swung shut, snapping off her words and Connie's answer.

"You made her happy." Gabe touched the dress laid out on her lap, his fingertips brushing the snowy-white collar. "You never agreed to come."

"To supper?" She could hardly think past the drum of her heart, chugging away like a train uphill. He did this to her, impressive and handsome, substantial and capable. He was all she saw, not the room, not Mary's dress, not the braided rug at her feet. Just Gabe Chapman, his chiseled good looks only part of the attraction. He tugged at her heart, made her feel things she had never known.

"Yes, supper." He reached out, his male-hot fingers brushing the curve of her cheek, then smoothing away the curls tumbling across her brow. How feather soft his touch, yet it made her blood heat, made her want more tenderness, more of his touch. "Give me this chance to thank you, Sara."

"I should be the one thanking you. You rescued me from the train and brought me here, shown me what I've—" She caught herself in time. *What I've never dared to dream of.* Time with her daughter.

"Supper's at six." He stood, withdrawing from her, leaving her cold and aching for more of his closeness. How she wanted more. "I live right across the road. The little log cabin. You can't miss it."

She stood, clutching Mary's dress in her arms, against her chest where her frantic heart thundered. "But I—"

"No buts, no arguments." Gabe lifted his coat from the pegs, the sincerity in his gaze drawing her like nothing could. "We want you to come."

How she ached at his words. He stepped through the threshold, leaving her alone.

Chapter Five

"I got a question, Pa." Mary skipped into the kitchen, her stick horse clutched in both hands.

"Let me have it." Gabe, used to his daughter's questions, gave the stew a good stir. "I'm ready for anything."

"Oh, Pa." Apparently not amused by her father's humor, she rode her play horse close to the stove. "Do you think Santa brought Sara to us?"

"I don't know. Seems to me Santa specializes in bringing toys, not people." He settled the lid on the kettle. "Where did you get an idea like that? From Aunt Connie?"

"Nope. Just wondered." Mary tilted her head to one side. "Maybe Santa brought the blizzard."

"The one that trapped the train?" Gabe tugged open the pantry door. "I don't think Santa brings blizzards."

"But what if he does?" Mary swiped at the yarn mane of her stick horse. "Sara's awfully pretty, don't you think?"

"Yeah, I do think she's pretty." Beautiful, actually, with a gentle way about her that made his insides curl up. He rifled through the pantry, looking for the basket of fresh biscuits Connie had donated for supper.

"And she's nice. She knows about clothes and how to sew 'em." Mary parked her horse against the corner, where it couldn't topple over. "She was much better than Aunt Connie at pickin' out stuff. She got me the lace collar and the ribbon to match. And the shoes. You didn't get to see the shoes, Pa."

"I have a feeling I'm about to."

With an elfin grin, Mary took off, clattering through the house like a wild buffalo.

Maybe it was one way to look at it—that Santa had brought Mary the opportunity for a new mother. Gabe decided he liked that viewpoint.

He set the covered biscuits on the counter, ready to be popped into the oven to warm at suppertime, and took a look around his kitchen. Checked curtains at the windows framed the view of rapidly falling snow. With the way it was accumulating, there was a chance the crew might not be able to clear the tracks before tomorrow.

And if they did, then all sorts of other events might conspire to keep her here. The engine might be broken. Another blizzard could hit.

The way Gabe looked at it, he ought to take advantage of such an opportunity. Besides, he'd rescued her from the train. He ought to have a shot at winning her heart. He was a lonely man, and not one woman he'd met since Ann's death had made his blood hot, made him feel good from the inside out.

"Look." Mary presented the pair of shiny black patent leather shoes. "And these stockings too."

The lace pattern was a close match to the dress, he would bet. Gabe knelt down to take a look. "She did a good job helping you."

"Just the way a real mother ought to."

Gabe's throat ached looking at the hope glistening in his daughter's blue gray eyes. Through a child's eyes, anything was possible. He knew Mary had watched other girls and their mothers in town walking or shopping together, seen the small touches a woman knew how to do, braid hair a fancy way or tie a ribbon just right.

"Maybe you ought to make Sara fall in love with you, Pa."

"Maybe we shouldn't condemn the woman to such a terrible fate. Jail would be better."

"Oh, Pa. Sara *likes* us."

"How do you know that?"

"Can't you tell?" Mary huffed, apparently exasperated at her thickheaded father. "She smiles when she's with us. If she hated us, she'd frown a lot."

"I'm glad you've thought this through."

"I've done a lot of thinkin'."

Any woman who spent time with his daughter without expecting anything, who did a kind deed for her, whose face changed simply looking at her was a fine lady in his estimation. He had noticed the fondness Sara showed toward Mary. Maybe it was because she'd been widowed so long, without children of her own, without the hope for any until she married again.

He gave the stew another good stir, satisfied with how it was simmering. "We've got some time before Sara shows up. What do you want to do?"

"Let's go play in the snow!" Mary set her new things on the trunk in the parlor, then dashed to the coat tree.

"We'd better get those snowmen built before another blizzard hits." Gabe's gaze slid to the windows. The snow had become a haze, blocking out the view of the street and the houses beyond. "Bundle up."

"Or I'll freeze up like an icicle, I know." Standing on

tiptoes, Mary tugged down **her** coat. "Pa? Maybe you ought to tell Sara she's pretty. That way she'll like you more."

"Thanks for the advice." Gabe knelt to help her with the small buttons. She might be almost five, but she was still little. "Now keep this snug around your throat. I don't want you getting sick."

"I know, Pa." Mary tucked her scarf beneath her coat's collar. She looked like a cardinal, bright red and eager. "Hurry up. We've got snowmen to build."

"I'll be right out." Gabe opened the door and Mary flew out, all pounding boots and excitement. The force of the cold air struck him to the bone.

Before he joined his daughter outside, he checked both stoves to make sure the fires would be warm when Mary clamored half frozen back into the house. Then he lifted his coat from the hook. Dishes sat ready and waiting on the table by the window. The scent of meat and vegetables simmering lingered in the air.

It would be nice to have a woman in his home again, someone to share the moments of his life with, one by one. He could only wish that woman might be Sara Mercer with her winter blue eyes and gentle smile.

"Pa!" Mary scolded, giggling as she dodged a big snowball. "You ain't listenin'!"

"I don't need a four year old's advice." Gabe dove to his knees to avoid Mary's surprisingly accurate snowball, which nearly hit him square on the forehead. "Not when it comes to romancing a lady."

"You don't know anything about girls." Mary packed more snow in her mittened hands, the yarn thick with clumped balls of ice.

"I know enough." Gabe already figured he wasn't going to charm Sara Mercer with his cooking. His stew was passable, nothing more, but just to have her in his kitchen, in his home, basking in the light of her presence . . . A cold white object struck him square in the face.

Mary's giggle announced her delight. "I got you, Pa."

"You sure did. A direct hit." He rubbed the snow out of his eyes, planning retaliation, and he heard the gentle bell of laughter.

Great, just great. He had been hoping on cleaning up, changing into his best shirt before she arrived, but it was too late. And too late to save his dignity. He turned to face Sara Mercer with a sense of doom. It was damn near impossible to look dashing with bits of snow clinging to his cap.

"Sara!" Mary shrieked with delight, dashing across the snow to catch Sara in a hug.

Her smile brightened. "Look what I brought for you."

"You finished the dress!"

"Just like I said." Liquid warm, those words, and as dependable as her promise. "I don't want to interrupt your game."

The wind snapped the hem of her skirts taut around slim ankles and played with the edge of her long cloak. She carried several packages—one he wagered was the special dress. "Maybe I'd better go inside and set these down. And Connie warned me to check on the stew."

"The stew." He flashed her a smile and liked the way she flushed, just a bit, as if she felt this too, this sense of rightness. "Let me carry those."

"They aren't heavy." She moved with an elegance, a grace that held him mesmerized, made it hard to look at anything but her.

She surrendered her packages. "Connie sent over a surprise."

"Let me guess." He heard the rustling inside the bag. "Popcorn."

"Yippee!" Mary jumped up, clapping her hands. "That's my very favorite."

"Mine too." Sara had had the treat a few times in her life.

"Don't go in yet, Sara." Mary's hold didn't lessen. "You gotta see my snowmen. You just gotta!"

"A few words of warning." Gabe tugged open the front door to the cozy looking log home. "Don't let her talk you into a snowball fight. She's got a good arm."

How handsome he looked, speckled with white, the left side of his face red from the icy snowball's impact. How dependable he looked, all solid man and tender smile.

Then he closed the door behind him, gone from her sight.

"We made a family." Mary tugged Sara over to the side of the house, where the three awkward snow people perched, stick arms raised in a perpetual greeting. "A father, a little girl, and a *mother*." Mary's voice caressed that word.

Sara remembered Mary's wish for Christmas. If she had a wish, what would it be?

Sara complimented the girl on her snow family, on the father with a mustache and the little girl with straw hair, but her gaze lingered on the mother figure, on the apron etched along the snowwoman's abdomen, the telltale depth of a child's finger, and the necklace at her throat. A locket. A heart-shaped locket, like the one hanging even now beneath her cloak.

"Hey, you two." Gabe stood on the porch, gloved hands curled around the post. "I've got the biscuits warming."

"Aunt Connie's biscuits." Mary grabbed Sara's hand and tugged her toward the steps. "Pa's are as hard as rocks."

"Hey, I heard that." Gabe reached out to catch Sara's elbow, helping her up the icy steps.

She looked up at him, surprised by the care he showed

her. How solid his grip felt, not possessive or bruising, but strong. So very strong.

"No matter what Mary and Connie say, I'm not that bad a cook."

"Sure, Pa."

"I've heard differently, Gabe." Sara swept across the threshold after Mary, and her heart felt so light. "This is a beautiful home."

"Come stand by me," Mary urged.

Sara felt Gabe behind her as he closed the door with a gentle whisper of hinges and the click of the doorknob. She heard his solid step on the wood floor. He was so close. Her skin prickled, and she shivered. She took a step away, unwinding her muffler.

"I'll take that." Velvet heat, that voice, and it warmed her from the inside, chased away the chill from snow and wind, made her see the man he was, both strong and vulnerable.

She did not want to see Gabe Chapman in such a way. It was enough he was a good father to Mary. It was what she had come to see, what she had had to know. Like a new bird testing its wings, she was uncertain of these feelings. Uncertain if she should be looking at Gabe and appreciating him as a man.

She would be leaving on the next train. Only a fool would think . . . No, there could never be any affection, any attraction between them.

"Let me show you your dress." Sara knew she was being rude, not allowing Gabe to help her with her coat, but she shrugged out of it quickly, then thanked him when he insisted on hanging it up for her. She avoided his gaze, her heart tearing, not knowing what to do.

Her hands trembling, she unfolded the dress from the bundle she carried. Smoothing the red velvet gently, Sara held up the garment.

"It's perfect." Mary's awe shimmered in eyes filled with delight. "Pa, come see. Oh, *thank you,* Sara."

Just to see Mary's happiness was more than Sara could take. She knew her eyes filled with tears she dared not show, with years of love for a baby no longer hers. The stolen pleasure she'd taken, doing this simple stitching. Never in her deepest dreams had she imagined sewing for her daughter.

"That's a fine job, Sara." Gabe hardly looked at the dress; he was gazing at her. And she felt his scrutiny like a touch, gentle as a winter's dawn. "Mary is going to have the best Christmas dress in town."

"Sara, you're a real good sewer." Mary shrugged out of her wraps. Ice tinkled to the floor and sizzled on the stone hearth.

"That's why I'm going to Missoula to work as a seam-stress." Sara's face clouded. "My mother taught me, you know. I was five years old—"

"I'll be five on January tenth."

Sara pursed her lips, the color draining from her cheeks. "My birthday's in January too."

"You should come to my party. Pa!" Mary twisted around to shout at her father, who had retreated to the kitchen. "Sara oughta come to my party."

"Maybe she'll be too busy with her new job, tiger." Gabe stepped into view, dark hair tumbling across his brow. He held a big spoon in one hand.

"Pa! That's not what you're supposed to say."

"Missoula is a long ways away." Sara's voice was rich with regret. "At least, to someone who's never traveled before."

Gabe knew his stew was boiling and the biscuits were probably drying out in the oven, but his feet felt bolted to the floor and his gaze riveted to the woman in his parlor. She lifted a slim hand to brush stray black curls out of her eyes, a graceful, simple movement, yet it made his heart hammer. Desire stronger than he'd ever known fired through his blood, driving with a force that knocked him breathless.

"We travel on the train a lot." Mary fingered the new lace collar. "Don't we, Pa?"

"Now and then." Gabe tried to sound normal, but how could he? It was as if everything had changed with Sara Mercer in his parlor.

"How exciting." Sara folded the dress neatly for Mary, her hands smoothing away every wrinkle with such care it made his throat knot, made every lonely spot in his chest ache. "This was the first time I've ever rode on the train. There now. This is all ready."

"For Christmas Eve," Mary breathed with reverence.

"It's a very important night." Sara stood, her skirts swishing to the floor to hide her slim ankles. "We'd better put this away before it gets wrinkled."

"Or dirty or somethin'." In agreement, Mary scooped up her shiny shoes and snowy-white stockings. "You gotta come see my room, Sara. Pa made my bed."

"He's a furniture maker too? Your father's pretty talented." Sara's voice grew distant as she followed Mary's skipping step down the hallway, but the tenderness in her voice did not fade.

Not from his heart, at least. Gabe grabbed the biscuits from the warming oven and plopped them into a bowl, then covered the bowl with a dishtowel to keep in the heat. Frankly, he had wanted to marry again, but there was a shortage of women in Montana Territory. And the few women he'd met—why, he hadn't felt that spark and hadn't been sure they would come to love Mary.

But Sara Mercer had a fondness for children that lit her voice, that resonated in her every act. From shimmering smiles to gentle laughter to sewing collars and cuffs on a little girl's dress—why, that kindness drew him, made his heart ache for that kind of affection in his life.

He set the biscuits on the table, content with the happy voices coming from Mary's room, the little girl's excitement and Sara's soft exclamations over the bed or desk or the ruffly curtains they had special ordered from Billings.

Mary's shoes drummed on the wood floor. "Pa? We're getting hungry."

"I heard you coming, buffalo gal." He set her bowl on the place by the window, near her stick horse tucked into the corner.

"Sara knows how to make lace, Pa." All sparkling awe.

They stood side by side, Mary's hand tucked in Sara's larger one, both woman and child slim and delicate of build. Looking at them together, he nearly dropped the steaming bowl he carried. Mary's shade of brown black hair was identical to Sara's, thick and bouncy, curling into ringlets when those unruly tendrils escaped from tight braids.

"I learned to crochet when I was your age." Sara gazed down at Mary, and only then did he notice the stormy blue of her eyes, saw how they matched Mary's. "My mother taught me. I remember in the winter, when the snow fell and it was cold everywhere but right near the stove, she would pull her rocking chair up to the hearth and bring out her big basket. It was full of wonderful threads and flosses and yarns. And I got to pick out the one I liked the best to work with. Mother would do the same, and she would settle into her chair and I would curl up at her feet and we would crochet until the afternoon became evening and it was time to start supper."

He stood captivated, the memory lighting her face the same way excitement colored Mary's. Why, they did look identical in this light, with that rare brightness in Sara's eyes.

A cold chill snaked down his spine. *It couldn't be, could it?* His heart skidded to a stop in his chest. Somehow he continued setting the bowls on the table. His thumb knocked a spoon and it clattered against the polished wood. It rang as it rocked, and he turned, his pulse thundering in his ears.

Mary, as an unwanted baby, had been born in the vicinity of Oak's Grove—at least that was what he'd been led to believe when his father-in-law had said he'd found an infant they could adopt. Gabe had never known the identity of Mary's mother. He had always assumed she had been a young woman, little more than a girl herself, who'd been disgraced. Could that woman have been Sara?

"Why, you're a better cook than you let on, Gabe Chapman." Sara swept into the kitchen, bringing with her a sweet apple-and-woman scent and the light of her smile. "That smells delicious. Let me help."

"Absolutely not. You're the guest."

"And really pretty," Mary spoke up, all impish grin, as she caught Sara's hand and tugged her in the direction of the table.

He looked again and saw only differences between Mary and Sara. The cut of the mouth, the cowlick in Mary's part, Sara's high cheekbones.

When Sara was told where to sit—in the best chair so she could look at both the window and the cozy parlor—Gabe could see a difference in the shades of those blue gray eyes. Sara's were darker, laden with shadows, where Mary's sparkled, a tad more blue than gray.

He gave the stew a final stir, before dishing up the last bowl. Before turning around to feel his heart thump at the way Sara watched him, gentle as spring rain. Surely his imagination had gotten away from him—that was all. Sara Mercer was a woman on her way to Missoula, stuck in a blizzard. It was chance she was here in Moose Creek, here in his kitchen.

Judging by the way his blood thrummed when he sat down near her, he had to believe maybe there was some truth to Mary's observations. He was too old to believe in Santa, but he did believe that things happened for a reason.

And maybe Sara—why, maybe she was meant for them. To give his daughter the mother she yearned for and to end the loneliness that banded tight around his heart.

Chapter Six

"I wanna play 'Silent Night' first," Mary informed them with a flick of her braids after their applause faded. "Wait. I gotta find the music."

Sara watched as the girl rattled through sheets of paper, then, with a bob of her head, smoothed the scored sheets of parchment. She set her small fingers over the ivory keys. Sweet notes, melody and harmony, blended together to make the solemn, familiar refrain.

Silent night, the piano strings toned, low and reverent. That was her daughter. Sara's chest swelled until it hurt with pride for the girl. A pride that could never be shown or spoken of, but it was real and abiding just the same.

"She's good." The words stuck in her throat.

Gabe nodded, pride bright in his eyes. "There's a music teacher in town. A woman we hired to come teach at the school, but she ended up married. She's taught Mary since her first lesson."

Music lessons, Sara marveled, unable to tear her gaze

away from the small girl on the polished piano stool, fingers deliberate and practiced.

Sleep in heavenly peace, the piano strings shivered, and the song ended. The final notes still lingered in the air even as Mary turned to accept her applause.

She played until bedtime, when Gabe sent her off to the necessary room to wash her face and brush her teeth and to change into a pink flowered nightgown.

"Come tuck me in, Sara." Mary held her hand tight.

Sara could not say no. This could be her last time spent with Mary and she wanted to savor every moment so it would last forever in her memories, treasured and rich.

Gabe brought out an illustrated book and read "A Visit from St. Nicholas." Sara had never heard the poem before, but Mary had, apparently many times, delighting in the father who threw open the shutters to hear Santa on his roof. She said the reindeer's names aloud along with Gabe, and her voice rose right along with his at the ending, " 'And to all a good night.' "

Gabe tucked the covers to Mary's chin as Sara watched, perched in the chair beside the large window, lace curtains brushed by the crystal lamp's glow. The child was surrounded by fine things, a beautiful bed and a store-bought dollhouse and a lovely quilt to cover her, but more important was the love in Gabe's touch as he brushed dark curls from her forehead and pressed a quick fatherly kiss there. It was love that made him her true father.

"Kiss me too, Sara!" Mary twisted beneath the quilt. "You want me to have sweet dreams, don't you?"

Sara laughed, unable to resist such a pleasure. "Of course I want you to sleep well."

"She's using every skill she owns to try to charm you." Gabe stood as she stepped close.

How wide his chest was beneath that dark blue shirt. Sara wasn't sure if she'd noticed it quite like this before.

His gaze kept trying to trap hers and she looked steadily at Mary, her elfin grin wide, happiness sparkling in deep blue gray eyes.

"I don't mind at all," she told Gabe and bent to press a kiss along the child's brow.

Such a sweetness filled her. Sara stepped back, stumbling. Gabe's strong hand snared her elbow and his presence, hot and unmistakable, lashed around her. Then they were alone in the hall outside Mary's closed door.

"I enjoyed the evening." Sara headed toward the coat tree, where her cloak looked so plain against Gabe's black wool jacket and Mary's berry red coat.

"We forgot to pop the corn." He strolled out of the shadowed hallway and into the lighted parlor.

The fire crackled merrily in the potbellied stove. The room glowed with the gentle light of several lamps. How inviting it looked, how hard to leave. But she must. With the way Gabe watched her—why, it made the strongest part of her weak.

"Maybe you and Mary can enjoy the popcorn tomorrow." Sara reached for her cloak. "It was a gift from Connie, not me."

"Stay." His fingers curled around the cloak's collar, holding the garment so she could not slip into it.

"I can't. It wouldn't be right."

"Why not?"

The shadows caressed the straight blade of his nose, the chiseled cut of cheekbone and chin, made mysterious dark blue eyes that raked hers with a question she didn't dare answer.

"We could sit by the fire and talk," he persisted. "I could boil some coffee or steep tea if you prefer."

"I plan to leave on the train come morning. Early morning." It was what she had to do, regardless of the yearnings

of her heart. "Besides, I've overstayed my welcome as it
is—"

"How can you say that?" His fingers brushed lower to
caress hers, leaving a sizzling trail of fire wherever his skin
touched hers. "You don't have to stay long. I just want to
get to know you better."

"I don't see why." She stepped away, letting him have
the cloak because to endure his touch—why, it tugged at
the deepest places inside her, untouched since her husband's death. And it hurt, because Gabe Chapman was the
one man she could never love, never have.

"How long has it been since your husband died?" So
understanding. He caught her hand with his big one. He
towered over her, blocking the light, leaving her in shadow.

"Five years."

"And you're afraid to love again." Sympathy shimmered
in his voice, true and genuine.

Her conscience stung. He thought she was still grieving
Andrew.

"It was rough getting over Ann's passing," he admitted.
"She felt like a part of me, and I was never the same after
I buried her. For a long time, I was afraid to love like that
again, because I was afraid I would do her an injustice.
And because I was afraid to lose my heart twice."

Gabe hung her cloak back on the tree, his face as dark
as the shadows. "But then I realized I had already risked
my heart. I had Mary, and because of her I was able to
move past the fear of loving another person again. But it
took me a long time and then I just hadn't met a woman
I wanted to be with."

"Gabe, you have no idea—" Her voice broke, full of
tears, but she did not cry. "I'm no longer grieving
Andrew."

"Then maybe Mary was right." A sense of rightness
burned in his chest, growing brighter until it engulfed

him, until he could see only Sara, her complexion pink from the warm parlor, her dark hair curled into tendrils that framed her face. A face he would be content to look at for the rest of his life.

She was like a candle newly lit, chasing away the darkness in his life. In a life where the evenings, after Mary was asleep, stretched like the night, long and lonely. And when he woke up, he was alone. He cooked breakfast, cared for Mary, and lived his life without a woman at his side, without the right woman.

Emotion shimmered in her eyes, as troubled as a stormy sky, and he saw there an old heartrending pain that brought silvered tears but would not let them fall. He knew the force of that kind of pain, and he hated how Sara must be hurting. She was so gentle and kind that she would sew for a stranger's daughter.

"Dear Sara." He dared to lay both hands along the delicate curve of her jaw, cradling her face against his palms. She felt like the finest silk; she smelled sweet like apples and cinnamon. "Maybe someone did send you to us."

Her tears brimmed, silent tears that rolled down her cheeks and touched his thumbs. He ached in ways he'd never known, wanting to protect her from the pain he read in her eyes, wanting to comfort her, wanting to make her his. He leaned forward and slanted his mouth over hers.

Their first kiss was like springtime after a long winter. Like the first touch of gentle sunlight to frozen earth. A tenderness welled within him at the brush of her lips. She was like velvet heat, and his pulse pounded in his ears. He felt as if he were drowning in the sensation from one small kiss.

And then she responded, her lips moving to meet his, and his chest kicked, his blood sizzled. A sparkling need for her telegraphed through his body and he pulled her close against him. She was all firm curves and soft woman, and he knew, as he dared to trace the seam of her lips with his tongue, that this kiss would never be enough. Or a second one. Not even a lifetime of kisses.

"Gabe." She broke away, her hands flying to her mouth. Her fingertips brushed his, for he still cupped her face and he could not bring himself to let go.

How could he let go of the first woman who made him feel alive inside? Who made him ache with desire, with hope? Maybe she could stay here forever in his arms, right against his heart. Tonight was the sweetest he'd known in many years, basking in the beautiful light of her presence, feeling special when she smiled just for him.

And how she treated Mary—why, she had captured his heart when she'd bent over to press a kiss to his daughter's brow. It was no superficial, perfunctory kiss, but a sweet tenderness that was just right.

How could he not fall in love with her? "Mary and I have been lonely, just the two of us." He could hear the emotion rumble in his voice, low and raw. "And I want"— he paused, trying to find the right words—"I want you."

"Oh, no." Panic filled her eyes, and she fumbled at the door, snatching her cloak from the hook. The coat tree wobbled, the door swung open, and she tumbled away from him out onto the porch and into the brutal night wind.

Not the reaction he expected. "Sara, come back here."

"I can't." She dashed across the porch and down the iced steps, slipping but not falling. She spun around, at the same time struggling into her cloak. "Supper was lovely."

He'd moved too fast. She was still grieving. Some things took time, but he knew in his heart what he said was true. Sara was right for them. She fit into their lives. "Wait. Don't leave."

"Good-bye, Gabe."

Not good night. But good-bye. As if she didn't plan on seeing him again.

The bitter chill lashed across his face, driving through his clothes to ice the skin beneath. He loped through the deep snow. "Sara!"

"Don't follow me, Gabe."

"I didn't mean to embarrass you. Or insult you." Damn, but she was fast. She was already to the road. He began running, closing the distance between them. "I don't know what's troubling you, but I promise you this: I have the best of intentions."

He halted in front of her, the cold night air burning his lungs, fogging his breath, and yet the night was so clear he could see the tears in her eyes, pooled and shimmering. He could almost feel how much she hurt.

"Please give me a chance." He took her hands and placed them between his, warming them, hoping to comfort her. Wanting her to know what lived in his heart. "I know this is fast. But the first moment I saw you, I was certain you were the kind of lady I'd been wishing for."

"No one has ever said such lovely things to me." She had to tilt her face to look up at him, and the faint starshine brushed her alabaster face with an angel's light. Her chin wobbled. "I can't love you, Gabe."

Her delicate hands slipped from his and she ran for the shelter of Connie's house, leaving him alone in the silent night.

Upstairs in the guest room Connie had made snug for her, Sara closed tight the door against the pleasant conversation down below. Connie and Jim had greeted her, and she had tried to be polite, but she knew her heart showed. How could it not? Connie had looked puzzled, but genuinely concerned. It was the depth of sincerity of these people, of Gabe and his sister, that troubled her the most.

They were good people, and she was deceiving them. Living in their house, eating their food and taking advantage of their trust. All to get close to Mary. If there were another place in town she could go, she would have done it. But there was no place else.

She didn't light the beautiful crystal lamps in the room. She much preferred the dark. Her heart aching, she hung up her cloak and muffler and pulled off her shoes. The room was chilly, but she didn't mind. Her chest burned, and she sat down on the window seat, the store-bought cushions and pillows so fine.

Outside starlight sheened on silvered blue snow. Like a picture in a storybook—that was how the world looked with the dark sentry of trees tipped with white, the shades and shadows of darkness shrouding houses and mountains as black as the night. All was as still as a hush, as the quietest whisper when the wind blew. She knew how that wind smelled, because it still clung to her clothes and hair, that fresh clean brightness mixed with the dark scents of wood smoke, of pine and cedar.

She saw Gabe ambling up the steps to his house, saw the slope of his shoulders, muscled and set, saw the bow of his head, slight, but unmistakable. She'd handled this so badly. Her lips still tingled with his kiss, with the hot brush of passion and need. Her chest ached remembering how exquisite it had felt to be held and kissed like a princess in a fairy tale, feeling precious and treasured.

And she'd given herself to him in that kiss, in that brush of lips and mingling of breaths.

I promise. I have the best of intentions. She watched Gabe hesitate on the porch, gazing through the darkness toward the house, to the window where she sat watching him. He couldn't see her, she knew, but she felt his question and his disappointment.

Please give me a chance, he'd said. Gabe Chapman wanted her—he'd said those very words. *You are the kind of lady I've been wishing for.*

Sara had loved her baby from the moment she knew she was pregnant, and when she was born—why, that sweet little girl had grabbed hold of Sara's heart and no force in the universe could break that love. What of Gabe and his intentions? Even now her heart still felt warmed by the evening of laughter and songs and bedtime stories.

And while she could not deny the attraction she felt for Gabe, what would it do to Mary? Giving in to her own desires for him—why, how could any good come from that? Her fierce love for Mary was what had brought her here and what gave her the strength to walk away. She would not change her child's life, could not break her trust, refused to deceive her.

Sara's heart twisted, as she remembered the privileges and the healthy and happy childhood Mary had with a loving and kind father. A far better life than Sara could ever have given her. And she would do anything to make sure Mary remained happy and treasured, with wonderful things like popcorn and piano lessons and store-bought dresses and shiny new shoes.

This was why she could leave, why she could go on, because her guilt and her shame no longer burdened her. She had made the right choice that cold winter's night when Mary was so tiny and helpless.

And maybe Sara could have a life in Missoula. With the clear weather, the train would be running tomorrow, maybe even by morning. She would move on, as she always meant to do, and she could find happiness for herself, maybe meet a kind man to marry, one with broad shoulders and dark blue eyes and a gentle easy humor. How she ached for such precious things, and maybe, one day, another baby, a real family of her own. If she had a Christmas wish—why, that was what it would be.

He'd moved too fast, Gabe knew that. As he boiled coffee and heated water for their morning oatmeal, he pondered Sara's hasty departure. He'd scared her off, no doubt, when all he'd meant to do was draw her closer. He was running out of time, if he wanted to try to romance her. The train could be pulling in by late morning as long as the weather held.

"Pa, you told her she was pretty, right?"

"I can't remember exactly, smarty." Gabe set the glass of milk on the table. "Here, drink up. I've got your oatmeal simmering."

"Did you get more jam?"

"In the pantry."

Riding her stick horse, Mary clattered across the kitchen. "Pa? Did you tell her we really liked her?"

"I tried to." He grabbed a thick cloth and lifted the kettle from the hot stove. "She may wind up leaving on the train anyway."

He hated the flash of disappointment on Mary's face. "I don't want her to go, Pa."

"Neither do I." Gabe set the steaming bowls on the table and leaned toward the window to get a good look at the sky.

"It looks pretty cloudy, Pa."

"That it does." Gabe grabbed the coffeepot and poured a cup, considering. Even if the train did come, he had the morning. It could be enough time, if not to convince Sara Mercer to stay, then at least he could try to win another smile from her and hope she would want to see him and Mary again. Missoula wasn't so far by train.

And besides, it did look cloudy outside. Maybe even cloudy enough for another blizzard.

Sara knew she could not delay any longer. Connie had called her, and she didn't want to keep them waiting. But she wasn't certain if she felt ready to say good-bye. There had been no more snow during the night, so surely the train was coming.

"There you are." It was Jim who spoke first, a kindly man, tall and lean, his spectacles glinting in the lamplight. He held up the china teapot. "Would you like some tea?"

"Please." Sara headed to the stove, where Connie was dishing out the food. "I'm sorry I'm late."

"You're not a bit late." Connie gestured with her chin. "Do me a favor and hold that platter for me."

"Sure." Sara lifted the delicate porcelain platter rimmed with cabbage roses and held it while Connie dished up the butter-fried potatoes.

"Here we are, the day before Christmas Eve, and I'm not nearly prepared." Connie scraped the last of the potatoes from the fry pan. "Would you like to come with me this morning? I have a few more gifts I need to get."

"It sounds fun, but it's possible the train might be coming in. Isn't that right?" Sara set the platter on the cloth-covered table.

"That's right." Jim gave his glasses a push with his forefinger, sliding them back up his nose. "The crew worked late into the evening last night, once the snow let up. There's a very good chance you could be with your aunt for Christmas."

"That would be wonderful." Sara held a second platter for the sausage and ham slices as Connie forked them out of another pan. "I haven't seen my aunt since I was young."

"Goodness, you can't spend a Christmas with a stranger,

even if she is your aunt." Connie set down the fry pan with a clunk of iron upon metal. True concern gleamed in eyes as dark as Gabe's. "Would it truly hurt your chances for this job if you just stayed a few more days with us?"

"What?" Sara's fingers slipped. The platter hit the edge of the stove. Shaken, she caught it in midair, saving all but one sausage, which rolled to a stop somewhere beneath the table.

"Good catch." Jim rose to grab a towel. "I'd hate to lose those sausages."

"Goodness, are you all right, Sara?" Connie dropped the pan on a trivet. "Are you burned?"

"No." Heat stained her face and she set the platter on the table. "I didn't mean to be so clumsy. Oh, Jim, I could have gotten that."

"That's my job, picking up after everything Connie misses." A good-natured grin accompanied his kind words, and he tossed the fallen sausage into the garbage pail.

"That's right. Men have their uses." Connie's glimmer of humor faded when she caught Sara's hand. "Are you sure you're all right? I hope my suggestion didn't startle you."

"No, I just—" Words failed her. "I truly can't jeopardize this job, no matter how much I appreciate your invitation."

"Couldn't we send a telegram to your aunt and ask her to hold the job for you?" Jim scooted his chair forward to reach for a platter of fried eggs. "I would be happy to send one for you this morning."

"Oh, I couldn't." She could feel the heat on her face, hotter than before. Besides, she couldn't afford the luxury of a telegram. They were expensive, and she fully intended to pay Connie and Jim for her stay. That left precious little in her reticule to see her through.

And besides, it wouldn't be right. Not to stay here intentionally, with these feelings so strong and bright in her heart, with her love growing stronger for Mary and for Gabe, love she had no right to. She was not Mary's mother, not in truth. Ann had been, the woman who had rocked Mary through endless nights and comforted her and cared for her. Who had taught Mary her first word and how to walk, then run, how to sing, and how to make a snowman.

"Surely your aunt doesn't need you until after Christmas." Connie reached for the salt and pepper, her gaze intent on Sara's face and eyes.

"She wanted me there a few days before to help with the rush sewing for the holiday." She needed that job. Her planned stay in Moose Creek had only been for a few hours, not days. It was hard thinking of leaving, but the truth was, she had to go. If she reached Missoula and her angered aunt decided not to give her the job—well, she would be in a real fix.

"For your sake, I hope the train is running this morning, but for mine—" Connie's gaze sharpened, and Sara bowed her head, certain the woman was studying her eyes. "Why, I have to admit I'm selfish and hope you stay."

Sara opened her mouth, not sure what to say, but a knock on the door spared her. The back door swung open and Mary breezed inside, bringing in with her a piece of sunshine. A man hesitated in the threshold, tall and iron strong, his blue gaze riveting Sara's the instant he stepped into the room.

"Gabe." The spoon clattered from her fingers, nearly landing in the sugar bowl.

"Didn't mean to interrupt your meal, but I want a private word with Sara." His gaze intensified, as if he could see clear through to her secrets, to the deepest part of her heart.

It was a place she didn't want him looking.

"You're free to use the parlor," Connie spoke up, reaching for the platter of sausages.

Jim and Mary looked at her expectantly and Sara didn't see how she could refuse. She stood, heart pounding. Had he guessed the truth?

Chapter Seven

Gabe held the swinging door open for Sara. She brushed past him, her chin bowed, her hands locked together. She wore a soft yellow dress, buttery and inviting, a color that made her black hair gleam and brought out the blue in her eyes.

She was still in mourning, even if she'd long ago given up wearing black. He had to remember that. He knew how hard this was, reaching out to another person, hoping to find love again.

"I'm sorry I scared you off last night." He wanted that out right away. He wanted her to know he wasn't about to push her if she wasn't ready. He was a patient man and more than willing to buy a few tickets to Missoula to visit her. "I didn't mean to be so direct. I thought you felt the same things I did."

"Gabe, I—"

"I know you need time." He could see it in her eyes,

the want so large not even her denial could hide it. "I'm willing to give you all the time you need."

"You have it all wrong." She wrung her hands, small and pretty hands slightly reddened from harsh lye soap, from a life of hard work. "I just want to leave."

His heart squeezed. "The train could be coming today, as long as the storm holds off. Once it clears the pass, there should be no more trouble the rest of the way to Missoula."

"That's what I want." She held his gaze steady, her eyes gleaming with a regret so big he could feel it in his own heart. "That's what's best. I hope you understand."

"I do." She wasn't ready. Or she didn't think she was. He knew about that too. "Mary and I enjoyed your company last night, Sara. Mary thinks Santa sent you here to be her mother."

"I know." She dipped her chin, and dark curls tumbled across her face, hiding the emotions that pinched her mouth. "I don't want to disappoint Mary, but I'm certain you two will find the right woman. I'm just not—" She hesitated, rubbing the curls from her eyes as dark as winter.

"You want too much, Gabe. More than it is right for me to give." She touched his sleeve, a brief but sustaining touch, and in that moment of contact he felt a sorrow so great it stunned him, left him reeling. Sara headed toward the kitchen, where Mary, a child who believed in Santa's magic, waited.

"I'm gonna sit by you, Sara." Mary scooted over a chair that belonged next to Jim.

"What? I've got boy germs or something?" Fond amusement sparkled in Jim's kind eyes.

"Well, you are a boy," Mary said as if that were a bad

thing she forgave him for. "I can sit with you at dinner-time."

"Thank you." Jim poked his fork into a bit of egg, hiding his smile.

"Sara, you're not going to leave when the train comes, right?" Mary looked up at her expectantly.

Sara let the door shut behind her. The fire in the stove crackled, and the teakettle bubbled on the stove, getting ready to whistle. The cozy room ought to make her feel wanted, as it had yesterday, but today she wanted only to escape. *Please let the train come this morning.*

"Your breakfast is getting cold," Connie reminded her gently. "We want to hear more about last night. Mary told us she played Christmas songs for you."

"Yes, she did." Sara forced cheer into her voice. "She's a very talented little girl."

"Nah, I just practice a lot," Mary denied, but pride beamed along her soft face, pink with pleasure. "Pa said my ma played the piano and she was real good."

Sara sunk down into her chair, her heart sinking like lead. "Is that why you wanted to learn?"

"Yep. Pa said my ma learned in New York with an important teacher."

"I never knew your mother, but I saw her a few times." Sara forced the words past the pain in her throat. "She was a nice lady and very pretty. I'm sure she was talented at everything she did."

"You know what my ma looked like?"

"Sara grew up in the same town as your pa and I did," Connie told Mary. "But I'm very glad she came our way."

Sara felt the tenderness of those words and saw the compassion etched on Connie's face. Her heart rocked to a stop as realization struck. *She knew.* Connie knew the truth and didn't blame, didn't suspect.

Overcome, Sara grabbed her teacup and found it cooled,

but drank anyway, one sip after another, willing the grateful tears away.

"I can still hop over to the telegraph office," Jim volunteered, relentless in his kindness.

Sara suspected he did not know her secret. "I wish I could ask you to, but I can't."

"Well, we hate to see you go." Connie reached for the teapot and filled Sara's cup. "But Missoula isn't so far away and we could write each other. Would you like that?"

"Very much."

"After all, it's fun to keep in touch. I could let you know how Jim and I are getting along. And tell you all that Mary is up to."

Sara set down the cup with a rattle, speechless at what Connie offered.

"Yeah, I'm up to a whole lot of things." Mary grabbed the jar of huckleberry jam and dipped her spoon in it. "I get a pony as soon as I'm five."

"A pony?" The words caught in Sara's throat.

"Yep. And I'm gonna learn to ride. And I want to learn to sew like you. And next year I getta start school."

"I know you are going to be my best student," Jim offered, scraping the fork against his plate.

"Pa says I'm smart like my ma."

"And as pretty, too," Connie added, her gaze landing on Sara.

Her chest hurt, her heart felt ready to shatter. How she wanted to belong here.

But Sara knew she didn't. She had to leave now while she still could find the strength to walk out that door.

Sara Mercer was all Gabe could think about that morning when he showed up at the office, where Clancy had the stove roaring and the coffee boiling. Still waiting on word from the railroad crew, his deputy explained, but it looked as if the tracks were clear. A crew of men, hired just to shovel snow, had returned to town about an hour ago.

Looked as if the train was going to beat the storm. Gabe glanced up from his desk, considering the northern horizon rimmed with gun-metal gray clouds. Maybe Sara was going to be able to leave, just as she wanted.

The front door swung open, bringing with it the crisp rush of a northern wind. "Sheriff. Got news on the train."

"Jesse Garrett. Come in and warm yourself. Feels like the temperature's dropping."

"It is. And I've come a long ways, galloped my mare all the way from the pass." The young man, his face pale from the cold, took the wooden chair Gabe offered and gratefully collapsed into it in front of the stove.

"Should I spread word the train is coming?"

"Not yet it ain't." Jesse tugged off his wool cap. "The engine's broke. Got a part being rushed out of Billings. Will take all day to repair."

"You don't say."

Gabe considered this new piece of information. Sara might not think she was right for him and Mary, but he could not deny the situation. The forces that be wanted to keep Sara in Moose Creek, in Connie's home, near him and Mary.

And who was he to argue with Santa Claus or even greater powers?

"Thanks for letting us know. Clancy and I will find out if we need to send more men to help. And judging by the storm gathering along the horizon, it will be a close call which will be here first: a blizzard or the train."

"Ain't that the truth." Jesse thanked Clancy for the steaming cup of coffee.

Gabe grabbed his coat from the peg, considering the possibilities. Sara Mercer would be stuck here for days.

He'd seen the fear in her eyes. She was just afraid to care again, to hand over her heart. Well, chances were he might have the time he needed to gently convince her otherwise.

"Sara, look at the cat." Mary gestured toward the gray-and-black tabby in the milliner's front window. "It's Mrs. Barry's kitty. Every morning she takes Winston to work with her. Can we go in and pet him?"

"I need to stop here anyway." Connie's smile was indulgent. "Careful not to run and scare Winston—"

Mary was already dashing through the doors and the striped cat, drowsing in the soft velvet background of the shop's display, hopped up, its tail stiff and back hair bristling. Then, recognizing the girl, he stepped forward ready for some chin scratches.

Sara tried not to watch, but her gaze drifted over to the girl and the cat, to the way Mary giggled, the sound lost through the thick glass.

"Elana Barry is the innkeeper's sister." Connie caught the brass doorknob and stepped inside. "Just like you, she thought she would be here for a brief time, and look, she's married and running her own business."

"Good morning." An elegant lady rose from her sewing machine, the black casement polished and gleaming in the lamplight.

Sara had never seen one before, but her aunt had purchased two for her shop in Missoula. In time, she would be expected to run such a wondrous machine.

"Why, you must be the woman from the train. I know everyone in this town, it's so small and friendly here. And let me tell you, word travels fast. Did you hear? Jesse just got back from the pass."

"The train. Is it coming?" She knew she sounded far

too eager, and she caught the puzzled frown on Connie's face and the disappointment on Mary's.

"Sara, you can't leave. You gotta stay and watch me sing."

"Oh, Mary." Her throat closed. "I don't want to leave, but I have to."

The bell on the door jangled. A tall shadow fell across the polished floor, broad of shoulder, substantial as the man who made it.

"Gabe." Sara's knees wobbled.

"Good morning, ladies." He tipped his hat, his sheriff's badge glinting in the lamplight. His gaze fastened on hers, dark and drawing. "I wanted to tell you in person, Sara. The train isn't coming this morning."

"What?" She leaned against a cabinet, vaguely aware of Connie and Elana conducting business. "Will it be coming later?"

"Fortunately for you"—regret tucked a frown at his brow—"they say there's a good chance the train will be here by suppertime."

Connie dug through her reticule and gold pieces clanged as she set them on the counter for Elana to count. "That isn't so long. Sara, it looks as if you might arrive in Missoula in time to save your job after all."

Relief filtered through her, but only a little. She still had today to get through. And with the way her heart ached every time she looked at Mary and Gabe, it would prove to be a very long wait.

"Darn, I forgot the candles." Connie dropped the canvas bag on the top of Gabe's kitchen table. "I swear, I'm getting so forgetful I'd lose my head if it wasn't stuck on my neck. I'll be right back."

"Can you bring back a lot more ribbon too?" Mary

begged, then closed the door behind her aunt. "Sara, do you know how to make popcorn?"

"Yes, I do." Sara glanced at the tree in the corner of the parlor, a safe distance from the stove, right in front of the big window. "But I've never strung popcorn."

"It's easy. Even I can show you that." Mary skipped to the table and inspected the array of ribbons and bells, peppermint candies and cranberries. She grabbed the sack of corn. "We got enough for the tree and lots left over to eat."

"I like the way you think." Sara took the bag from Mary's firm grasp. "Come help me get the fire stoked, and we'll have the skillet hot by the time Connie returns."

"Pa keeps the kindling here." Mary hauled a basket of dried cedar shavings from the lean-to. "Do you know how to open the stove?"

"I sure do." Sara knelt and turned the handle. The dank scent of ashes filled the air. She lifted the poker from its hook and carefully uncovered the top layer of gray to reveal the gleaming red orange embers beneath.

"Take the littlest ones," Mary advised, both small hands gripping that basket tight.

"The littlest ones." Sara spread the slivers of wood over the embers and they smoked, then sizzled, bursting into flame.

"Now the bigger ones."

Sara obliged, although she didn't need Mary's advice. She had tried to keep her distance from the girl today, for both the child's sake and her own, but Mary had been hard to resist.

Soon the flames inside the stove were healthy enough to add sticks of wood, carefully stacked to let in enough air. Heat radiated against Sara's face as she shut the door, then adjusted the damper.

She stood, swiping the slivers of cedar and bits of moss from her skirt.

"There's a broom right next to my horse." Mary dashed across the kitchen to carry it back, handle held high.

"It's getting dark awfully fast." Sara noticed she could hardly see the mess she'd made on the floor. "I'd better light a—"

The house shook, and the last of the light ebbed from the room.

"Mary? Are you all right?"

"It's a blizzard." Tentative fingers touched hers. "Are you scared?" How small that voice sounded.

"No. Just surprised." Sara reached out with her free hand and felt the edge of the table. She remembered there was a lamp in the center. By feel, she found the match drawer and lit one. Meager flame chased away some of the dark as she removed the glass chimney and lit the wick. The light grew and danced until it was enough to see the worry on Mary's dear face.

She ached to draw the child into her arms and give her comfort, but she could not. Mary wasn't her child to hold. Not anymore.

"Aunt Connie!" Mary raced to the window. She pulled back the gingham curtains but there was only twilight gleaming blue on a wall of snow and wind.

"Connie is very capable. I'm certain she is safe." Sara had to believe it. "I've never been in a blizzard like this. Look, the wind is driving the snow through the door."

"Yeah." Mary rubbed her eyes. "Where do you think Pa is?"

"He's safe too."

"But I don't like waiting for him to come home."

"What would you like to do while we wait? I could heat some milk. I noticed some chocolate in the pantry."

"No, I wanna pop popcorn." Mary looked a little brighter.

"We've already got the stove heating. Why don't I see if I can get the fire in the parlor lit?"

Already she could see her breath—the temperature had dropped that quickly.

"I can help." Mary trailed after her, just a step behind.

Sara didn't need to guess there would be no train. Maybe she ought to be grateful, having this time alone with Mary. But she felt awkward, because the longer she stayed, the closer she became to Gabe and Mary, the greater the deceit. And now, if Connie knew . . .

She struck a match to light two more lamps before kneeling down to stir the embers into flame inside the potbellied stove. With two fires going, the log house, its walls thick and well chinked, was warm in no time.

Mary advised Sara on which fry pan to use and which lid to cover the pan with. Then Sara dropped a dollop of lard into the skillet and held it above the heat until it melted.

"Quick, add the corn." She held the pan low so that Mary could pour in the kernels. "Wait! That's too much."

"Oops." Mary managed to right the bag, spilling corn on the floor. "Is it gonna make a mess?"

"Probably." Sara lifted the pan back onto the heat. The oil surrounding the golden kernels sizzled. "Maybe you'd better find a really big bowl."

"I don't think we have one." Mary dropped to the floor to look through the cabinets.

Sara covered the pan with the lid, leaving it slightly ajar. The first kernel popped. Then another, and then a multitude started, filling her ears with the happy sound.

"Pa!" Mary hopped to her feet and took off.

Gabe was home? The workday couldn't be over. "Mary, I need—" A white froth rose up beneath the lid. "Mary—"

"Looks like you got yourself into a little trouble, ma'am." Gabe's presence, tingling and male hot, brushed her back. "You let Mary help, didn't you? That's okay. I've made that mistake before."

"Pa!"

A popped kernel shot from the pan, raining to the floor. More followed. "A bowl. I need a bowl."

One appeared at her elbow, held by strong hands. "Good thing I'm here to come to your rescue."

Her entire body felt on fire simply being beside him. Sara tried not to look at him as she tilted the lid just enough to pour some of the wildly popping corn into the bowl he held. White fluffy pieces shot out, like rocks from a slingshot, all in a thousand different directions. Hitting Mary's forehead, tumbling down Gabe's collar, landing on the table, the chair seats, the floor.

"Quick, another bowl!" A kernel plugged her in the chin.

Gabe scrambled to his knees and corn tumbled down on him, fat and fluffy. He stood up, popcorn pieces tumbling off his head and shoulders to land on top of his boots.

"This is out of control." He held out an empty bowl.

Sara tilted the fry pan enough to keep the popping kernels inside and let out the already popped corn. He caught it with the bowl, then produced another when it was full. He was prepared this time. Still, more kernels popped, muffled beneath the lid Sara held.

Her eyes shimmered with suppressed laughter. "Goodness, look at this mess. I think this is finally quieting down."

"You have some in your hair." How pretty she looked with her cheeks flushed from the heat and dark tendrils curling around her face, lustrous against her creamy complexion. He plucked the popped corn from the crown of her head where pieces had become tangled in those fine silken wisps. His foolish heart thundering, he gazed down into her eyes.

They were so wide, filled with yearning. She said she didn't want him. But she had lied about that. He could see what she wanted, see those needs as plain as the ceiling over his head. "It's darn nice having you in my kitchen."

She caught her breath, and he could see her chest rise, see the strain on her face. "I need one more bowl."

So he wasn't wrong. Sara Mercer liked him. His chest filled with that knowledge. He wanted her. How he wanted her.

"Pa, I picked up all the popcorn." Mary had piled the pieces that had fallen around the room into an empty kettle, perfect for stringing up. "Pa, do you think Connie's safe at home?"

"I know she is. I went to her house before I came here."

"To get me?"

"Yep. But your aunt said you were over here with Sara. You three were going to decorate the tree without me. Run and get a sweater on. That wind is getting colder."

"Okay." Mary's shoes drummed on the floor.

"She's louder than the blizzard." A smile sweet on her face, Sara upended the last batch of popcorn and filled his last bowl. "I didn't mean to make a mess of your kitchen."

"No problem." He held out his hand, gesturing at his clean floor. "Mary picked it up. We should start decorating the tree."

"And it's time for me to leave." She avoided his gaze, dipping her chin, but he wasn't fooled. She wasn't abrupt, but a quiet want lingered beneath her words. "You and Mary enjoy your decorating."

"You can't leave, Sara."

"Connie is just across the road. I can make it. I've lived my whole life in Montana. I can handle one small blizzard." She took a step, all grace and winsome elegance, but beneath her words was a hard stubbornness, as if she were waiting for him to argue. As if she wanted him to. She reached for her coat.

"The wind is stronger than when I came home." He grabbed the butter from the pantry. "Look, I bet you can't even see Connie's lights from here."

"I can't stay here, Gabe. It wouldn't be right."

"Because of your reputation?" He spooned a heaping chunk of butter into a small pan.

Because I don't belong here. Where seeing Mary had once been her dream and spending a day with her an unimagined privilege—now it was torture. Sara knew she didn't belong here and never would. And with the way she was falling in love with Gabe—why, what good could come of that?

Oh, she thought she was so smart, but in truth, she couldn't hold back her heart. This man was from her dreams, strong and gentle, handsome and brave, infinitely kind.

The love she felt was for Gabe Chapman, the man, and not because he was Mary's father. The gleam of affection nestled in her heart—so bright and vibrant—was for him, all for him. For the man with the lopsided smile and easy humor who made her feel as if she'd never been truly kissed, never honestly loved before.

Chapter Eight

"Mary loved having you here to help tuck her into bed again." Gabe ambled down the hall and stepped into the light of the parlor. He liked seeing Sara sitting on the sofa, making snowflakes for their tree, her skirts fanning around her slim frame. "I think she would have rather stayed up much later and learned how to do that."

"This? Oh, it's just tatting." She held out the little wonder that Mary had marveled over less than an hour ago, made of string and Sara's ingenuity. "I think that looks about right, don't you?"

"Just like a snowflake." He wanted to reach out, wanted to pull her against his chest and cradle her in his arms, just to hold her. Well, in truth he wanted to do more than that, but holding her would be a nice place to start. A very nice place indeed.

She somehow knotted the end of string and added another snowflake to the pile. "I think Mary will be excited to wake up tomorrow morning and see how these turned out."

"You make her very happy, Sara. And me too." He lifted the kettle off the stove. The single lamp in the room illuminated the polished table, the leftover bowl of popcorn, and Sara's soft, honest beauty.

Light sheened on her dark hair, like starlight chasing midnight shadows, and shone in her luminous eyes, round with want and worry. That light caressed her as he could not, brushing the gentle curve of her cheek and jaw, touching the tempting shape of her Cupid's mouth, playing at the curves of her breasts and hips.

Now he could see the advantage in a Montana blizzard. Sara was trapped here, unable to even cross the street without great risk of becoming disoriented, even lost in the storm. Gabe felt particularly grateful because, as the evening progressed, he knew now for certain she was the woman he wanted to spend the rest of his life with.

"You wouldn't happen to have any starch?" Sara asked, her head bowed over her work, already spinning the little silver object she held around the white length of string. She twisted it and turned it and made magic, made snowflakes, delicate and intricate and all for Mary's tree.

"You never know what's in my cabinets. I'll check in the lean-to for you." He hated leaving her sight, but her smile warmed him for the few frigid minutes it took to rummage around in the cold lean-to and find the container of starch. The kitchen smelled like steeping tea and the lingering scent of popcorn.

"It feels right, you standing in my kitchen." He set the jug on the counter, unable to take his gaze from her, instincts warning him to go slow. His touches and spoken feelings had scared her off before, and so he held back what burned in his heart, sweet aching affection that seemed to grow every time he looked at her.

"I know you're searching for a mother for Mary, but just because I'm here doesn't mean I'm the right candidate." She tried to smile but failed. How dark her eyes were, how troubled. "Let's just sit by the fire and let me finish these snowflakes for the tree."

"See the difference you make just by being here?"

"What difference?" A frown puzzled her brow. She truly did not know what she had done here.

"Magic." He gestured toward the tree in the parlor, shrouded by lamplight, wearing snowy-white popcorn strings and bright cranberry beads and plump red ribbons. Presents sat beneath it, wrapped in colorful paper and tied with ribbon and string. "Our tree has never looked this good."

"Be careful, Gabe Chapman. I'm likely to believe your flattery." Sara set down her nearly completed snowflake to check on the tea. Enamel clinked against enamel when she lifted the small lid.

"I'm not trying to flatter you, Sara." His hand covered hers. "I'm trying to win your heart."

"Why mine?" So huge, her eyes, so unknowing.

Didn't she know what she did to him? How she made him wish for her, not just any woman, but her? With her quiet smile and quieter humor and the generosity of her heart?

"You drew me the moment I saw you step down from the train, so independent and vulnerable. You stepped into my empty life and filled it up."

"I think any woman could do the same, and many would be a better choice." She pulled her hand away, taking the teapot with her, turning her back to search for cups in the cabinets.

"Not any woman. You're not convenient, Sara. You're special. Mary knows it and so do I. Things happen for a reason. The train getting stuck on the pass and your coming to Moose Creek were both by chance. You didn't plan to come here."

Her shoulders stiffened and she didn't answer.

"Look, I know how hard it is to put aside your grief—"

"I told you before, I'm not grieving Andrew. I'll always miss him and feel sad he's gone, but that's not the reason—" She bowed her head, her spine stiff. The light caressed the back of her neck, where soft dark tendrils curled at her nape, fallen from the intricate knot of her molasses-dark hair.

"Then what is it?" He dared to lay a hand on her shoulder. He could feel her tension, feel how something bothered her greatly. "I don't mean to hurt you."

"Then stop trying to court me."

"What's wrong with a little courting?"

"You don't want me, Gabe. Believe me." She shoved a cup into his hand and dodged him. Her shoes drummed with her retreat and her skirts swished. His blood thickened from wanting her.

How he wanted her, only her.

Cradling both her tatting and her tea, she sped across the room, finding refuge on the sofa near the lamplight. She'd said it before, that she had moved past her grieving. Then what was the problem? She had mentioned no engagement, and he was fairly sure she would have said something after their kiss if her heart belonged to another man.

The parlor echoed with the happy memories from this evening, when they'd decorated the tree, singing Christmas carols and any other song they happened to think of while they strung the popcorn and cranberries. Mary's excitement seemed to linger in the air, like the fresh scent of pine, her happiness a bright luxury. Having Sara with them tonight only made the evening more special.

And he had been happy too, truly happy of heart and

soul for the first time in a long, long while. Sara made him laugh, made him feel deep and true, made him ache for her touch and to be touched, made him want to lay her down beneath him and make her completely his.

"Do you think I'm ugly?" He set the tea on the table and crossed the room.

She didn't look up from her work, another snowflake taking shape beneath her sensitive fingers. "No, Gabe. I don't think you're ugly."

"Do you like my house?"

Her gaze flicked up to his, her mouth a tight line. "You have a beautiful home."

"And I know you like my daughter."

She bowed her chin, concentrating hard on her work. "You know I do."

"Then will you tell me what the problem is?"

Sara's fingers stilled. Oh, he was a cocky man, far too sure of himself. She knew what he up to. "Just because you're handsome doesn't mean a woman has to fall at your feet."

"I never said I wanted you on the floor." Humor sparkled in eyes as dark as dreams and played along the edges of his mouth, hinting at dimples.

He strode across the room, unflinching and determined, the golden glow from the lamplight limning his height and his strong sturdy breadth. Sara tried to keep her heart from beating faster, her breath from growing thick, her blood from zinging with want as he sat down beside her, crossing one booted ankle to rest on his knee, leaning one elbow against the arm rest.

Her blood zinged, her breath thickened and her heart beat faster.

"This is what it would be like if you married me." How deep and rich his voice. How inviting, tempting her with a happiness she could never have.

But he didn't know that. Sara tied off the string and made a quick double knot, then hid it neatly. "This was a very pleasant evening."

"Because of you." His hand settled on her forearm, hot and tempting and just short of possessive.

Selfish want gathered inside her, in the secret place where she dreamed. Want for a life with this man who made her blood scorch, who made her melt at the simple touch of his hand. "Don't do this, Gabe. Please."

"You're happy with us. I know you are."

"How do you know?"

"Your face is too honest. It's there in your eyes, even now, how happy you are. That's one thing I like very much. You wear your heart."

"That just proves how wrong you are." She twisted away from his touch, guilt rising, and concentrated on starting another snowflake. Look what he thought of her, unable to deceive, unable to be dishonest.

"Tell me why I'm wrong?"

"What's wrong isn't any of your concern, no matter how you try to make it." So soft those words, brushed with sorrow. "Can't you see that I plan to leave tomorrow on the train? I'll never return to Moose Creek. Ever. So we can't have a relationship. Don't you see?"

"I believe we can make a place for you in our lives."

Before she could argue further, his lips claimed hers in a kiss infinitely tender and oh so passionate.

She could feel his desire for her in the way he treasured her mouth with his. How she wanted him. Her chest thundered with desire for this man so true and tender. She tipped her head back, reveling in the sensations, both hot and sweet, of his kiss. Velvet heat and brushing tongues and trembling pleasure. Her whole body burned with it.

His hands wrapped around her neck, his fingers caressing the escaped curls at her nape. Hot sparks jolted down her spine. A want so great wrapped around her chest and banded tight, stealing her breath and all protest. She dared to press her hands to his chest and feel the rock-hard span of muscle and bone. How fast his heart drummed beneath her palm.

"You seem to like the way I kiss," he murmured against her lips, their breath mingling, before he pressed kisses over her chin, along the line of her jaw, down the length of her throat.

"I do." In all her life Sara had never felt like this, tingly soft on the inside, melting like butter on a hot stove. She wanted to wrap around him and hold on, to feel the iron-hard weight of his body pressing hers to the ground, to know what it would be like to make love to him, to share with him that bright, thrilling intimacy.

"You feel like silk." His lips brushed her collar, where somehow a few buttons had loosened. "You taste like dreams."

Dazed, she tipped her head back as she felt more of her bodice give way beneath his tugging fingers, buttons easing through fabric, first her dress, then her chemise until she was naked to his touch. His eyes widened, glittered with approval and then he touched her, tentative and tender and thrilling.

"You're so exquisitely made." His breath teased her nipples and then his tongue flicked around one pebbled tip.

A tight band of pleasure twisted straight through her abdomen. Sara closed her eyes, savoring the wondrous feeling. Her hands curled around the back of his neck to hold him against her. His dark locks tumbled through her fingers, soft and luxurious. When he drew her nipple into his mouth with his tongue and suckled deeply, the pleasure nearly shattered her.

Over and over again, he suckled and licked, teased and

laved until her body trembled with wanting him, until she felt charged and aching. Then his hands were on her thighs and lifting her skirts. The touch of his fingertips to her leg pierced through the daze of pleasure.

What was she doing? She had no right to love this man, not when he didn't know the truth about her. She straightened up, not knowing what to say. Embarrassment—no, shame—heated her face. She couldn't look at him. She felt him move away, felt the brush of fabric instead of his touch against her thigh.

"You're right. We should wait. I got carried away." His lips brushed her brow, infinitely gentle.

Why did he have to be so understanding? Her body still trembled, her blood hot and scorching. She wanted him, how she wanted him.

"Remember, you can tell me anything."

"Not this." Not this one huge thing.

"Whatever it is, I promise it won't change one bit how I feel for you." The kindness in his voice, low and inviting, made her look up. His eyes were dark as temptation, intimate and sparkling. Golden lamplight haloed him and illuminated the great affection he held for her, a great respect.

She'd done nothing to earn it, but there it was, a rare precious light. She almost believed he could be that understanding, that he could see how a woman, impoverished by her husband's death, had to return home to her father's strict household, how she could not keep her beloved baby. She believed Gabe, the man, just might understand.

But not Gabe, the father.

"You can take the bedroom." He stood, towering over her, such a good man. "I'll go find a few extra blankets for the sofa."

"I would rather sleep here, if you don't mind."

"You're my guest, Sara. Your reputation be damned, I

can't let you sleep out here. It isn't as warm or comfortable."

"I had hoped to finish Mary's snowflakes." Thinking of how she could surprise the girl chased away some of the tightness in her chest.

"There's tomorrow for that." Tender as night, his hand brushed her chin. "You need your sleep. The storm may be over tomorrow. Either way, it's Christmas Eve and you should celebrate with us. Look, there are presents for you under the tree."

"Why, no, I—" Her gaze strayed to the packages both Mary and Gabe had set out just after supper, talking and laughing. She hadn't expected presents. "I couldn't accept anything from you."

"These are gifts from our hearts, Mary's and mine." He pressed a kiss to her brow. "I'll get the bed ready for you."

How he cared for her, cared about her. No man had done so in a long time. "Truly, I don't want your bed, Gabe. I often have trouble sleeping at night. If I'm out here, I can make myself a pot of tea."

"As long are you're sure." He pressed another kiss to her brow and moved away, a man of steely might and tenderness, a combination she so admired.

He returned with an armload of bedclothes. Together they tucked in the sheets and spread the wool blankets and thick quilt. "I've bolted the doors, so you should be safe. I'm just down the hall if you need anything, anything at all."

"Thank you, Gabe." She didn't want to love him, but heaven help her, she loved him more than words could say.

* * *

It's Christmas Eve and you should celebrate with us. Gabe's words seemed to echo in the pleasant silence of the sleeping house.

This is what it would be like if you married me. She could have a real home, these people who made her feel safe and wanted, cared for and cherished as her family. She could have the privilege of raising Mary.

Sara cherished all the memories she had saved up so far, her first sight of Mary, come to fetch her for breakfast. And the joy of shopping with her, the stolen pleasure of sewing for her own daughter, the evenings spent in song, of tucking Mary in, of showing her a quicker way to thread a needle . . . How the memories collected, filling her heart, shimmering moments already more precious than any treasure.

What if she were to stay silent? Sara nursed her cooling cup of tea, the smooth enamel comfortable in her hand. What if she were to share this table with Gabe and Mary for every breakfast, every supper? What if she could call him her own? Have the right to show him her love? To wear Gabe's ring and take his name and share every night with him, basking in the pleasuring heat of his touch.

Sara felt cold inside despite the tea, as cold as the dying storm. What was she going to do? Not tell Gabe the truth? Nothing good could come of a love that was not honest, of intentions that were not sincere.

Yet how could she tell him?

The storm withered, the howl of the wind dying into a rustle, then a whisper. In time, moonlight peeked between parting clouds to gleam silver blue on the snowy world, hushed and reverent and infinitely peaceful.

There would be no train tomorrow. Sara poured the last cup from the teapot, treasuring these final moments in Gabe's house—the muffled tick of the parlor clock, the crisp scent of pine, the velvety darkness without lamplight to diffuse it, the soothing taste of peppermint.

She could not truly deceive Gabe, and she was ashamed she'd even thought of it. Ashamed she'd come here intending only to look. But given the opportunity, she broke her word to remain uninvolved in Mary's life, to never make contact, to never try to claim her.

If Gabe knew the truth, that was what he would think, what the father in him would believe. How could Sara blame him? It looked as if she came to town to take Mary, or to capture Gabe's affections intentionally just to get close to her lost child.

Heartbroken, Sara savored the last bit of tea and gazed out at the pristine world, brand-new and shiny with moonlight. She would leave before dawn, train or no, before she deceived Gabe one more day, before she came to love him and Mary a little bit more.

The tatted snowflakes, stiff with starch, fluttered on a string from sofa to wingchair in front of the cooling stove. She pushed back the chair and carried the tea things to the kitchen.

It was time to go while she still could. Time to leave Gabe and Mary to their lives. Missoula awaited, a job and independence such as she'd always wanted. She would have the letters Connie promised to write, telling her of Mary.

It ought to be enough, much more than she ever dared to wish for. And yet as the night faded, Sara knew it could never be enough.

The moment he opened his eyes, he knew. Sara was here. A happiness curled around him and it wasn't nearly so difficult throwing back the warm covers, climbing out of the comfortable bed, and facing the frigid morning.

He'd get the fires going, water boiling, maybe ask Sara

what she wanted for breakfast. He liked the idea of cooking for her. Or better yet, cooking alongside her. Last night's kiss lingered in his memory, in the intimate touches she'd allowed. Sweet heavens, he didn't think he could get enough of a woman like that. Loving her could satisfy him the rest of his life.

He shivered into his clothes. The winds had stopped, the brief fury of the storm left a morning still and crisp. He peeked out the window and figured a good foot or more of snow had fallen last night. Enough to keep the train from running and Sara in Moose Creek through Christmas.

The parlor was silent. He crept on stockinged feet to the kitchen, where he opened the stove as quietly as he could, although the hinges squealed. He found the fire not too long banked, the embers glimmering hot.

Sara must have had trouble sleeping with the wind howling outside the door and made tea. He added kindling, then wood, feeding the fire, pleased she made herself right at home. It was his intention to make this a permanent arrangement.

"Pa? Where's Sara?" Mary stood in the shadows, rubbing her eyes.

"She's sleeping on the couch. Quiet, so we don't wake her."

"No, she isn't. And her sewing box is gone too."

"What?" Gabe swung around. In an instant he saw her cloak and muffler were both missing from the coat tree. "Maybe she's at Aunt Connie's house."

He didn't like the fact that she'd left without a word, but he knew a woman's reputation was important. And yet, she could have left a note—

"Pa?" Mary's voice sounded close to tears.

He found her in the parlor on her hands and knees before the tree. The first pink gleam of dawn brushed through the window and illuminated the tears sluicing down her face.

He knelt, his arms reaching out. "What's wrong?"

"Sara's gone." Mary flew against him and buried her face in the hollow of his shoulder.

"There's no place for her to go, except back to Aunt Connie's." He didn't like this, how Sara had made Mary cry, but he wasn't sure if the woman realized how they cared for her, treasuring the rare happiness she'd brought to their lives.

"Then why did she leave presents?" Sobs shuddered through Mary's delicate body.

"Because today is Christmas Eve." Gabe held her all the tighter. "Why, look at that. Did you see all those lacy snowflakes she made for you? They're to hang on the tree."

"I w-want Sara to help me hang them."

Sara. She'd slipped out of their home without a word, without regard to how it would affect Mary. How could she do this to a child? To him?

One thing was for certain: He wanted answers. He would find out why Sara had run off without a word, one way or another.

Chapter Nine

"Sara's things aren't in her room." Connie descended the staircase still in her wrapper and nightgown. "There's not a place in town to stay. Where do you think she's gone? And in this weather."

"On to Missoula is my guess. Paul down at the livery rented her a horse and sled at dawn's light. Said he didn't want to, but she told him about her job, how her aunt expected her today. And even then, she had only half the funds. Gave him her aunt's name and promised to send the rest of what she owed him."

"Then she's truly left." Connie rubbed her brow, her face tight, her mouth pinched. "I at least wanted to say good-bye. I wanted to keep in touch with her. Jim's still asleep. Want me to put on some coffee?"

"I'd sure appreciate it, sis." Gabe unwound his muffler but left his coat on, for the house was cool. He'd rousted Connie from her bed, and the fires in both stoves were still banked. "Let me help."

"Goodness, would you look at this?" Surprise softened Connie's voice.

Gabe pushed through the swinging door into the kitchen and saw, even in the unlit room, the objects on the table: gifts wrapped for Christmas Day.

Glass chinked and a match flared as Connie lit a lamp. She turned up the wick and lemony light showed a hastily written note, a stack of small bills, and gifts for Connie and Jim.

"Oh, Sara." Connie brushed a tear from her eyes as she unfolded the paper and began to read. "She says she's afraid to lose her chance for this job and to forgive her, but she cannot stay. She wants to thank me for sharing my home and my family with her, for this brief but treasured time."

Gabe's throat filled. "Surely her aunt would hold the position if not even the train can get Sara there on time."

"That's my thought too. Maybe she's a stern woman, but surely she would have to be fair." Connie's fingers brushed the lace ribbon tied around a wrapped gift, hand-made and as delicate as the woman who'd crocheted it. "Maybe there was another reason she chose to leave."

"Leave? She ran off like a woman with something to hide. A secret. Something she was ashamed of." He thought of how charmed Sara had been by Mary, how shy of him, swearing she was over grieving—that wasn't the reason she refused to love him.

You don't want me, Gabe. Believe me. Her words had troubled him then, but even more now that she'd fled in sub-zero temperatures and ten-foot-high snowdrifts with no one to help her find her way.

He remembered the moment two evenings past in his kitchen when he had looked at his daughter and Sara side by side.

Kneeling before the range, Gabe added kindling to the

embers and watch them burst into flame. "Connie, do you remember anything I might have told you about Mary's adoption?"

"No." Connie, her nose in the panty, pulled down the grinder, but her spine stiffened, her shoulders tensed. "I'm not the one who adopted Mary."

"No, but I just thought . . . " He reached for a stick of cedar, his pulse rushing in his ears. "Women talk, and I was led to believe the baby had been just a week old. Whoever gave up that baby had to live fairly close to Oak's Grove."

"Only stands to reason." Connie set the coffee grinder on the counter.

"You know how women talk, and you were active in several charities at the time. Surely you knew of a young woman who'd gotten in trouble"—he added more cedar and stepped back as the radiant heat scorched his face, making the skin feel tight—"or one who was forced to give up her baby."

"Because of a husband's death?"

Gabe closed the stove's small door, the hinges squeaking. A gust of wind shot down the pipe and the burners rattled, sending up tiny puffs of smoke.

His gaze landed on the wrapped gifts on the table. "Ann fell in love with Mary the first moment she was placed in her arms. I'll never forget that day. I became a father and Ann—why, she finally had her greatest dream. A baby to call her own, to love and raise."

"Ann loved Mary as her own, no doubt about it." Connie set the canister of coffee beans next to the grinder, her motions automatic, but her voice—how emotion deepened it—rang raw and tender. "But I image Mary's real mother—the one who held and loved and nursed that baby for her first week of life, then had to give her away—why, think of how much she must have loved little Mary."

"Yes." The knowledge clamped tight in his chest, balled in his throat. "Ann wanted to forget another woman had given birth to our baby, so we never asked. And I never knew."

"Well, now you do." Connie dumped a handful of beans in the mill.

Damn, he felt like a fool. He should have guessed, should have seen it. Hell, he had. He'd noticed it when Sara and Mary had stood side by side, the same unruly hair the exact dark shade of deep molasses and their eyes, both blue and gray, although Sara's were more gray, maybe because she carried with her a great sorrow, a great sadness of having given up her baby so many years ago.

Her baby. Gabe felt struck by lightning, off kilter, as if his entire world had shifted suddenly and nothing would ever be the same again. Sara might have innocently been on that train, innocently stranded like the other passengers, but had she used the situation to get close to Mary?

"Where are you going?" Connie sounded panicked as he headed toward the door.

He didn't answer. He didn't have time. "Watch Mary for me. I don't want her to know anything about this. Not one word, Connie."

He waited for his sister's nod, and then he was outside, wading through the high drifts to saddle his gelding. A few lazy flakes swirled in the air and he studied the clouds, scented snow on the low wind.

Another storm was brewing, but how bad, he couldn't tell.

"Whoa, boy." Sara eased back on the thick leather reins looped between her fingers, which were numb despite the two pairs of mittens she wore. "Easy, now."

The big black gelding tossed his head, just short of panic.

This was the fifth time the little sled had fallen through a snowdrift, made unstable by the grass or pockets of air beneath it. It made for slow going.

The sun had already stretched beyond the zenith, and it was now rapidly disappearing behind diffuse clouds. The snow had changed too. First, light flakes had danced on the air, falling with a lazy ease; then they blew more seriously until the tracks behind her disappeared and the horizon ahead faded to a nebulous shroud.

Sara unloaded the simply built sleigh, then heaved and tugged until the vehicle was righted again. She checked the traces and leather buckles before harnessing up the skittish gelding. The big animal looked at her with worried eyes, for no doubt he could sense how the storm could worsen and trap them here on the desolate mountainside.

She'd had little choice in leaving, as difficult as this trek away from Moose Creek had been. She had wondered throughout the day how Mary was doing, how Gabe might feel when he discovered her missing. She'd hurt him, she knew. But it was far better hurting him this way, with an unexplained departure. She could not risk hurting Mary, who did not even seem to know she was adopted.

No, Sara was doing the right thing. She had no doubts. From the deepest part of her, she knew it. But that didn't mean it was easy. Unshed tears ached in her throat, a great ball of grief and loss that hurt with every breath she took.

The gelding gave a snort, sidestepping in his traces as he tossed his head. "It's okay, boy," she soothed, then glanced over her shoulder.

A dark spot stood out against the miles of pristine snow—a horse and rider. She'd met no one on the trail today—that is, if she was still on the trail. It was impossible to tell with the drifted snow, for it had erased all signs of a road.

"Come on, you darn sled." She pulled and tugged, her muscles straining, until the vehicle tipped off its side to rest back on its runners. Now she just had to get the sleigh out of the hole and back up onto solid ground.

As she patted down the uneven snow, she glanced over her shoulder. The rider was closer, more distinct as he crested a rise, then disappeared into a gully.

Being alone in the vast wilderness with a stranger riding close wasn't all that safe. Sara slapped the reins against the black's rear and the animal gave a little lunge, hauling the sled back up onto the hard packed snow.

"Whoa, boy." She pulled him to a stop, then fetched her satchels. Bitter wind burned her face and teared her eyes as she looked behind her, toward Moose Creek and the people she had left behind.

The rider had not crested the next small rise, and so she settled back onto the small sled's seat, tossed a wool blanket over her lap to cut some of the wind's bite, and sent the gelding into a quick walk.

The horse balked now and then, a little spooked from finding a few unstable spots in the snow, but she calmed him, talking low. She tried to keep the urgency out of her voice, but it stayed in her heart, thumping hard with each beat.

The tingling feeling at the back of her neck told her the rider had closed the distance between him. Gabe. She knew it was him before she twisted around to make out the square cut of his jaw or the broad dependable line of his shoulders. He rode fast, a hat protecting his face from the pelting snow, his clothes patched with icy-white flakes.

"Get up, boy!" She sent the black into a faster walk, but the animal neighed and the ground gave way beneath them. For an instant she felt airborne and then the sled hit bottom, bucking her from the seat and into the icy snow. Brief pain skidded up her side and burned in her arm.

"You've caught the edge of the slew." Rumbling and

dark that voice, without a trace of his usual humor or kindness.

Sara swallowed the groan on her lips and sat up, dusting the bits of white from her skirts. "I didn't know there was a slew. I guess that explains why I keep going down. I'm riding on nothing but reeds and air."

"Let me help."

"I can do it myself." Sara stood, determined to hide the bite of pain in her ribs as she rescued her satchels, thrown clear of the sleigh. "Easy, boy."

The gelding reared, squealing in fear, plunging around in the uncovered reeds.

"Easy now." Sara reached for the fallen reins. "Let me get you unharnessed."

"You need help." She heard Gabe's saddle creak slightly as he dismounted.

Her heart plunged in her chest. "No, I'm doing well enough by myself."

"I know. You don't need me. You told me that before." His boots squeaked on the snow.

She knelt to release the buckles. The traces came free and the gelding calmed. "That's a boy."

"Here, give me the reins and I'll tie him." Gabe's gloved hand reached out.

"I can handle this." She walked the gelding, stomping down the snow to make it more stable, then led him up the incline and back onto solid snow.

"He'll run off."

"He hasn't yet." Sara did not dare lift her gaze to Gabe and see his strength or remember the heat of his kisses. Keeping her heart cold, she climbed back down to the fallen sled and concentrated on her work. "Why did you come after me? You shouldn't have left Mary. You should have stayed home where it was warm. It's Christmas Eve."

"Why did you leave the gifts?"

"You rode all this way to ask me that?" She curled her fingers around the sled's sideboard and yanked hard. The vehicle refused to budge, lying on its side, wedged nearly upside down.

"You didn't answer my question."

She squinted up at him through the thickly falling flakes, white flecks of cold that tumbled like rain to the ground. "It's Christmas. Giving gifts is customary."

"Not when you leave without a word and never expect to return." He strode down the incline, his brows furrowed, his jaw clamped tight.

She whipped back around and took hold of one sharp runner. "Get back on your horse, Gabe. My future isn't in Moose Creek."

"It's not in Missoula either." He nodded toward the horizon. "Another storm's blowing in. We've got to find shelter before it hits."

"Then you head back to town alone. I can take care of myself." Sara struggled to turn the sled, her muscles straining, tears building in her eyes. She would not accept his help, would not lean on him. Besides, she could never return to Moose Creek.

"Scoot over and let me get a good hold on that runner. It's wedged tight in the snow."

She moved over, but she didn't leave the job for him to do. He had to give her credit for her stubborn will. So independent she was, even resigned to needing his help. They counted to three and pulled together, the sled moaning and giving a bit.

"This isn't working." Sara swiped the snow gathering on her lashes with the back of one mittened hand. "Maybe you could push while I pulled."

He'd thought of that too, and circled around her, but she would not meet his gaze. Her back stiffened as his sleeve brushed hers. Stubborn and independent and strong. He liked that combination, especially in this woman who did not assume, who did not want much for herself.

She gripped the runner and baseboard of the sled hard. When he pushed, he could feel how strong she was. She had done hard work on the farm, he guessed. Working together, they finally were able to roll the sled over onto its runners.

"Thank you for your help." Already she was kneeling down, hitching up.

Gabe caught the leather straps on his side of the sleigh and quickly tugged and buckled. "You can't make it to Missoula before the storm."

"It's already storming." Fat chunks of snow drove on the wind.

"It'll only get worse. Come on. Let's go back."

"It's my decision to make, Gabe. Tell Mary"—her eyes clouded, so gray with bleak sorrow—"Merry Christmas."

She snapped the reins and the gelding grudgingly stepped forward. The sled eased up out of the broken snow and onto safer ground, runners squeaking on the shadowed ice. He watched her go, a stubborn woman determined to cling to her course, the only future she had.

He could understand that. He knew all about pride and loss and being afraid.

The falling snow obscured the towering mountains, graceful foothills and the stands of timber as far as eye could see. The snow blanketed the land, a gray white shroud that cloaked Sara's retreating form so that she was only a splash of black and gray against the webby-blue shadows of dusk.

How she must have grieved, losing her new husband the way she had. And since she hadn't been able to keep her baby, it must have been damn hard to keep right on living, feeling with her heart, believing happiness could happen to her again.

He kicked his gelding into a brisk lope. "You aren't going to make it to Missoula—not like this."

Her chin shot up. She held herself so tight, not just from the frigid wind, but as if she were ready to break from the inside out, to fracture into a million pieces.

"I don't want you here. I didn't ask you to come after me." She tried to sound fierce, but her voice remained thin and wobbly, shaky with emotion. "I said good-bye. Why can't you leave it at that?"

"I just thought you'd like to know you're on the wrong road."

"Then it's my problem, Gabe, and I'll find my own way." She bowed her head, squeezing her eyes shut. A muscle jumped in her jaw. "It's Christmas Eve, so go home and spend it with your daughter."

"I'm not going home alone." Gabe caught hold of the rented gelding's bit and drew the animal to a stop. He circled his horse around to look at her, covered with snow, her face white from the cold. "I know, Sara."

"What?"

"I know you're Mary's real mother."

A terrible shaking sluiced through her, and Sara wrapped her arms around her stomach. Had Connie told him? No, she was the kind of woman who wouldn't betray a confidence, even an implied one.

He'd guessed on his own, because she stayed too long, indulged herself spending time with Mary, time she had no right to.

"I know I broke my agreement. I signed papers—it was legal. I said I would never try to contact Mary." What he must think of her. Sara's heart cracked, piece by piece until her entire chest filled with pain.

She could not look up and bear to see hatred mark Gabe's handsome face or sour his beautiful mouth. She did not want her memories tarnished with this horrible truth, this terrible thing she'd done.

"I never would have told her. I only meant to stay in Moose Creek a few hours."

"I know. I spoke with the clerk at the railroad station. He said you traded in your ticket to Missoula this morning. I asked to see it." He walked his horse closer until he towered over the small sled, tall and intimidating. His shadow, faint but unmistakable, fell over her. "You came to see her intentionally."

"That's all I wanted. Just to see her. Just to see the little girl my baby had become." How selfish it sounded now. How shamefully, horribly selfish. "I swear this to you, on my own mother's grave. I would never have let Mary know. I did not come to change her life."

Gabe said nothing for a long time. Snow tapped in the silence between them, a thousand constant whispers as perfect white flakes met frozen ground. The rented horse snorted, releasing his breath in one long whoosh, bored of standing still.

"It could start blizzarding anytime. You don't have a choice in this, Sara. There is no shelter ahead on this road. It leads across the pass north to the abandoned gold camps." Gabe swung his horse around. "We have to go back to Moose Creek."

She let him turn the rented horse around. Tears filled her eyes and froze on her lashes. The storm was worsening, and she had lost her way.

Chapter Ten

Moose Creek was dark and frozen when they arrived. Snow accumulated in thick white bands on porch rails and storefront awnings and the lengths of hitching posts. Unlit windows made the town look abandoned, maybe forgotten. A peaceful calm seemed to envelop this piece of the world; the silence was broken only by the hush of snowfall and low wind.

A glow sheened on the snow, drawing them farther down the street. The light grew, spreading a golden haze, shrouding the edge of the forest with a brightness, a sense of hope on this desolate night. Smoke puffed from the chimney, promising warmth to weary travelers. Gabe drew the horses to a halt at the line of hitching posts, just brushed by lamplight from the glittering windows. The faint sound of children's voices filled the air, merry with joy, lifting in song.

"I'll see to the horses. Go on ahead and get out of this cold." Gabe took the reins from her numb hands, not looking at her. Saying nothing more, just as he had during the grueling journey home.

Knowing she deserved his silence, she did as he asked. She did not belong at his side anyway, tending horses or anything else.

Alone once again, Sara bowed her head against the driving cold and hurried up the shoveled steps, following the sound of voices rejoicing this holy night.

She struggled with the doors against the wind, but when she stepped inside the vestibule and into the heated light of the church, she heard the solemn blend of melody and harmony, of soprano and alto, pure and sweet.

Her gaze riveted on a splash of red velvet. There was Mary, in the first row, her dress only a small part of her precious beauty. She held a candle in both hands, the gentle light brushing a golden glow across her pixie face. The choir around her quieted and she lifted her voice like an angel's, clear and bright as she sang, " 'Sleep in heavenly peace.' "

Tears wedged in Sara's throat, big grateful tears of pleasure and pride. That was her daughter, her baby girl. Another child's solo rang solemn and low, but Sara could not tear her gaze away from Mary or the white lace bow crowning her dark curls or the shine of the heart-shaped locket hanging around her neck, the locket Andrew had given Sara for her birthday, just before they married. Now it gleamed like a great treasure in the soft golden candlelight. Presents she had left for Mary beneath their Christmas tree.

A hand settled on her shoulder and she jumped. Gabe's voice, low and rich, caressed the back of her neck. "Mary wanted to open your gifts. She didn't understand why you'd left."

Words and feelings, meant to remain unspoken, swelled in her chest. How could she speak of her heart?

The last notes of the song faded, low and reverent. The children filed from the front of the church back into the pews. Mary rushed down the main aisle, braids and bright skirts flying and ran straight at Sara, arms outstretched, smile beaming.

"You came!" Mary wrapped her arms tight around Sara's waist, holding on hard, with a child's might. "Pa said he would bring you back to see me sing. Was I good?"

"Very good." Sara could not help wrapping her arms around the child, this precious child, holding her despite the unbearable pain in her heart. "You were the best singer."

"And the prettiest girl." Gabe knelt down to accept an ardent hug from his daughter.

"Aunt Connie and I worried all day." Mary stepped back, tilting her head to gaze up at them. The rustling sounds of the church surrounded them, the excitement of children getting stockings of candy at the big tree tucked in the corner. "It snowed real hard and we got scared the wind would turn into a blizzard. So Connie and me made gingerbread men, and after, when I was still scared, I wanted to wear your presents."

"The bow looks beautiful in your hair." Sara brushed her hand across Mary's brow, felt the silken texture of those wayward curls and the satin softness of a child's skin, both so dear. So very, very dear.

Mary's small fingers closed around the locket. "I like this best. I got a present for you. Pa helped me decide what to give you. You just gotta come open it. Please?"

Sara felt Gabe's gaze on her face, as unreadable as his silence. He had to be angry with her, had to think the worst of her reasons for being here. She couldn't blame him. He loved Mary. He did not want her hurt.

"It's late, Mary. I don't want to disappoint you, but—"

"You gotta come." The girl tipped her face up, dark curls cascading everywhere, a look of sheer affection so bold on her face it brought tears to Sara's eyes. "You just gotta."

"Sara!" Connie's merry voice interrupted, arms wide to cradle her in a hug. "It's good to see you're safe and sound. I can't tell you how we worried."

"You shouldn't have, but it's nice to have someone to worry over me." She stepped away, regretting the distance she had to put between her and Connie.

"You'll still need a place to stay. Even though the blizzard we feared didn't hit, the engine wasn't fixed in time. The hotel and boardinghouse are still full." Connie fiddled with the strings on her reticule and then plunged her hand inside. "Here, take this. It's the front door key."

"I can't. I just can't impose on you anymore."

"Nonsense." Empathy lit Connie's eyes. "You need a place to stay, and you're always welcome in my home, Sara. Always. Don't you ever forget that."

She didn't understand how Connie could be so generous. It felt amazing and yet she was grateful for it too. So she accepted the key with a strangled thank you, not trusting her voice to say more.

"Now I'm off to Jim's mother's house for a midnight supper. It's tradition in his family, so I guess I'm off to feast on a roast ham." Connie pressed a kiss to Mary's brow. "Now mind your pa and keep out of the rest of those presents. I know you're dying to open them."

"I wanna see if I got the dolly Pa promised me."

"I don't remember any promise." Gabe's smile softened his handsome face but did not reach his eyes, eyes dark and inscrutable, as hard to read as midnight shadows. "Have a good time, Connie. I'll see Sara home."

"No, Gabe. I can take care of myself." She tried to keep her voice light, tried not to let the sorrow and shame in her heart show. "Tomorrow's Christmas. Mary needs to get to sleep so Santa Claus can come. I don't want him to miss her house because I kept her up too late."

"Santa isn't bringing me presents," Mary declared with a grand note of confidence. "He's bringing me a mother, just like I asked."

Mary's words haunted Sara's conscience all the way to Connie's house. Although it was late, sleep wasn't about to come anytime soon. So she fed the embers in the kitchen stove until they were flaming and crackling, driving the cold air from the cheerful room. She set water to boil, found cold sliced chicken in the pantry, then made a small sandwich.

The tea was ready by the time she was done eating. She cradled the cup, savoring the feel of the steam against her face, breathing in the fragrance of fresh honey and lemons and expensive tea. Such a luxury. Alone in the kitchen, she tried to think of what she had, of the good things in her life.

A good job waiting for her, or so she hoped. The chance for a real future. Maybe, if she saved hard, she might have a little house of her own one day to decorate and make cozy like this. Maybe she would find a man to fall in love with, one who could make her forget Gabe Chapman and his lopsided smile and his gentle strength.

With Mary tucked in bed, her faith in Santa Claus stubborn and unyielding, Gabe turned his attention to banking the fires so she would be safe while he slipped outside. The embers buried, he fetched his coat from the hook and shrugged into it.

His gaze landed on the tree in the dark corner, limbs widespread, holding unlit candles and sprays of ribbon, strings of popcorn and cranberries. The scent of pine teased his nose, just as the memories tugged at his heart. Memories of Sara in this room, her gentle affection for Mary like a single flame in the darkness chasing away shadows.

This room had been filled with happiness and song, with her sweet, low laughter and Mary's giggles. How good it felt, how joyful, to have had her here. He would never stand in the parlor again without thinking of her and of what could have been.

He knelt to snatch the gift from beneath the tree, one with her name on it, one of many she had chosen to leave behind.

He headed out into the heavy snow, flakes blinding him as he crossed the road. The wind cut through his clothes like a knife. He felt frozen by the time he stomped the snow off his boots on Connie's back porch. Only the kitchen light was on. He pushed his way into the lean-to and rapped his knuckles against the inside door.

"Gabe." She stared up at him with dread dark in her eyes. "If you've come to tell me to leave, I want you to know that I have already made arrangements to go first thing in the morning."

"You sure took care of that fast."

"I only wish it were sooner. Mr. Hawkins has a wagon load of goods to deliver north of Missoula, and he's agreed to take me if the train isn't running." Her voice wobbled, and she kept her chin bowed as she retreated farther into the kitchen. "So you don't need to stay. Mary shouldn't be alone."

"Mary is fine for a little while. Look. I can see the house from here." He wished he could hate Sara Mercer for her deception, but how could he hate the woman who had made it possible for him and Ann to raise their own baby? How could he ever hate the woman with eyes the same color as his daughter's? "I could use some of that tea."

Her hands shook as she lifted another cup from the cabinets. She kept her back to him, spine stiff, chin set. "I never meant to harm Mary. I want you to know that. I just wanted to see her, just once. That was all."

The cup clanked on the counter and the lid of the china pot rattled with her nervousness. "A woman I worked with at the laundry had attended Connie's wedding last year, and told us all about it. Nobody knew about Mary, of course, but they did talk about you, since you had grown up in Oak's Grove, and how you had settled in Moose Creek too. I can't tell you how wonderful it was to learn such a small detail about my little baby. I didn't know about Ann's death. When Aunt Ester offered me this job, I couldn't believe my luck. Moose Creek was a stop on the railroad line. It seemed too good to be true."

She set the steaming cup on the table near him, then retreated. Her gaze stayed low, and her hands nervously worried a loose thread at her cuff. "I should never had been so selfish."

He tried to imagine how hard it had been for Sara to give up her baby, one conceived in love. She must have held every dream of raising her beautiful daughter herself before her husband's death. Not to be forced to hand the baby over to strangers and never know what had become of her.

He set the box on the table, wrapped in gay red paper, Mary's choice.

Sara tried to imagine what Gabe could mean by offering her a gift, one that had been left beneath the tree all three of them had decorated together with happiness and song. It was a small package. It couldn't contain much more than a folded length of lace, maybe a small handkerchief.

"Go ahead. Open it."

It was so hard to judge the tone of his voice. Her stomach felt tied in knots. She was braced for his anger, for his suspicions, for worse. Not a gift as Christmas morning arrived, dark with the quiet bong of the clock and the pop of the fire inside the stove.

The box was light in her hand. She carefully untied the red ribbon, a length of the same yardage Mary had chosen to trim her new velvet dress. She would save this always. When she felt lonely for her daughter on any night to come, she would have memories and this gift.

The paper folded away easily to reveal a plain white box. Sara lifted the lid and something winked in the low lamplight, something bright and dazzling. On a bed of velvet sparkled a ring of rubies, rich and priceless, the same color as Mary's dress. She had never seen valuable gemstones before but knew as they winked and glittered how expensive the rubies must be.

"This was my mother's." Gabe's step tolled as he circled the table, ambling into the shadows where the single lamp could not reach. "Mary wanted you to have it."

"It's a wedding ring." She slipped the lid back on the box. "I can't accept anything so fine. Mary should keep it."

"She wanted you to spend Christmas Eve with us and to have you open the gift before we went to church. She wanted to ask you to marry us."

Mary was bound to be disappointed when she learned Sara could not be the mother she asked Santa for. "I don't know how to fix this. I wish I'd never . . . "

No, she was glad she'd come. She felt stronger for knowing how loved her baby was, that Mary's life was good and her happy smile genuine.

"I do know how to fix it." Gabe's hands covered hers, big strong hands that looked capable enough to solve any problem, no matter how great.

"I already plan to leave."

"That wasn't the solution I had in mind." He towered over her, a man of strength but of goodness too. Without a drop of hatred in his eyes as true as forgiveness. "Accept the ring and marry us."

"Marry you?" Sara choked. Pain seared down her windpipe, spread through her chest. "How can you ask me such a thing?"

"I know you never came to hurt Mary or to try to take her, or work your way into her life. If you had, you would have done it differently, not tried to leave every chance you got."

A smile touched his lips, lopsided and so drawing she could not look away. He was all she saw, mighty man and sturdy kindness, the kind a woman could depend on all her life.

"I can't imagine how painful it must have been to give up your baby. Or how you've longed for her all these years." His voice broke, a low rumble of emotion that came straight from his heart. "I know you just wanted to let go, to see the little girl you loved."

"That's all I wanted, Gabe. I feel so guilty. I seized every chance to get to know Mary more when I should have asked you to find me another place to live. But I stayed here with Connie, right in the middle of your family. I lied to you all. I'm ashamed I did, but to see Mary . . . "

Her chin wobbled, and her big beautiful eyes silvered with tears. "How can I ever find the words to thank you for being her father? You've given her a life I could never dream of providing her. I can't tell you how grateful I am. To know that in giving her up, I gave her you."

"Sara." How his heart rent seeing her tears, seeing the pain she kept tucked inside. The years had not been easy, longing always for the baby she loved so much. He cradled her hand, so feminine and delicate, and pressed kisses to her slim knuckles. "You seem to think that I've done something, but all I did was be a father, nothing more. It's nothing like what you have given me."

"What could I possibly give?"

She didn't know—he could read that in her eyes, puzzled and lost, so lost. And he would show her the way home.

"You gave me Mary. You brought light back into our lives made dark by Ann's death. And gifts of laughter and songs and something more, something better." He laid his hand against her jaw, cupping her dear face. "You've shown us an unselfish love, one so true and pure I've never seen the like. You have placed Mary's happiness far above your own, and you have captured my whole heart, Sara Mercer. I love you and I'll be damned if I'm going to let you leave."

She eased into his arms, pressing her cheek against his chest. A great satisfaction licked through him, growing stronger until all he felt was his love for her, bright and shining and without end.

"You truly want me to stay?"

He nodded, and Sara squeezed the tears from her eyes, unable to believe.

But with one look at his face, she saw the truth of his words, the brilliance of his love as sure as the light in the room.

He wanted her, this man with a heart big enough to see the best in her, to offer a love rare and true. He kissed her and fire flitted through her chest, heated her blood, fueled sparkling desire. For him, for this man she would love the rest of her life.

Gabe scooped the ring from the box, glinting and shimmering, and slipped it around her ring finger. She stared at her left hand, overcome.

"Marry me," he whispered tenderly.

"Yes." Joy filled her. She was going to be Gabe's wife. It was that simple, and yet it was everything. "But what about Mary? What will we tell her?"

"We'll tell her the truth." Gabe took Sara's hand and led her to the window, where the storm had dissipated into a gentle snowfall. The clouds parted to allow a few brilliant stars to shine upon them, silvering the silent night, bringing peace to the world.

"The truth? I don't want her hurt, Gabe. I don't want her to forget Ann."

"She needs to know, Sara. She needs to know that years ago a woman had to give up her beloved baby. And came at Christmas time to see her little girl, just to see her, thinking she wasn't wanted."

He wrapped one arm around Sara's shoulders, sheltering her against his strong body, holding her close. "But what the woman didn't know was that she brought with her a gift the little girl had been waiting for, and her father too."

"What gift did I bring?" Sara looked out at the house across the street where Mary slept, where they would live together as a family, a real family, a place where she finally belonged.

"You gave us your love, Sara." His lips brushed her brow, gentle and reverent. "It was as though we were living in darkness until you came. And now all I see is the future with you and me and Mary."

"And maybe another baby one day."

"Maybe."

Arm in arm, they watched the snow stop, the last flakes dancing and whirling weightlessly to earth. Calm settled over the land, and the reverent brush of the starlight made the snow gleam like silver, rich and rare.

"Come, Sara." He took her hand. "Let's go home."

WHEN ALL THROUGH THE NIGHT

by

Tracy Sumner

Prologue

Richmond—1851

She was being punished.

"Dammit, Kat. Let me in!" Tanner bellowed, standing somewhere beneath her second-story window.

Katherine Peters swallowed a sob and pressed her forehead against her quaking knees. Her back hurt from crouching between the rosewood wardrobe and the pine-paneled wall, but this was the only place she felt safe. At the moment. As a child, she'd hidden from her mother, her nanny, and later, her tutor in this very spot, but she'd never taken tears with her. Fear, certainly, and guilt, over a shattered vase or incomplete lessons, but never tears.

Now they coursed down her face in alarming streams, dampening the neck of her cream wool dress, making her skin feel sticky and puffy. She scrubbed at her eyes and tapped the bridge of her nose in confusion. Her spectacles. Sitting beside the newspaper.

Reaching out with a trembling hand, she traced the indecipherable lines of text. Dusty ink blotches stained her skin. She crushed the newspaper in her fist. In her mind, the ink ran bloodred—her blood splattered all over cheap newsprint for all of Richmond to see. A broken heart and a bleak future lay between those meaningless letters.

Kate flung the newspaper to the floor. Tanner Barkley, a bloody newspaperman. A deceitful, fraudulent bast—

A rock sailed through the open window, skipping across a marble-topped washstand and knocking a candle sconce to the floor before coming to rest on her sister's prized Wilton rug. A hoarse shout followed. "Kat, please! I need to talk to you. If you'll just let me explain!"

Kate wrapped her arms around her knees. *No, no, no.* Not after what he'd done—lying about his profession, lying about everything, it seemed. Spending time with her, debating politics, walking along the James River, teaching her to play chess . . .

Oh, dear God, Kate, you let him do much more than play chess with you. And she was paying the price, for her naiveté. For her complete lack of judgment.

She sniffed, wiped a soggy sleeve beneath her nose, the stink of damp wool filling her nostrils. Taking a deep breath, she squeezed from her hiding place. The rock was in her hand before she knew what she intended to do with it.

Walking to the window, she leaned out, bracing her belly against the frame. A gust of humid air attacked her, whipping hair into her face. A metallic clink off brick jerked Tanner's head up. His pale blue eyes drilled into her. Probing, pleading. A lock of black hair fell across his brow and her traitorous hand actually wanted to lift it to brush it aside.

He raised his arms, entreating. "Please, Kat. Just listen to me. For one minute."

"You had two months to talk to me, two months to tell me the truth," she whispered, unsure if he could even hear her. She gripped the rock until her skin stung, her knees cracking against the wall with steady thumps.

"Goddammit, Princess. You're being foolish." Tanner's words echoed off the courtyard walls. Foolish. *Foolish.*

Fury gripped her, swept a hazy red glow before her eyes. "*Foolish.* If I *never* lay eyes on you again, it will be too soon!" Cocking her arm, she aimed as well as she could without her spectacles and hurled the rock at his head.

Tanner cursed, ducked, flinched, and cursed again when the rock struck his shoulder. Kate slammed the window into place, flipped the stiff latch, and sank to her knees. A shiver worked its way from her toes to her shoulders. She gasped for breath, stunned and defeated.

Thank heavens her sister, Eliza, had chosen to attend the opera this evening.

How could Kate explain the loss of employment, fiancée, and lover all in one day?

Chapter One

South Carolina—1852

They burst from the still settling stagecoach like two cats from a burlap sack, spitting and clawing. Kate stumbled through a cloud of dust and snapped her flounced skirt with a vicious flip of her wrist. "Dear God, what did I do to deserve this? I simply asked for a quiet Christmas." She glared at the sky, as if she expected to see an answer scrawled across the clouds.

Powerless to stop himself, Tanner stepped forward, halting when she stepped back. "I told you I was sorry. Three times, in fact. The cheroot simply got away from me. The wind"—his hand shot out, circled—"just ripped it from my fingers. My good arm is tangled up in this sling, you know." He lifted his injured arm, suppressed a wince of pain for his trouble.

Kate seized the tuft of auburn curls trailing across her cheek, tried unsuccessfully to contain them behind her ear. "Mr. Barkley, you have never been anything but a thorn, worse than a thorn, a ragged piece of glass, yes, *glass,* cutting into my side. Luckily I only have a singed shawl to show for it this time." Dipping her chin, she fingered the black-edged hole in the shawl draped around her shoulders.

Tanner frowned, wondering if he should offer her his coat. He glanced down. Frayed seams, a peculiar odor. Then again, maybe not. "Jesus, I'll buy you a new one."

She flicked her gaze from his head to his feet. "I don't know if I would go that far, Mr. Barkley. Paisley is quite . . . expensive. Above and beyond a newspaperman's wage, I imagine. Although you never looked this frightful. If this is all you're able to afford"—she wagged her pinkie in his direction—"I would surmise that you've taken a headlong leap into indigence. Not getting enough stories thrown your way?"

"You don't know what you're talking about," he said, his voice one breath below a snarl. "You never did. You could have let me talk to you. Explain the situation. And I tried, dammit. Supplicated—"

"Please. No need to use such grand words with me." She raised an arched brow in that arrogant way of hers—something that never failed to bump his fury two notches higher. "And about this threadbare topic," she added in a bored tone, amber eyes holding his, eyes brimming so sharply with intelligence that they almost took away from the beauty of her face.

He took a fast step forward, slapped his hands on either side of the coach, hemming her in. Though he'd planned to get the hell off the stagecoach and leave her standing in the swirl of dust generated from his rapid departure, he found it difficult to follow through with that look, almost a gloating smirk of achievement, twisting her features. God, he absolutely hated when she used the brow arch *and* the bored tone together. "Kat, you're better off without Abel Asher, if that's what you're still so angry about."

"Better? Is it better to open the door one morning and have your fiancé, whom you have known since childhood, standing on your front step, screeching that you ruined his business? Ruined his life? Screeching loud enough to draw a crowd on the street?" Swaying forward, she struck Tanner's chest with a closed fist. "Is it better to have your engagement ring practically ripped from your finger?" *Pound.* "Better to have your name publicly muddied by your involvement with an overzealous newspaperman?" *Pound.* "And all for a newspaper article. An article about misappropriation of funds that everyone in Richmond knew was happening."

He grabbed her hand, used it to pull her against him. "Everyone knowing didn't make it right, Kat. Asher deserved what he got. I told you that you were not a part of it. Were never a part of it."

She tipped her head and laughed, shrill and thin. "Never part of it. I was Abel's bookkeeper. What do you think he thought?"

"Are you pining over him, Kat? Is that it? Did you love him that much?"

"Love? I wrote him a letter the night before, you idiot, breaking the engagement. Abel and I were *never* in love. A convenient arrangement between families, nothing more. You knew that. Do you think I would have ... would have ... with *you?* If I was in love with *him?"* She muttered a furious oath, gave a forceful shove, and brushed past him. "But in your notably gauche fashion, you corrected the situation before I could, didn't you?"

"Princess, I never meant—"

Kate whipped around so quickly Tanner felt a rush of air slap his face. Her skin dulled, pale as parchment.

"Don't you dare call me Princess. *Never* again." Her hands grappled, tangling in her shawl, twisting.

Her breath, warm and sweet smelling, crept into his nostrils. He watched her lips flatten, the bottom one slinking between her even white teeth. A stab of raw yearning, absent for so long he almost didn't recognize it, rocked him in his size-too-big secondhand boots. "Kat," he said in a strained voice, reaching out, his fingers fisted to hide the tremors shaking them. He had no idea what he appealed for.

A heavy step sounded behind them; a strong hand clasped Tanner's shoulder. "You were mighty lucky, Tan, the stage being only two hours late."

With a startled twist, Tanner turned, and forced a smile, relieved and flustered. "Adam." He nodded to the black sling looped around his neck. "I would shake, but as you can see . . . "

Adam's eyes widened as he looked his friend over from head to foot. He seemed to remember himself and returned the smile, though Tanner could tell it was forced. "Where is your trunk?"

Tanner shrugged, the movement sending a slicing twinge up his arm. "No trunk. Traveling light these days."

"Let me guess. You raced out of Richmond with a band of ruffians on your heels," Kate muttered as she passed them, heading for the rear of the coach, where her trunk was being hoisted to the ground by the driver.

Tanner jerked his head, the ends of his sling smacking his neck. "No, a jealous husband this time. After all, sweetheart, you claim to know me so well."

She shuffled to a stop. "All I can say is, what a surprise."

Tanner bowed as low as he could without sending another spear of hell up his arm. "Yes, isn't it?"

She blinked, screwed her beautiful face tight, and looked away.

The same intractable, exquisite woman. Damn her.

Tanner looked back to find Adam glancing back and forth between them. He nodded, seeming to make up his mind. "Tanner, the Four Leaf Clover is a block down. On the left side of Main Street. Which is about all there is to Edgemont. Only saloon in town—can't miss it. I'll meet you in ten minutes." A hostile scowl and a firm shove accompanied the dictate. Turning, he stepped forward, blocking Tanner's view of Kate.

Tanner grunted, scuffed his boot through the dirt. *Fine.* The illustrious Four Leaf Clover. He refused to stand around like some fool, waiting to talk to a woman who looked at him as if she wished he had never been born.

As he trudged along, a wild gust of air ripping at his shabby Chesterfield, the declaration resounded in his mind as it did every time he thought of her. As it did every time he watched her race across a crowded Richmond street, nearly stumbling in her haste to evade him.

To hell with you, too, Kat Peters.

Tanner glanced up as he reached the start of the boardwalk. Wreaths of red-berried holly and some grayish leaf he couldn't identify dangled from every wooden post and whitewashed storefront. A heavy pine scent lingered, a scent that called to mind childhood holidays spent round a roaring fire, the air thick with cigar smoke and candied yams, he and West sneaking sips of Syllabub and Madeira.

Christmas. He hadn't realized it was so near. What day was it anyway? Nineteenth? Eighteenth? Hell. Another Christmas without his family. His mother would cry; his father would rage. Why hadn't he come home . . . the bank needed him . . . blasted newspaper business . . . dangerous. Tanner glanced at his arm, reached to touch the scar on his chin.

He stepped onto the boardwalk, unable to miss the saloon, as Adam had said. The Four Leaf Clover announced itself in grand style, ornate green letters spilling across a filthy window. Curling ivy draped the entrance and was wound in tight spirals on the posts outside. It was the most guileless looking saloon Tanner had ever seen. He paused, looking down the narrow street. Wagons lugged by sway-backed nags, women in worn gingham, baskets bobbing against their hips. A mercantile, a livery, a millinery. He leaned back, raised his hand to shade his eyes. Peters' Millinery. He snorted. Just his goddamn luck.

Shouldering past the swinging doors, he held his arm protectively against his side, and ducked a fat twist of mistletoe. The calming mixture of tobacco and whiskey wafted over him. He smiled. Now that was more like it.

A woman flaunting generous curves and a thatch of tangled blond hair stepped forward, snagging his good arm before he reached the bar. Her adequate bosom lapped over the edge of her bodice, inviting closer inspection. Tanner smiled, let his gaze linger before lifting his head. Cheap perfume, sweat, powder entered his nostrils on his next breath. Ah, well, what could he expect?

"Howdy," he said, presenting a practiced introductory smile. First time he'd said *howdy* in his life.

She giggled and leaned closer, pressing her bosom into his elbow. He shifted, kneaded, felt her nipple pucker into a tight bud. He'd have to remember the word if it worked this well.

Red lips parted. "Oh, honey. Are you a cowboy?"

"No." Tanner lowered his chin, his voice. "A newspaperman," he said, giving the title the stamp of a lover's caress.

Cowboy-lover's shoulders drooped, sucking her breasts inside her dress. "Dang. I've been wantin' to meet a gen-u-ine cowboy for a long time. I heard, well"—she wrinkled her upturned nose—"I heard they're fun. Too far out here to meet a real one. Plenty of farmers, though, and farmers *are* a healthy bunch. Pretty fun, farmers."

"Newspapermen are even more fun. Guaranteed." Another elbow caress might get her going. A couple of drinks. He sniffed. A bath for both of them. Clean sheets.

Cowboy-lover skimmed a chipped nail up his sleeve. "Honey, you look tired."

Tired? God, for two months, he'd slept on grimy warehouse floors, prowled Richmond's docks like a starved cat, conversed with dregs and tramps, and all for a story that had nearly gotten him killed. He'd run to Edgemont to let things calm down a bit and run straight into Kat Peters.

Cowboy-lover tilted her head and smacked her lips. "Don't worry none, honey. I'll fix you up fine and dandy."

"Two whiskeys, Doris. From my bottle. We'll be at the usual table," a deep voice instructed.

Cowboy-lover flashed a sour smile and marched behind the bar.

Tanner managed a short laugh. *Adam.* Invariably, men in love with their wives disapproved of trollops. He turned, groaned low in his throat. "Perfect timing as always, friend."

"Not much has changed with you either, I see."

Tanner shrugged and smoothed his hand over the top of the bar. Seeing his fingers tremble, he clenched them into a fist.

Adam's gaze lowered, then jerked high. He gestured to a dark corner in the back of the saloon. "Come on. To say the very least, you look like you could use a drink."

Cowboy-lover swept past them, slapped glasses on a scarred table, rubbed her hip against Tanner's, sniffed at Adam, and pranced away.

"You've made her very happy, Tan," Adam said.

Tanner slid into a chair, grimaced when he banged his arm against the wooden edge of the table. "Oh? How's that?"

"Doris doesn't get a lot of . . . attention around here."

Tanner took a sip of whiskey, rolled it from one side of his mouth to the other, swallowed. It blazed a fortifying trail, settling quite nicely in his gut. "Well, she's not so bad, if that's all you have."

Adam slapped his hand on the table. Leaning forward, he searched Tanner's face. A shot of discomfiture snaked along Tanner's spine. He didn't know what lurked in his eyes, was afraid to look closely—avoided mirrors for just that reason. Shoving his buttocks back as far as he could without toppling from the chair, he lowered his gaze to his glass.

"What the hell is going on, Tan? You look like you haven't slept in weeks, bathed in weeks, eaten in months. Chrissakes, your *clothing*. Hanging off you in tatters. Whose is it anyway?"

Tanner shifted, the oil lamp's glare lighting amber fires in the liquid in his glass. Amber. Like Kat's eyes during— *"Nothing.* Nothing to worry about," he said, slowly lifting his head. He cleared his throat and repeated it in a steadier voice.

Adam's gaze jumped from his arm to his face. "Yes, I can see that."

"Anyway, I'm sorry to rush down here without more notice. I telegraphed as soon as I could." He tilted his glass back and forth. "I didn't even realize how close it was to Christmas."

"Tanner, I've been asking you to come for two years. We have plenty of room since I added on to the house." Adam paused, took a deliberate sip. The dancing flame illuminated the calculating glint in his eyes. "Maybe you can find time to write an editorial for the *Sentinel* while you're here. God knows, we could use it. Besides, Charlie is so damn excited to see you, she can't sit still."

Thank you, God. A safe topic. "Charlie," Tanner said, fingering the chipped rim of his glass. "How is she?"

"Wonderful. Beautiful. A pain in my ass." Adam grinned and Tanner felt a moment's envy at the look of love on his face. "Ever since you put her on that train in Richmond and told her what you thought of me, she's considered you a true friend. Truthfully, I would have liked it just fine if you hadn't been quite so honest."

"Yes, well, standing in for you that day was really unpleasant. I had to get some enjoyment. Ruining your good name with the woman you loved worked for me."

"I've paid heavily for my cowardice, believe me."

Cowboy-lover's heels clicked against the plank floor as she swabbed the bar and whistled "Camptown Races" in an off-key chirp. Adam's shoulders hitched, fell. He blew out a breath, looked at Tanner, looked away.

Here it comes. Tanner's stomach sank to his boots.

"Tan, what did I intrude upon today? By the stage-coach?"

Tanner smiled, a slight smile, the best he could manage; then he drained his glass in one swallow. "Why do you think you *intruded* upon anything?"

Adam's jaw jumped as he ground his teeth together. "Fine. Don't tell me. None of my business. But let me remind you that this is a small town. So goddamned small you can stroll from one end of it to the other and not finish a cheroot. If you have a problem with Katherine Peters, it'll be hard to avoid it, or her, in Edgemont. And Kate's mother—you remember Charlie's chaperone in Richmond, don't you? Mrs. Peters owns a fripperies shop just down the street."

"Yeah, yeah, I remember. The old shrew. I saw the sign for her store. Just my luck to have this happen, you know." Tanner licked a drop of whiskey from his lip, scrutinized his empty glass with marked intent.

Adam rolled his eyes and poured a half measure. Tanner

frowned at the stingy allotment. Adam sighed and slid the bottle out of reach.

Adam propped his chin on his fist, leaned forward. "Charlie's having some kind of Christmas tree decorating dinner. If you don't show, she will kill me. And I know for a fact Mrs. Peters is invited. Her daughter is sure to be there too. Can you handle that without upsetting the guests? One lovely guest in particular."

"No problem."

"Are you sure?"

"Look, I knew her once. Okay?" Tanner slammed his glass to the table.

"How well?"

How well? Well enough for dreams of her to wake him, turn him into a pathetic person desperately searching a cold bed for a warm body—a brutal reminder of her absence. Some days, when his loneliness seemed like a living, breathing entity inside him, he could smell her scent on his sheets.

"How well, Tanner? I guess I should know if I'm gonna have to stand between you two again."

"How well?" He tipped his glass high, emptied it. Welcome warmth flowed through him. "Pretty well. About two years ago."

Adam's hand shot out, entreating. "And?"

"Suffice it to say, the lady isn't as charmed with me as old Doris over there. At one time, maybe, but some well-intended lies, a series of articles in the *Times*, and a bit of belated, ham-fisted backtracking botched that rather well."

"With both of you in Richmond, seems like—"

"Seems like nothing. Close proximity hasn't helped. The woman literally dashes the other way when she sees me coming. In any case, even if"—he shook his head—"even if I wanted to give it another try, she has someone. Saw them twice. On the street. A few weeks later, at the opera.

The second time, I asked my host who he was." The bastard, clinging to her side, hand resting possessively on her arm. "Crawford somebody or other. A damned society boy. I certainly don't reside in his circle, so I'm not acquainted with him. Too lofty an assortment for a lowly newspaperman."

"Maybe—"

"Listen," Tanner interrupted, setting a severe look on his face that he hoped would convey his exhaustion with the subject. "I'm way past wanting Kat Peters to be a part of my life. She's nothing now except a faded memory."

"Faded memories make you act like you did by that stagecoach?"

Tanner grunted. "She just made me a little angry, is all." He closed his eyes, the meager amount of whiskey he'd consumed clouding his mind. Maybe food would help. When had he eaten last? Two days ago, three?

"Tanner?" Adam's voice called to him from the end of a long tunnel. "Tanner, are you all right?"

Tanner blinked, Adam's face swimming into view. "Just tired, hungry. The last few weeks have been rough ... working on a story. Hiding out. The beard, the clothes—all part of it. A few days ago, I got caught in some trouble." He paused, wiped his hand across his mouth. His fingers trembled against his lips. "I—I had to leave town."

Adam rocked back in his chair. "Are the police looking for you?"

"No. God, no." He shook his head. "Nothing like that. I didn't do anything illegal. I just picked the wrong place at the wrong time. Trust me, a very wrong time."

"Your editor?"

"He knows. Suggested I lie low for a week or two, take a rest. So here I am."

Adam sighed. "Well, you're safe here. This is as close to the end of the world as it gets."

For the first time in nearly a week, the flame of panic in Tanner's chest dimmed, and he slid lower in his chair. Somehow, he knew he could place some of his burden on his friend's capable shoulders. "I just want to sleep. Forget about writing for a few nights. Forget what a newspaper looks like." Forget he'd ever known Kat Peters.

"How about we stop by the barber, then get you home? Tan, I think you need a few years' sleep, never mind a few nights'. We can work the rest out tomorrow."

Tanner groaned. "A trollop, a barber, *and* a bed? Whoa, this place might be too much for me."

"Barber first. Bath a close second. No wonder Katherine Peters was in such a rage. Locked in a stagecoach with you smelling this . . . terrible."

Kat. Just a few doors down. Long limbs tangled in silk sheets. Her glorious rust-colored hair flowing down her back. God, she was so close he could almost feel her, simmering deep in his bones.

I don't care about her anymore, Tanner assured himself, shoving his chair to the floor with a clatter.

What the hell difference could one more lie make?

Kate closed the bedroom door in her mother's glowering face, turned, and slumped against it. Her legs didn't want to support her, her feet didn't want to move, but she forced them to, her knees finally cracking the wooden bedstead. Flopping to her stomach, she buried her face in the downy coverlet.

Dear God.

Tanner Barkley. In this trifling, puny nothing of a town. Tanner Barkley.

Wrenching to a sit, she yanked off her right boot and

flung it against the wall. She had avoided him for a year and a half. Except for a few haphazard confrontations. Outside Palmer's Antiques: willowy redhead. On the lawn of Capital Square: petite brunette. Chisom Taylor's ball: voluptuous blonde. Spring races. Hmm . . . she squinted, wound a strand of hair about her finger. Ah. Another blonde.

With a yank, Kate hurled the other boot to the floor.

Groaning, she slumped to her side, thrust her head beneath a feather pillow. The casing reeked of lemon verbena. Her mother loved lemon verbena. All at once, Kate felt like retching. Or leaping from the upper porch she had glimpsed from the walkway below.

What was she going to do? What in the world was she going to do?

Buck up, Kate. You shared a stagecoach with him. For over three hours.

Yes, that was true. The longest three hours of her life. To avoid looking at him, she'd recorded the number of scuff marks on her boots, identified every variety of shrub among the frost-covered tangle they passed, and calculated the latest interest rates in her head.

But as the coach bounced, so had her gaze.

Tanner looked dreadful. Emaciated. Pale blue eyes hollow in their sockets, normally bronze skin the color of chalk. Arm supported by a dirty sling. A nasty red scar snaking beneath the heavy stubble on his chin. His good hand shaking as he lifted his cheroot—which he'd not asked permission to smoke—to his lips. The wind had snatched it from his fingers and thrust it, smoldering angrily, atop her paisley shawl.

Stomach churning, she wrapped her arms around her waist and hugged tight. What did it matter? She hated Tanner. She really did. But she didn't delight in his looking so frail. Crazy when, not so long ago, she'd wished to see him at his worst: strung from the highest limb in Richmond, dragged down Bank Street behind a galloping horse, tarred and feathered and forced to run naked through Town Market. *Naked.* She shivered and closed her eyes as an image of his muscular physique, as clear as any daguerreotype, popped, unwelcome, into her mind.

Scratch the tar-and-feather idea. Kate could almost visualize the mob of tittering women, plucking feathers and pinching Tanner's tarred behind. She punched the pillow, clenched her fist tighter, and punched again.

And his face, still so handsome that when she'd gotten her first good look—a shaft of light spilling over him, making him appear all innocent and golden—a breath of air, thick as cotton, almost choked her.

Kate flung the pillow to the floor and let her gaze rove the dim room. Faded doilies and somber furniture hemmed her in, made her dreadfully breathless. Oh, and the colorless prospect of marrying Crawford—a man she did not love. A man who had requested an answer upon her return to Richmond. A debacle she'd fumbled once before, maladroitly, but with a sincere measure of naiveté. At the time, true love had monopolized her thoughts. Now, naiveté could not be blamed. Fear, perhaps, but not naiveté.

But why, dear God why, did the same man seem to be once again standing in her way?

"Sweetheart, tell me you didn't."

Charlotte Chase pressed her lips to her husband's shoulder and snuggled against him. The teasing scent of leather drifted from his skin. He released an exasperated groan, but slid his hand from her knee to her waist, drawing her in. She smiled. Perhaps this wasn't going to be so bad after all. "You've been busy writing the feature on"—she kissed his chin—"Harriet Beecher Stowe and"—the corner of his mouth—"with the amount of work here, I just figured—"

"You just figured you'd stick your nose in Miss Peters's business," Adam finished, disgust lacing his words.

She sighed. "If you must put it so bluntly, I suppose, yes."

"Oh, Charlie."

"Oh, Charlie, nothing. This will keep Kate occupied while she's here. The project interested her very much. Besides, September was the last time you tabulated our subscription accounts. Heavens, she's a bookkeeper in Richmond, perfectly qualified to review our piddly records. A bookkeeper when she can find work, that is."

"I hear the edge. Another crusade for the independent woman?"

"No, but"—she tapped her fingernail against his chest—"you should have seen her mother's face scrunch up nice and tight when I suggested it. Tongue clicking against those hard-edged teeth. Mrs. Peters is as likely to approve of her daughter as she is to sprout wings and fly to the moon. Plus, I like Kate. She has spirit." *She shook my hand when she met me,* Charlie remembered, laughing softly.

"Wait till Mrs. Peters realizes Tanner is in town. They'll hear her shrieking on her flight to the moon."

Charlie popped up on her elbow. "Tanner? How do you know about Tanner and Kate?"

"Came across them clawing at each other by the stagecoach. Pretty obvious something was going on. No woman would be that angry unless emotions were bubbling just beneath the surface."

"Just tell me, did you get any information out of him?"

"Tanner said they knew each other before, something about a newspaper article. He lied to her, tried to explain things, I guess. Hell, I don't know for sure. The man looked ready to pitch to the floor. I didn't ask anything else about it.''

"Why get a boy to do a man's job?" she muttered. "And you waited this long to tell me?"

He slipped his hand around hers, squeezed. "Yes, I waited. I wanted to avoid some harebrained scheme. Like this one. Tanner just happens to stop by the office to write an editorial and who is there but Kate Peters, doing the subscription accounts for the newspaper.''

Mercy, he knows me well, Charlie thought and plopped to her side, the bed ropes squeaking in protest. "Well, she does have quite a mathematical mind. Even Mrs. Peters said so, and she wasn't giving praise, I can tell you. Intelligent *and* beautiful. What more could the woman want in a daughter?''

"Yeah, well, you know that old crow. I guess Kate told you about Tanner, huh?"

Charlie grinned. "Not exactly. I mentioned that we had a guest for the holidays she might enjoy meeting. Both unmarried, attractive. I thought I would give it a go." She ignored her husband's amused snort. "Anyway, Kate told me that she knew our guest and had no wish to know him any better, thank you very much.''

Adam stiffened. "You didn't invite her to your damned tree-decorating party, did you? I already told Tanner about it—"

"Of course, I invited her. You know how I hate those things—even my own. Pointy pinkie fingers and fragile china I always end up breaking. Dry wafers getting stuck in my throat. I figure Kate will throw a few sparks in and brighten this one a little.''

"Charlotte Chase, are you trying to kill me before I make it to thirty-four?"

"Of course not. But what's wrong with having a little fun and helping true love along the way?"

"Didn't look at *all* like love to me—looked like a bad case of the hates." He laughed and pressed a kiss to her brow. "True love? Tanner Barkley and Katherine Peters? Sweetheart, I think you've lost what's left of your mind."

Chapter Two

Kate slid her spectacles into place, adjusted a curved arm behind each ear, and plunged into the ragged rows of numbers before her. Her mother kept the worst record book she had ever seen. Blotches of black ink stained every sheet; the pages were wrinkled and torn. Figures consistently miscalculated or simply left out. Nevertheless, it presented a creative challenge, much like designing bonnets did for her mother. Moreover, it kept Kate's mind from scuffling with her disturbing predicament.

With a deceptively merry doorbell jingle and a deep laugh that brought to mind images she'd hoped were long dead, Kate's disturbing predicament strolled into the millinery, the scent of lilacs and leather trailing just behind. Kate's hand jerked, her rapid progress across the page skidding to a halt.

"Why, thank you, Mr. Barkley. I didn't know how I was going to open the door carrying this load of Christmas packages." A tinkling voice, witlessness oozing from every breathy word. *My, he attracts them like flies to honey—or manure,* Kate thought and gripped the pen until her knuckles whitened.

"My pleasure, ma'am. I'll just put them on the counter. I'll even help you carry them to your buggy if need be."

Kate recorded the last set of numbers in a faltering scribble, merely because they still sat in her mind. How she'd arrived at them she could not recall, but she could see them clearly enough, even if they were a bit red tinged. Three, six, nine.

"Mr. Barkley, surely you've seen a pointsettia before. From Charleston." Kate heard the faint shuffle of leaves, an enticing laugh. "Takes a special . . . *touch* to keep them happy. Lots of darkness, a little pampering. Much like . . . "

Tanner laughed at whatever the woman whispered, their voices overlapping, intertwining, becoming a mindless warble in her ears. Kate clenched her teeth and pressed down hard on the final curve of the six. Ink spurted across the page, dribbled from the tablet to mahogany. "Damn."

"Tsk, tsk, Kat. Such language," Tanner said, amusement riding high in his voice.

Kate dabbed at the puddle of ink, then rose, forcing a look of indifference to her face. For the benefit of the woman at Tanner's side, she curled her lips. "Can I help you, Mr. Barkley?"

Tanner bent over the counter, poked at a taffy-filled cornucopia. After a moment, he cocked a chin naked of yesterday's heavy stubble and caught her gaze. Unwrapping a piece of candy, he popped it into his mouth and rolled the wrapper into a ball between his thumb and forefinger. He blinked, ridiculously long lashes brushing his skin, jaw flexing as he chewed. "I hoped you could, Kat. I need ribbon." He paused, considered a moment, chewing slowly. "Red. About a yard."

Kate swallowed, tasting the remnants of her morning

cup of coffee. "Don't tell me you need to purchase a lover's trinket at this early date? Been in town, oh"—she tipped the watch pinned at her waist—"thirty hours."

He shrugged his good shoulder, flicked the wadded wrapper to the floor. "Certainly, entertainment is hard to come by in this"—he glanced at the package-laden woman glued to his side, flashed a charming smile, then looked back at Kate, his smile thinning—"well, let's just say I work quickly."

Kate worked hard to keep her smile in place, felt it slip, and dropped her chin, staring at his chest. A tattered wool coat hung from his shoulders, the sleeves dangling past his wrists. Strange. Tanner had always taken an almost feminine interest in his attire. "Nice clothing," she said, looking up, pleasure flooding her as she watched his lips flatten, his eyes narrow.

The woman at Tanner's side released a sigh of impatience—clearly finished permitting another woman to govern the male attention in the room—and swept a lock of white blond hair from her face. She looked from Tanner to Kate and back again. Her gaze traveled to the top of Kate's head, inches above her own, then settled on Kate's spectacles. "You must be Katherine, Mrs. Peters's daughter. She's told me so much about you. I'm Lila Dane Walker. Of course, your mother's mentioned me. I'm her best customer."

"Yes, of course she has." Katherine lifted her hand above the counter. "I'm sorry to have you wait, but I don't know a thing about bonnets."

Lila glanced at Kate's ink-stained fingers, raised her gloved hand, hesitantly.

Tanner laughed. "Shake it, Mrs. Walker. Masculine affectation. Suffragette pretense. Don't worry—the impudence won't rub off. Thick skin holds it in."

Kate shot him a sharp look. *Shut up, you.*

He arched a brow, one corner of his mouth kicking.

Again, Lila glanced from one to the other, confusion skipping across her face.

Kate sighed and rolled her eyes, itching to jerk Lila's creeping hand over the counter. Finally, Lila grasped the tips of Kate's fingers, wagged once, and dropped the offensive digits as if they burned her skin.

The formalities taken care of, Kate turned, said sharply, "Mother, Mrs. Walker is here."

"One moment, dear," her mother called.

Kate pressed her hand to her stomach. One moment. One moment in hell was what it felt like. She could *smell* him from here. Smoke and leather. And man. She knew his scent, really knew it, had tucked it into her memories, a sliver beneath her skin. If she had to, she could select it from a thousand others. Easy when it used to cling to her clothes, to her hair, to her skin. To her sheets.

Horribly vivid images assaulted her as it traveled from her nostrils to her brain.

Please, Mother. Please hurry, she whispered and turned to face the couple, whose mingled laughter crowded the small shop.

"Why, Mr. Barkley, just for a newspaper article? And all that with a broken arm?"

"I didn't break the arm, darling. Someone shot a hole through it."

"Shot?" Kate gasped, leaning forward before she could stop herself.

Tanner's pale blue eyes shifted to her, held. Until a subtle cough forced a break. He turned, smiled into Lila's upturned face, shrugged.

Lila twisted the beaded fringe dangling from her purse around her finger. "All this craziness over a newspaper. Grief! My family is in a *respectable* business." She lifted her chin. "Banking."

Tanner slipped a cheroot from his coat pocket, grasped it between his teeth. "Respectable? I'm not sure I agree, although my family's heart pumps along the same veins." He leaned, dipping the twisted tip into a sconce sitting atop the counter.

Lila frowned at his obvious lack of courtesy and waved her hand before her face. "Veins? Is your father a doctor?" She coughed, low and dainty, to no avail.

What an idiot, Kate thought with a half turn, focusing her attention on the drooping ribbon hanging from the poinsettia's basket. Unwilling to discuss Tanner's family with him, she could not deny her curiosity about them. Beyond the basics, he had never told her anything about himself.

"Doctors?" He shook his head, laughing. A bit of gray ash drifted from his cheroot. "No doctors. Banking. My grandfather, my father. God help me, even my poor brother."

Lila preened, spiked up on her toes in rapture. And interest. "A *large* bank?"

"Fairly." He blew a breath of smoke in Kate's direction, although his gaze remained on the woman standing too close to his side. "Sloane-Barkley."

"Sloane-Barkley?" Lila frowned, heels slapping the floor. "I've never heard of them."

"Sloane-Barkley," Kate repeated, choking on a whiff of smoke. *Sloane-Barkley?* Tanner's family was the Barkley in *Sloane-Barkley?* Stocks and bonds Sloane-Barkley? Textbook case study Sloane-Barkley? And the little blond imbecile, her mother's best customer, had never even heard of them? Dear God.

"Something wrong, Kat?"

She swung her head up. "Wrong? What could possibly be wrong, Mr. Barkley?"

"Just thought I saw a hint of surprise cross your face." He scrutinized as he spoke, then forced a smile in place.

"Surprise? Why *shouldn't* surprise cross my face? You never told me anything. About yourself, about your family. You could be a traveling circus performer for all I know. A gypsy. Oh, no, let me guess. A newspaperman. A newspaperman who is an heir to a small banking fortune." She snapped her fingers. "Oh, yes, that's it."

"Sorry to find you gave up the heir for—what is his name again? Crawford?"

She flinched and turned and walked out the back door before a complete thought could form in her mind. The wind snatched her skirts as she crossed the weed-choked alley behind the row of shops and elbowed past a string of prickly shrubs, ripping her sleeve on a stubborn branch. Beginning to shiver, she started running. Ran until her lungs ached, until her skin stung. Cotton stockings and thin wool did little to protect her, even worse with a faint layer of perspiration dampening her skin.

Damn him. She bowed at the waist, gulping air. Memories, and pain, flooded her mind. *Damn him.* She yanked her spectacles from her face and rubbed her eyes, her hand trembling. The sound of pounding footfalls reached her ears.

"Kat? What the hell are you doing?"

She whipped around. "You bastard," she cried and flung her spectacles at him.

Tanner stepped back, dropped his gaze to his feet. Stooping, he slipped his arm from his sling and extricated the silver frames from the dirt. The wind lifted his hair, whipped it against his face.

"Tell me you didn't come out the back door," she said, disturbed to find her voice shaking as much as the rest of her.

Cleaning her spectacles against his sleeve, he cocked a brow. "How else do you think I got out here?"

Dear God, she wanted to hurt him. Wipe that taunting half smile from his lips; lower his hitched brow with her fist. Before she'd met him, she had never once imagined hitting a man, kicking him . . . well, in the nether region. "My mother. Did you see my mother?" Feeling like a naughty child, Kate nonetheless implored: *Say no. Please say no.*

"See her? Why, she's holding my cheroot for me."

Fury ripped through Kate. "I hate you," she screamed and rushed at him, slamming her fist into his shoulder. She heard his grunt of pain as they stumbled to the ground. Pummeling his chest, she closed in on his neck, teeth bared and snapping. Gasping for breath, she flailed, legs kicking, arms swinging. He captured them between his, halting her struggles. As black began to spot her vision, she dropped her head to the ground, tried to draw the meager amount of air her corset would allow into her lungs.

"Easy, Kat. I was only joking," she thought she heard him say.

The air worked its magic, confusion flowing out, awareness flowing in. Awareness of his body, pressing into hers from knee to chest. His warm breath cuffing her cheek, his solid heartbeat, drumming chest to chest with hers. She groaned, turned her face into the grass, smelled dirt and winter and him. "I hate you," she said, voice breaking for real this time.

His arms tensed, his chest hitched midbreath. "I hate you too, you little witch."

She bit the inside of her cheek, tasted blood, concentrated on it. Finally, this pain outweighed any other. Outweighed the feeling of him lying atop her. A familiar enough sensation to send a spiral of desire through her mind, her body. She tensed. "Get off me."

Tanner sighed, and finally, his weight lifted. Kate rolled her head, flicked her lids, blinked when bright sunlight spilled into her eyes. He braced his elbows on either side of her; his snapping blue eyes fixed firmly on her face. She dug her backbone into the ground to escape. A moist chill seeped through wool, producing a shiver she could not suppress.

"What the hell is wrong with you? Running out here in this skimpy getup?" His chest rose and fell, misty air surging from his lips. "Are you really this distressed to find you let a better prospect than your beloved Crawford get away?"

"Get away? Where did you get the idiotic idea I let *you* go? Your duplicity pushed me away."

"Well, you didn't grieve for long."

Grieve? For months, every time she'd closed her eyes, images of Tanner were there, taunting her. Galloping beside her, hair gleaming as richly as his sorrel's dark coat. Daring her to make love in a field of wildflowers along the banks of the James River. Teaching her to play chess and grinning with delight the first time she beat him. Winking at her across a crowded dance floor, a circle of admirers surrounding him, the gentle play of pleasure curving his lips reserved for her.

Or so she had believed. Foolish belief. Foolish woman.

She jerked beneath him, placed her hands against his chest, and shoved. "Get off me, I said. Get off me now."

He shook his head and leaned in, shifted, settling between her thighs. She felt him then, long and hard. And hot. Purposely, she'd bet. He wanted to draw her in, wanted to remind her what it had been like between them. But she remembered well enough without his blunt provocation. To prove it, her desire no longer crept—it raced.

He whispered near her ear, "Remember the first time I kissed you?" He laughed softly, his breath warming her skin. "The vacant storeroom at the Governor's Ball." He nipped at the edge of her jaw. "We slipped away into that darkened corner." He sucked her skin between his teeth, and a groan slipped from his throat. "The first time I realized how tall you were. An astonishing realization." He ground his hips against hers. "We fit well together, Kat. A perfect fit."

She expelled a breath. "I forgot you two years ago. Forgot all that."

He lifted his head, his eyes glowing, sapphire blue. As she watched, his face paled beneath a passionate flush, intensifying the crooked scar on his chin. "You've forgotten? Well, damn you, I haven't." Angry now, his hands skimmed her neck, her face, tangled in her hair, turning her head as he fit his mouth to hers.

"Open for me, Princess. I want to kiss you, really kiss you." His lips moved against hers. Gentle, soft.

Feeling a measure of surprise at her weakness, she started to, knowing she would be lost.

Suddenly, he swayed and lifted his head. Just enough for her to peer into a chalk-pale face. He lowered his brow to hers, shadows obscuring her view. Warm skin. Too warm. Moist. With a jolt of alarm, she realized he leaned against her to steady himself. She shifted. "Mr. Barkley?"

A violent shudder shook him. "Miss . . . Peters." A bead of sweat rolled from his face to hers. It burned across her cheek, trailed into her hair.

"Are you ill?"

He managed a laborious, choking laugh, but nothing more.

"Please, if you're ill," she whispered, growing more distressed. She had known he was, ever since she watched him climb into the stagecoach with uncharacteristic caution. "If you're ill, you must let me see what's wrong." No matter how much she hated the man, she could not let him suffer in some field behind her mother's shop.

Groaning, Tanner rolled to his back, flopped his arm across his face. Kate shoved to her knees, frantically searching his shoulders, chest, arms.

Dear God. Blood soaked the bandage circling his injured arm, trickled in a thin line down his wrist and between his fingers, coating the grass beneath his palm red.

Tears sprang to her eyes, blurring her vision, stinging her lids as she tried to blink them back. She bit her bottom lip and tasted tobacco and him. She rose to her feet, knees shaking. "I think you need . . . I think you need a doctor. I'll go get a doctor."

Against his brow, he clenched his fingers into a fist, veins protruding, muscles flexing. "No. All I need is . . . a drink."

"Are you crazed? You're bleeding. You need a *doctor*."

Tanner's chest rose on a weak breath; then he smiled, a flimsy show of white teeth and mulishness. His fist shook, so he closed it tighter. "I need a . . . woman. And if you won't . . . oblige me, there is one . . . at the saloon. She calls me Cowboy."

Kate stumbled back, as wounded as he looked. Deep in her chest—right below the blood smeared across her bodice—she felt as if the wind had been knocked right out of her. She blinked, pressed the heels of her hands into her eyes. "When did you get this cruel? When?"

He flung his arm from his face, fixed her with a cold gaze. "Cruel? Why, after you, sweetheart."

Turning, she plowed through the shrubs, caring little if her dress got ripped to shreds, telling herself she cared little if Tanner bled to death in the damned field behind her mother's shop. She bowed her head, praying she had gotten away before he saw the tears streaming down her face, and dashed toward the newspaper office.

*   *   *

"You damn fool." Adam's shadow spilled over the table, shading Tanner.

Tanner waved him away with a flick of his wrist and blinked against the sudden darkness. "Fool? What da' you know?"

"I've been looking for you for over an hour, Tan. Did you see the doctor?"

He laughed and hooked his ankles atop a chair, his heels dangling off the edge. The chair wobbled and he wobbled with it. "Let Cowboy-lover take care ovit. May let her take care ovit all." He raised his glass in salute and emptied it in one swallow.

"Kate came to see me. Right after she left you apparently."

Tanner straightened, clumsily untangled his boots, and dropped his feet to the floor. "Cowboy-lover!" He grinned as Doris twitched her generous hips, skirted tables, pinching fingers, and grasping arms, and slipped into his lap, rosy lips drawn, exposing teeth the color of fresh corn.

"Hey, Cowboy." Leaning forward, she poured more whiskey in Tanner's glass.

"Howdy, darlin'." Tanner slipped his good arm around her waist. Somewhat fleshy, not as lean and tight as his princess, but she would do. He sniffed. No scent of sandalwood and cinnamon. No ink stains on her fingers. Or eyes the color of whiskey and violent sunsets.

"Doris, get off his lap. *Now*. And, Tanner, what in the name of God is that stupid-looking sling?"

"Cowboy, you gonna let him say my sling is stupid looking? I ripped apart a new petticoat for that thang. Broderie anglaise and all."

"Don't talk to her like that. Prettiest sling I ever saw." Still he gave her a firm shove, a bit relieved. Doris's substantial weight, coupled with the cloying scent of sweat and perfume, was beginning to offend the dry part of his brain. "Later, darling, later. Me an' Newspaperboy gotta talk."

With an eager hug and a clumsy hop, Doris departed, navigating the maze of immodest groping and brazen cat-calls.

"Chrissakes, Tanner." Adam yanked his fingers through his hair and flung himself into a chair.

"What? What? What?" Tanner took a sip of whiskey, his gaze roving the room. He would be damned, double damned, triple damned, if he'd let Kat Peters tangle him up in the deadly knots she had before. Or let his best friend push him around. Go whining, would she? Well, she could go whining to the whole town for all he cared. Go whining and—

"What's that in your pocket?"

Pocket? Tanner raised a hand and plucked at his shirt. Probably a frilly trinket Cowboy-lover had—

Oh . . . he'd forgotten about those. He dropped his arm, shrugged. "Nothing."

"Kate's spectacles." Adam slapped his hand to the table. "Give them to me."

"No."

"She's coming over early tomorrow, before the party, to help Charlie make Christmas decorations. I'll return them to her." A persistent tap against wood. "Give them to me."

"I said no!" Tanner jerked to his feet, his chair banging against the wall. "I'll be there. I can . . . I can give 'em to her." Except he did not want to see her, did he? God, he hoped he didn't.

"From the looks of things, you don't need to get near her, and she doesn't need to get near you."

"Don't interfere, Adam. Not in this." Of course, Adam

was right. He didn't need to get near her. He *knew* that. He just didn't like anyone *telling* him not to get near her.

Adam slid his hand in a lazy circle, dark gaze probing. "You're here, bloody and drunk, and she's out, or *was* out, riding my horse hell-bent for leather. Why shouldn't I interfere?"

Tanner bolted a step forward, upsetting the table. The whiskey bottle danced off the edge and shattered on the floor. Jagged shards of glass crunched beneath Tanner's boots as the smell of whiskey surrounded him. "Taber? You let her ride Taber?"

Adam grimaced and stood, pulling soaked cloth from his legs. He shook one foot, then the other. "For the love of . . . " He rounded the overturned table, grasped Tanner's shoulder, and propelled him across the crowded saloon.

"Careful, Newspaperboy, careful."

"Doesn't your precious Doris know you're a news-paperboy?"

"I'm a *newspaperman*," Tanner said and stumbled past the swinging doors with a hop and lurch. He stopped his forward motion thanks to a wooden post and an uneven board wedged against the toe of his boot. His arm circled the post, tangling in a strand of ivy garland, and knocking a holly wreath to the ground. He pressed his brow against rough wood, the boardwalk tilting beneath his feet. *Jesus, for a breath of air not tainted with the scent of pine.* "Damn decorations."

A strong grasp steadied him. "Can you make it down?"

He nodded. Peeling off the post, he righted himself with more strength than he would have imagined he possessed.

"You want me to get a wagon, Tan?"

"No, no. No wagon."

"Doc Olden—"

"No doctor." Tanner yanked his fingers through his hair, pulled his damp collar from his neck.

"Your arm—"

"I popped a few stitches is all. The bleeding stopped hours ago."

"But—"

"To the homestead, Mr. Chase." He tumbled off the boardwalk, a fresh layer of sweat glazing his skin with each step. He needed to get off his feet before he landed on his face in the dirt.

Adam muttered a curse and caught up to him. Tanner shook off the hand that crept beneath his elbow.

Moonlight washed over them, throwing tilted shadows across their path. Dry footfalls and the occasional squeal of a passing wagon were the only sounds. Tanner watched his breath cloud before his eyes and wondered why his world felt as if it was shattering at his feet. Same as his mother's Bristol glass goblet—the one he had thrown at his brother after a particularly rousing childhood argument.

"Kate was very upset when she came to see me, Tan."

Tanner's steps faltered. He dug the heel of his boot into a wheel groove, spoke so softly he barely heard his words. "I never intended to hurt her, you know."

A step ahead, Adam paused, turned.

"I was investigating a story. Falsified government contracts. Bribery. Involved a family business, which I in-infiltrated. Asher Incorporated. You may 'member the name—one of your father's associates, I think. Anyway, I met Kat at a company banquet or party or something. Before either one of us realized it, we were spending a lot of time together. Walks along the river, intimate dinners at a small restaurant I frequented, three-hour chess matches." He laughed. "She was a damn good chess player. Anyway, I didn't tell her. I never had the chance to tell her ...

about the investigation. Didn't tell her anything about the newspaper. Just acted like I worked for Asher, nothing more, nothing less.'' He kicked a lump of dirt into the withered scrub brush lining the road. "Except there was more to it than her just working for Asher. She"—he glanced at Adam, then at his feet—"she was supposed to marry him.''

"*Marry* him?''

"Sounds really bad, doesn't it?''

Adam rubbed his hand across his mouth and closed his eyes on a worn sigh. "Tell me you didn't use her for information.''

"I didn't. God, Adam, I found more than enough on my own,'' he said and lurched forward.

An accusing silence, fraught with guilt and the severe snap of half-frozen straw, settled between them.

Adam cupped his hands around his mouth and blew into them. "She found out by reading your article? Couldn't you have told her first, before the damn thing went to press?''

Tanner paused, tilted his head, and gazed at the sky. Thousands of stars, more than he had ever seen, winked from black velvet folds. "I went to my editor with the story, told him everything. How I infiltrated the company . . . about my friendship with Kat . . . that I needed time. One week. I asked him to wait to print. He agreed to give me a blessed week. The next morning I . . . we . . . Kat and I had a luncheon appointment. I dressed, opened the newspaper over coffee and . . .'' He shook his head, unable to finish.

"He printed.''

A grim laugh burst from Tanner's mouth. "Under my byline in bold black letters. Largest type I'd ever been given.''

"Couldn't you have explained it to her? Did you even try?''

"Of course, I tried. Pleaded. Me"—he rapped his chest— "Tanner Barkley. *Pleading.* With a woman. Went rushing to her house, all the way there practicing all these desperate explanations. Been planning to tell her for weeks. Gathering courage to tell her, I guess." Tanner didn't mention arriving at the *Times* office later that day, drunker than he had ever been in his life, arguing with his editor, breaking the bastard's nose. Or stumbling into the jeweler's on Tenth Street and picking up his grandmother's engagement ring—resized to fit Kat's dainty finger. A ring now sitting in the top drawer of his desk. "Kat was pretty coldhearted. Returned my letters. Refused my calling cards, which I had to dig out of my moldy university trunk, mind you. Threw a rock at my head from a second-story window. Hell, I even sent a telegraph to her crab of a mother."

"Mrs. Peters?"

"Who else?"

Adam clapped his hands over his eyes. "Heaven help us all."

"Come to think of it, she *wasn't* pleased to see me this morning."

Adam groaned. "Charlie's decorating party is going to have more spark than she can handle."

"What?"

"Nothing. Nothing." Adam dropped his hands by his side, shoulders slumping. "So you haven't spoken with Kate since then?"

"No. Except a distant greeting at some fancy ball. Outside a shop. A crowded street. And only if I sneak up on her. Catch her unaware. If she sees me coming, forget about it."

"You could try again."

"No, I damn well will not try again. Not after she ran right out and hooked old Crawford like a limp fish. I know

I hurt her when she deserved honesty. But at the time, I didn't think I could afford to give it. I also know the blame lies with me, yet . . . " Yet he'd come to think she had hurt him even worse than he had hurt her. She hadn't been the fool who fell in love, left holding an empty bag of dreams for the future. And an engagement ring he could not even bear to lock away in his bank deposit box.

They continued along the road through a dense copse of towering loblolly pines. Moonlight lit the path in scattered patches, but Tanner followed Adam, stepping blindly, not sure how far they were from the house.

"Left here, Tan."

They turned onto a narrow drive, centered by a rounded ridge of brown grass. Tanner forced himself to place one foot in front of the other, focused on the flickering light showing through a slit in a curtain. A crisp breeze raised damp hair from his collar. He coughed, shivered. Glancing to the side, he caught Adam's frown.

Looking away, Tanner searched the shadowed porch, finding two empty rocking chairs and a large orange cat. "She's not here, is she?" he asked and blinked, the edges of his vision fading. If he made a fool of himself, collapsed or some stupid thing, he didn't want to do it in front of Kat. If he woke to find her touching him, gazing at him with those mysterious amber eyes, he honestly didn't know what he might do.

"No, she's not here. I met her at the livery, looking . . ." Adam halted, stuttering and fidgeting with the lapel of his coat. "She looked a bit wild-eyed. Big John didn't have any horses available, so I let her take Taber. I remember what I endured with Charlie. I thought it might help her to ride. Always helped me."

A flash of anger flared in Tanner's belly. "She doesn't need your damn horse. She's fine. More than fine. Crawford-what's-it sees to that."

"Tan, she didn't look fine. She looked frantic. Blood on her dress, her hair tangled. Grass, leaves stuck in it. I don't know what happened today. I won't ask. Somehow, you have this all mixed up in your mind. I think she cares more than you believe she does. More than I believed she did. Charlie . . . Oh, never mind."

Tanner stared across rolling hills awash in silver moonlight, his mind reeling. Still cared? His gut tightened. Could it be possible? After what he had done to her? Isn't that why he had followed her behind her mother's shop? A test. Baiting her, waiting to see her reaction. No, well . . . *yes*.

Only, the pain on her face had been a surprise. Anger, he had expected. But pain? Could it compare to the pain he felt every time he looked at her? Thought of her?

Dammit, was it possible *he* still cared?

No. *Oh, no.* The only women he cared about were the ones who didn't expect more than a silver coin or two the next morning. Women like Doris, who didn't have the power to rip a man's heart from his chest. Besides, Kat loved this Crawford person, didn't she? Hell, she was probably redecorating her bridal suite at this very moment.

"Pain confuses memories, Tan. And believe me, time will not lift a finger to correct the mistakes. You have to do that yourself."

Tanner shrugged. "Confused or not, memories are part of the past, and I don't want any part of the past." Flashing amber eyes and cinnamon-scented skin. Damp sheets and teasing smiles. Unreserved laughter and genuine friendship. The anguish, the deafening despair, he had felt when he realized he'd lost her. "Huh-uh. No, thanks."

"If you believe that, Tan," Adam whispered, skepticism evident in his voice.

"I believe it. Don't you worry—I believe it."

Except his heart was not so sure.

Chapter Three

A fierce gust of wind ripped across the porch, loosening the chignon at the nape of Kate's neck, slinging strands of hair into her face. She plopped her basket on the scarred planks, slammed her ruched silk bonnet atop her head, and tied the ribbon beneath her chin with a firm tug and twist. When her mother arrived at the Chase's after closing the millinery, she would take one look at Kate, click her tongue in that bothersome way, and insist her daughter recoil the lopsided lump of hair into some semblance of order. Then she'd try to follow her to the nearest mirror to make sure she did it.

Kate took a deep breath and lifted her hand, disturbed to see her fingers quivering. Two fainthearted raps on wood. Strangely enough, no elaborate knocker graced the door, just a trailing ivy wreath. Her mother had mentioned, on more than one occasion, the lack of pretense surrounding the wealthiest couple in Edgemont. Kate considered this praise; her mother did not.

Footfalls echoed, followed by a gusty laugh. Kate squared her shoulders, reclaimed the basket, and veiled her trembling hands in the generous folds of woven flannel overlapping the edges.

Calm down, Kate. You can do this.

Can I? Can I endure an evening of flirtatious foolishness, watching every woman over twelve and under eighty disintegrate into a witless dither? Can I forget Tanner kissed me—albeit a brief, feeble kiss—and how I burst into flames like a pile of dry hay? Can I—

The door flew open, banged against the wall.

"Oh, Kate, I'm glad you're here," Charlie said, tugging her inside. She kicked the door closed with her heel, the swirl of black atop her head flying in all directions.

"Hello," Kate replied, somewhat confounded by the exuberant greeting.

Charlie bounced on her toes, plucked Kate's shawl from her shoulders, and flung it on the hall tree's highest hook. Helplessly, Kate's gaze jumped from her hostess's tattered sweater to the black trousers hugging her lean hips. Charlie caught the look, threw back her head, and emitted a bark of laughter more suited to a sailor than a woman whose nose barely reached Kate's bosom.

"Don't worry. I'll change into an appropriate gown for the party. I think you may be a little early or, heavens, I'm a little late. Can you imagine the reception I would likely receive from your mother wearing this?" Charlie's eyes widened as her hand flew to her mouth. She took a step forward. "Hellfire, I didn't leave her on the porch, did I?"

Kate halted, the basket perched in midair, a burst of laughter as indecorous as Charlie's slipping from her. "No. No." She gasped, pressed the back of her hand to her lips, the basket to her stomach. "She had to close the shop."

Charlie smiled, shrugged one slim shoulder. "Oh, good. I mean, uh . . . " A blush worked its way across her cheeks.

Kate waved her off. "Believe me. I understand. I love my mother, but she . . . she's a rather staunch defender of appropriate feminine conduct. If it makes you feel any better, she's quite disappointed by my refusal to act like a brainless ninny when it would work so much better for me. The old adage about attracting more flies with honey, I imagine."

Charlie leaned over the basket, flipped the flannel aside. "Oh, gingerbread, a pecan tea cake." She poked around. "What are these?" She drew her hand out, holding a wrapped ball between her fingers.

"My mother calls them Secrets. Bonbons with a note inside. A parlor game they played when she was a girl. A *suitable* parlor game, she says."

Charlie walked backward a few steps, flipping the ball from one hand to the other. "Parlor games! I hadn't even thought of it. And your mother did, bless her heart. You know, she believes I can't organize a real party. I guess she's right. I'm treating this like an indoor picnic in December, and imagine, she wanted to lend me her china." She winked and turned, her warm laughter echoing down the hallway.

Kate followed close behind, her kid leather boots creating a whisper of sound compared to Charlie's black brogans and hooflike cadence. Stopping at the first open doorway, Kate peeked around the molded border. *Empty.* Her shoulders slumped as she released a breath she had not known she held. One room down. Her goal: the kitchen, where she hoped to hide for most of the evening.

Her gaze skipped from the maroon rug to the beam ceiling. At the back of the room, a fire blazed in a hearth of tan and black stone. Unusual. Part parlor, part den, furnished with a mixture of furniture and colorful bric-a-brac. Shaded silver sconces bathed the room in warm light—golden streaks gleaming off polished wood.

Kate walked forward, her face appearing in the bull's-eye mirror hanging above the stone mantel. She squinted, frowned. Pale skin, bonnet crooked. Plunking her basket on the nearest table, she bit her lip, pinched her cheeks, yanked the bonnet from her head, and smoothed her hair. A deep breath, yet her heart continued to bump against the wall of her chest with enough force to billow her bodice. Or so it felt anyway.

Why in the world should she care if a man who had once been her lover resided in this very house, right this very minute? Naturally, this situation occurred all the time. Polite society frowned upon such things, but a little frowning didn't keep them from happening. She was as sure of that as she was of the broad strip of sunlight spilling over the toe of her boot. Hell, she didn't need sunlight—*she* was proof.

Kate wrinkled her nose and stared hard at her reflection, seeing instead blue eyes and a lock of black hair falling across a smooth brow.

Her summer with Tanner had been a devilish, captivating period of her life. The only time God had thrown a boulder into her path and she had chosen to climb over it instead of retracing her steps. Although the boulder *had* disintegrated halfway up and she'd landed, quite painfully, on her rump.

Afterward, she had searched for something, *someone*, to heal her shattered heart. Searched for a thread of happiness in her life. She had looked, assessed, analyzed. At every party, on every street corner, even during preaching, she had appraised men. Looking for the rare jewel, clear facets, and a perfect cut. A jewel to ease her heartache. But one was too tall, another too short. Too skinny, too stupid. Wrong hair color, wrong eye color. Voice too deep,

voice too high. A kaleidoscope of dissatisfaction. Vexation
with this objective had encouraged her to accept Crawford's offer of friendship. And marriage offer or no, friendship it remained.

Tilting her chin, she smiled at herself in the mirror. She
would like to make Tanner suffer this time. The deceitful
scoundrel. Yes. She nodded. She could do it. Better him
than her. Or at least she could ignore him altogether.

She turned, feeling smugly determined, to find the
deceitful scoundrel watching her from the doorway.

He looked healthier. Color had returned, in part, to his
face. Shadows lurked, but not deep ones like before. The
promise of a beard darkened his hollowed cheeks, his firm
chin. A white bandage circled his arm; she could see it
peeking from a crisp cuff. He'd disposed of the crusty
sling. She squinted. Definitely his clothing. A black cutaway
coat sloped over broad shoulders, rounding out from a
lean waist. A checked waistcoat topped a chest she remembered well—one covered with thick hair and firm muscle.
Gray trousers braided in black set off a pair of mile-long
legs crossed at the ankle.

Oh, hell, she had *almost* forgotten his blessed good looks,
how splendidly packaged he was when he wanted to be.

Tanner smiled, slow and easy. "Like what you see?"

Pivoting on her heel, Kate plucked her basket from the
table, looped her arm through the handle. "Just thinking
that you're looking well, Mr. Barkley. New clothing, I see.
Interesting for a man who brought no trunks with him.
As you said, you *do* work quickly."

His face colored, a muscle in his jaw jumped. "Drop the
Mr. Barkley, will you?"

"So sorry, but I'm not willing to drop anything for you,"
she said and started forward.

He unlocked his ankles and stepped wide, blocking her
escape. "I wanted to apologize, dammit. For the other day.

I''—he flipped his coattail away and shoved his hand in his pocket—"I . . . um, the thing I said about the . . . "

"The harlot, Mr. Barkley."

No reply, only a narrowing of his eyes.

"I thought so."

A white rim appeared around his mouth. "Yes, that."

"That?"

"You know what I mean. String me up if it makes you feel better. I'm sorry is all."

"Why apologize for speaking truthfully?" She pinched a silk fingertip, tugged, and slid her glove from her hand. With effort, she shoved aside the disquieting picture of Tanner in another woman's arms. She tipped her head, forcing a smile. "Funny, I'll be damned if I thought you had it in you. To tell the truth, I mean."

"It wasn't the truth."

"You mean, there *is* no harlot."

"Well, no—"

"You mean, she didn't call you Cowboy or some such nonsense?"

His Adam's apple bobbed, a rosy circle bloomed on each cheek. "Well, no."

Kate pinched and tugged the other glove. "Oh. You mean you did not or"—she glanced down, then up, meeting his crystal blue glare—"you could not." She laughed behind a loose glove.

"I couldn't," he said between clenched teeth.

"Interesting." She shrugged. "I suppose."

"Isn't that exactly how you remember me, Kat? An inferior lover."

She flicked the silk glove against her palm and locked the smile in place. All the while, her stomach muscles tapped against her boned corset. "There have been so many since then I'm not sure I can accurately recall," she heard herself say. Now where had that come from?

Tanner ripped his hand from his pocket and stumbled forward. Kate stepped back. And back again, into a table, the wooden grove jamming into her spine. He grabbed the basket from her hand and tossed it to the floor. Closing in, he cupped her face in his palms, his fingers sliding into her hair. Either she trembled or he did—she wasn't sure which.

"How many, Kat? How many men have known you like I knew you?"

She shrugged, prayed he could not hear the wild beat of her heart. "Lovers—lovers are easy to come by, Mr. Barkley. Surely *you*, of all people, are not surprised by that."

He tipped her head, searched her face, analyzing her expression. A thin smile crossed his face and he leaned in quick, his breath cuffing her cheek. Tobacco. Mint. "You're lying. I can see it. Therefore, I will call your bluff. Lovers *are* easy to come by, sweet, but I don't think you speak from experience."

"How dare you . . . " She pressed back, frantic, having nowhere to go between hard wood and firm muscle. "How dare you question me when you've had a different flavor on your arm every time I've . . . " She snapped her mouth shut and dropped her gaze to the flawlessly knotted Byron resting in the hollow of his throat. *Easy, Kate. Don't let him into your mind. Take a deep breath and say something ugly to get him away from you.* She tried, but all that came out was: "You indiscriminate, presumptuous boor. How dare you."

"I do dare, Kat. Because I see the truth shining in your eyes. Like it or not, I *know* you." He shook her, causing her chignon to loosen, the knot of hair tumbling to her shoulder. "I know the taste of your lips, what the inside of your mouth feels like, how arousing the rough edge of your teeth scraping against my tongue is. I know how soft the hair on the inside of your thighs is, that you like your feet tickled and your fingers sucked, that you're afraid of spiders, but love snakes. I know you'll eat vanilla ice cream but refuse strawberry every time. I know you play a damned tough game of chess but throw a ball like a girl, can swim like a fish but hate fishing. I know the color your hair turns in the summer and the way your cheeks pink and freckle in the sun. I know what your face looks like, dreamy and lost, when you tighten around me. I know what color your eyes turn when you go over the edge. And you should know the same things about me, damn you. Ask yourself the same question, Princess. How dare *you* believe what you have believed for two years.'' His voice broke, his fingers curling, digging into her skin.

Dear God, she thought, astounded, bewildered—completely stunned. *Dear God.* She squeezed her hands into fists, snaring wool and silk between her fingers. Should she know him that well? Did she know him that well? She couldn't think, couldn't make her mind complete the circle. Not when it hurt this much. Warm, her skin was too warm, her knees too weak. She trembled, swayed toward him, self-doubt plaguing her.

She was a fool. After everything, a fool, to feel anything for this man.

Tanner jerked his head, awareness lighting his face. His gaze found hers, held. His hands clenched, crawled lower, closed around her elbows. He opened his mouth, his teeth stark white, his skin flushed. *"Princess."* Slowly, his head lowered. Black curls and soft lips, the scent of soap on his skin, blocked everything except the word ringing in her ears. Princess. Princess.

Princess.

First one glove, then the other, tumbled to the floor. Kate raised her arms, rammed her palms flat against his chest, and shoved him with surprising force. He lurched to the side, dazed, a big enough stumble to allow her to pass. She raced through the doorway, whacked her elbow against the wall.

Princess.

She clapped her hands over her ears, paused, teetering from one foot to the other. The sound of metal clanging. The kitchen. Surely—*please, God!*—he wouldn't follow her there.

The smell of burnt sugar smacked Kate in the face as she plunged into the humid room. She paused, stared, gulping air and fighting tears. Turning a slow circle, she stared at the destruction, a feeling of insensibility tugging at her. Flour and cinnamon lay sprinkled upon oak countertops like day-old snow with a good portion of dirt thrown in. A rolling pin lay half on, half off the counter, interrupted from its topple to the floor by a butter mold dribbling sticky gobs. Smashed raisins, slivers of apple, and two pulpy lumps of pumpkin lay on the floor.

Charlie stood in the middle of this confusion, calm and self-possessed, a bit soiled, a giddy grin earmarking her face. She shrugged and lifted a knife, shoved another across the table using the tip of her finger, as if she didn't want to touch it. "These are different. Hellfire, what the blazes are they for?"

Kate stepped forward, wringing her hands, ready to welcome debates about silverware or flying bats diving into her hair—anything that would redirect the turmoil, the dread, consuming her. She stumbled, snatched the knife from the table, and twirled it end over end. A distorted image of her face appeared in silver, pale and wide-eyed. She imagined her ears lifting as she listened for the echo of Tanner's step.

"Do you know what that one's for?"

Kate jerked. "Um, this one's for meat. Or fish maybe. I don't really know why they're different. Not a lesson I ever wanted to learn or did learn. I guess . . ." She sucked er bottom lip between her teeth to stop her babbling, gripped the knife, her knuckles cracking.

The kitchen door creaked, a board in the floor snapped. A heavy footfall and a voice that sent a shiver of dread racing along Kate's spine.

"Charlie, I thought you might—you might need this." Tanner stood in the doorway, Kate's basket dwarfed in his large palm, deep groves etching the sides of his mouth, his skin stretched taut over his cheeks. His head swung toward Kate. For a brief moment, a scorching blue hell burned into her from across the room. Then, with a sudden, rapid blink, it skipped away.

"Kate, your hand!" Charlie grabbed her arm.

Kate glanced at the glossy red bubble spurting from a gash on her finger. Come to think of it, she *had* felt a sharp prick about the time Tanner intruded. She flexed her hand, a line of blood coursing down her palm. For some reason, the situation struck her as funny, and she laughed.

Before she had time to think, or move, or speak, he appeared by her side. Lifting the knife from her hand, wrapping a crisp cotton handkerchief around her finger, his coattail flapping against her waist, his minty breath stealing into her nostrils. "Hold this. Tight. Until the bleeding stops. Don't release the pressure." Kate brushed his hand aside and flipped back the corner of the handkerchief. A monogram, stitched in black thread. TSB. She skimmed the pad of her thumb across the letters. Tanner Sloane Barkley, she now knew. Funny, she had never seen one of his handkerchiefs before. Might have raised questions he could not afford to answer.

"Are you all right," Charlie asked.

"I'm fine," she whispered, a growing circle of red staining the cloth as she pressed harder. Tears pricked her eyelids, burning, stinging. Oh, how she wished they were tears of pain. Her control nearly depleted, she grasped a the last bit by a flimsy thread, wishing Tanner did no stand so close that she could see the neat tucks in the wais of his trousers, the black braid edging the legs.

"Kat," he said, a gentle whisper for her ears alone.

She shook her head, refused to look at him, focused instead on the piece of apple touching his boot. "Go Please leave me alone. *Please.*"

A sound, somewhere between a groan and a sigh, rum bled low in his throat. He rocked back on his heels dropped his hand by his side, and curled his fingers int a fist.

Why did he have to smell so good? So clean and mascu line? So damned *familiar.*

Bulky black boots appeared beside Tanner's, squashed the apple sliver to bits. Charlie said, "Go on. I'll take care of this. A dab of my famous, foul Indian ointment, as my dear husband calls it, and she'll be good as new. Although she will stink for a while. You go find Adam and help him with that blessed tree. Remember moist sand in the bucket. Dig it in good and deep. And try not to break any branches."

Blinking rapidly, the first tear trickled down Kate's face, and paused on the curve of her cheek. *Hurry.*

"Go on, Tanner, scat. Adam's probably tearing his hair out by now."

"Fine," he said, pivoting on his heel and stomping across the room. He slapped the door open, his footfalls echoing, each heavy clomp a burst of sunshine penetrating a black cloud. The door rocked with disintegrating creaks, finally expiring like a spent breath.

Kate swiped her hand beneath her eyes and whispered a silent prayer for Charlie Chase.

"My, my, temper, temper. Men." Charlie laughed and peeled the cloth from Kate's finger, dabbed at a smudge of blood. "Not bad, at all. Probably won't even scar, if you're worried. My miracle salve will fix this up just fine. No need for tears."

Kate sniffed, wagged her head. "It's not that."

"I guessed as much. You don't look the kind to snivel about a stupid cut on your finger. I can see there is more to it. But, it's not my place to interfere. That said"— she tapped her ugly boot on the floor—"I would love to interfere if you'd let me."

Kate lifted her head, dried her face with a bell-shaped sleeve. "Forgive me. I don't have a handkerchief. Except for the bloody one wrapped around my finger."

Charlotte grinned and strode away, disappearing into a small pantry. The sound of jars banging and boxes shifting drifted from the darkened doorway. "Handkerchief? What in the world does having a handkerchief at a crucial moment ever do for anybody?" she called. Tromping back, she raising a round tin above her head, signaling victory. "Stinks to high heaven but works like a charm. Sit. I'll smear it on while you have a much needed glass of Syllabub."

A beveled glass, filled with liquid the color of spring roses, hit the table before Kate could protest. She sipped as Charlie dabbed, an indelicate touch, cautious but clumsy. Like a man's. Kate sniffed, gagged. The stuff smelled worse than *high heaven* could smell.

"I'm guessing that you were acquainted with Tanner before coming to Edgemont," Charlie said, a glint of curiosity showing on her face. As if she realized this, she glanced down and set to wrapping a narrow strip of cloth around Kate's finger.

"Yes, I knew him. In Richmond. For one summer. I guess it was almost two years ago, a year and a half more like, that we became"—she took a long sip—"unacquainted."

Charlie's hand stilled for a moment; then she finished
tying off the ragged ends. "A year and a half? That long.'

"Yes, that long," Kate said, watching a flood of late
afternoon sunlight roll over the edge of the table and
puddle on the floor.

Charlie patted Kate's hand and slid into the chair beside
her. "After two years, y'all still spark off each other like a
match against flint. Hmmm . . . "

Kate shook her head. "You have it all wrong."

"Do I?"

"Yes, of course."

"Well, you didn't see his face when he saw blood on
your hand. Hard to disguise alarm when it rips wide like
a seam in a pair of tight trousers."

Kate coughed, choked, Syllabub burning her throat.
"Didn't have to . . . see his face. I know those looks. Charming. Concerned. Tanner Barkley has the unique ability to
make you believe you're the only person in the room.
Then you see him the next night, using the same persuasive
smile on someone else. I promise you, and thank God, let
me tell you, you don't know him as well as I do."

Charlie licked her lips and banged her glass on the table.
"Maybe for him you *were* the only person in the room."

Kate snorted, rolled her eyes toward the ceiling.

"Are you so sure about him, Kate?"

"Sure enough." She nodded her head, then said more
firmly, "Yes, very sure. Positive."

"He saved Adam's life once, you know."

"Well, he's even then, because he ruined mine." Kate
grasped a spray of rosemary from the center of the table,
lifted it to her nose so quickly it slapped her cheek. The
scent of pine hit her, heavy and immediate.

"There must be—"

"His *name*, Charlie, printed in big black letters. And
mine—only smaller. His article referred to us as colleagues.

Very formal. Not too hard to imagine the informal term used in every drawing room in Richmond." Kate laughed, tapping the greenery against her glass. "I won't go into detail about the people who cleared a wide path around me for the next year. I think my former fiancé's mother fainted when she heard the news. At the largest ball of the year too, no less."

Charlie sputtered, a dribble of pink bubbling in the corner of her mouth. "A fiancé"—she smacked her hand against her chest—"I thought . . . "

"Dear God, it sounds terrible, I know. My parents arranged it. I was sixteen. I had known the family, known Abel, since childhood. I wasn't in love with him or even close to it. And he did not love me. In fact, I wrote a hundred letters breaking it off before Tanner ever came along. I wanted, more than anything I have ever wanted, to simply *love* my husband. And when I finally did fall in love, it was with the wrong man. It hit me like a windstorm—exciting and absorbing. I couldn't sleep or eat. Take a breath without thinking about Tanner. Suddenly, he was in my life, and I didn't know what it meant, what to do about him, what to do about Abel. You see, Tanner and I never discussed the future. Nothing serious, or truthful, if you must know, ever passed his lips. But I waited. For him to open up his heart, declare his love for me, you know. I even wrote a letter the day before that damned newspaper hit my doorstep, and I think I would have mailed it. I had finally convinced myself that I loved him. No mistake about it. And then—well, you can guess the rest."

Charlie rested her glass on her wrist and slowly shook her head. "I can't believe it."

"Believe it." Kate snapped the rosemary in two.

"How horrible, how humiliating. Why . . . how. What a . . . ohhh!"

Opening her fist, Kate examined the cracked sprig lyin
in a rude twist on her palm. She shrugged with mor
placidity than she had ever felt about Tanner Barkley. "
told you.''

Chapter Four

"Chrissakes, Adam, they're a mess." Tanner wrenched his gaze from the doorway, his ears from the hum of voices raised in occasional song and frequent laughter. Charlie's guffaw. Kate's giggle. He frowned. Kate was not—had never been—a giggler.

Adam leaned to the side of the cumbersome pine tree they were cramming into a bucket of wet dirt, his mouth flattening into a scowl. "I'll be holding Charlie's head over a bucket tonight and somehow—I don't know how exactly—but somehow, this is *your* doing, Barkley."

Tanner reared back. "My doing?" The tree tipped forward, butting Adam's shoulder.

"Easy, Tan!"

Tanner grabbed the closest branch and yanked. "My doing? Your wife and my . . . and Kate are stumbling around from too much eggnog and Syllabub, both of them giving me the evil eye, and it's somehow *my* doing?"

"Yes, somehow."

"Well, hell."

Adam glared over the top of a limp branch, one they had broken while dragging the tree up the porch steps. That side would face the corner. "You're in love with her"—he grunted, centering the trunk in the bucket—"and all you can do is throw sophomoric glances her way and bellyache about her flirting with Tom Walker, who is so in love with his wife he can't see that she's chasing after you as hungrily as a bitch in heat." In response, the tree swayed, bouncing off Adam's chest. He shoved it back and snarled, "You're useless—you know that?"

"Lila Walker isn't chasing me."

"Ha!"

Tanner closed his hand part way around the trunk, bark biting into his palm. "And I'm not useless. I only have one good arm to work with here, dammit."

"Now you're going to deny being in love with her. Go ahead."

Tanner closed his eyes and struggled to hold the tree steady, his arm shaking so badly he couldn't control it. Pine needles plinked off the top of his head, slithered past the collar of his shirt. He exhaled, smelled whiskey and tobacco on his breath, and whispered, "I can't."

Adam swung his head up and loosened his hold for one stunned moment. The tree teetered to the left and upended with a violent cough of dirt. It whacked the ceiling before landing in a heap on the maroon-and-gold carpet, the tip settling between two blazing logs.

"Chrissakes, Tan. Pull that thing out of the fireplace."

They each grabbed a limb and tugged. Emitting a spray of orange sparks, the tree skidded across the floor, carpet wadding beneath it. A thin trail of smoke swirled amidst the stench of burning pine.

"Dammit," Adam said and gave the closest branch a

swift kick. Thinking better of it, he threw a glance over his shoulder.

"Don't worry, coward. She's not there."

Adam tossed a defiant glare in Tanner's direction, kicked the tree again for good measure. "You're in love with her." Blatant disgust laced his words.

"I suppose so . . . yes." He had known it from the beginning. Admitting it was another story.

"For how long?"

He shrugged, plucking at a pine needle stuck to his sleeve. "Two years. Although I never told her. Since the first day I met her . . . I guess."

Adam yanked one glove, then the other, from his hands. "Drowning love in a sea of milky-white breasts didn't work?"

"Does it look like it worked?" *A sea of breasts*. Close to it. Tanner cringed as a line of women paraded before him, as they had when Kat called him—What was it? An indiscriminate boor?

Adam eyed him for a moment, then shook his head. "That bad, huh?"

"Bad? Well . . . " Blondes. Brunettes. Redheads. Misshapen feet, chipped fingernails. Hoarse laughter and awkward endearments hissed across wrinkled sheets. No matter how he'd searched, not a speck of amber to be found in any of their eyes.

"You'll never change, Tan."

"I changed two years ago, dammit," he said in a tight voice and jerked his shoulder, sending a sharp stab of pain up his arm. "Well, are you going to help me or not? I need to talk with her. Catch her alone somehow. Maybe Charlie can corner her in that filthy kitchen of hers."

"I don't know about enlisting Charlie's assistance. Kate seems to have won her over." Adam sighed, staring at the tree sprawled across his feet. "Besides, you messed it up pretty good all by yourself. I don't know if your relation ship—whatever it was—can be salvaged."

"Don't you think I know that?" Tanner leaned down to grasp a limb, needles crackling beneath his boot. "I have to talk to her. Her mother stands guard at her shop." With a gritty twist, he embedded the trunk in sand. "And I can't get near her in Richmond. Believe me, I tried."

Adam wiped his wrist across his brow, grabbed the cluster of moss Charlie had scoured the woods for, and settled it around the thick trunk. Sitting back on his heels, he examined the arrangement, his gaze thoughtful. "I don't know, Tan. If Kate's trying to stay away from you, how do you know it's not for the best?"

Tanner tugged his fingers through his hair, let his lid drift low. Laughter—shrill, low, indifferent—trickled from the parlor. Charlie, telling someone to dip the string of cranberries in red wax, the dried peas in green. Kat laughing, saying she would dip hers in both, thank you very much. Lila—who *was* chasing after him like a bitch in heat—complaining about a drop of wax on her satin boot.

Wearily, he rubbed his eyes, his jaw. Lord, he felt lonely to the pits of his soul, standing there in a cold library in the middle of nowhere. A shiver shook him, but not one from the wintry bite in the room. He shivered because he felt so removed—from love, home, family. It had been almost a year since he had last talked to his family. An argument with his father—or was it his brother? He had not seen his niece, his brother's only child, since her chubby legs had just begun to catapult her across a sprigged blanket.

Of course, he could abandon his pursuit of Kat Peters. Raise a white flag in defeat. Let her return to Richmond, marry Crawford whose-it. Stumble upon her on a crowded street, carrying a plump child in her arms, a downy auburn head snuggled against her breast. Her beautiful amber eyes inspecting his face, then dodging away.

No. Kat belonged to him, dammit.

Tanner shook himself from his musing, found Adam's attention centered on him. Too perceptive, as usual. He sighed and shoved his hand in his trouser pocket, digging deep. Closing his fingers around metal, he drew the hairpin from his pocket, flipped it into the air with his thumb.

Catching it, Adam twirled it between his fingers, then angled a dubious look at Tanner. "A hairpin?"

"I went to Kat's house the afternoon the story came out. She was leaning from a window, threw a rock at my head. The hairpin landed beside me on the brick walkway." He felt his face heat, shrugged for lack of a better explanation. He knew what he wanted to say, but couldn't force his vocal cords to comply.

Adam turned the hairpin over and back, arched a dark brow. "You've carried a rusty, crooked hairpin"—he waved it airily—"*this* hairpin, in your pocket, for two years?"

Tanner cleared his throat, coughed. "Yes, I mean . . . most times . . . or in my desk drawer. I don't know why exactly. I guess it made me feel closer to her when I got to missing her well . . . badly. Also, um, I have this ring. My grandmother's. I planned on giving it to her, before the story, before I had a chance . . . " His voice faded. He felt inane and childish, embarrassed and angry. Flustered, he stamped his feet and kicked the bucket, causing the tree to sway violently.

Adam's lips curved in a deliberate, sweeping smile. He tipped his head and laughed, long and deep.

Tanner's temperature soared with each chuckle. He fisted his hands by his side, jerked his shoulders, a drop of sweat rolling down his back. "Just forget it. All right?"

Lips twitching, Adam tossed the hairpin back to Tanner. A mischievous expression crossed his face. "Oh, don't go

getting your dander up. I'll help. Somehow, I'll help
Because damned if you are not the most lovesick pup I'v
ever seen. A hairpin. For two years." He slapped his hand
on his knees and bowed at the waist, laughter pourin
from him.

Tanner pocketed the hairpin and swung away. At leas
one of them could enjoy his misery.

A pleasant hum buzzed in Kate's head by the time th
tree decorating began. Little bursts of artificial bravad
pulsed through her veins, giving her the courage to ignor
Tanner. Handsome, scowling Tanner, who kept trying t
wedge himself between her and—she squinted, glance
at the man beside her—oh, hell, she couldn't remember
But he seemed nice enough, whatever his name was. Harry
maybe. Or Joe? A little short, Harry-Joe, but who reall
needed a tall man? And Harry-Joe's eyes weren't as strikin
as . . . but who really needed to gawk at a set of eyes blu
as a summer sky?

Kate teetered, bounced on the balls of her feet, and wit
a wild fling, threw the end of her popcorn garland at
branch just above her head. It sailed high and snagged
quite inelegantly, she thought, on a different branch tha
she had intended. She tugged, tugged again, but it stuck
"Excuse me," she said to Harry-Joe. "Could you help me
My garland is caught."

Harry-Joe smiled and stretched—barely able to reach i
himself—grasping it between two thin fingers, and bring
ing it to her, where he presented it like a trophy.

"Jesus."

Kate jerked, leaned down and in, peering between
broken-branched hollow. Tanner—eyes narrow and, damn
it all, very, very blue—peered back at her. They stared, s
still Kate could hear pine needles scraping against her cheek

She even imagined she could hear Tanner breathing, kind of harsh, raspy. Behind her, Harry-Joe coughed, touched her elbow. She started, bumping into the tree, rousing a chorus of groans and bouncing ornaments.

"Would you like some Syllabub, Miss Peters?" Harry-Joe asked.

"Yes, thank you." Though the last thing she needed was more Syllabub.

Kate watched Harry-Joe scurry off, sighed with relief, and reached into the wooden crate by her side. Crocheted ornaments, paper-link chains, holly sprigs, cornucopias overflowing with candy. She chose a delicate lace star, considered it a moment, then hung it in a bare spot. Stepping back to see how it looked, she encountered a hard chest. She did not have to turn to know who stood there. She *smelled* him. Tobacco, mint, man.

"Mr. Barkley, what a surprise," she said, nudging the star a little straighter. Her words echoed in her ears. Surprisingly, they sounded quite steady.

Tanner stepped beside her, his elbow brushing hers, a crocheted snowflake dangling from his extended finger. "Do you need any help with your garland, Miss Peters?" He waggled the snowflake in her face.

She knocked it away, snatched a green sprig from the crate, and had it halfway to the tree before she realized it was mistletoe. She held her breath, raised her arm higher. A log splintered in the fireplace; her skirt rustled across the top of Tanner's boots. All disturbed the rhythm of her pulse. Her hand quivered, the branch quivered, and the damned mistletoe fluttered to the floor.

Kate blinked and angled her chin to find Tanner watching. She could not escape the look. Or what it meant.

"Come here," he whispered.

She shook her head as he leaned in. Leaned in tight, until she could see black whiskers sprouting from his jaw,

the ragged edge of a scar trailing across his chin, flecks
yellow crowding the outer edge of his pupil, white teet
between his parted lips.

Oh, no, she thought, the words quite possibly escaping
His breath touched her just before his lips did. A feathe
light press, gentle. His fingers invading her hair. A cuppe
hand sliding, tangling, forcing her forward. She stumble
against him. Left shoulder, right knee, left hipbone. H
cradled the crown of her head, walking them back into
darkened corner, then flush against the wall.

She resisted—she truly did. Kept her lips sealed tigh
her hands fisted by her side, her spine ramrod straigh
Unfortunately, the wine she'd consumed had strengthene
her resolve in some areas and weakened it terribly in oth
ers. And it had been so long since he had kissed her lik
this, an animal, starving for the taste of her. When h
tongue flicked against her lips, she sighed, releasing a burs
of air and restraint. He brought his hand to her waist, hi
snowflake hitting the floor. His tongue circled, crept insid
her mouth, cautiously, as if he feared rejection.

Rejection. She almost laughed—instead, she showed hir
how ridiculous she found the idea. Rising on the tips c
her toes, she brushed her fingers along his cheeks, his neck
his shoulders. Gripping, his muscles straining beneath he
hands, she slanted her head, her tongue entering hi
mouth with eager sincerity.

He groaned—so low she wasn't sure if she heard it o
felt it—and tightened his hold, winding one arm aroun
her. His fingers spread over her rib cage, detailing eacl
groove. His thumb pressed into the hollow at the nape o
her neck, tilting her head. Deeper. The taste of whiske
and Syllabub mingling. Deeper. Into each other, into th
corner. Deeper as a shudder worked its way up her spine
through her mouth and into his.

Closer, a restless compulsion to get closer controlled

her. He felt it, responded, leaning over her, shoving her against the wall. She pulled him in, fit her thumbs in the buckle and strap at the back of his trousers. Cool metal against her skin failed to arouse her mindfulness of the possibility that they would be discovered. Conversely, she focused on savoring the sensations guiding her, and on pushing aside thoughts that would interfere.

A rough edge on his front tooth. The taste of gingerbread. The scent of soap on his cheek. The edge of his brace biting into her breast. His thumb brushing the underside of her arm, sliding lower, hand curling. His fingers tangling in her dress, his skin scorching her.

Another minute . . . just another minute. Maybe she whispered it.

Tanner froze, closed his hand about her arm, and shook gently. His breath cuffed her cheeks in harsh bursts, launching loose strands of hair into her face. Kate swayed, absorbed in the symphony of colors swirling around her, kissed his cheek, sucked at the skin along his jaw. Lifting her lids, she found his gaze, wide and dark, slipping low, to her breasts.

"Kat, stop." He pushed her away, tugged his hand through his hair. "Stop. Before someone sees us. While I can still think clearly. Dammit."

In reply, she pulled his head to hers and kissed him, openmouthed. No remorse, no modesty. Lips, tongue, teeth. The colors behind her lids exploded. Bright yellow and red. Dark blue, the exact color of his eyes when they had made love in that narrow bed of his. Elbows and knees cracking paint-chipped walls. Feet dangling off the end. Rumps bumping slack bed ropes. Once, they had even rolled off, slick skinned, to the floor.

Oh, if only they were in his bed again, she thought and groaned low in her throat.

"Christ," he whispered, ragged and breathless, and

shouldered her into the wall. His lips left hers, trailing a moist path across her cheek. He sucked her earlobe into his mouth, his tongue hot and rough, seeking what she struggled to give. A wave of heat washed over her—from her toes to her earlobe. She remembered this feeling, a feeling as clear and familiar as his voice. The attraction between them was not an illusion, a fantasy she'd created to excuse her recklessness. It was real.

"Princess." Laying his lips against her cheek, he gasped, "Princess." He stepped back just enough to let a whisper of air slide between them, enough to cool her skin. Pressing his forehead to hers, he sighed, shivered.

A heavy step sounded behind them, followed by a shocked stutter.

The promised glass of Syllabub had arrived.

Tanner drew a final breath of sandalwood and cinnamon, the first true contentment he'd felt in almost two years trickling away. Opening his eyes, he forced himself to remember just where the hell he was. He searched Kate's face, fighting the urge to smooth the uncertainty from her brow. Lifting her bandaged finger to his mouth, he placed a kiss on her fingertip, and smiled. Her hand reeked of Charlie's miracle salve.

I love you, he said in his mind, willing her to understand. He prayed she did. *Please, Kat, please understand.* But she only blinked and stared, face pinched and pale.

Pasting on a counterfeit grin, he turned to face the damned garland retriever, who stood, mouth gaping, gaze shifting. Tanner sighed and stepped forward, grasped the man's free hand and pumped, Syllabub splashing to the floor. "Congratulate me, sir! The little filly's finally agreed to become my wife. Months of hard courting, I can tell you, but I plumb wore her out. Wore her slap out." He pumped the man's hand again. Baby-soft skin.

"Congra—"

"Oh, thank you, sir, thank you. I know you mean it."
Tanner nodded to the glass. "Do you mind?" Without
waiting for an answer, he snatched it from the raised hand
and slung back the contents. *Ugh.* He stifled a grimace.
Honest to God, he needed a drink more than he needed
air right now, but this stuff? God-awful. Whoa.

"What is this?" Tanner shoved the glass into the still
raised hand. "Oh, right." He elbowed the garland retriever
in the ribs, winked. "A woman's drink. I get it. I get it."
Leaning in, he whispered, "Do you mind giving us a little
privacy, sir? I might just have me another little ol' kiss to
commemorate this wonderful occasion. I was fixing to, you
know, when you showed up. Stuck here in this corner and
all. The happiest night of my life, I tell you."

The garland retriever blinked and pivoted on his heel,
stumbling straight into the Christmas tree.

Tanner shoved his hand between the branches and
yanked the tree steady. A muffled laugh had him turning
faster than the garland retriever, almost unsettling the tree
again.

Kate stood, one arm circling her ribs, fingers splayed on
the side of her breast, hand clasped over her mouth.

Tanner felt a smile plump his cheeks, lift his lips from
his teeth. "What?"

"You." She dipped her head. A swift headshake released
rusty strands into her face.

Tanner lifted his hand, watched it close in upon her as
if it were not his own. Just to wind a velvet curl about his
finger, brush it across his lips. Lift it to his nose and breathe
her into his soul.

*Take care, Tanner. You'll have her running the other way if
she realizes what you're thinking.*

Suppressing a sigh, he shoved his hands in his pockets—
his injured arm contracting in protest—aware of a growing
need to pull his trousers from his groin. He fought to keep

his hands to himself, harnessed the urgent compulsion he felt to touch her.

For now, he would be content to look. *For now.*

Oblivious to his frustration, Kate raised her head, wiped a finger beneath each eye. "Where in the world did you come up with that awful accent?"

Tanner shrugged, a meager bounce due to the stitched skin that pained him in escalating amounts. "I spent a few months out west. Listened, practiced. Use it occasionally for a story."

Kate's cheeks smoothed as her smile shriveled. The light their kiss had sparked in her eyes dimmed. "Well, at least you didn't lead me to believe you were from a godforsaken territory. A farmer or something. I really would have felt foolish seeing you swinging some sweetheart on your arm while charming her with a crisp Northern pitch."

"Wait a damn minute." He snatched his hands free and closed in on her, her twig of mistletoe snapping beneath his boot.

"Don't," she said and halted his movement, her palm flat on his chest. She shoved him back for emphasis. "Don't."

He reached to take her hand, but she snatched it back before he could. "For God's sake, Kat." Shifting his gaze to the flame flickering above her head, he rubbed his hand over his face, sniffed. Her scent clung to his skin. Somehow, this primitive awareness fortified his resolve. Leaning in before she could dash away, he tipped her chin until her eyes met his. "Admittedly, I deserve your censure. Most of it anyway. I made a few tactical errors. Lacked judgment at times. Misread responses—yours *and* mine. Acted impulsively instead of intelligently. I admit all that. But you can trust me when I say—"

"I can't trust you as far as I can spit, Mr. Barkley."

"That's a little harsh, I think. And drop the Mr. Barkley, will you please?"

"Harsh?" She jerked her chin from his grasp. "I entrusted you with a precious gift. A gift you threw out like day-old rubbish. A gift that's given to you so often that you think nothing of it. While I . . . I thought"—she glanced away—"oh, what does it matter to tell you now?" Her mouth flattened into a thin line. "I thought I loved you."

"Love? Me . . . Kat . . . what? What did you say?"

She snapped her head around, said between clenched teeth, "I thought I loved you. Dear God, how could you have believed anything else?"

"Love?"

"Yes, love. Absurd notion, isn't it? After all, I did not even *know* you." She laughed—a ragged, disagreeable sound.

Tanner nearly tripped over his feet getting to her. He gripped her shoulders, hands shaking. "No, no, Kat. It's not absurd." He could hardly bear to hear her bitter laughter ringing in his ears. Not laughter that followed her telling him she loved him—*had* loved him—for the first time. He feared he might scream from the top of his lungs. Instead, he swallowed his self-directed fury and asked in a dull tone, "Why didn't you ever tell me?"

She tilted her chin, flashed a mocking half smile. "Oh, that would have been an amusing tale around the club, wouldn't it?"

"No, Kat." He pulled her close. "Don't you see? I loved you too. I tried to tell you that all those times you turned me away."

Her smile curled into an ugly twist. "Of course, you did."

The shatter of glass across the room had them whipping their heads around. Tanner glanced back to find Kate studying her bandaged finger. He sighed. "How, god-dammit, can I convince you?"

"Doesn't matter what you do, what you say, Mr. Barkley. That summer is as dead as Charlie's Christmas tree will be in another week." A huff of breath—laugh or sigh—slipped from her. She tugged at the tattered cloth. "Although, I must confess that the attraction between us seems to linger. Strange how one cannot control things like that. Wouldn't you know, my mother was right? She always told me the charming ones are the vipers."

"You don't honestly believe that."

"Try me," she said and shrugged from his grasp, stumbled, her breasts jostling his chest.

The persistent twinge below his banded waist increased to a flat-out ache. A different ache than the one in his arm, but an ache just the same. He took a moment to study the mistletoe beneath his boot, time to allow the pounding in his head to slack off, the steady pulse beneath his skin to abate. Inhaling deeply, he looked into her face. Color reddened her cheeks, her eyes rounded, wary. He was getting nowhere quickly. Stepping back, he raised his hands in surrender. She glanced around him, no doubt plotting her escape.

"Kat, we need to talk. You must see we *have* to talk. Not now, not with all this"—he lifted his shoulder, gestured to the crowd of people on the other side of the tree—"going on. Meet me tonight. After the party."

She frowned, her brows nearly touching. "Talk? I don't need to talk."

"Is that right?"

"What happened between us tonight"—she threw her hand out, watched it tremble for a moment, then jerked it by her side—"is your idea of talking."

"No . . . no kissing. I won't—oh, all right, I won't touch you. Okay?"

She snorted.

"I swear."

"Like hell."

Chrissakes, what a mouth she had. "We can talk about . . . about what happened. In Richmond. Anything. I'll tell you anything you want to know. I just want you to give me some time to try and work this out." Tanner sputtered to a halt, his voice low and strained, intense. Scared he would frighten her further, he coughed and swallowed. Tried again. "I'll meet you behind your mother's shop. Eleven o'clock."

Kate blinked once. "I'm to freeze to death for this belated, and rather precipitous, spectacle of honesty?"

"Twenty minutes."

"No."

"Ten." Jesus, he hated her for making him grovel— respected her for making him grovel.

She shook her head, but he could see that the movement lacked conviction.

"I'll be there, so you might as well show up."

The wall sconce flickered, spilling golden light across her face. She drew her gaze to his, her eyes gleaming brightly. Too brightly. She pressed her lips together, sucked the bottom one between her teeth. Her tongue flicked out, then disappeared inside her mouth. Tanner had never felt a stronger urge to kiss anyone in his life.

Jesus, he loved her. If he could only make her understand. Make her believe him.

"All right," Kate whispered, but she glanced away immediately after saying it. "Oh, here, I almost forgot." She shoved a wadded square of cloth into his hand and brushed past him, head down, shoulders slumped.

As a hollow ache gripped him, Tanner followed her retreat, the gentle sway of her hips, the delicate whisper of wool across a needle-covered floor. Glancing down, he relaxed his fist. His bloodstained handkerchief, the black monogram stark against white linen. Crushing it, he stared, seeing nothing, hearing nothing.

I thought I loved you.

Tanner blinked the mist from his vision, threw his head back, and swallowed deeply. Kat had loved him once, and oh, God . . . if he had only known.

Could she again? He had a sinking feeling that she had spoken the truth. For her, at least, their love *was* as dead as Charlie's Christmas tree was doomed to be.

Kate pressed her brow against glass, let the frigid cold dull her skin. Chipping a piece of ice from the bottom of the pane, she watched Tanner pace the length of her mother's store, hands knotted behind his back, head bent, seeming to search the ground before him. Halting, he tilted his chin, and glared at the row of windows above him. His eyes glittered in a sudden splash of moonlight. Fortunately, he didn't know which window was hers. She would not put it past him to climb the ivy trellis and pound on it until it shattered.

A steamy cloud spurted from his mouth, his lips forming the one word able to pierce her soul: Princess.

She pressed her hand against her chest, burrowing her fingers into wool, her heart tripping beneath her palm. Shrinking back, she dug her shoulder into the corner, but not before she saw him sway on his feet, lift a shaking hand to his face. Dear God, he didn't need to be standing outside in the freezing cold, feverish and exhausted.

Oh, Tanner.

A tear crept down her cheek, then another, and another still. Her skin felt shriveled and dirty, sticky from the tears she had shed since returning home. She scrubbed at her cheeks, rolled her tongue over her teeth. Only the faintest hint of whiskey, of him, remained. If only the same could be said for her heart.

Doomed. She was doomed to remember this evening for a lifetime. As if she'd needed more memories of Tanner Barkley to shove in a trunk already chock-full. Little about him, about their wondrous summer together, had faded with time. No matter what lies she told him. Remembering, she closed her eyes. Sunlight pouring over him. Black hair tangled round her seeking fingers. His tongue laving the warm hollow at the base of her throat. The weight of his chest, his hips, his legs, driving all judgment and worry of consequence from her mind. She flexed her hands, untangling the imaginary strands.

Dear God, memories were dangerous.

After Tanner's newspaper article, after she'd realized what Tanner had done to her, she had ceased all contact with him. For months, he had tried to destroy the barrier she'd erected between them. Letters she returned unopened, dog-eared calling cards she threw in the rubbish bin, abrupt visits to her sister's home she ignored. Heaven help him, he'd even sent a telegraph to her mother.

Finally—and it was absurd on her part that she hated him for it—he had given up. What did she expect?

Blinking back tears, she leaned forward and looked out the window, her breath clouding the glass. Squinting, she searched the grassy path behind the shop, found only a yawning expanse of gray.

Gone. Given up. Like before.

Kate shuddered. She had come to Edgemont seeking answers—about Crawford, about her future, about her life. Instead, she had found she still loved Tanner Barkley and that their love still brought a price she would not pay. Could not bring herself to pay.

Flinging her arms loose, she stumbled to the bureau tucked against the bedroom wall. She swept her hand across the marble top, scattering her mother's bric-a-brac. A cologne bottle dropped to the floor, shattering at her feet. The scent of violets cracked the air. Kate did not blink, didn't care if she sliced her feet to shreds.

Where was it?

There. Stilling, she lifted her hand before her face, traced the edge of her hairpin. She brought it closer, but didn't really need to. Enough moonlight spilled into the room. Regardless, she did not see the crooked hairpin she held, but the one that had bounced off the bricked courtyard by Tanner's boot. He had bought the hairpins for her—an impulsive purchase on one of their rare trips to the city—two weeks before . . . well, two weeks before her world shattered into as many pieces as that damned cologne bottle of her mother's.

She curled her hand into a tight fist, a rusted edge nicking her skin.

Tanner had kept her hairpin all this time. And he'd admitted it in front of a roomful of strangers. During a stupid parlor game, of all things. Oh, how she wanted to believe that meant he loved her, had always loved her, but she'd come to think, long ago, after months of grief and denial, that Tanner Barkley could not possibly love anyone.

And the notion that she still loved him scared her too much to consider.

After all, what could be worse than loving a man who could not love you in return?

Concealed by shadow, Tanner assumed Charlie couldn't see him. Then he remembered the glowing cheroot wedged between his fingers and sighed. The porch swing tilted when Charlie grabbed the chain securing it, groaned when she settled beside him. He sucked smoke into his lungs, rolled away from her, and released a charcoal puff into the darkness. A motionless night, brittle, icy teeth nipping at his fingers, his nose and cheeks. To make matters worse, his arm seemed to throb with each fragile snowflake that drifted to the ground.

"Kate didn't show?" Charlie asked, the creak of the swing almost blotting out her words.

Tanner flicked ashes from his thumb and lifted his gaze to the sky. Blue black, a thousand stars. Woodsmoke. The sweet scent of rosemary. He lifted his shoulders, dropped them in a soundless sigh. "No."

Charlie's feet shuffled. Her lips parted, closed, parted.

Sliding his buttocks back, Tanner straightened his spine, preparing for the advice she readied to give.

"I think Kate might have done it until that stupid game," she finally said.

"Before she went home, she made me give the hairpin to her," he said. "Ripped it right out of my hand. It's all I have of her, all I *had*. Except a slew of faded memories. She probably tossed it in the weeds on her way home." He laughed, sensed how fragile it sounded, and tried again. No better.

"Tanner, maybe I should help you to—"

"*No.*" Twisting his heel, he extinguished his cheroot, and rose to his feet. For a moment, black colored his vision. Closing his hand about the wooden railing, he gulped cool air like water. "I don't know ... I don't know what I was thinking. Playing a damned parlor game. Answering a direct question honestly for once in my life." He still couldn't believe the question *or* his answer. Who in the hell needed to know the contents of a man's pockets? And what each item signified? *Jesus.* Telling a roomful of people he kept a former lover's hairpin in his pocket? With the former lover in the room? He was losing his mind. Simply losing his damn mind.

"You love Kate, Tanner. Why do you think you can

control that love? You didn't ask for it, choose it, and you can't make it stop. You can't make it disappear. Believe me, I tried. Tried to hide my love for Adam. And he tried to hide his love for me. You remember escorting me to the train station in Richmond. Oh, I reveled in my martyrdom. My supreme sacrifice. Then I came back to Edgemont without him, and my days didn't matter if he wasn't in them. And my nights . . . '' The creak of the swing mingled with her soft laughter. "What did our stubbornness get us but three miserable months apart? What has it gotten you? And Kate?"

Tanner angled his head, glanced over his shoulder. Vague shadows revealed the lower half of Charlie's face, the tender, loving smile gracing her lips. Her gaze rested on her bedroom window, making him wonder if she missed her husband even now. Pushing the swift jab of envy aside, he turned his head, stared across fields awash in silver and white. "So you've decided I'm in love with her?" he asked, stretching, catching a snowflake on his finger.

"Oh, Tanner. Those lovely blue eyes of yours smolder when you look at her."

"Well, maybe they do, but dammit, I'm not groveling at her feet, some pitiful dog begging for scraps."

"You have to admit what you did to her wasn't—well, it was awful."

"I tried, Charlie. I did everything in my power to talk to her after . . . '' He dropped his face to his hands, smelled cinnamon on his skin, and swallowed the emotion clogging his throat. "She didn't understand that the man she knew was the only man inside me. I know she looks back on that summer, the things we did—hell, the simple things, playing chess and riding horses—looks at it all like a deceptive dream. I foolishly believed I could tell her, *would* tell her tomorrow . . . the next day. Next week. While loving her with my whole heart, giving every part of myself I deemed worthy."

"She didn't tell me . . . didn't say you—"

A bitter laugh popped out as he lifted his head, misty air rising before his face. "I'll just bet she didn't," he growled. A dizzying burst of anger, not all self-directed, flooded through him. He blinked and leaned against the railing to steady himself. He waved Charlie away when she started to rise. "Kat doesn't trust me. And I need to face the facts. She never will. I thought I could get her past it, thought if I tried hard enough she would forgive me. But tonight, standing behind that bonnet shop, staring into an endless expanse of black, her vacant window taunting me, like a bolt out of the blue, it hit me. I finally realized that she's in love with another man. In all likelihood she's *marrying* another man. Even if she's not, her love for me is gone. I killed it. And here I stood, a desperate fool, trying to talk to her about what happened two years ago. A relationship she wants to forget." He tucked his hands beneath his armpits and shivered. "I thought telling her about my family, that goddamned bank, university, my life, my feelings for her would bring her back to me."

"You're convinced it won't?"

"Didn't you hear me? She is marrying another man. I'm finished dancing a jig to her music."

Charlie lowered her chin, kicked a black boot high. "What about the kiss? You think she would kiss a man she didn't love like that?"

"How do you know—" He waved his hand, dismissive. "That doesn't—well, we were always good like *that*. At that. Nothing more, nothing less."

He lied well, but they both knew the truth.

"You're quitting then?" Charlie asked.

"Yes." The word dropped, dull and final, between them.

Charlie threw a quick glance his way. "When will you leave?"

"Day after tomorrow maybe. I promised Adam I'd do an editorial for him. Going into the *Sentinel* office in the morning. Some story about an agricultural"—he sighed—"whatever."

She jerked her head, a flash of surprise, perhaps, or delight, streaking through sapphire. "Oh! The *Sentinel* office. Tomorrow." Chewing her lip, she focused on a point high above his head. "I mean, you can't leave day after tomorrow. That's Christmas day. Tomorrow is Christmas Eve." She shrugged. "No stages. Plenty of time to write an editorial. Plenty of time. And, well . . . good. Plenty of time."

Tanner could swear he heard something—wicked amusement maybe—threading her rambling speech. He tried to decipher her expression but her fidgety movements and a profiled half smile told him nothing.

Slumping against the railing, he released a powdery breath. Christmas. In two days. He wished he could summon even a glimmer of happiness about that. He missed his family and desperately loved another man's woman. A woman who used to be *his*. A woman who'd loved him once. Or so she said.

Oh, yes, Merry Christmas.

Chapter Five

Tanner stepped inside the *Sentinel* office and stopped short. Kate sat behind a scarred wooden desk, spectacles perched on the bridge of her nose, pencil tapping against the record book sprawled before her.

Wonderful.

Charlie's secretive glee the night before suddenly made sense. Loads of sense.

"Shut the door, Charlie. It's almost dark, freezing out there," Kate mumbled without looking up, fingering her round silver rims.

He closed the door and walked forward, trying to mask the heaviness of his step. Pausing before his knees smacked the desk, he searched her bent head, her tidy chignon. No sign of the rusty hairpin. *His* rusty hairpin. Probably have better luck searching the ditches along Main Street for the thing.

"I've almost finished the subscription accounts for"— Kate glanced up, stumbled—"for last month." Her grip on the pencil tightened; a streak of rose crossed each cheek.

"That's good. Excellent."

She stared for a moment, reached to brush her fingers across her lips, then dropped her head, gazing at the record book. A shiver she probably didn't want him to see worked its way up her arm. "If you're following me or—"

"I didn't know you would be here," he said. "Honest." He hitched his hip on the edge of the desk, threw a hand out. "I didn't plan this. Charlie's grand idea. Tell you what, Kat, just ignore me. Pretend it's like that evening we sat through dinner at the Chisoms' ball. Our eyes met twice, I think. In one evening. Hell, you're easy to ignore."

She grunted as her pencil bobbled over the page.

"Actually, I would have arrived earlier in the day, but making up for lost sleep, you know. Standing around in a poor man's excuse for an alley. Half the night. In the freezing cold. Waiting for"—he tapped his finger atop the slanted figures marking the page—"waiting for . . . Oh, what the hell was I waiting for?"

Her head lifted, amber eyes glowing in a pale face. Her anger was easily definable. Whatever else she felt, she tucked close. "I don't owe you a blessed thing, Mr. Barkley. Not ten minutes behind my mother's shop or sixty seconds in here. Your effrontery never fails to amaze me. Truly, never fails. Why . . . oh . . . " Her pencil arched across paper, the tip snapping when it bounced off the desk's surface.

Tanner smiled, felt a responsive, aggressive tightening in his gut. He'd felt this way many times. During one of their chess matches or, if they been in a bit of a combative mood, just before they made love. Well, he and Kate had been heading toward this confrontation for a long time. Two years. Two lonely, silent years. He was ready. "Last night, you said you would be there. Listen to me. Give me a chance to work things out."

"I lied."

"Obviously. Getting pretty good at that, aren't you?"

Slapping her hands on the desk, she jumped from her chair, leaned in until the tips of their noses brushed. She ripped her spectacles from her face, whacked his cheek, and flung them down with a crack. A broad band of sunlight washed over her, igniting her hair, bronzing her skin. She looked formidable and magnificent. "You bastard. I never lied to you then. Not once. I gave you everything I had to give and more. What a fool, oh, what a fool I was."

He released a breath, delayed taking another. The scent of sandalwood surrounding her confused his thoughts, did strange things to his insides. Sighing, he whispered, "Don't you think I know that? Why I tried so goddamned hard to talk with you. Explain—"

"Explain?" Her eyes widened, white circling amber all the way around. "Explain? Explain how you, explain how you . . . oh, dear Lord . . . " She brought her hand to her brow and squeezed, as if she could expel her thoughts.

"I never used one word you said, Kat. Not one. Hell, I didn't need you to get inside Asher's business. I didn't need your information. Not one bloody thing you told me showed up in any of those articles. Your name, yes, but I didn't plan that, Kat. I swear." His fist hit the desk, sending papers to the floor in a jumbled flutter. "By God, didn't you read them?"

"No. Not after that morning." Her fingertips pressed hard, making pale dents in her skin. "I couldn't endure it."

Again, he pounded his fist on the desk. "Goddammit, Kat. You didn't read them? No wonder then." All the time they had lost . . . . "I'd been bellying up to Asher for more than three months when I met you. Occasional games of poker at the club, late-night political discussions over whiskey, constantly needling him to hire me. None of those articles had anything to do with you. I told Asher the truth, partially. Presented myself as a jaded heir to a banking fortune, needing an office to waste a few hours of the day. He understood my situation all too well. Mirrored his. And, Sloane-Barkley wasn't a bad contact for him to have. I had protected myself, my identity, and I knew it. My byline hadn't run in the *Times* for three years. Not under my own name anyway. He never guessed for a moment that I was not who I said I was."

Kate lowered her hand, her eyes sweeping across his face. "That made two of us."

Leaning in, Tanner grasped her chin, drawing her gaze to his when she would have pulled it away. Soft skin, the softest he'd ever felt, her pulse skipping beneath his fingers. "You weren't something I planned on, Princess. Things would have been much simpler had I never met you."

Her mouth formed a startled "oh" as she wrenched free. Tanner prided himself on rarely making mistakes, but he realized this one and rounded the desk, blocking her exit. Closing his hands around her arms, he yanked her to him, forced her up on her toes. Standing chest to chest, she glared, chin high but quivering, harsh breaths mingling with his.

God, he loved her, felt it fill his heart, weigh heavy in his chest. Loved the raw courage, the frank intelligence, shining in her eyes. Loved the proud tilt of her jaw and the way she worried her lip rather than give in to tears. While thoughts of what he *could* say circled in his mind, surprisingly, he heard himself say this: "I will never regret the time we spent together, Kat. *Never.* You were the best thing that ever happened to me. And I knew it. I always knew it. I planned to tell you many times, about my family, the newspaper, anything you wanted to know. But I was close, so close to finishing that story, one I'd worked on for almost a year. Just one more day, I kept telling myself. *Just one more day.* I thought I had time. I thought *we* had time."

Her throat worked, her chin jerking as she tried to lower it. "Time for what? More . . . intimate discussions in that tiny bed of yours? A rousing game of chess sitting on feather pillows stacked on the floor? Quiet dinners on your three-legged coffee table? I remember that microscopic apartment. Really, I found it terribly charming." A shot of laughter lifted her lips. She twisted for release, but he held firm. "Let me guess. You own the building."

Tanner clicked his teeth together, feigned a look of pique. Raised brows, wide eyes, slightly parted lips. The whole bit. Truthfully, he *did* own the building, but he would crisp in the pits of hell before he admitted it. That was all she needed to hear right now. He made a mental note to arrange to sell the thing the day after Christmas. Shaking his head, he laughed. "Don't be silly. Own the building. Not very likely."

Her lids drifted shut as her bones seemed to melt. She sagged, a slim shoulder settling on his chest. Her breasts lifted, warm and full against him, then fell on a sigh. "Tanner, it just doesn't matter anymore. I don't love you anymore," she said, voice muffled against his coat.

His breath caught, but only for a moment. *Tanner.* She'd called him Tanner. Leaning in, he brushed his lips across the top of her head, smelled strawberries. And ink. She had not called him by his first name for a long time. Too long. Perhaps, she didn't love this Crawford fellow after all. Maybe *he* had a chance. A wonderful second chance to make her love him. "It does matter. We matter. I want you to understand." He paused, staring at a splintered crack in the wall.

Now or never, old man. "Kat, I—I want to tell you, always meant to tell you, that I . . . how much I—"

She angled her head, up and away. "Whatever it is, it's too late."

"Too late? What do you mean? Too late?" He set her back, searched her face.

Kate faced him squarely, but pain registered in her eyes, loud and clear. And so did controlled tenacity. Numb conviction. She looked awfully certain of something. Certain enough to have Tanner's stomach knotting, his fingers itching, begging him to let them explore her body, or shake some sense into her. Surely, she was not . . . would not . . .

"I'm marrying Crawford, Tanner. I telegraphed him early this morning. He's been pushing me to accept his proposal. So I did. A bit rushed, I admit, but he had a rather public scrape with a married woman, a colleague's wife, a year ago, and his family is desperate to secure loose ends. One of the loose ends being marriage. To a woman with her own scandal skulking about, but not one as harmful as his. And not as recent." The words tumbled from her lips in the most emotionless stream he'd ever heard.

"Do you love him?" he demanded, shaking her, her hips settling against his thighs.

Blinking, she tried to lower her gaze. Tanner cupped her cheeks with both hands, bent his knees so she couldn't look anywhere but into his face. Staring, he repeated, "Do you love him?"

Her lips moved, he felt the drift of air but heard no sound.

"Do you, Kat? For God's sake, do you love him?" *Do you still love me?*

She nodded weakly, brow bumping his chin, and whispered in a ragged voice, "Yes . . . yes, I love—"

He slammed his mouth over hers, determined to halt

her rash admission. She struggled, brought her hands to his chest and shoved, but he fought back, gathering her close, trapping her in his arms. He would prove his love this way, if she would not listen, if she would not let him *tell* her how much he loved her.

You don't love him, Kat. You don't love him. You love me. A dizzying chime, a maddening recitation. Ringing in his mind, resounding in his ears as her lips bloomed beneath his, as her fingers danced over his chest, his ribs, her hands locking behind his back. A groan he could not contain surged from his throat. She responded with a sigh and a wiggle, unintentionally nestling his erection firmly against her.

Oh, Princess. You don't love him. Can't love him.

I don't love him. I . . . do . . . not . . . love . . . Tanner Barkley. She repeated this in her mind, even as she brought her hands to his chest, fisted her fingers in the coarse material, nudged, and with his help, propelled his coat to the floor.

Deep kisses getting deeper, rough hands, smooth fingertips, his, hers, everywhere at once. God, she remembered him just this way, handsome, aroused. Vivid images flooded her mind as his hands cupped her bottom, pulled her flush against him. He nibbled her cheek, her neck, the tender skin beneath her ear. Her head dropped back, exposing her throat to his mouth, his teeth. She gloried in his familiar touch, his familiar scent. All so enticingly familiar that he slipped past her defenses as easily as a hushed whisper.

"You don't love him." His tongue flicked inside her ear. His knuckles skimmed the rounded fullness of her breast. "You love *me*," he breathed, dauntless and decisive, the rush of hot air against her cheek making her shiver and squirm.

"No." Her head lolled to the side, her shoulder rolling toward his seeking mouth, his probing fingers. *"Lust."*

She tugged at his shirt, yanked when necessary. A button, two, plinked to the floor. Slipping her hand inside, she tangled her fingers in the springy curls covering his chest. She recognized his pursuit, his goal. To bend her to his will. He used what had always been, in his mind, his greatest source of power over her. Thank God, Tanner didn't know she had lied about marrying Crawford, that she loved him too much to ever marry another man. There lay the greatest power of all.

He choose that moment—as if he sensed her dismissal—to pull the ties of her corset, tug it lower, expose her breasts to his expectant fingers, his ravenous mouth. Cool air puckered her nipples; then his lips arrived, warming her to the depths of her soul. Shattering her control.

Arching, she complied with his demands, reason and thought fleeing, ardent need rushing in. Need her body remembered even if her mind didn't want to. Broken images swirled. Ones that felt foreign, as if they belonged to someone else. Fevered sighs, tortured sounds of longing. The scrape of stubble against her skin . . . his tongue circling, flicking over her nipple . . . her fingers splayed across his lean belly . . . sliding lower, tracing the trail of hair . . . his hands plucking at her corset . . . it dangling, falling to the floor . . . his lips, moist and desperate, licking, sucking, moving lower . . .

She groaned in anticipation.

He came up for air, gasping, and threw his head back. "Princess . . . the shades are drawn, but . . . " He faltered, gazing into her eyes, dipped his head, and captured her lips again. She complied, pressing close, wanting to climb inside him, have him climb inside her. Her pulse pounded in her head, her heart in her chest. Loud and unsteady. Curling her arm around his neck, the one beneath his shirt circled his waist. Quivers shook the muscles in his back, shook the arms that held her. Moist skin. Hot. Sliding, bending, his hips met hers and began a deliberate grind, his tongue matching the rhythm. He tasted of mint and the remnants of coffee.

Or was that her taste mixed with his?

Cupping her breasts, he kneaded and caressed, slid his hands to her buttocks and lifted, pulled. Closer, closer, nestling himself between her tender folds. A ragged sound crawled from his throat as he kissed her, teeth and tongue and lips. She mimicked his movements until they rocked together in perfect accord. His passion, his rigid erection, did not frighten her, instead made her skin sizzle and sting. Made her wish again, *desperately,* for that narrow bed of his.

"Princess," he said against her mouth. "The office door"—he sucked her bottom lip between his teeth—"isn't locked." His hands rose to her bared breasts, his thumbs teasing her nipples in time with the cadence of his hips.

Pulling his shirt free of his trousers, she began tugging at the buttons on his fly. "Closed. The office is closed. No one"—she freed one button—"no one will come in." With trembling, eager fingers, she worked hard on the next.

He reared back, chest heaving, air ripping from his lips. She watched his gaze slither low, then lift. A moist sheen sprinkled his jaw, his eyes glowed, deep blue and wild. Releasing a shuttered breath, he searched her face, which she'd lifted, steady and sure, for his inspection. "Thank God," he whispered, evidently finding whatever it was he'd needed to find.

Glancing into each corner, he suddenly grasped her hand, pulled her, stumbling behind him, into a cramped room filled with reams of faded newsprint and the faint smell of decay. Lifting, placing her bottom on a desk shoved against the wall, he kicked the door closed and half turned, crushing his mouth to hers before she could knock her heels against the wide drawers. The desk provided the perfect accompaniment, bringing her face, and most especially, her hips, level with his.

"I want you," he said against her lips, his hands cupping her jaw. His fingers quivered, tensed. "So damn much. God, I can't tell you how much."

Agreeing, she slipped his braces from his shoulders. His crisp cotton shirt followed. She wanted to purr, wanted him to growl, tried to make him by streaking her nails across his bare chest. His heartbeat hammered beneath her palm. "Take . . . me . . . then," she said.

And she meant it.

He tipped his head, dropped his brow to hers. The scent of soap clung to his jaw. "Oh, God, I don't want to make a mistake . . . with you. Ever again. I just can't think clearly right now. I never expected to be with you, like this, again."

She could not bear to imagine what he meant by that, or how troubled, how sincere, he sounded. Dear God, if she had to endure life without the man she loved, why not take another beautiful golden memory with her?

Wasting no more time to try to reason it out, she decided to play dirty and slid her hand into his gaping trouser fly. Through a paltry woolen layer, he pulsed, hard and long and warm. She traced the rounded tip, skimmed her fingers along the length, rubbed her thumb over the swollen vein ridging the back. She remembered, oh, she remembered, what he liked. Knew how to push him over the edge before he realized what hit him. Or had time to deny what he wanted. What *they* needed.

"Jesus, Princess," he rasped, yanking her against his chest. His head lowered, his lips sought. His hands ripped fistfuls of skirt, petticoat, and chemise to her waist. Splaying her legs wide, he fit his groin in the pocket between her thighs, cupped her bottom and drew her close, flush. He rubbed himself against her, rocking back and forth, on his feet from heel to toe.

A faultless, two-pieces-of-a-puzzle fit.

A fit that curled her toes inside soft leather, sensitized her skin. Every inquiring brush of his fingers, every sweep of his hair against her naked breasts, every nip of his teeth against her skin, had her hopping and writhing, as if her bottom rested on a flaming grate. This was enough to throw her into the fires of perdition—or so it seemed—but he pushed, deepening the kiss. Openmouthed, predatory, hostile. As if she had destroyed his wavering intent.

It had not only wavered, it had disintegrated. In a flurry of fevered touches, ardent moans, the whisper of cloth crushed between damp, grinding skin, the creak and wobble of the desk.

"Now," he said, bending, drawing her nipple between his teeth, and sucking, tongue teasing the outer edge. "I need you now, Princess, before . . . " His words faded into vague, meaningless murmurs, muffled against the plump mound of her breast.

He shuddered when her hands curved around his buttocks, nails digging deep. She acted on instinct alone, her mind a tangled jumble, her world encompassed by a pulsing heartbeat, a firm chest, and rigid arms. Scooting forward, her bottom met cool wood, her feet dangling. She brought her hands to his hips and trailed kisses along his temple, the hard curve of his cheek. Salt and soap lingered on her tongue. "Now, love," she pleaded, stubble biting into her cheek.

He lifted his head, his hair tickling her lips, the tip of her nose. He found her mouth, distracted, bracing his knees against the desk, fiddling with his trousers. She felt the brush of a hard knuckle, the press of metal buttons— a sharp contrast against heated skin—then his erection sprang free, nudging her thigh. Pausing, his piercing blue gaze searched her face, dipped to her breasts, lifted.

He's beautiful, she thought, raising her hand, tracing the angry scar on his face, skimming her thumb across his lips. He turned his head, pressed a soft kiss to her wrist, black hair glistening against his flushed cheek.

His fingers danced over her, seeking, probing. She gasped and arched as he slid inside, arranged a gentle, steady rhythm. Her legs quivered, felt loose, disjointed. Marionette boneless. She knew if she stood, she would go crashing to the floor in a broken heap. Gripping his arms, she dropped her head to his shoulder, drew a ragged breath scented with an intimate blend. "Please," she heard herself say, one leg climbing higher, tangling in his dangling brace, locking in place just below the rounded curve of his buttocks. Pulling, she urged him closer.

God, she was wet. Slick. Near to peaking. A low whimper burst forth, her lips moving against his neck, her head twisting on his shoulder. With impatient jerks, she propelled him forward. He laughed, loving her uninhibited exuberance. Loving *her.*

Afraid he would hurt her—recalling her delicious tightness—he forced his mind, his body, to go slowly. He tipped her hips, guided himself through crisp hair and moist folds, until he met her center. Squeezing his eyes shut, he thrust slowly, moving inch by inch—a disciplined glide along a sleek canal. Her hands tensed around his arms, her head knocked against his shoulder. Soft mews vibrated in her throat as he came to rest, hip to hip.

It hit him just as hard and he shuddered, felt the quiver snake its way from his toes to his lips, releasing in an unbridled moan. Being with her, buried deep, filling her, made every other woman he'd been with seem absurd. Meaningless. For two years, he'd taken her in the darkness of the night, her sighs filling his ears, her taste filling his mouth. Her love filling his heart.

He flexed his hips and withdrew as far as he could. She shifted and sucked him back in like a drawn breath. *Damn, this old desk is the perfect height,* he thought. He tried to picture all the desks he'd seen in his life, tried to think of anything but the feel of her stretched around him, pulsing, thigh muscles jumping, heel digging into his buttocks, pointed nipples scratching his chest.

She nipped his neck, her hands gliding down his back, taking hold of his hips, and rocking. "Harder," she whispered, driving against him, frantic bursts of air batting his cheek. "Harder . . . ohhh, Tanner . . . you remember."

"I remember, Princess." Unable to deny her, unable to deny himself, he clasped her to him and began a steady, pounding rhythm. Deep, fluid strokes, which she matched without hesitation. Compliant harmony. Colors burst in a shower of brilliance behind his eyelids; his skin tingled, tightened, felt too small to contain him. The scent of sex crowded the dusty air, coated his skin. *Not long. Not long for either of us.* Tangling his fingers in her hair, he took command of her lips, desperately wishing he could reach her nipples.

With a final brush of his tongue, he pulled away, enough to see her face. Cheeks flushed, eyelids fluttering, lips pursed, then parting on a sigh. She was the most exquisite woman he'd ever seen and, even if it killed him, he would *never* let her go again.

"Open your eyes, Princess," he said softly, the words fraying at the edges.

She blinked, head tilting forward, eyes unfocused. Below, his fingers found her, flicked over the sensitive bud of skin. Back and forth, his thrusts slowing to long, creeping strokes. Resolute, he ignored her efforts to reverse the decision.

"You're mine, Princess. *Mine.* There won't be a marriage to anyone but me. I'll die before another man knows you this way." As he lips brushed her ear, he buried himself in her, then withdrew to the tip. "No one could love you as much as I do. I promise you that. I'll promise you that every day for the rest of your life if you let me."

Her eyes widened, lost a little of their befuddlement. Tanner refocused his efforts, concentrated on making her peak with his words ringing in her ears. A bit Machiavellian perhaps, but after all, desperate men took desperate measures.

She opened her mouth to speak, emitting a tortured half groan instead.

Hammering the nail in deeper, he dipped his head, mouthed close to her ear in a barely audible voice, "No one, Princess. Remember that while you clench tight, give yourself to me again, flood us both with—" She arched in response, crushing his hand between their bodies. Triumphant, he felt her spasm around him.

She threw her head back, neck muscles taut, lips parted, swollen. He peeled himself from her, claiming his right to watch her. He felt her passionate cry, in his chest, in his soul, as if she'd plunged it in with a sharp blade. Whimpering and panting, she tucked her head into the nook between his neck and shoulder, shivering in his arms.

He thrust deeply and her leg tightened around him. His heart pounded in his head, pounded out thought, pounded out everything except his Princess. His vision faded, dimmed to black, flashes of gold sparking the edges. A loud roaring filled his ears as the air thickened like dense summer heat. Straining, he grasped pleasure with both hands, teeth bared, arms clutching, binding her to him, attaining a pinnacle he'd never hoped to reach again.

Moments later, coming down, Tanner slumped against her, chest hitching, greedy lungs battling for air. A bead of sweat rolled off his chin, slid to her brow. Kate swabbed it off, missed the first time because her hand trembled. Seeing it, she rolled her fingers into a fist, shoved.

Gazes locking, they stared. Faintly, he realized his arm throbbed, his trousers hung around his ankles, his knees ached from banging them against the desk. She blinked, brushed a limp strand of hair from her face, her expression one of disbelief. Of course, she looked beautiful, but he felt no pleasure looking at her. Her cautious expression made it painfully obvious that she still didn't trust him.

Fury nearly lifted his head from his shoulders.

Tugging his hand through his hair, he brushed a drop of sweat from his cheek and smelled her on his skin. Disengaging—not wanting to—he spun around, yanked his trousers to his waist, irate and flustered. "You're going to marry that bastard, aren't you? I can see it, written all over your face. After this"—he fastened elusive buttons, his fingers still wet from her—"you still don't believe me. My bleeding heart ripped from my chest isn't enough for you, is it? How long, Kat? How long would you make me suffer before I earned the right to love you again? Two years, four? An eternity?" Grabbing his shirt from the floor, he shoved his arms in the sleeves, wincing when his stitches stretched. "Well, I'm finished begging. Finished."

He heard her feet slap the floor, felt her gaze burning into him. Covering his face with both hands, he drew a breath of tainted air, dropped his lids, fighting his love for her.

"Love? What in the world would you know about love, Tanner? Like a bauble you're denied, you covet me. Covet, lust, not love." Clothing rustled, her slippers shuffled. "You destroyed me once. Maybe I even let you. Assisted. Enthusiastically at times. But I won't—I can't risk that again. I cannot risk loving you again."

He lowered his hands, tipped his head, and stared at a

cobweb spanning an entire corner of the ceiling. "Kat, I've
loved you since the first day I met you, I think. Truthfully, I
don't know what I can do to make you believe that. I know
you're scared. God, do you think I'm not?" He laughed,
heard how thin and ragged it sounded, and cringed. "You
assume you were the only one hurt by that article. Well,
you have no idea."

His anger increased with her silence. Stalking forward,
he grasped the doorknob, gave it a furious twist. The door
whacked against the wall, hinges snapping.

Kate followed, plucking at his sleeve. He flinched, tugging it from her fingers. "Tanner, please. Please try to
understand."

He turned, chest rising and falling. "You love *me*, you
goddamned fool," he growled, waiting again for some
change in her expression. No such luck. He yanked away,
away from her eyes, glowing from their lovemaking, away
from her skin, glistening from his touch. "What we share
isn't something you could share with anyone, Kat."

He tilted his head, slid a tight glance her way. "You said
you'd had legions of lovers. So many you couldn't *accurately
recall*."

"Well, yes—I mean, I haven't . . . that is, I loved them . . .
loved them all. That loneliness you speak of"—she waved her
hand, almost able to hide the shaking—"is not an emotion I
can identify with."

Jamming his hands in his pockets, Tanner vowed to keep
them to himself. "Really, Kat? The kind of love that makes
your knees quiver, your stomach flutter? Makes your heart
feel like it will burst from your chest? Alters you so much
that you don't recognizable yourself in the mirror? I can
tell you the first time I felt that way. It was the first night
you spent in my flat. I woke with the sun, excited, as eager
as a pup. Wanting to wake you and"—he laughed and
shook his head—"and *talk*. Talk about your day, what

you wanted to eat for breakfast, what you'd read in the newspaper the day before. Jesus . . ." His voice faded. He coughed, shrugged. "Maybe you don't understand. Maybe I'm the only one who felt that way. Or maybe what I did ruined us. Completely ruined it all. You know, it's funny really. I've never had much patience for mistakes, and yet, I've made so many with you.

"Where the hell is my coat?" he muttered—arm throbbing, head pounding, chest aching—and stalked to the desk. It lay in a crumple on the floor, reminding him of Kate's urgent desire, her *need*—the need she refused to acknowledge—to strip his clothes from his body. He slipped it on with jerky movements, finally beginning to notice the confusion of sounds coming from outside. Glass shattering, hoarse shouting.

Some elemental warning, an alarm ringing in his mind, had him running to the door. Wrenching it back on its hinges, he saw flames licking the edge of a second-story window in the Four Leaf Clover, great billows of gray smoke spewing into the sky.

Good God, the town was burning down around them.

Chapter Six

Tanner raced outside, glanced across the street. A few wobbly-footed bystanders milled about outside the Four Leaf Clover. Other than that, the town appeared deserted; most people were at home preparing for the holiday.

A distraught scream, shrill and feminine, hit his ears. "Great." He snatched his gloves from his pocket and jammed them on his hands. "Just great."

Kate caught him as he stepped off the boardwalk, gripping his sleeve in her fist, slowing his stride to a confused stumble. "Don't go. Don't do it," she said, voice breaking. In the fire's reddish glow, her skin shimmered, her eyes gleamed. She looked charmingly ravished. Enchanting.

Enchanting and determined to marry another man.

Tanner ripped his sleeve from her grasp, shoved her away. "Stay here. Out of trouble," he threw over his shoulder and dashed toward the meager crowd swarming in front of the saloon.

Plunging into the throng of men, he grabbed the first

person he encountered and turned him by a ragged cuff. "The fire rig? Is it coming?" He had to shout above the confused rumble of voices, the roar of flames consuming parched wood.

The man he'd chosen—ninety if he was a day—cupped his hand around his mouth, shouted, "No fire rig! Town's been saving for one. Cake sales, miscellany auctions, nigh on two years. About there, I reckon. Got a water wagon though." A whiskey cloud floated from his lips, tangling in the dense patch of whiskers dotting his face.

Stunned, Tanner slapped his gloved palm against his head, and spun around on his heel. "About goddamn there. Holy . . . " He jerked his gaze to the window, watched orange fingers dance around the edge of the shattered frame, a feeling of dread knotting his stomach. Still controllable—hadn't spread to the roof or the other rooms. *Yet.* Sweet Jesus, Edgemont didn't even have a fire rig. How in the hell could they extinguish a fire on the second floor without one?

Twisting around, Tanner snagged the old man by the wrist and thrust his lips by his ear. "Water wagon? Where is it?"

The old man hitched his thumb high, yelled, "Big John's Livery. Just a spit and a holler. Out back, behind the stable."

Tanner leaned back, met the rheumy brown eyes blinking up at him. "Go! Get that damn thing down here. I don't care how. If you can't do it, find someone who can. *Now.*"

Tanner seized another sleeve, looked into another bewildered face—not as rheumy as the last, but exceedingly ruddy from drink. "Blankets," he ordered, searching the face for comprehension. "Buckets. Water. Sand. Whatever you can find. Anyone you can find." The man nodded and staggered off.

A young boy—nine, ten at the most—crashed into Tanner's knees, nearly sent him tumbling to the ground. "I'll help, mister," he gasped.

"Son, you know where Adam Chase lives?"

The boy wiped his nose, snapped his fingers, and nodded, mint green eyes glittering in a dirty face.

"Get him. Alert as many men as you can along the way. And a doctor—find a doctor. Just don't get *near* this building. Understand?"

"Yes, sir!" the boy shouted and disappeared in a sea of smoke and darkness. Tanner's most energetic volunteer yet.

A piercing shatter filled the air. Shards of glass rained down upon Tanner's shoulders as a wave of scorching fury washed over him. He tilted his head, saw flames nibbling at a second upstairs window. *Jesus.* He had to get in there, make sure everyone had gotten out.

Striding forward, he issued orders to the three men scrambling by his side: Form a bucket brigade, do the best you can with any water coming in, stand watch, keep women and children away. Evacuate the buildings next to the saloon. *Hurry.*

Figuring it provided meager protection, but better than none, he buttoned his coat, stumbled because his fingers were numb from the cold, yet sweat poured down his face, his back. As he neared the Four Leaf's entrance, a viscious crest of smoke and heat spewed forth, smarting his eyes, burning his throat, scorching his skin. He grimaced, sucking bitter air he wished he could do without into his lungs, and started forward.

Kate clawed at the stick-thin arms circling her waist. "Let me go, you fool," she cried, shouldering against the rigid hold. She watched helplessly as Tanner paused before the saloon's gaudy crimson doors, pressed a palm flat against one, then nodded with apparent relief and disappeared inside. "Oh, no. No, Tanner." Her chin bumped her chest, tears making sticky tracks down her face.

The old man yanked her to the side as a swarm of men raced past, formed a brigade, and began hurling buckets of water against the Four Leaf's whitewashed front. "Ma'am, the colonel tole me to keep woman and children back. Got the water wagon ready, passing pails, jus' like the colonel ordered."

Scrubbing at her face, she laughed, heard the hysteria present. "He's not a colonel, you buffoon. A newspaperman. Tanner's a . . . newspaperman." There. She'd said it. Out loud. With pride threading her words. True pride. A newspaperman—she loved a newspaperman. And he had disappeared inside—inside a building with flames just starting to poke through the roof. "I've got to go," she said and shoved hard.

The arms around her tightened, a bony elbow digging into her ribs. "Easy now. I know he ain't no colonel, but he looks a darn sight like a colonel I once knew, I reckon. Back in 'fifteen. Battle of Orleans. Colonel by the name of Perkins. From Baton Rouge. Or was it Natchez?"

The front window of the saloon exploded in a shower of glass. The men closest to it jumped back, shielding their faces. One screamed in pain and clutched his hand, blood dripping between his clenched fingers. Resisting, Kate twisted her head, drilled her keeper with the coldest glare she could muster. "You get your damned hands off me *right now* or I'm going to break one of your skinny damned arms. Do you understand?"

Her keeper's brows reared high, retreating under a canopy of filthy white. "Ma'am?" His hold loosened.

"*Let . . . me . . . go.*" She swung her fist, smacked it against his shoulder. A jolt of pain swam up her arm, reverberated in her shoulder.

"Goddern crazy bitch," he muttered as she struggled to break free.

"Let her go, Jose. I've got it."

Adam. Kate sagged, her eyes filling with relieved tears.

"She hit me, Chase!" the old man yelled.

"I said I've got it."

Jerking free, Kate stumbled forward. "Adam! Dear God, Tanner's in there!" She took two furious steps toward the saloon; then Adam wrenched her off her feet and held firm. Unlike the old man's frail grip, this one she could not break even if she tried. Heart pounding, stomach churning, she glanced over her shoulder. "Adam, *please.*" The violent splinter of weakening wood blocked her words.

"How long?" Adam's gaze jumped from her face to the saloon, which had begun to blaze quicker than dry kindling. "Not long, I hope," he said and cursed, his hand tensing about her arm.

"Five minutes. At the most."

He nodded. "I'm going in." Halting, he turned, reached out, and shook her. Hard. "Dammit, Kate. Go over by the water wagon. And stay. We need as many people as we can get to work the brigade. Charlie's rounding up more men. If we can, we'll keep this blessed town from burning down around our ears. No fire rig, for the love of . . . " Shoving her toward the group bellowing orders and passing buckets, he jumped onto the boardwalk, and plunged through the saloon's doors. A mad swing, then one door clattered to the boardwalk.

Swinging about, Kate lifted her skirts and rushed to the water wagon, merely an oversize barrel on wheels. Shards of glass cracked beneath her slippers as she skidded to an abrupt halt, grasping the rough edge of the wagon for support. The smell of charred wood and spilled whiskey filled the air, filled her mouth with a sour, biting taste she wondered if she would ever forget. She inserted herself in the line, ignoring the startled looks she received, vowing to do anything to help Tanner get out of there. *Anything.*

When he did—because he *would*—she would do all the things she'd promised God as she watched Tanner plunge into that burning building. Honor her mother, her sister. Have more patience with people. Attend Mass twice a week. Curse less often.

Or had she promised not to curse at all?

Twisting, she passed a bucket to the next person in line, water seeping through her skirt, dribbling on her feet. Pausing, she squinted, staring at the saloon's roof, now engulfed in flames—tongues of destruction crowding a star-filled sky. While she watched, a section at the north edge crumpled in a furious cough of sparks.

Shaking her head—shaking off the hot tears flooding her eyes—she grasped another bucket, hoisting it high.

Dear God, please protect him. Please.

Cowboy-lover went limp in his arms, blonde head flopping against his shoulder. Stumbling past a sea of splintered chairs and overturned tables, Tanner collided with a muscular body, jostling the woman in his arms. He blinked, streaking tears down his face, blurring his vision.

"Tanner?" A fierce bellow.

"Adam?" Tanner tried, but could not speak above a hoarse whisper—not loud enough to be heard above the furor of igniting wood. He swallowed, tasted cinders and hell. "One more in here," he mouthed, blinking away the moisture, seeing Adam's perplexed frown. Shaking his head—there wasn't time to do more—Tanner shoved Cowboy-lover into Adam's arms. Thankfully, his friend relieved him of the burden.

Struggling past the tangible barrier surrounding him, Tanner lurched forward, plowing into the bar he remembered ran the entire length of one wall. Melted varnish stuck to his fingers, the wood seeming to pulsate beneath them. A whiskey bottle exploded, showering him with liquid.

"Dammit, Tan, we've got . . . " A violent reverberation swallowed the rest of Adam's words.

Part of the roof, Tanner guessed, and without doubt the stairs to his right, had collapsed. A rush of heat flooded the room, struck his face like a slap.

One more minute. A man. Here somewhere, alongside the bar. Cowboy-lover had whispered this when Tanner found her, shaking and screaming, in a dark corner near the stairs. He stretched his arm out, reaching, searching. Broken glass, puddles of liquor, splinters of wood. A flaming cinder popped against his hand, sizzled. Belatedly, his brain registered the pain. Gloves? They must have fallen off somewhere along the way.

"Where are you, goddammit?" he screamed, gulping air, coughing, choking. With a burst of agony, he knew he would have to leave the man to die. Already, his thoughts came much too slowly, his actions even further behind. Hunkering low, he weaved toward the door, or where he remembered the door being. He stumbled over a chair leg and tumbled to his hands and knees. Reaching blindly, he gave it one last go, finally grasping a man's boot. "Thank God," he whispered and slung the man over his shoulder. With a grunt, he heaved to his feet, felt the stitches in his arm strain in painful protest. Wiping his eyes, he covered his mouth, and limped toward the door.

Following a narrow shaft of moonlight, Tanner concentrated on keeping one foot in front of the other, concentrated on ignoring the howling pain in his arm. A rush of cold air, the sound of voices raised in alarm. Plunging outside, Tanner collided with Adam, his elbow popping off a wooden post, a wilted wreath flopping into the ashes at his feet.

"Chrissakes, Tan, where did *he* come from?" Adam mercifully lifted the weight from Tanner's shoulders and shoved him from the boardwalk, where he'd halted, too befuddled to move.

Blood pounded in his head, his skin throbbed, felt frozen and blistered all at once. He tilted his face to the sky, snowflakes landing on his cheeks, melting, soothing. Out of nowhere, the scent of sandalwood drifted to him. Incredible that any smell other than smoke could enter his singed nostrils. Leaning on the arm slipping round his waist, his lids fluttered as his vision dimmed. A tiny pinprick of light, a voice calling to him from a distance.

Kat.

Her beautiful face flashed in his mind as darkness claimed him.

"Tell her to go to hell," Kate said, lifting a damp cloth from Tanner's brow. "I'm not leaving until he wakes up. What more do I have to say to make her understand? What do I care about the *appropriateness* of the situation?"

Charlie stepped into the dimly lit room, closing the door behind her. "I'll express your concerns. Not quite that way perhaps. I'm too frightened of your mother to tell her to go to hell right to her face, even if her daughter sent the message. She'd insist on escorting me to church every Sunday for a month as penance."

Kate dipped the cloth in a bowl of water and wrung it out, her hands chapped from the repeated procedure. Heavens, no matter how much she washed Tanner's face, his body, the scent of charred wood remained.

"How is he?" Charlie perched her hip on the rosewood

bedpost, smoothed a hand over the bodice of her calico day dress.

"Better. His fever is lower. His breathing is finally clear, thank God. I thought I'd go crazy listening to that rasping wheeze, as abrasive as sand ground against a chalkboard. Watching his chest rise so slowly, almost like it was an afterthought." She sighed, tilted her head, neck cracking from the uncomfortable position she'd imposed upon it the last two days. "Still as death though. But that's what the doctor told us to expect." He had also informed them of the possibility that Tanner would never wake up. Kate refused to consider *that* option.

Charlie sighed. "If only he hadn't been unhealthy before. So—"

"Exhausted. Stitches and gunshot wounds. Told Adam he'd hardly slept in weeks." Kate squeezed the cloth, a sudden, angry reflex, drops of water falling to the pine floor. "Fool man. Running into a burning building, playing hero. One of those characters he pretends to be, researching one of his beloved articles."

The post creaked when Charlie lifted from it. "Hellfire, Kate, he *is* a hero. Two people would have died in that fire if he hadn't gone in. That bunch of drunkards couldn't find a pitchfork if it protruded from their bottoms. Adam and the rest of the men would have arrived too late. Much too late."

"Yes, a hero. My, how will—what does Tanner call her? Cowboy-lover?—repay him for his gallantry?" She grunted, swabbing his cheek with a bit more vigor than necessary. "By reaching inside his trousers—that's how." She turned, flashed a tight smile, felt her cheeks heat, no doubt color.

"Oh, Kate." Charlie pressed her hand to her lips, laughter bubbling forth. "I'm sorry," she said, shaking her head. Her hand lifted, revealing a broad smile. "Oh, Kate . . . you do love him."

Kate glanced down, searched Tanner's face. Restless, pulsing lids, dark lashes curling where they met skin. She brushed a lock of hair from his brow, let the silky softness glide through her fingers. "Yes." She tried to ignore the dull ache in her chest, the tears pricking her lids.

"But your mother said—she was trying to give me the stagecoach schedule. You're not—does that mean . . . you're not leaving, are you?"

Slowly, Kate turned her head, met Charlie's questioning gaze. "As soon as . . . as soon as I know he's all right."

"Why?"

Why? Because the fear of losing him, loving him scared her to death. She was scared to death of life, she supposed. She wanted to be stronger, but the misery that had come with loving him before had nearly killed her.

"Don't . . . even . . . try . . . " A hoarse croak, the words disjointed. A shaft of pale sunlight flooded the room, throwing shadows into Tanner's hollowed cheeks. His eyes opened, lifted slightly, narrow slits revealing a sliver of blue. His hand tensed, bandaged fingers raising an inch, trembling, then falling to the mattress. Releasing a raw sigh, his lids drifted low.

Kate stared, unable to speak, unable to think beyond the mad rush of relief she felt. She lifted his hand to her mouth, pressed a kiss upon his fingertips, peeking above the white bandage, skimmed her chin across the inside of his wrist. Vaguely, she heard the door shut, footfalls echoing down the hallway.

Tanner's mouth opened. His lids fluttered. His throat worked as he swallowed.

"Shhh . . . you need to rest. Don't try to talk."

" . . . got me . . . "

She leaned in, her ear brushing his lips. A whisper of air, sooty and dry, cuffed her cheek. Below the scent of smoke, she smelled *him,* and the scent made her stomach clench tight, made the hair on the back of her neck stand tall.

"I . . . can't win now. Beg, keep you"—Tanner coughed, chest hitching beneath the cotton sheet—"from leaving." He licked his lips, breath rasping, voice thin. "But . . . watch over your shoulder . . . Princess. Watch for . . . me." Words thickening, his head sank deeper into the feather pillow, his hand going slack in hers. "Just when you think I won't . . . I'll be there. I will. Because I told . . . you the truth."

Chapter Seven

Watch over your shoulder, Princess. Watch for me.

Kate did every few minutes, seeing only tilting shadows cast from the astral lamp burning by her side. The seamstress had left her more than thirty minutes before in the dressing room of this monstrosity of a shop, the largest in Richmond. Left her to pace the cool floor in nothing but a lightly boned corset and a pair of cambric drawers. Left her to twiddle her thumbs and stare at the walls and wonder what the hell she was doing.

Left her to wonder when Tanner *would* appear.

She shivered, goose bumps rising, and rubbed her arms to dispel them. Naturally, she did not *want* him to appear— all her mother needed to go completely mad—only Kate couldn't help pondering if he would. His voice, the intractable tone, the warning in his words.

I'll be there.

However, as Kate wanted, *truly* wanted, she had not seen hide nor hair of him, had not heard so much as a peep, a deep dammit. When she first arrived in Richmond, she'd cloistered herself in her sister's home like a nun awaiting sanctification, her mother standing stoic guard outside her bedroom door. She'd feared looking out her window— but had looked quite often—afraid Tanner would leap from behind a tall hedge, swoop down, and pluck her up like a hawk. But the days passed, and she realized, of course, that a feverish, delirious man had spoken those words. Pure drivel.

Walking to the window, she pressed her chin against the frosty pane. Her breath misted; the world outside blurred, indistinct.

The door behind Kate opened as the seamstress returned. A floral whiff rushed into the room. What kind of flowers? She shrugged. Who cared? "I hope the dress is ready," she grumbled, streaking her fingers across glass. "It's quite cold in here, you know."

"No doubt it is in that getup." The door clicked shut. "Be damned if I don't like it though."

Kate's breath stalled in her throat. She spun around, bumping the table holding the astral lamp, causing shadows to leap across the floor. Across hollowed cheeks, black hair, and a broad smile. *Tanner.* Lounging in the doorway, ankles crossed, shoulder perched against the wall, lean body held at a slight pitch.

He arched a brow, glanced at the tottering table. "No more fires. How about it, Princess? Just recovered from the last one, matter of fact."

Kate's mind went blank, completely blank. She struggled to form a sentence while he leaned at the waist, scraped a match across the heel of his boot, cupped his hand around his mouth, and lit a cheroot—pretty as you please. "Hope you don't mind," he said, the damned thing dangling from his beautiful lips.

Dear God, he looked good enough to eat. No, better than

that. Good enough to dive into feet first. His hair, recently trimmed, gleamed. His face, filled out in the two weeks since she'd seen him, bloomed with healthy color. His lips—oh, his lips. Powerless, a little desperate, she licked her own, watched him watching her. His lids drooped for just a moment, sheltering his pale blue gaze as he shifted, peeled off the wall.

She stumbled back, her knees quivering with . . . well, certainly not excitement. Excitement? How absurd. But what if he did stride over on those powerful legs and—and touch her?

Ruining her fantasy, Tanner halted in the middle of the room, rotated a chair with the toe of his boot and straddled it, all the while smiling that easy, delicious smile of his. "Looking mighty nervous, Princess." Laying his arm along the back, he lifted the cheroot from his lips, flicked ashes to the floor. His head tilted back, his gaze drilling into her. Probing. Intense.

"Nervous?" Kate laughed and backed up another step, bottom smacking stone. His distinct scent—soap, mint, and leather—wafted past her nose, sneaked, uninvited, into her nostrils. She twisted her itching hands into fists. "I'm simply trying to think—"

"Don't. Please." He grimaced and blew a breath of smoke toward the ceiling. "That's what has gotten us into trouble all along."

"I can't imagine—"

"Go ahead, Princess. *Imagine.* I would have guessed you'd been imagining for two weeks now." He shrugged, calm and unconcerned. "I told you I would come."

"Yes, but—"

"A bit delayed, I'll admit. Train from Wilmington was held up for two days. For a time, it looked like I'd have to saddle a horse and ride like hell—oh, excuse me"—he nodded in her direction—"to get here, but my luck held and with your lovely sister's help"—he snapped his fingers, the edge of his mouth kicking high—"here I am."

Fury, swift and sharp, nipped at the back of her eyelids. Fury *and* the damned excitement she tried to deny. She sputtered, finally screeched, "Here you are to what? *What?* Don't smile like that at me! Oooh, get that crooked grin off your face. There are four loudmouthed ninnies who have hardly spoken to me in months, waiting outside this room"—she stalked forward, shaking a pointed finger—"waiting for *me*. A woman trying hard to erase one gigantic black mark from her record. A black mark in your handwriting. If you've messed this up, so help me, Tanner Barkley, I will kiss . . . I mean I will kill—oh!"

Laughing, Tanner shoved the chair away and caught her about the waist as she raced for the door. "Whoa, love, whoa," he said while she struggled to break free. "We don't want to bring the ninnies scurrying in here thinking someone is abducting you, now do we?" Dragging her against his chest, he pressed a kiss to her neck, instantly reducing her struggles. His lips trailed to her ear, tugged on her earlobe, his tongue flicking inside. Feeble struggles. Cupping her breasts, his thumbs worked her nipples in expanding circles.

Struggles ceased.

Daring her knees to hold her weight, Kate sagged against him, felt his arousal nudging her bottom. Battling a fierce rush of desire, she couldn't quite halt her hips from wiggling, settling her against him. Around him.

"All right, enough games," he whispered, a rough edge to his voice. Turning her in his arms, he covered her mouth, slid his tongue between her lips before she could think to argue, which at this point she probably would not have. She swayed, lifted on her toes, and wrapped her arms around his neck. Deep and openmouthed, tangled round each other, they kissed. Starving, desperate kisses. Kisses of shared loneliness. Kisses of painful separation. Kisses of heartfelt love and renewed fascination. Hip-rocking kisses, blood thickening and gun-metal hot.

Tanner came up gradually. "I have five things to say to you. And you're going to listen." He dipped his head, claimed her lips in a brief, urgent kiss, before drawing back. His eyes blazed. Blue. Ocean blue.

Fuzzy headed, feeling drunk and befuddled, Kate angled her chin, blinked and squinted, reached to touch the spectacles that were not there. He smelled so good she wanted to bottle his scent and sprinkle it on her sheets, pour it in her bath water. Glancing around, she had to shake her head and concentrate—dear God, really *concentrate*—to remember where she was. "Tanner, I—"

He tapped his finger against her mouth, silencing her, pausing to stroke his thumb across her bottom lip. "Hush," he said, his voice thick with—she smiled for the first time that day—suppressed passion. "One. Cowboy-lover did not show her gratitude by reaching into my trousers, as you so delicately phrased it. Nor did she *ever* come close to having the pleasure. Reserved for you, Princess. Although she did give me a rather exuberant hug on my departure from Edgemont."

Kate snapped back in his arms, but he yanked her hard against his chest and actually had the nerve to flash one of his tasty grins. Dropping a kiss to her brow, he lingered a moment, his lips warm, slightly chapped. "Two. Because you seem to think this is information I purposely withheld, I finished at Oxford in"—he trailed his fingers through her hair, nibbling at her jaw—"1841. Then spent two miserable years toiling away at Sloane-Barkley. Writing loan agreements, persuading old men to take their savings from beneath feather mattresses and deposit it in a secure metal vault." He sucked a patch of skin into his mouth, groaned low in his throat. "Two years of dry bank forecasts and financial records that had no end. Absolute drudgery."

"Oxford?"

He cupped her breasts, squeezing gently, lifting them above the lace edge of her bodice. "You think my Western accent is adequate? This one is my bloody best," he said next to her ear, in a perfect English intonation.

"Hmmm . . . "

Sliding lower, his hands closed about her hips, drawing her tight against him. "Three. My editor promised to hold the story for one week, Princess. You remember, we had a lunch appointment. At the Pale Lily on Market Street, I think." A slow grind, wool and cambric not enough to keep his heat from flooding into her, liquefying, preparing her for him. Following the curves of her body, he gripped her arms and set her back. "I swear I planned to tell you. *That* day. I'd been rehearsing it for days, weeks."

Kate stared, unfocused amber, a confused crook to her lips, the remains of a battered chignon grazing her cheek. Tanner grinned ruefully. Perhaps his persuasive techniques *were* a bit overzealous.

Rooting around in his waistcoat pocket with one hand, he lifted hers to his lips with the other. "Four." He slipped the ring on her middle finger, turned her hand in the lamp's golden glow. A perfect fit. He had known it would be. "I had this with me the day the story came out. Just picked it up from the jeweler's the day before. Had it resized. It belonged to Grandmother Sloane. My mother's mother. Notorious for plump digits, Grandmother Sloane. Had it tucked in my pocket when you hit me in the shoulder with that rock, truth be told."

He felt her hand tremble, her fingers begin to curl into a fist. "Tanner, I—"

"Marry me, Kat. Now. *Today*." A jolt of fear hit him. Surely, after all this, she would not refuse. "I don't want to wait. I don't want to live without you. Not for an hour, not for one minute." He captured her hands, hauled her against him, and kissed her until she shoved against his chest, gasping for air. Tipping her chin, he held firm. Her lids fluttered wide, her gaze finding his. "I love you, Kat. I love you more than life. More than I've ever imagined someone could love another person. More than I ever wanted to love someone. Plus"—he glanced down, laughed, shrugged—"I'm dressed for a wedding. My family is too. They're taking up an entire pew at St. Andrew's on Fifth."

She lifted her hand before her face and fingered the ring as if it would shatter into a thousand pieces. "Family? But . . . a wedding . . . Crawford . . . he and I, we have an agreement to—to break off our friendship at an appropriate time . . . gossip, you know . . . "

Tanner coughed and rocked on his heels. "Well, you see, I took care of him."

Her gaze flew to his, her skin paper white. "Took care, oh, you didn't kill him, did you?"

"Dear God, I'm no murderer," he said, raking his hand through his hair. Jesus, his Princess thought highly of him, didn't she? "I just transferred a modest amount into his bank account. You were a rather good deal, I think."

"You *bought* me?"

Her sharp tone had him stepping back, arms raised, fingers splayed in defense. "No, not bought. Just a small contribution to keep his mouth shut nice and tight. Avoid some of that gossip you mentioned."

"You paid for me! Like a horse or something."

"Much less than a horse. Unless I bought an old nag. Or a donkey maybe."

"Damn you!" Kate shrieked and raced toward the door.

With an easy stretch, Tanner caught her and hoisted her over his shoulder, legs kicking, body bucking. He laughed, then sighed, and finally slapped the firm bottom writhing quite enjoyably against his cheek. "I've had about enough of this, Kat. Either you love me or you don't. Do you?" Another gentle slap. "Well?"

"Yes! I love you. I always have, you arrogant—"

Another slap, followed by a lewd caress. "Marriage? Today?"

Her head bumped his back, bottom rocking high. "Yes, yes."

"A deal then," he said and let her slide down his chest, against his hips, his aching arousal. His head dipped as he gave in to the kiss he wanted above all else at that moment.

"Tanner," Kate whispered against his lips. "What about number five?"

Laughing, he tucked a stray curl behind her ear. "Ah, yes, I almost forgot. A bit belated, but . . . " Tilting her chin, Tanner stared straight into her eyes, a soft smile curving his lips. "Merry Christmas, Princess."

Put a Little Romance in Your Life With
Janelle Taylor

Put a Little Romance in Your Life With
Fern Michaels